three souls

three souls

JANIE CHANG

WILLIAM MORROW

An Imprint of HarperCollinsPublishers

P.S.™ is a trademark of HarperCollins Publishers.

THREE SOULS. Copyright © 2013 by Janie Chang. All rights reserved. Printed in the United States of America. No part of this book may be used or reproduced in any manner whatsoever without written permission except in the case of brief quotations embodied in critical articles and reviews. For information address HarperCollins Publishers, 10 East 53rd Street, New York, NY 10022.

HarperCollins books may be purchased for educational, business, or sales promotional use. For information please e-mail the Special Markets Department at SPsales@harpercollins.com.

First published in 2013 in Canada by HarperCollins Publishers, Ltd.

FIRST U.S. EDITION

Designed by Diahann Sturge

Library of Congress Cataloging-in-Publication Data
Chang, Janie.
    Three souls : a novel / Janie Chang.
        p.   cm
    ISBN 978-0-06-229319-0 (pbk.)
    1. Young women—Fiction. 2. Future life—Fiction. I. Title.
PS3603.H35729T43   2014
813'.6—dc23
                                                                    2013031946

14 15 16 17 18   OV/RRD   10 9 8 7 6 5 4 3 2 1

For my mother, Mao Lei

three souls

Part One

Pinghu, January 1935

We have three souls, or so I'd been told.

But only in death could I confirm this.

The moment the priest spoke the last prayer and sealed my coffin, I awoke and floated upward in a slow drift of incense smoke, until I could travel no farther. I settled in the rafters of the small temple, a sleepy wraith perched in the roof beams. I had knowledge, but no memory. My first thoughts were confused, for clearly this was the real world. But surely I no longer belonged here. When would I take my journey to the afterlife?

Below me, pale winter sunlight from an open doorway illuminated the temple's dark slate floors. Men and women in white robes crouched in front of an altar stained by decades of burning incense sticks. Noise assailed me from all directions. The tapping of wood-block instruments, the wailing of paid mourners, the chanting of acolytes. On the altar, a wooden tablet gleamed, gold-painted characters carved into its newly varnished surface. An ancestral name tablet, carved for a family shrine.

Song Leiyin. Beloved Wife. Dutiful Daughter.

I recognized that name. My name.

It was when the priests had finished their chanting that I saw my souls for the first time, three bright sparks circling in the air beside me. They were small, shining, and red as embers, but I knew that to the living they were as invisible as motes of dust.

One of the sparks floated in a lazy arc to rest atop the varnished tablet. A delicate rustling at the back of my mind said this was my *yang* soul. I could feel its presence, stern and uncompromising. My *yin* soul wafted down to settle on the coffin, a careless, almost impudent movement. My *hun* soul stayed beside me, watchful as a cat in a strange neighborhood.

I turned to my *hun* soul, a question forming in my still-sleepy mind, when a small, pale face in the crowd below caught my eye. A little girl in mourning robes of white, white ribbons woven through her braids. She knelt behind a man bent so low with weeping his forehead touched the slate floor. The girl shuffled on her knees and the elderly woman beside her put a warning hand on her back. Obediently the little girl stooped down again, her expression blank but for the slightest quiver of her lips. Her dark eyes were dull and rimmed with red. They should have been bright, alive with curiosity.

How did I know that about her eyes?

Memory flickered and I recognized the little girl. My daughter. Weilan. She was so still, so silent. I snapped into wakefulness and in the next moment, I was beside her on the slate, my arms around her thin shoulders.

Mama is here, my precious girl. I'm still with you. But I couldn't feel her. I drew back, suddenly cautious. I didn't want to frighten her. I was dead.

She took no notice of me and that made me weep, my relief struggling with disappointment, for although I longed to hold her, I didn't want to give her nightmares about her mother's ghost. I stayed kneeling beside her, whispering all the pet names I used to call her: *Small Bird, Sesame Seed, My Only Heart.*

I hoped for a tiny gap between our worlds, a crack that would allow my comforting thoughts to reach her even if words could not. She was only six, so young to be motherless. Who would listen to her chant her times tables now and rub her cold hands on winter days? Who would arrange a marriage for her and teach her how to embroider cloth slippers as gifts for her husband's family?

A restless, elusive tugging sensation told me I didn't belong in this world, but I vowed to resist for as long as possible. If there was any way I could take care of my child, even if I couldn't be seen or felt or heard, I wouldn't abandon her until it became impossible for me to stay.

Borne aloft on the sturdy shoulders of hired mourners, my coffin left the courtyard. I followed, drifting beside my daughter as the funeral procession traveled through the streets of the town, my *yin* soul riding on top of the coffin. Beside my final resting place, I watched the ceremonies. The man who had been weeping arranged food offerings in front of the grave. Weilan lit a bundle of incense sticks, her small hands nearly blue with cold.

Tense and anxious, I watched as the coffin was placed in its grave. Surely once my body was buried, I would be snatched away to the afterlife.

But nothing happened. I was still here.

I returned to town with the funeral cortège, but my *yin* soul remained behind at the grave, and in my mind's eye it shared with me what it saw. Workers were piling earth into a smooth mound on top of my burial spot.

When they finished, however, I didn't drift upward, nor did my consciousness fade into oblivion. When was I supposed to begin my journey to the afterlife?

At the front gates of the estate, fewer than a dozen people entered, all that remained once the mourners had been paid off.

"Come, Granddaughter," said the old woman. Her voice sounded tired, strained but kind. This was, had been, my mother-in-law. She would be the one to bring up my daughter now. "I told Old Kwan to have some sweet-date soup waiting for us. Let's go and warm up in the dining room." She led Weilan away.

I stood waiting by the temple, my mind full of questions. Finally my *yin* soul returned, sliding along a thin shaft of winter sunlight. It joined the two other sparks in a slow circling above the altar.

I'm dead and buried, I said to them. *Am I not supposed to leave this earth now? Or will the gods let me stay to watch over my child?*

But they ignored me and I drifted among the rafters of the temple, silent and perplexed.

❧

My souls spiral down and come to rest on the altar.

We are ready now, says a stern voice, and there is a taste of mustard at the back of my tongue. My *yang* soul. Although his red spark remains balanced on the wooden tablet, an elderly man wearing a round scholar's cap appears beside the altar. He resembles my grandfather as I've seen him in photographs, with steel-rimmed glasses and a goatee. He is dressed in a high-necked *changshan* gown of deep blue silk over loose black trousers.

Yes, let's begin. A new voice tinkles like wind chimes, accompanied by the scent of camellia. The bright ember of my *yin* soul dances in midair, circling the confines of the courtyard. She comes to rest beside the old scholar, a schoolgirl of fifteen with deep brown eyes below wispy bangs, a long pigtail thrown over one shoulder. Her ankle socks and navy uniform blazer match perfectly, her white blouse is spotless.

Leiyin needs to remember, says a third voice. My *hun* soul flies down from the beams overhead and I feel my hair being pulled, a light, playful tug. Its image joins the other souls. It manifests as a silhouette of light, shaped like a human, as brilliant as the morning sun and as featureless. *Before she can ascend to the afterlife, she needs to understand the reason for her detention in this world.*

This is punishment? This doesn't look like hell, I say, feeling a wave of panic. *Where is the underground maze? What about the fanged demons, the chambers of torture? What is this twilight existence if not the afterlife?*

This isn't hell, nor is it the true afterlife. My *yang* soul turns to me, a slight scowl on his seamed face. *You could say it's the after-death. And you're still here because in life you were responsible for a great wrong.*

I don't remember anything about a great wrong. Bewildered as much as indignant, I want to remember my life. Surely I was not, had not been, a criminal.

Soon you'll remember everything and so will we. My *yin* soul pulls the ribbon off her pigtail and shakes out her hair. She begins braiding it again. *Relive your memories. Only then will you understand what you must do to ascend to the afterlife.*

And why do I need to ascend anyway? I know I sound sulky, rebellious.

As soon as I ask this question, an eager swirl of emotions radiates from my souls. In my mind's eye I see them, three red sparks lifting into the air toward a portal that spills golden light over the horizon. Beyond the portal flicker tantalizing glimpses of grassy landscapes, mountain lakes, and eternally blossoming orchards. This vision makes me yearn to rise up toward that portal and join my souls. Now I understand the restlessness that invades my being, an upward pull I can't follow so long as the manacles of my sins weigh me down to this world.

We must ascend. Reincarnation awaits us in the afterlife. My *yin* soul spins so that her pleated skirt twirls up around her, a circle of navy blue. *There, we will have a chance for new lives, new hope. But if we stay too long in this existence . . .* As her voice trails off, I hear in it a small tremor.

First, she must remember, my *hun* soul interjects. It reaches out a shining limb and pulls my hair again, this time a firm and peremptory tug. *You must understand the damage you did. Then you must make amends to balance the ledger. Only then can we ascend together to the true afterlife.*

So we will go together? You won't go now and leave me here? Relief.

We are your souls, we're part of you, my *yang* soul snaps. *We can't leave until you do.* He glares at me through moon-shaped lenses.

Don't mind yang, says my *yin* soul, who has finished braiding her hair. *He's not happy unless he's berating someone.*

Where should we begin? my *hun* soul asks. *On the day of the party?*

Yes, the day of the party, the other souls agree.

The day you first stepped off the path that had been paved for you, my *hun* soul says.

I have no choice. How else can I reclaim my memories, discover what to do next? At this moment I can't even remember what Weilan looked like as a baby.

My *yin* soul sinks to the floor and tucks her knees under her skirt, a child waiting to hear a story. My *yang* soul settles on a stool near the door and brushes a cobweb from his black trousers. My *hun* soul drifts to the altar, and with a single bright fingertip gently strokes my name tablet.

Suddenly I'm standing on a street lined with sycamore trees and high, whitewashed walls. I'm watching a schoolgirl climb down from a rickshaw. But in that same moment, I'm also that girl, my foot about to touch the curb.

I know everything about my life before that moment.

I know nothing of what is to come.

1

Changchow, 1928

*F*or once I had been eager to leave school and get home. I jumped off the rickshaw as soon as it stopped outside the walls of our estate and darted through the wicket gate, dashing past Lao Li, who sat on guard just inside the entrance.

"No need to rush, Third Young Mistress," the old gatekeeper called after me. "The guests won't be here for at least two hours!"

For the party, he would change into an immaculate house uniform of gray tunic and trousers. He would push open the huge front gates while other servants swarmed to the entrance to guide carriages and sedan chairs into the forecourt and out again, smooth and practiced as clockwork.

The party wasn't my only reason for hurrying. Father had promised to give me his decision today. I sprinted through the courtyard, then past the formal reception halls, and through to the next garden. I had just turned seventeen and was trying to be mindful of my dignity. I hadn't jumped the boxwood hedge in years, but on this day I hiked up the skirt of my *qipao* and prepared to take a shortcut.

⌒⌒⌒

Hold, I beg my souls. *Hold this flow of memories and let me look at my home again.*

I want to see the entire property as it was that day. The world of my childhood lies enclosed within its walls: recollections of bare feet on cool moss, a grove of green bamboo, my face pressed against tall windows, watching raindrops gather in pools on a marble terrace.

Obligingly, my *hun* soul halts the stream of memories and together we rise above the gray roof tiles to view my home as it was. I see myself below, pigtails streaming and skirt yanked up my thighs, about to hurdle a two-foot hedge. I see my family's estate, its perimeter bounded by whitewashed brick walls, the heavy wooden gates banded with brass studs. I catch glimpses of quiet streets outside, lined with tall, leafy sycamores and other walls, other homes.

The Old Garden is at the center of our property, a huge private park with a man-made lake at one end large enough to contain an island of reeds and willows, home to families of ducks. Arranged around the Old Garden are a dozen courtyard houses, each nestled beside its own, smaller garden.

In that moment of suspended memory, one of my great-uncles is halted in midstep on his stroll around the lake, a servant boy behind him toting books and a canteen of water. Two of my aunts rest in the shade of the bamboo grove, admiring a stand of blue irises. On one of the terraces facing the Old Garden, my nieces skip rope, arms raised, motionless.

I turn my gaze across to my own home, built thirty years ago when my father returned from university in Paris, in love with honeycolored stone and all things French. We lived in a villa surrounded by a green lawn that rolled down to rose gardens bordered by boxwood hedges. It was all straight lines and precise geometry, even to the clipped Italian cypresses lining the walls. The rose garden blooms in masses of color, extravagant and gaudy compared to the restrained serenity of the Old Garden.

Then my *hun* soul allows the stream of memories to flow again.

I watch my memory-self leap over the hedge, and at the same time, I feel boxwood leaves brush past my ankles and the giddy, unreserved joy of being seventeen again.

❧

I ran into the villa and nearly crashed into Nanny Qiu.

"*Wah, wah,* Third Young Mistress! Why are you running inside the house like some mad animal?"

"I need to see Father. Right now. Is he in his study?"

"Yes, but the Master is with your brothers."

That meant Father was discussing family finances.

"Oh. Has Eldest Sister arrived?"

"She is helping Second Young Mistress get dressed."

My sister Gaoyin was home from Shanghai for the party. I

nearly slipped on the cool marble of the circular staircase as I dashed up to the western wing of the house, where my second sister, Sueyin, sat at her dressing table. Gaoyin stood behind, pinning up her hair. They both turned to me, smiling in welcome.

∽∾∽

How could I have forgotten their lovely faces, even for a moment, even in death?

Everyone agreed that my mother had been the most beautiful woman ever to marry into our family. I was four when she died, and retained only the haziest of impressions of her: a pale oval face, the scent of osmanthus blossom. Her exquisite features lived on, celebrated in family legend and preserved in a few sepia-toned photographs.

Before they turned sixteen, my two older sisters, near replicas of our mother, were famous already in Changchow. Their faces were perfect ovals, their eyes longlidded beneath delicately arched eye brows. The most nuanced of details differentiated their features and those details bequeathed to Sueyin an unearthly beauty. Her nose was just slightly longer, her mouth a little wider than Gaoyin's. I'm considered pretty, but beside my sisters, I was quite ordinary: my eyebrows heavy, my forehead a bit too high. But we Chinese like groupings of three, so I was lumped in with them and we were known as the Three Beauties of the Song Clan.

Thus when elderly aunts or servants chastised me, they might say, "Your mother, whose skin put white jade to shame, always stayed out of the sun," or, "Your mother, whose graceful walk poets compared to the swaying of willows, never would have galloped down the hall like a demented mule."

Their words never failed to remind me that I could only aspire to such perfection, for in addition to an excess of beauty, my mother had been blessed with a sweet nature and fertile loins, delivering two sons before both she and her third son died during childbirth. That she also bore three daughters was of little consequence.

⌘

"Let me look at you," my eldest sister said.

But I was the one staring in admiration. Gaoyin's long, glossy hair, once habitually twisted up in a knot, now grazed her jawline in soft waves, a modern and sophisticated hairstyle like those we saw on models in the Shanghai fashion magazines. But she was far more beautiful than any of them.

She hugged me, an embrace of bergamot and jasmine.

"How delicious, Eldest Sister. What's that new perfume?"

"It's called Shalimar," she said, pleased. "Shen brought it back for me from France."

"What does Father think of your short hair?"

She tossed her curls. "Shen likes it, and my husband's opinion is what matters now. But tell me, little bookworm, what are you reading these days? Is it something I would enjoy?"

"Probably not. But at least you wouldn't need to read it in secret, since you're married. It's a translation, a Russian novel called *Anna Karenina*. It's banned from the school library."

"But you bought a copy anyway?"

"No, a classmate lent it to me."

Gaoyin's laughter sent her curls bouncing against her neck. She turned back to pinning up Sueyin's hair, which she had arranged into a knot secured by jeweled combs.

Even barefaced and wearing the dowdiest of dresses, Sueyin turned heads. Gaoyin and I shared her pale skin, but our elderly aunts assured us that Sueyin was the only one who had inherited my mother's lustrous complexion. I never understood the point of envying Sueyin. She was simply unattainably beautiful. Tonight her face glowed radiant as white jade against the high neck of her emerald green *qipao*. The dress was a modest ankle length but cut close to show off her slim figure.

"Well, Third Sister," said Gaoyin, "what will you wear tonight?"

"I'll just wash my face and go down in this." My hand swept the front of my dress, a plain *qipao* of navy blue, its only ornament a row of turquoise cloth-covered buttons fastened across the bodice.

"Third Sister! This is Sueyin's engagement party, not a family dinner."

"All right, then. I'll change into my formal school uniform, you know, the blue blazer and plaid skirt."

Before Gaoyin could open her mouth to rebuke me again, Sueyin spoke up.

"Please, Little Sister. Wear something special." Her perfect eyebrows drew closer in the tiniest of frowns. "Or you'll look like a high school student."

"I *am* a student." But Sueyin, selfless as she was beautiful, hardly ever asked me for favors, and I relented. "For your engagement party, Second Sister, I'll wear a nice dress."

When Sueyin turned eighteen, a flood of matchmakers began arriving at our gates from as far away as Hangchow and Shanghai. Father had settled on Liu Tienzhen, the only son of Judge Liu, whose family was even wealthier than ours. The judge was famously traditional and hadn't wanted the betrothed couple to meet before the wedding. But in deference to Father's request, Judge Liu had agreed to allow Sueyin and Tienzhen to meet beforehand so they wouldn't be total strangers on their wedding day. That was the reason for this evening's party. Gaoyin insisted on calling it the official engagement party.

I hoped Father would put off any engagement or marriage for me until I'd finished my education. I sat up on the bed.

"I need to see Father. Right now."

They both turned to me, with identical inquiring looks.

"Father said he'd give me his decision today. Whether I can attend teacher's college. I've applied to Hangchow Women's University."

"His answer will be no." Gaoyin's self-confident tone made me want to stick my tongue out at her.

"Third Sister is always top of her class. There's a good chance Father will agree." Sueyin smiled in my direction.

At that moment old Nanny Qiu came puffing to the door.

"*Wah, wah,* Third Young Mistress, what are you doing? The Master wants to see you now. Then you must take a bath, you must be covered in sweat after the way you galloped up here. Your mother—"

"Yes, yes." I got up hastily. "Nanny, will you come in later to fix my hair?"

But I had a parting shot for Gaoyin.

"Just because you didn't go to university doesn't mean Father won't let me. For one thing, my grades are much better than yours ever were."

She threw a pillow at me. I ducked and ran out, giggling.

༄

The door to Father's study was ajar and I could hear my eldest brother's voice.

"Chiang's army lost so badly to the Japanese in Jinan earlier this month. I'm sure it's added to Japan's certainty that China is theirs for the taking. The Japanese may be trying to downplay the whole thing by calling it the May Third Incident, but I'm sure it means war with Japan, sooner or later."

"We need to consider both Hong Kong and Singapore. The Japanese wouldn't dare invade British territory. Our assets would be safer overseas."

"I agree, Father, but I still think we should buy property in Hawaii or San Francisco. America is even safer."

The voices belonged to my father and my eldest brother, Changyin, who were both standing over Father's big lacquered table, looking down at piles of paper. I knew the civil war was ruining many families, some even wealthier than ours. But with Father and Changyin looking after our investments, surely we would be all right.

Father was plainly clothed, as always. It was hard for me to reconcile this dignified presence, whom I had never seen in anything but a traditional *changshan* gown, with photographs of Father as a student in Paris, a grinning young man resplendent in striped shirts and embroidered waistcoats. Tonight, because of the party, his gown was silk, dark gray woven with a design of bamboo leaves. He wore shoes with cloth soles, a pair that Stepmother had finished making just the day before. His goatee was newly trimmed.

My eldest brother was the only one of us who took after Father, with his heavy, square face, heavy eyebrows, and square, solid build. Like Father, Changyin wore a *changshan*. But unlike Father, who wore loose trousers beneath his *changshan*, Changyin favored a half-Western look. Tailored gabardine trousers showed below his ankle-length gown, their cuffs neatly settled on polished black wingtip shoes. Changyin was only twenty-seven, but to me he seemed decades older. He shared with Father the work of managing our family's wealth and I could already see the strain in his ruddy complexion. His carefully trimmed hair showed signs of thinning and would be as gray as Father's before he turned forty.

My second brother, Tongyin, lounged in an armchair, staring out the French doors and not even trying to conceal his boredom. Tongyin had long since abandoned traditional dress. His summer suit of pale linen was brand new and his yellow paisley tie matched the hatband on his straw panama hat. His hair was shiny, slicked back. He had become even more of a dandy since attending university in Shanghai. Much as I detested him, I had to admit Tongyin was very handsome; he had inherited our mother's cheekbones and her long, delicate fingers. At the moment,

the straw panama twirled on one of those fingers. He exhibited
no interest in our family finances beyond what was deposited in
his bank account each month, yet Father always included him in
their discussions.

"Are you going to the party wearing *that*?" Tongyin had noticed me at the door. Although he was only two years my senior
he always treated me as though I were a child.

"No. Are you going to the party smelling like that?" I couldn't
help it. Tongyin was the vainest person alive. And he tended to
dab on too much cologne.

"*Eh.* That's enough." From the other end of the table
Changyin shook a finger at us. An order from Eldest Brother was
as good as an order from Father and we held our bickering while
Changyin and Father finished talking.

Dismissed by a casual wave of Father's hand, my brothers left
the room. I stuck my tongue out at Tongyin, and then quickly
composed myself.

"Father, how are you feeling today?"

He smiled, an indulgent and affectionate smile. Surely he
had decided in my favor.

"Third Daughter. Sometimes I forget you are already a young
woman. Where have all my little children gone?"

"There's still Fei-Fei, Father." He nodded, but I knew that Fei-
Fei, who was the daughter of his concubine, my stepmother, held
a smaller place in his heart.

"The house feels empty already when I think of Sueyin getting
married. It would be even emptier if you went away to school."

My mouth opened, but I bit my tongue.

"Third Daughter, you do not need a career. So there is no

point in spending tuition fees and boarding-school fees on more education."

I looked down at my lap, struggling to hide my disappointment. Hadn't I made it clear to Father how much I wanted to attend university? I had plans already to share a room with my best friend, Nanmei. What would I tell her now?

He lifted my chin with a forefinger and tapped me playfully on the nose. "No sulking, little bookworm. You're a clever young woman with many interests. Tomorrow or next week you will find another pastime worthy of your intelligence."

"Father, I don't consider teaching a pastime."

"Leiyin, you will be a wife and mother. You won't need to earn a living."

His tone was mild, but he had used my name. There would be no further discussion.

I just had to convince Father that university wasn't a frivolous whim. Then I looked at the table, the stacks of paper, and the old abacus with ivory beads that had once belonged to my grandfather. I looked at Father. He had so much on his mind. But there had to be a way.

"Now go see your stepmother," he said. "She wants a word before the party."

I was dismissed.

Stepmother sat at one of the three round tables in the small dining room. Lu, the head house servant, stood beside her, as upright as a general on horseback, the pleats of his trousers as sharp as bayonet blades. He gave me the slightest of bows and continued addressing the house servants lined up along the wall. They stood at attention, shoulders stiff and straight, hands crossed behind their backs.

"Finally, if a guest asks for something and you don't know where it is or what it is, just bow and say, 'Right away.' Then come and get me immediately. I'll be at the side entrance of the dining hall. Now go wash up and put on your best uniforms. Girls, remember to pin up your pigtails."

They filed out under Head Servant Lu's critical gaze. I counted sixteen. Stepmother had borrowed staff from other houses for the party. Lu made his bow to Stepmother and another, deeper one to me and then joined the end of the departing troop.

Stepmother was thirty-three, only six years older than Changyin. From a distance, however, her old-fashioned gowns and matronly hairstyle gave the impression that she was a generation older. Her looks were comfortably plain, her smooth flat features serene as a Buddha's and just as impenetrable. Her eyes were remarkable, large and deep set. Hers was a demeanor that soothed tempers and quieted arguments.

If we hadn't been so fond of Stepmother, we would have called her by the lesser family title of Yi Niang, for she was only Father's concubine and not eligible to be addressed as Stepmother. If she had given birth to a boy instead of little Fei-Fei, Father might have married her and she would be his first wife now. I knew that Stepmother, who was from a family of cloth merchants, had never expected to be made a wife, even after our mother died. If Father married again, it would be to a woman of our own class, but I hoped he wouldn't. I'd hate it if a new wife proved unkind to Stepmother and little Fei-Fei.

"You wished to see me, Stepmother?"

"Yes, Third Stepdaughter. Once your second sister is married, you'll be the only daughter of the house. You'll have to take on hostess duties, so you could begin tonight if you're willing."

"Of course, Stepmother. Tell me what I have to do." I sighed. I'd have to stay for the entire party. When would I find time to finish *Anna Karenina*?

"Leiyin. Your father expects it of you." Her amused smile said she knew I wasn't enthusiastic. "Just take this list and study it before you come downstairs to the party."

I glanced at the list, then over at the door. The scent of Shalimar announced Gaoyin's entrance.

"Stepmother? Ah, Third Sister, you're here too." For a moment, Gaoyin looked strangely shy. "It's not important. I just wanted a few minutes with Stepmother."

I stayed in my chair. Gaoyin indicated the door with the slightest tilt of her head.

I rose reluctantly. "Well, I'd better go upstairs and bathe before Nanny gets upset with me again."

⌒⌒⌒

The party didn't need my attention. I doubted the servants needed any supervision, given how thoroughly they had been drilled by Stepmother and Head Servant Lu. I scanned the drawing room anyway, just to be sure.

Three crystal chandeliers, their prisms and beads polished to dazzling clarity, formed the centerpiece of the drawing room. Porcelain vases filled with flowers from the garden decorated every alcove. Framed by potted palms, a string quartet churned out popular tunes. They sounded rather dispirited, so I smiled to show I was paying attention, and the tempo picked up.

A maid moved through the crowd, emptying ashtrays almost as soon as they were dirtied. So silent and unobtrusive that they were nearly invisible, servants in cloth-soled shoes padded over the shining parquet floors carrying trays of shrimp toasts, tiny blintzes topped with caviar, and deviled quail eggs. The dinner itself would be Chinese, of course. It was fashionable to serve Western-style appetizers, but we couldn't inflict an entire meal of foreign food on our guests.

Gaoyin wore a cocktail dress of dark gray silk that would have looked matronly on anyone else. I knew she wanted to be sure Sueyin wouldn't be upstaged, but really, there was no need to worry. Sueyin looked like a heavenly handmaiden from the court of the Jade Emperor. Her fiancé hardly took his eyes away from her. Liu Tienzhen wasn't as tall as my brothers, but he was very handsome. He had smooth skin and the sleek features of a matinee idol. He inclined his head toward her with a gentle but slightly possessive air. The soft, dreamy look in his eyes when he gazed at her pleased me. Of course he adored her already, how could anyone not? They made an impossibly beautiful couple.

Tienzhen didn't quite take her hand, but he did touch her elbow as Sueyin led him outside to walk in the garden. The sky had turned cobalt blue, now dark enough for the moon to be seen, a shy crescent of silver. The evening air was heavy, it would rain before morning; but the peonies and early summer roses were in bloom, and the garden would be steeped in fragrance.

If the loud drone of conversation indoors was any indication, the guests were mingling very well. Father and Changyin had included several poets and writers on the guest list, regular attendees of Father's renowned weekly salons. Father always said one could rely on passionate literary types to liven up conversation. The party was going so well I wondered if I could slip away to finish *Anna Karenina*. I had to return it soon to Nanmei, for there was a long queue of girls waiting their turn to read this scandalous book.

Circling the room, I caught fragments of conversation. On the banquette, my father and Judge Liu were deep in a discussion about the legal system of the Song Dynasty.

"I put it to you, honored Judge, that despite the turbulence of the era, the Song legal code was essentially the same as the legal code of the Tang Dynasty."

"Both were based on the Northern Zhou codes, I agree, but you must admit the Tang adhered more strictly to the Confucian rules of social order."

Next I passed by Changyin and Gaoyin's husband, Zhao Shen, who were with a group of men engrossed in a loud debate about the conflict between the Communists and the Nationalist government.

"The Communists are recruiting college students as activists. Pay their tuition, let them finish school, then send them out to the countryside as teachers to spread Marxism."

"After the Nationalists carried out that purge last April, round-ing up members of the Communist party and executing them like that, you can bet the Communists will never trust them again."

"The Reds are calling it the Shanghai Massacre, you know. I'd be nervous if I was a member of the left-wing faction of the Nationalist party. They're next in Chiang's line of fire, for sure."

"That coalition of three factions was never going to hold together. Now they're each claiming a different capital city. Peking, Nanking, Wuhan—how do you think that makes us look to the rest of the world?"

It made my head hurt keeping track of our politics, but I did try. After all, I was born the year the Nationalists overthrew the Qing Dynasty and we became a republic. For a decade, Nationalists and Communists had been united, and some of the Communists had even joined the Nationalist party to form a left-wing faction. Then Sun Yat-sen died, the alliance fell apart, and I still wasn't sure why each side accused the other of betraying Sun's Three Principles of the People.

The one thing I did understand was that I had to do my part to bring our young nation into the twentieth century. Our class had studied an essay written by Madame Sun Yat-sen about women taking an equal role in building China. Ever since then, Nanmei and I had been determined to become teachers. I just had to make Father understand.

If I had a hard time keeping up with politics, Tongyin didn't even try. Outside, a handful of young men lounged on the terrace, slouched in the wicker chairs, their fashionable shoes propped up on the coffee table. One of them flicked a cigarette butt into the peony shrubs. Half-finished drinks cluttered the marble paving.

In the mild evening air their laughter rang noisy and raucous. Tongyin was the loudest of the lot, and even though his back was to me and I couldn't hear his words, I knew he was telling a smutty story.

The scent of Shalimar told me that Gaoyin had come to my side. She swept her gaze across the terrace. The young men facing us noticed her scrutiny, and there were a few wolf whistles, quickly hushed. One of them bowed in exaggerated courtesy.

"Let's go inside." She pulled me around. "Come meet my friends."

It was evident from the bursts of laughter and shocked gasps we heard as we approached that the women gathered in the corner were catching up on gossip.

"My goodness, is that Yen Hanchin?" A woman I knew only slightly, dressed head to toe in pink, asked the question, avid interest evident in both her tone and the gleam of her eyes as she gazed across the room. "That *is* him, isn't it, Gaoyin? Over there, beside your brother? I'd heard he was back from Russia."

Yen Hanchin. His name was on my copy of *Anna Karenina*; he was the translator. I stared in the same direction. Across the room a stout, slightly balding man leaned in confidingly toward my brother, cigarette ash dropping on the Persian carpet as he spoke. So that was the translator of the forbidden novel. How disappointing. I had imagined someone more haggard, a starving writer and political activist. The Chinese version of Levin's brother Nikolai. I'd heard Yen Hanchin harbored leftist sympathies, another reason why his book was banned from our library.

"Yes, Changyin knows Yen Hanchin slightly," Gaoyin said.

"They met at a poetry reading. Yen's a very fine poet, apparently. But he's only become famous since he translated *Anna Karenina*."

"I suppose that's better than being infamous for other things," said the woman in pink.

It had been a mistake to stare for so long. Gaoyin noticed my curiosity. "Would you like to discuss *Anna Karenina* with Yen Hanchin, Third Sister?"

"No, Eldest Sister. Anyway I haven't finished reading the book."

I didn't want to get trapped talking to some middle-aged scholar, infamous or not. He might drone on about prerevolutionary Russia and its depiction in the modern novel. Our headmistress had tortured us once with a lecture by just such an academic and Nanmei had had to pinch me every five minutes to keep my head from nodding onto my chest.

"Come." Gaoyin took my arm. Her eyes glittered and her cheeks were flushed. When she drank wine, no amount of face powder could hide the effects.

"Oh, Eldest Sister, I'm supposed to be supervising the servants."

But she pulled me across the room, her high heels giving her more purchase on the Persian carpet than I had with my slippery flat soles.

"Yen Hanchin, here is someone you should meet."

One of the men turned around at her greeting. It was all I could do not to gasp.

Not the stout balding man. Not a Nikolai.

A Vronsky.

Tall, with hair just a bit too long. He was in his late twenties, perhaps as old as thirty. His shabby linen jacket made all the other men, in their tailored suits and silk ties, look merely ornamental. He was lean and lightly tanned. Beneath intense brown eyes his cheekbones were sharp, angled escarpments. He was both beautiful and intoxicatingly masculine. He was a poet. For several moments I couldn't take my eyes away from him. Was this the feeling that swept over Anna each time she beheld Vronsky?

He smiled down at me, the smile of a man accustomed to the admiration of women.

⌘

As soon as the flow of memories reveals Hanchin's face to me, my souls rustle in agitation, and somehow we know he's the reason I remain trapped between worlds. We don't know why, not yet, only that he's important to my escape from this inadequate spirit world.

Say nothing, I command my souls. *I don't want your commentary right now. Just carry on with the memories.*

To my surprise, they stop rustling and although I can almost hear them protest, they settle down quietly in the roof beams of the temple and the evening continues.

⌘

"Mr. Yen, this is my youngest sister, Song Leiyin. She's a great admirer of your latest work although she isn't supposed to be reading it."

"So now I've met the youngest of the Three Beauties." He gave me the slightest of bows.

Gaoyin beckoned us to follow her to some chairs by the French doors. She reached over to the low table and opened an enameled cigarette case.

"This little beauty has been neglecting her hostess duties and needs to compensate by entertaining you with clever conversation. She's by far the cleverest of us all."

"Not when it comes to conversation." Under the high collar of my silk *qipao*, my neck was hot, and I badly wanted an iced drink. I also wanted very badly to keep this man's attention.

"The secret to good conversation, Third Sister, is to ask lots of questions." My sister leaned over, immaculately posed, so that Yen Hanchin could light her cigarette. "Thank you, Mr. Yen. Then the other person answers your questions, does all the talking, and thinks you're fascinating. Now, I must return to my friends."

We watched Gaoyin walk away, slim hips swaying. She was so elegant. Why had I instructed Nanny Qiu to dress my hair in a single long braid down my back? I looked like a child, a high school student.

Yen Hanchin didn't seem at all uncomfortable in the silence. He gave me a slow, slightly amused smile that made me press my hands against my stomach. My mind groped for something to start a conversation. "I hear you've just returned from Russia. What's Moscow like?"

"Bitterly cold."

"I see." More silence. I stole a look at his hands, elegantly shaped, tanned. I hoped I wasn't blushing. Changyin's friends treated me like a little sister. I didn't want Yen Hanchin to think of me as a little sister.

"I do have one question, Mr. Yen. Then you can return to talking politics."

"Maybe I prefer being fascinating to talking politics."

"Now you're making fun of me. I'm not a child, you know. I've nearly finished high school."

"My apologies. What's your question?"

"Why is *Anna Karenina* considered such a great novel? It's all about adultery and the unhappiness it causes, nothing unusual in novels, surely."

"Did you skip over the parts about life in rural Russia, industrialization, the Slavic campaign?"

Now I did blush. "Yes. But I borrowed the book and have to give it back soon. So I'm just following the love stories."

"Perhaps you could read it again when you're older."

When I was older. I groaned silently.

"The novel's about family relationships, class, and social change. It's important because it is considered the first realist novel, a true depiction of life, not romanticized or idealized."

"Is that why you translated it?" I wanted him to keep talking, so I could listen to his voice, watch his lips move.

"Partly. But also because it mirrors some of our own struggles to turn China into a modern nation."

"I don't know why people think it's so scandalous. Some of the classics, *The Scholars*, for example, are about courtesans and even allude to love between men."

Did he think it was daring of me to use such words? *Courtesans. Love between men.* Hanchin didn't seem shocked. But after all, he was a poet and an author. He considered every subject from a literary point of view. I couldn't wait to tell Nanmei about this evening, to say I'd been discussing *Anna Karenina* with its handsome translator.

"Well, I suppose they think that Western decadence is more corrupting than the Chinese kind," he said. "If you're interested in Russian literature, try Turgenev's *Fathers and Sons*. There's also *The Brothers Karamazov*. I found it surprisingly modern for a nineteenth-century novel."

He reached for the enameled case to help himself to a cigarette. "Tell me, Miss Song, what will you do once you've finished high school?"

I wanted him to keep talking, not turn the conversation to my suddenly inadequate life.

"I plan to go to teacher's college."

"Excellent. China needs more teachers. The college in Hangchow or the one in Peking?"

"Oh! Hangchow of course, the one affiliated with Zhejiang University."

"That is indeed a good school." He nodded, and a warm current flowed through my chest. I wanted to hear that tone of approval again, to know he considered my plans worthwhile. *China needs more teachers.* I would tell Father that my wish to attend university wasn't just a whim, it was for our country.

My mind devoid of anything intelligent to say, I waved over a maidservant to offer Hanchin some shrimp toasts. She leaned down, the platter neatly balanced.

"My favorite," he said, looking up appreciatively. He smiled his thanks and the maid blushed deep scarlet. Servants just aren't used to guests paying them any attention.

When I handed a napkin to Hanchin, our fingers touched,

his cool and dry, mine hot as melting candle wax. I turned to dismiss the servant and caught a glimpse of the woman in pink across the room, watching.

I hold on to this scene for a while. My *yin* soul and I shiver slightly with pleasure at this memory of falling in love for the first time. My *yang* soul isn't so approving. My *hun* soul seems to be paying no attention at all, circling the drawing room inspecting flower arrangements.

You do realize it was lust, says my *yang* soul, stern as an ancestral portrait. He pulls a square of white cotton out of his sleeve and polishes his glasses.

Yang, I can't believe you just used that word. My *yin* soul giggles.

I was seventeen and unmarried, I remind him. *I didn't recognize those feelings back then, but now that I'm dead, why bother feeling ashamed? Yes, I admit to lust.*

How could you expect her to recognize such a tangle of feelings? says my *yin* soul, her brown eyes still fixed on Hanchin. *She was just a girl. She wouldn't be the first person to confuse lust with love. Nor the last.*

No, no, I object. *Not merely lust. By the time Tongyin interrupted our conversation, I knew I was in love. As certainly as Anna knew she couldn't live without Vronsky.*

My brother held his hand out to Hanchin. "Sir, I'm Song Tongyin, Changyin's brother."

I restrained a scowl. Second Brother and I were close in age, but we were not close in any other ways. When we were younger, he played little tricks on me, filling the toes of my shoes with small stones or hiding chunks of hot ginger among the pieces of fruit that Nanny put into my bowl. Now we merely ignored each other.

"Sit, sit." Hanchin waved at the seat between us. "Changyin tells me you're interested in Russia."

"Sir, perhaps you could come out to the terrace and meet my friends," Tongyin said, giving me a dismissive glance that made me want to kick him. "You needn't bore yourself entertaining my little sister."

"On the contrary, Leiyin and I have become great friends. I hope to turn her to the Socialist cause." He smiled at me, and again, heat rose from the center of my being.

"Ah. Ha, ha. A good joke, sir. A splendid joke. Yes, she'll make a fine peasant rebel in that silk dress."

Hanchin turned to face me. "It's been a pleasure. If you have problems finding those books, Miss Song, write to me care of the *China Millennium Journal* office. I'm sure we have spare copies lying around."

Tongyin looked startled. I gave Hanchin my widest smile. "Thank you so much, Mr. Yen. You're very kind."

I watched Hanchin stroll through the French doors with Tongyin. Then I walked as fast as decently possible out of the drawing room and ran up the stairs to the first landing. From behind the heavy silk drapes I peeked out the tall windows that overlooked the terrace. I watched him, drank in the sight of him. Outside, torches scented with citronella lit the terrace and their softly pungent fragrance drifted up. Hanchin was seated in a wicker chair, his long legs crossed, gesturing with his hands as he spoke. Hovering around him, an admiring circle of young men, their summer suits pale as moth wings.

※ ※ ※

The Liu family was the first to leave the party. We gathered to see them off at the front gate. After our repeated promises that we would visit their home very soon, they got into their motorcar and departed.

"A fine old family," said Father, "with good habits. Early to bed and early to rise."

"Well now, Second Sister." Gaoyin slipped an arm around Sueyin's shoulders as we returned to the villa. "Liu Tienzhen seems very nice."

Sueyin said nothing but when we entered the front door, she darted up the staircase in a near run. My father and brothers, who had gone ahead to rejoin our guests, didn't notice.

"What's wrong with her?" said Gaoyin. We hurried upstairs and found Sueyin sobbing on her bed. Gaoyin knelt beside her.

"What's the matter? We still have guests to entertain, Second Sister."

"Second Sister, what is wrong?" I had begun to wonder at her fiancé's early departure.

Sueyin turned to us, eyes red, expression bitter. "Didn't you notice? Couldn't you see?"

"Notice what?"

"Tienzhen left early because he missed his pipe. Father has betrothed me to a man who takes opium." Her voice was low, trembling with the effort required to keep hysteria from creeping into her words.

"Are you sure?" Gaoyin was shocked. I slumped against the bedroom wall, my fingers running over the flocked surface, pale green leaves on vines.

"He asked me if I also took opium," said Sueyin. "So yes, I'm sure."

How could we not have noticed? The soft, dreamy gaze that we had thought was directed at her beauty, the languid movements that had seemed so refined.

Sueyin kicked off her shoes wearily and sank onto the bed, a crumpled swath of emerald silk. She turned her face away from us. "I'm not going down to the party again."

❦

I turn to my souls. *I should have stayed with Sueyin to console her, not left her alone. But I was seventeen and self-centered.*

Yes, look at you, my *hun* soul agrees. *There you go to your room, to devour the rest of* Anna Karenina.

My two other souls say nothing, but my *yang* soul shakes his gray head and my *yin* soul gives me a shrug. I taste salt, catch the faintest whiff of pipe tobacco, and look at them. My *yin* soul shrugs again.

Taste is yang, *the scent is mine,* she says. *We can't hide our feelings from you.*

So that's what it is, I say. *And how does my* hun *soul show displeasure? Unpleasant noises?*

No, it says with a shrug of its gleaming shoulders. *I would just slap you.*

~~~

When I lay in bed that night, Sueyin's predicament didn't occupy my thoughts for long. My brain seethed with schemes. Next time, I would be ready. Next time, I would have read all the books Hanchin had mentioned. Next time, my hair would be pinned up and I would look older. Next time, I would have read all the recent issues of *China Millennium* and know what to say to him.

The following morning I took my time waking up. Hanchin would wait for me to finish university before proposing. We'd give readings where Hanchin would recite his poetry, some dedicated to his muse, his young wife. He'd give lectures all over China and I would travel with him as his secretary, his helpmate.

Nanny Qiu's stage whisper cut through my drowsy daydreams.

"*Wah, wah,* Third Young Mistress. Get up, get up!" A firm hand shook my shoulder.

"Oh, Nanny, let me sleep some more."

"Your eldest sister and eldest brother are in the Master's study, arguing with him."

Immediately, I sat up and swung my legs out from under the covers. Changyin never challenged Father's decisions. Nobody did. I pulled on my dressing gown while my toes searched the floor beside my bed for slippers.

"What are they arguing about, Nanny?"

She held my feet still and pulled a slipper onto each foot. "It's about your second sister's marriage. But once they shut the door, I heard nothing. I have no reason to be in that part of the house." She looked at me very pointedly, her face bland and virtuous.

I hurried to the east wing of the house just in time to see Tongyin quietly pull open the balcony door. He glared but I held a finger to my lips. Our curiosity proved stronger than the animosity between us, and he shrugged, letting me join him. The long balcony ran nearly the full width of the house, sheltering the French doors below from all but the worst gusts of rain. We crawled along and crouched beneath Father's study window, which he kept slightly open even on the coldest days. Knees drawn up to our chins like children, we strained to listen.

"He would need to be a man of enormous willpower to overcome the habit, Father." Gaoyin's voice was shrill, agitated. "His mother gave him opium when he was only a child; he won't be able to give it up."

"Father, he'll bankrupt his family. As all opium addicts do. What would happen to Sueyin then?" Changyin, reasonable and calm.

"He couldn't bankrupt that family's wealth in three lifetimes," said Father. "The betrothal has been official for years. The marriage will go ahead."

"Father, we beg you. Any man in China would give thanks to the gods for a wife like Sueyin," Gaoyin pleaded. "Please, don't marry our sister to a man who will only shame her."

"Enough!" Father's voice, like thunder.

Although we were safe outside, both Tongyin and I winced. Inside, the silence was absolute. I had no doubt my brother and sister had dropped to their knees at Father's bark of displeasure.

"Are you saying your father does not know what he is doing?" There was no reply. He wasn't asking a question.

"Are you saying your father did not think this through? These are dangerous times for China. We will see far worse turmoil soon. We must be well-connected to survive. The judge's integrity is respected by even the most corrupt officials. Do you understand? Sueyin isn't marrying the son of Judge Liu, she is marrying into his *family*."

Another brief silence.

"Now let us go down to breakfast."

We waited outside until we heard them leave the study. Tongyin slid to the balcony door to take a peek, but before he reached for the handle, I pulled him back.

"Second Brother, why would Madame Liu give opium to her own son?"

"Liu Tienzhen is an only child, you idiot. She doesn't want him to leave home for a career or to travel. The pipe keeps him docile."

He slipped through the balcony door and ran silently down the staircase.

༄༅

I shake my head. *Father looked down on opium users. He scorned families who allowed opium in their homes. He said it was a cer-*

tain sign the family would lose all their wealth and standing. He despised the drug.

So would anyone, my *hun* soul says, *who understood how Western nations gained power by holding China ransom over opium.*

Father told us about classmates and friends of his who had taken up the pipe and set aside ambition, I recall. *I thought that surely once he knew about Tienzhen, he would have called off the marriage. But he didn't.*

No, *he did not,* my *yang* soul says. He looks a little uncomfortable. *In unpredictable times, wealth and connections matter more. The Judge had both and his son was the price.*

A *price Sueyin has to pay.* Her voice is sweet but there is a bitter note to my *yin* soul's words, like the fetid, sweet opium smoke that drifts past my nose.

Once she's married, Sueyin's days and years will belong to her husband's family, says my *hun* soul. *Her husband's opium habit makes it that much worse.* Its bright silhouette glitters.

A *woman's life is never her own,* my *yin* soul says. She puffs out her pink cheeks to blow incense ash off the altar. *She depends first upon her parents and then upon the husband they choose for her.*

I don't need my souls to tell me that a young wife's fate is set from the moment she crosses the threshold of her husband's home. She addresses her in-laws as Jia Po and Gong Gong, Mother and Father. Her survival depends on a carefully serene, powdered face, her happiness on the way her in-laws treat her. Until she delivers an heir, her status is tenuous. If she proves infertile, concubines may displace her, family members will bully her. She will struggle to stay afloat in the fickle waters of the inner courtyard, buffeted by forces beyond her control. Her only salvation is to deliver sons. She waits for the older generation to die. Then and only then can she take her turn as matriarch, her every whim a command, her lightest remarks an affliction to her sons' wives.

If you had bothered to remember this when it came to your own situation, your life would have been quite different. My *hun* soul shimmers, a shining form without features. I can't discern its expression. Its voice, however, sounds sad rather than accusatory.

2

The next day, I told Wang Nanmei everything at lunchtime. We sat in a corner of the dining hall, but our classmates' laughter and talk were so loud we could barely hear each other, so we slipped outdoors to walk in the schoolyard, arm in arm. Nanmei squeezed my fingers, her mouth opening in excitement when I described meeting Yen Hanchin, his voice, his beautiful hands, his eyes, our conversation.

"Oh, Leiyin, I'm so envious! The actual translator! That's almost as good as meeting Tolstoy!"

"I'm sure Tolstoy isn't anywhere near as handsome."

She eyed me and I blushed.

"Are you in love with him, Leiyin?"

"Well, at least a crush." That was all I cared to admit for now. "But I have something else to tell you."

Her plump, pretty face fell when she learned of my father's decision.

"It's a waste of your intelligence if you don't use it to help our country," she said. Nanmei never minced words. She was a merchant's daughter. Her father owned several silk and cotton mills and she tended to categorize things simply, as either wasteful or worthwhile.

Both of us admired the beautiful, American-educated widow of the Father of our Nation, taking to heart Madame Sun Yat-sen's words to seek higher education. It wasn't hard to see myself standing by the blackboard, chalk in hand, or bent over a young pupil to correct her writing. I imagined a class full of earnest faces, taking in my every word, wanting to please me the way I always wanted to please my teachers.

"I need to convince Father I'm serious about university," I said. "He seems to believe it's just a passing whim."

She grabbed my hand. "Let's go to the library. I know what to do. You need to win a scholarship!"

On the long table by the door of the school library were boxes holding application forms, each box labeled with the name of a university. One form remained for scholarships to Hangchow Women's University.

"There's one left. It's fate," she said, snatching it up. "When you win this scholarship, your father won't have to pay tuition or boarding fees. He'll be so proud—Hangchow Women's University is so prestigious. He'll realize how serious you are, and how much others value your achievements."

"Oh, Nanmei, I've been trying to figure out what to do for days and you've just solved my problem! Do you really think I can win a scholarship?"

"Of course. Hangchow Women's wants the best and brightest young women, and if you're not that, I don't know who is."

Then she leaned over to whisper mischievously in my ear. "And just think how much it will impress Yen Hanchin."

I hadn't even thought of how a scholarship could elevate me in Hanchin's esteem. But Nanmei was right. How could I expect Hanchin, with all his degrees from Chinese and Russian universities, to marry a mere high school graduate? An education was critical to my plans for a future with Hanchin.

Already, Nanmei was seated at a library table, scanning the form. How lucky I was to have her as my friend. She looked up and flashed a smile, her beautiful eyes bright and happy.

"We'll go to university together," she said. "We must. We're the generation of women Madame Sun Yat-sen is counting on to bring China out of the feudal era."

⌒⌒⌒

Sueyin went to Shanghai for two weeks. Her wedding was set for the middle of June, and this visit with Gaoyin would be her last taste of freedom, for once she married she would need permission from her husband and in-laws to travel away from home. Sueyin returned from her trip with a trunkload of clothes and gifts, seemingly in better spirits.

"How beautiful." I held up a pair of gloves, thin kid leather in navy blue edged with tiny silver studs. "Have you worn these yet?"

"Yes. I went to a film premiere with Gaoyin and Shen. The

gloves match this." She pulled a navy blue handbag out of a box. "I met the director, Cheng Puhkao. He asked me to audition for his next film."

"Oh, you should, Second Sister! You're far more beautiful than any of those film actresses."

"What do I know about acting?" She shook her head. "I've never even acted in a school play. Anyway, Judge Liu would never allow it. Don't be foolish, Leiyin. I'm getting married."

She lifted a pasteboard box out of her trunk and set it on her dressing table, then raised its lid to reveal an interior divided into two sections. One held a stack of writing paper, heavy and cream colored; the other held matching envelopes. Silently she pulled out an envelope and opened it to reveal a lining of navy blue tissue paper. It was the finest stationery I had ever seen.

"Gaoyin ordered this especially. She has a box of the same stationery."

⤳⤳⤳

I can tell this gift matters more to her than all the beautiful clothes Nanny Qiu is putting away in her trunk. I want to reach out and hug Sueyin, an impossible task for my incorporeal body.

Of the three of us, Second Sister was always the most compliant, the most sweet-natured. She was as transparent as water and utterly without guile. I study the scene in her bedroom: two sisters chatting, looking through one's purchases. There is something different about Sueyin.

There is an edge to her voice now, so unfamiliar, my *yin* soul says, twisting a pigtail around her finger. A wistful scent of jasmine tea fills my nostrils.

I study Sueyin's features again and see a new hardness in the set of her lips, the lift of her chin. She is as beautiful as ever, but there is something smoldering beneath her features and a touch of something else, another expression.

Rebellion, my *hun* soul says. It glows quietly beside me. *I think Sueyin harbors mutinous thoughts.*

Nonsense, says my *yang* soul. He strokes his goatee, a complacent look on his face. *Never Sueyin. She is the most obedient of daughters.* He registers approval, sweet lychee juice washing over my tongue.

∽∼∾

After that first evening on the terrace with Hanchin, Tongyin began quoting Marx the way a downspout gurgles out rainwater. Normally he spent his days sleeping until noon, loitering around the house for a few hours before going out with friends. After the party, however, he spent more time at home, mostly in the library. Father had reservations about the Chinese Communist Party, but he had no objections to socialism residing on his bookshelves, saying we needed to understand before we were qualified to criticize. The low table beside Tongyin's chair was piled high with books about Russia and socialist philosophy, and news magazines—including issues of *China Millennium.*

Tongyin asked Father to add Hanchin to the guest list for the next salon. Then my brother actually made a trip to the kitchens to make sure shrimp toasts would be on the menu. If I had been wheedling for such favors, the entire family would have known about my infatuation. For once, I truly appreciated my otherwise useless brother.

∽∽∽

I dressed carefully for the next salon, choosing a pale green summer frock with lace at the neckline. Nanny Qiu twisted my hair into a chignon, the style Gaoyin used to favor before she bobbed her hair. My mother's jade bracelets hung on my wrist, tinkling sweetly whenever I raised my arm.

"I thought you were eating supper with Stepmother and Sueyin," Tongyin said with a scowl when I came downstairs. Although his voice was casual, I could tell he was nervous. He was using even more cologne than usual.

"Tonight I'd like to sit in on the salon."

"You're very dressed up." His eyes narrowed.

"This is my coolest frock. It's very hot today. You already have sweat beads on your upper lip, Second Brother." Helpfully, I offered him a handkerchief.

He snatched one from his own pocket and wiped his face. There was no sport in making Tongyin self-conscious about his appearance, it was too easy. But before he could snap at me, servants opened the front door wide to signal that guests were approaching, and Tongyin hurried to join Father and Changyin.

I retreated to the terrace and sat under the shade of the cassia tree. In the heat, its blossoms were dropping prematurely, covering the wicker furniture with limp golden petals. Shielded by the high back of the peacock chair, I peered through its woven wicker and watched the guests arrive in small groups: a dozen in all, mostly men, only three women. I caught no more than a glimpse of Hanchin before he entered the house, Tongyin glued to his side.

Once the guests were settled in the small drawing room, I slipped in and stood against the wall, so that Hanchin was in my line of sight while I pretended to watch the three poets seated at the front. While they read, I feasted my eyes on Hanchin. He'd had his hair cut since the night of the party. He wore linen trousers and a short-sleeved cotton shirt, as did most of the others in this hot weather. His bare arms were lightly tanned, lean and muscular. I wondered if his torso would be as brown as his arms. From time to time, he closed his eyes to listen and I could tell when he liked what he heard because he would tilt his head slightly and nod. Tongyin sat on his left, and a woman on his right. She leaned over constantly to whisper in his ear. She was thin, with a blotchy complexion, I was pleased to notice.

When the readings were over, a few guests clustered around Father, but most were out on the terrace, where the evening air was cooler and servants were bringing refreshments.

Hanchin and some of the others stood at the far end of the terrace. Tongyin was with them. My brother's face was earnest and his eyes were trained on Hanchin. The rest of the group kept glancing over at the table, where servants were arranging platters. The three women sat on the wicker chairs beneath the cassia tree, conversing. I could tell the thin one wasn't really paying attention to the others, her eyes kept straying to Hanchin. As did mine. I had to appear disinterested, pay no more attention to him than to any of the other guests.

But I found myself making my way across the terrace and stopping in front of the group surrounding Hanchin.

"Gentlemen. The food is ready, please don't be so polite. Help yourselves."

Although snacks were appropriate for this hour, Stepmother always served hearty fare in addition to the small morsels and sweet pastries. White steamed buns, both plain and stuffed with pork and vegetables; curried-chicken pastries; and slices of roast pork. And, on this evening, shrimp toasts.

Years ago I had remarked that some of these guests ate enough for a week. Stepmother had replied very gently, "For some, it's the most food they see all week."

There was a hesitant but eager shuffle to the buffet table. Even the women in the wicker chairs behind us abandoned their seats. Now I was almost alone with Hanchin. And Tongyin. I held my hand out to Hanchin.

"How nice to see you again, Mr. Yen. Can I bring you something from the buffet table?"

Jade bangles tinkled, traitors to my body's shaking. He held my hand by the fingertips and bowed slightly. He didn't kiss it in the French style, as I had hoped, but he held on for a moment longer than necessary, I thought.

"Thank you, Miss Song, but I find it difficult to eat when it's so hot."

"Oh. Perhaps a cold drink, then?"

"You're interrupting, Little Sister. We were just talking about Japan's influence on the socialist movement in China." My brother's tone implied I wasn't equal to the conversation.

"Yes, Japanese writings on socialism made a lot of impact in China in those early days." I smiled serenely and refused to budge. Tongyin's eyes bulged at this.

"There's an article from *China Millennium* on this very topic," Hanchin said. "The mid-April issue, I believe. There's a quote in there I wish I could show you, Tongyin."

"Oh, we have that issue, it's in the library. Let me get it." And with that, Tongyin hurried off, leaving me to stand there, facing Hanchin.

"Are you secretly a socialist, Miss Song?" He said this lightly, in a teasing voice. He knew quite well, as did everyone in Changchow, that Father was staunchly for the Nationalists.

"I'm not sure. Mostly I'd like women to do more for China. Get better educations, take more roles in government. I want to teach."

"Well, socialism holds out more hope on those issues. Once you've graduated from university, will your father allow you to teach?"

I blushed and looked away. How could I tell him that even my plans for university might come to nothing? There were times when a teaching career seemed like a bright but uncertain dream, a blurred horizon of beautiful colors. If I managed to graduate, would my father even allow me to earn a living?

He must have sensed my embarrassment.

"An education is never wasted," he said. His smile. Oh, his

smile. "You may lose all that you acquire, but knowledge and wisdom remain yours forever. One of my favorite sayings. By the time you graduate perhaps your situation will be quite different."

I couldn't believe that all around the terrace, people were eating and drinking, engrossed in their own conversations. It seemed impossible that they weren't looking at us, the tension radiating from my body in near-tangible waves. I could barely breathe from the effort of holding back my hand, from reaching out to touch his face.

Finally I blurted out, "Tongyin will be a long time finding the mid-April issue. It's in my bedroom."

We both burst out laughing. And then, people did look.

⌒⌒⌒

My souls and I examine the scene.

Look at the expression on his face. That was when I truly began to believe he might be able to love me. His words were so kind. And as for the situation being very different, well, if we were married, it would be my husband's opinion that mattered. Hanchin would let me work by his side, or teach.

You believed he would love you, my *hun* soul remarks, its tone a little dry. *After all, you loved him, how could he not love you back?* It pinches me, but its shining fingers are playful, not spiteful.

Adoration glistens in the eyes of my memory-self. On Hanchin's face, there is enjoyment. And something else. Is it tenderness or relief? I don't recall seeing that look the first time. But on that day, I realize, Hanchin's smile and, above all, the intensity of his gaze, conspired to convince me that he too was falling in love.

❧

I thought about Hanchin even more, if that was possible. I imagined my student life, when he would come to visit me whenever he had a lecture to give in Hangchow. Effortlessly I slipped into daydreams about the conversations we would have about poetry, politics, and our future together. I was bursting with the need to tell someone about my feelings. Normally I would have confided in Sueyin, but this time I didn't trust her to take my side. She saw only Yen Hanchin, a poor poet, the infamous translator of *Anna Karenina*, an unsuitable alliance for a family such as ours.

There was only one person I had entrusted with my secret. With our convocation soon to come, I had a good excuse to spend hours with Nanmei at her home. We were responsible for two speeches at the ceremony: Nanmei was to thank our teachers on behalf of the graduating class, and I was writing the valedictory speech. We had decided my speech would urge our classmates to pursue careers in the service of our country. The work went slowly, however. I couldn't concentrate.

"Stop thinking about Yen Hanchin!" Nanmei's voice was impatient but she laughed when she poked me with the eraser end of a pencil. I blushed and pushed back the chair.

We were in her father's library, which was much smaller than ours. Its shelves contained more popular novels and *wuxia*, martial arts tales, than Tang Dynasty classics. When we had come in, her father had been half asleep in an armchair, a newspaper draped across his lap. I had hesitated, but Nanmei woke him up with a rustle of the paper.

"Father, we have schoolwork to do and you're just taking a nap. You can do that in your own room."

To my astonishment, Mr. Wang merely shook a finger at her, greeted me with a smile, and left with his newspaper. In a million years I couldn't imagine taking such liberties with Father.

"I have an idea!" Nanmei's pretty eyes were as lively as tadpoles. She put a fresh sheet of paper on the table in front of me and cleared away the rest of my scribbles. "Since you seem to spend most of your time imagining conversations with Yen Hanchin, pretend you're writing him a letter explaining why it matters so much for women to seek higher education and careers."

After that, the speech writing went much better.

❦

"Where is Tongyin? Is he still in bed?" Father asked. We were having lunch and Stepmother had just placed slices of fish and tofu on Father's plate. Then she rotated the circular inner table so that the dish rested in front of Changyin and his wife, Geeling, who had made a rare effort to walk over and dine with us.

"I was in the garden when Second Brother left the house this morning," said my sister-in-law in her tiny voice. "It was eight o'clock." And she ducked her head to stare into her rice bowl, as though waiting to be scolded for speaking.

Geeling had been betrothed to Changyin since childhood, but it was not until Changyin was older that he had declared he would never marry a woman with tiny feet. Her parents had to loosen her bindings after they had been set. Sometimes the letting-loose process resulted in painfully deformed bones. Geeling carried herself with a shyness that seemed equally painful. My sister-in-law barely spoke, and when she did, it was in a whispery, hesitant voice. She seemed comfortable only with her children and rarely left their house.

A servant was dispatched to speak to our gatekeeper and returned with the news that Tongyin had taken a rickshaw to the *China Millennium* office.

"I have no idea what would inspire him to get up early, but if he has gone to see Yen Hanchin, I have no objections." Father helped himself to some pickled radish.

"Father, I'm a little worried," Changyin said. "Tongyin is very impressionable. Yen Hanchin is from a good family, but he leans to the left since his return from Russia."

"First Son, don't be too concerned," Father went on. "Yen Hanchin is probably just interested in the philosophy behind socialism and other political systems. He is an intellectual. When he gains more recognition for his fine poetry, he will forget about politics."

I glowed at Father's praise for Hanchin's poetry. When the time came, I would appeal to Father's soft spot for poets.

❧

That evening, Tongyin arrived home shortly after supper, flushed and talkative. I was reading a translation of *Eugene Onegin*, one of the books Hanchin had recommended to me the night of the party. Father and Changyin were reading newspapers, and Stepmother and Sueyin sat on the sofa, gathered under a pool of light from the floor lamp behind them. They were embroidering bags of red silk to give to the most honored wedding guests. Sueyin didn't need my second-rate embroidery skills.

Tongyin waved off Stepmother's attempts to order him a supper tray.

"No need, no need at all. I ate at *China Millennium*'s offices. We had noodles sent up from a street vendor. Delicious."

I couldn't believe that my brother, who scorned all but the smartest cafés, would eat street food. But apparently Hanchin's company had influenced him. I felt a twinge of envy. I imagined the camaraderie at *China Millennium* to be like that of the officers' quarters in Vronsky's regiment.

"Father, I'm going to be Yen Hanchin's assistant." He looked ridiculously happy. "A magazine is a busy place, and he says I can be useful just running his errands."

Tongyin had never spoken of any ambitions. For him, university was no more than a place where he could meet his friends every day. By some miracle, Hanchin had inspired Tongyin to take on responsibility.

"Is he paying you to be his assistant?" I asked. My pang of resentment was now a full, aching jealousy.

"Not at all. No. I'm not staff, I'm just a volunteer. An apprentice of sorts."

"Second Son, I am pleased that you want to help Yen Hanchin," Father said. "I am less pleased, however, that you're associating with a magazine that often prints editorials sympathizing with the left."

Tongyin sat on a leather ottoman beside Father, his face earnest.

"It's not a problem, Father. Not at all. Actually I'll be managing Hanchin's lecture schedule. He's in demand and it's quite a job keeping track of all his commitments. I'll only be at the magazine's offices because that's where he works all day."

Father relaxed. "Second Son, I approve. But your name must never be associated with that magazine."

"Of course, Father, of course." Tongyin's voice then took on a wheedling tone as he turned to Changyin. "Tomorrow evening Hanchin is giving a talk at a school. About modern Russia. Why don't you come, Eldest Brother? We'd still get home in time for a late supper."

Changyin shook his head and returned to his newspaper. "I'm busy already."

I spoke up. "I'd like to attend that lecture. We've been studying Russia and I could learn something useful. Father, may I go?"

"Third Daughter, you may attend if you are chaperoned by one of your brothers," Father said, standing. "Good night."

"Good night, Father," we chorused as he left the room.

"Well, I'm going back to my house now," said Changyin, folding his newspaper. "Since Tongyin is obviously going, consider yourself chaperoned, Third Sister."

Tongyin glared at me, but Changyin had said his piece.

Sueyin looked up from her needlework. "Leiyin, you were coming with me to the Yuans' garden party tomorrow night."

I knew Sueyin wanted to spend as much time as possible with me before she moved to the Liu estate.

"Second Sister, please forgive me and give my apologies to the Yuans. I really would like to go to this lecture."

She nodded without reproach and went upstairs, taking her sewing box with her. I noticed how much thinner she had grown, how heavily the box seemed to weigh her down.

Stepmother gave me a long look.

How cruel we can be to the ones we love. I plunged back into my book.

3

To add credibility to my story, I went to Hanchin's lecture with a notebook and pen. As our rickshaw lurched along potholed streets, I received a stern speech from Tongyin.

"Don't say anything, Third Sister, not a thing. If you embarrass me, I'll never take you anywhere again."

"You never take me anywhere anyway. What do I have to lose?"

"Third Sister Leiyin, I'm warning you."

"You make it sound as though I *want* to embarrass myself. Stop worrying. Why don't you tell me a bit about Hanchin's lecture? Then I might not need to ask questions by the time we get there."

"It's fascinating, truly fascinating." His face grew animated. "Hanchin says it all comes down to class struggle. Just like prerevolutionary Russia, most of our population is rural. China is still an agrarian economy."

Tongyin's account of the parallels between prerevolutionary

Russia and contemporary China impressed me, mostly because of his passion. Hanchin had roused my indolent brother into taking an interest in something other than hair pomade.

The rickshaw took us into the Clocktower District, then through a maze of streets lined with shops, now closed. We stopped in front of a low, shabby building. Painted on the wall beside the door were the words DISTRICT PRIMARY SCHOOL 47. We entered a corridor that led between empty classrooms. I thought at first we had come to the wrong school. At the end of the hallway, light streamed from an open doorway where some plainly dressed men stood, talking and smoking.

"I thought you said this was a school lecture." I was sure this wasn't at all what Father had imagined. The building was so run-down. And where were the students?

"It's being held at a school, isn't it?" He sounded defensive.

When we looked inside, Hanchin was at the front of the room, busy chatting with a group of young men. I scanned the crowd and was glad I'd worn a plain *qipao*. In his linen suit, Tongyin looked like a foreigner among the drab grays and blues of a mostly student crowd. There were a few women there, all wearing *qipaos* in conservative dark colors.

My brother waved to the men at the front. I recognized some of them and tried not to stare openly at Hanchin. Unlike some of the women in the audience, I noticed.

"We saved you a chair," said one of Hanchin's friends as we moved closer. "Right here, at the front. But, ah, you brought your sister with you. Miss Song." And he bowed. "Please, take my seat."

"I'm happy to stand by the wall."

"Please, I insist."

There was an exaggerated courtesy about him that didn't sit well with me even though he had a handsome face, square-jawed and masculine. His manner was slightly mocking. I now recalled his name. Cha Zhiming.

"No, Zhiming, that won't do at all. Not at all. I'll stand and my sister can have my chair." Turning to me, Tongyin hissed, "Go sit. Now. And shut up."

I sat down in the front row, opened my notebook, and un-capped my pen. Hanchin took his place at the front of the room, glanced around, and smiled. A warm, intimate smile that heated the blood in my veins, for I was certain the smile was for me. There were perhaps sixty people crammed into the room and within the first few minutes they were all silent, spellbound. I could have sat forever in that rundown classroom with its rows of battered wooden chairs.

My notes from that lecture were brief, a few scribbles:

Social change. Peasants and property.

Industrialization. (Circled several times.)

Free education. (Circled several times.)

⌒⌒⌒

He certainly has a quality about him, my *yang* soul says, his grudging appreciation evident in the wash of a sweet fruit taste across my tongue. Red plum. *A fine speaker.*

My souls wander through the classroom. Reluctantly, I turn my eyes away from Hanchin to look at my brother, leaning against the wall to my right. Tongyin's face is slightly flushed and his lips are parted, moist. His eyes, fixed on Hanchin, glitter. I notice that almost all the women in the audience share this same rapt look. And so do I. Had I been so obvious?

There is something else also, and my *yin* soul catches the question in my mind, turns to me with a query in her deep brown eyes.

There is something not right about this crowd, I say. In the grip of my infatuation, what had I seen and heard that evening except Hanchin? But now I scan through the crowd and see faces that don't match the humble clothing they wear. New cloth caps pulled over well-cut hair, hands too smooth for factory work, clean-shaven chins.

Hanchin speaks in an even, gracefully cadenced voice, so perfect for reciting poetry, not at all a rabble-rouser, but calm and reasonable, with an occasional flash of wit to keep his audience alert. His words couldn't possibly be used against him. He praises education—surely the safest ploy of all, for what Chinese can argue against education? He speaks of a minimum wage as one option to improve working conditions, unions as a way of opening civil discussions between workers and employers.

You were so sheltered, my *yin* soul points out. She is seated on a low bench against the wall of the classroom, arranging her pleated skirt. *It was a complicated and dangerous time.*

Hanchin was being watched. And he knew it, says my *yang* soul. His round eyeglasses reflect an image of the single naked lightbulb dangling from the ceiling.

It means your brother was being watched as well, says my *hun* soul.

At the end of the talk, the audience clapped wildly. Tongyin, along with a few others, circulated through the crowd to take subscriptions for *China Millennium*. I remained seated, pretending I wasn't staring at Hanchin while he shook hands and answered questions, smiling and assured.

Beside me, Cha Zhiming stretched out his hands to rest them on a chair. He looked thoughtful, no trace of mockery on his face. I was pleased but not surprised. How could anyone not be moved by Hanchin's words?

"Well, Miss Song, which part of the talk made the biggest impression on you?"

Eagerness to talk about the lecture overcame my dislike for him. After all, what did I really have against Cha Zhiming except for the fact that he was my brother's friend?

"I was thinking that China has such a long tradition of valuing education. Surely it would be easier to achieve universal literacy here than in Russia."

He nodded, as though in agreement. I warmed to him slightly.

Then he asked, "What about Tongyin? Why do you suppose he's interested?"

It was obvious to me that Tongyin had developed a schoolgirl crush on Yen Hanchin, but I wasn't going to disparage my brother in front of an outsider, so I just shrugged. Tongyin, who had finished canvassing the crowd, stood by the door, where Hanchin was shaking hands with departing admirers. After a few words with him, my brother hurried over to us.

"Some of us are going around the corner to have a quick supper with Hanchin. Leiyin, you need to go home now. I'll call you a rickshaw."

"You're supposed to chaperone me at all times. I'll go with you to supper." I held back my eagerness.

"Absolutely not. No, that's impossible. Teahouses are no place for a young girl."

"Then you have to take me home."

Tongyin appeared on the brink of a tantrum.

"I have a suggestion," said Cha Zhiming. "Let me take your sister home. I can't stay for supper anyway."

"But if Father finds out I wasn't chaperoned . . ."

"Your father will never know I was the one who brought you home. The rickshaw can drop you at the gate and continue on. You can tell your family that Tongyin brought you home and went off again."

Tongyin's face brightened. "Cha Zhiming, you're a true friend."

I couldn't bicker with my brother in public, especially with Hanchin there. But if I had to leave, I would make a graceful exit.

"All right. But before we go, I'll congratulate Mr. Yen on his speech."

I marched up to Hanchin with a mask of confidence I didn't feel.

"Miss Song, what a nice surprise it was to see you here." Again, that warm and knowing smile.

"You were wonderful." My cheeks felt hot, my stomach unsettled. "Now I want more than ever to bring literacy to all our citizens."

"I'm so very glad to hear you say that. Teaching is the most fulfilling career anyone could have. Ah, Tongyin. You'll both be joining us for supper?"

"No, she can't stay. Cha here is taking her home," my brother said quickly.

"Well then, Miss Song. Perhaps we'll meet some other time."

Tongyin glared at me. If it were up to him, there wouldn't be another time.

In the rickshaw, Cha Zhiming and I made small talk. Gaoyin would have been proud of me. I asked a few questions, then hardly needed to speak at all. Cha Zhiming told me about his father, a general in the Nationalist army, his mother, who had died when he was in his teens, and his half brothers.

"I have three younger brothers," he said. "Were those your sisters I saw at your home? Such pretty little girls."

"I have a half sister, Fei-Fei. The others are my nieces. But tell me about your plans for university next year."

The dim streetlights hid his expression, but his voice was resigned. "I prefer the arts, but this fall I'm transferring to Whampoa Military Academy. My father let me attend university in Shanghai for a while before starting a military career, so I should be grateful."

On the street outside our home, I slipped off the rickshaw, knocked on the wicket gate, and Lao Li let me in. I didn't give Cha Zhiming a second thought.

The next afternoon, Sueyin and I were walking in the Old Garden, making our way around the lake to feed the ducks, when Nanny Qiu came charging up the path, calling out in the voice she reserved for pronouncements of doom.

"*Wah, wah,* Third Young Mistress. Your father wants you in his study. Immediately."

I hurried back to the house, leaving Sueyin surrounded by anxious ducks. When I arrived, Tongyin was in Father's study, seated on the leather sofa and looking gloomy. Father paced up and down the Turkish carpet. He motioned for me to sit beside Tongyin.

"One of your eldest brother's friends was at Yen Hanchin's lecture last night."

No wonder Tongyin looked so unhappy. The friend probably saw me get into the rickshaw with Cha Zhiming.

"Second Son, the lecture was about politics. With leftist messages. Now a daughter of our house has been seen at a political meeting."

"Sir. Not so, sir. Let me explain." Tongyin's hands plucked at his monogrammed handkerchief.

"Second Son, no explanations. I'm tolerant of your interest in politics. It is part of being a student. But your sister's reputation is another matter. When the time comes to arrange her marriage, there must be no hint of any interest in Communism. It would be extremely detrimental to her prospects."

I opened my mouth, then closed it.

"Second Son, you're an adult, but also a son of this house. You must avoid public events of a questionable nature. If Yen

Hanchin speaks on literature, or reads his poetry, you may attend. But not if the speech is about unions or socialist ideologies."

How could Father think that Hanchin's poetry was independent of his political beliefs? In *China Millennium*, it was clear that Hanchin's ideals inspired his work. Even his poetry alluded to politics and social change.

"Third Daughter, no more of this going out to working-class neighborhoods. The location of that school should have warned you, but it was not your fault. No more lectures from now on unless they're through your school."

I nodded, both disappointed and relieved. At least Father didn't know about Cha Zhiming taking me home. Tongyin tried not to look too pleased that I couldn't follow him around anymore. Behind Father's back, he made a face at me.

⸙

My *yang* soul shakes his gray head. *You were dreaming to think he would approve of your marrying such a man.*

I see that now. I sigh at the memory.

But you did so enjoy being in love. It's like being pleasantly ill, my *yin* soul says. *Drugged and excited, all at once.* She throws her arms in the air and dances along the terrace of the family shrine.

Anyway, don't you remember Father saying he believed that once Hanchin's poetry gained more recognition, he would move away from politics? I believed that everything would work out.

My *hun* soul laughs, a brittle tinkling sound. *Oh, Leiyin. Your father might have admired starving poets, but that didn't mean he wanted his daughter to marry one.*

❧

Finally, I mustered the courage to write my first letter to Hanchin:

> *Dear Mr. Yen,*
>
> *I have attached some questions about the April issue of your magazine regarding the proposal to simplify written Chinese. Please don't write back, because Father reads our letters. He would object to our correspondence—not to you specifically, but to any man who isn't a relative. I hope we'll be able to discuss these questions at the next salon. Thank you for understanding.*
>
> *Song Leiyin*

The letter was in my bag the next day when I went to see Nanmei. Nanny Qiu accompanied me as usual and I was debating whether I could go to the post office after seeing Nanmei. Could I trust Nanny to keep my secret? Once we entered the gates of the Wang estate, she headed for the servants' quarters to see who was free to enjoy a good gossip.

"What do you mean, your nanny might tell?" Nanmei looked puzzled when I asked her to post the letter for me. I realized again that her family was far more casual than mine.

A light rain had started falling, so instead of strolling in the

Wangs' gardens, we walked along the joined verandas of four houses that bordered a large courtyard. A small bamboo grove and pond amplified the sound of the raindrops.

"She might mention to my family that I'd mailed a letter at the post office."

"But that's what one does at a post office."

"At home, we leave letters on a tray in the foyer and Father's secretary posts them after Father reads them," I explained, embarrassed.

Nanmei looked shocked. "He reads your personal letters?"

"Well, personal means for the family. When Gaoyin writes to Sueyin, it's really meant for all of us."

She shook her head, incredulous, then examined the address on the letter.

"That's really close to our shoemaker's. Mother's taking us all to get measured for new shoes tomorrow. I could even deliver it personally to *China Millennium*'s office."

"Oh, Nanmei, that would be so good of you. Mail service is terrible these days. Will your mother mind if you slip away for a few minutes?"

"*All* the women of the house are going for new shoes." We both laughed. Between Nanmei's mother, her sisters, sisters-in-law, and assorted female cousins, the shop would be in chaos. She could disappear for an hour unnoticed.

"Besides, I may finally catch a glimpse of your beloved." She sounded wistful.

ᔔᓇᔕ

After every lecture, Tongyin would go out with Hanchin and a few friends for a late supper. There had even been a few nights when Tongyin hadn't come home until morning. On this evening, he returned early, just as we were finishing supper. He waved away the servant who put a bowl and chopsticks in front of him.

Tongyin pulled a book out of his satchel. "Look, here is Hanchin's latest translation. *Eugene Onegin* by Pushkin. It's fresh off the printing press."

"Isn't there already a translation?" I asked. "I've been reading *Eugene Onegin*."

"You're correct. Absolutely right. But the original by Pushkin was a novel in verse, and that first translation was in prose. Hanchin translated it in verse. He said it's the hardest work he's ever done. It took him six years. He gave me a copy as a gift."

He handed the volume to Father as though it were fine crystal. The book made its way around the table. I was the last to take a look. Hanchin had inscribed his name on the flyleaf, but just his name; there was no personal message to Tongyin.

I turned the pages slowly and carefully, scanning through the verses. This was the novel about the young girl in love with an older man. I wanted to read it all on the spot, inhale Hanchin's words until they seeped into my blood, soaked into my brain. Tucked between the pages, I found a slip of very thin paper, almost onion skin, of palest blue. A bookmark or a price tag, something the printer had left behind. Reluctantly, I gave *Eugene Onegin* back to Tongyin.

Well, I had something to show the family too, now that we were finished eating.

"Third Daughter, what time does your convocation start?"

Father interrupted my thoughts. "It's the day after tomorrow, am I correct?"

My uniform was already hanging on my closet door, the plaid skirt ironed in perfect pleats. Nanny Qiu had ribbons for my hair the exact same shade of navy blue as my blazer. Alone in my room, I had practiced giving the valedictorian speech several times.

"It starts at ten in the morning. But, Father, I'll need to arrive an hour in advance, since I'm on the student organizing committee."

"Third Daughter, you may take the motorcar and then send it back to fetch us. What awards can we expect my little bookworm to win?"

"I'm fairly sure I'll win the prize for Literature, and also for History and Geography." This was my opening.

"And the headmistress will be announcing something else, Father. I've got something to show you." I held out the envelope I'd been hiding beneath my chair.

That morning, the headmistress had called me into her office and handed me a letter from Hangchow Women's University offering me a full scholarship. I managed to hold on to my dignity in front of her, but a few minutes later when I showed the letter to Nanmei, we both screamed in jubilation, dancing up and down the hallway while our teachers looked on tolerantly.

I had managed to wait until now—after supper, when the entire family was together—to make my triumphant announcement.

"Ah, Third Daughter. More good news?" Father sounded pleased already.

"Yes, Father. My grades were good enough to win a scholarship. Here's the letter from Hangchow Women's University. Four years of tuition, all provided for."

Father read it and handed it back with a nod of satisfaction.

"A scholarship, Third Daughter. Well done, very well done. If you would like to invite some classmates for a celebration, you may do so. Or if you see something you like in a shop, put it on our account."

"Thank you, Father." I beamed. He was so pleased, as I had known he would be.

"But write to the university as soon as possible to decline so they can give this scholarship to another deserving student."

Something rose in my throat. But I held my voice steady.

"Father, what do you mean? I applied for a scholarship because you said you couldn't afford tuition. But with this scholarship, it won't cost you anything."

"Third Daughter, I'm very proud of your accomplishments, but you are not going because there is no need. You will not be working for a living. You have a comfortable future as a wife and mother."

My mouth went dry. Under the dining table, Sueyin delivered a warning kick.

"But, Father, I *want* to work. I want to be a teacher. Madame Sun Yat-sen says China needs more teachers. It's . . . it's my patriotic duty."

The dining room fell silent, an uneasy hush. Father chuckled, as though reasoning with a small child.

"Third Daughter, always so idealistic. But families such as ours do not need our women to go out and earn money. What would people think of you teaching peasants?"

"Then why did you bother sending me to school at all? Why did you bother caring about my grades?" My voice sounded strident, harsh. Father's eyes narrowed at my angry tone. Sueyin kicked me harder.

"I sent you to school because you will marry an educated young man who will want an educated wife. High school is sufficient. As for grades, in any effort, one should always strive for the highest achievement."

"And after such high achievement, all you want is for me to get married and . . . and *breed*?"

Appalled at myself for shouting at Father, I ran out of the room sobbing—angry and frightened.

∽∾∽

My *yang* soul regards me with disapproval. I bristle, but inside I am hurt.

You argued with him. Worse, you did it in front of the family. Could you not at least have disagreed with him in private? He shakes his gray head, exasperated. The taste of ginger bites at my tongue.

Father always took such pleasure in my achievements at school. He arrived early to every recital and awards ceremony. He always sat in the front row, where I could see him applaud. I can't tell you how often I saw him turn to another parent and mouth the words "That's my daughter." But those achievements meant nothing to him, in the end.

He was proud of you, my *hun* soul says. We're on the terrace outside the family shrine, and I pace back and forth, still seething at the memory.

It continues. *But a career can be a difficult burden, daily drudgery. He wanted you to have a comfortable life.*

It's so unfair! My yin soul defends me. Look at Tongyin. For him, university was just another place to have a good time. But there was never any question that he would go. He was a son. You can't blame Leiyin for being angry. What else was she to think, when Father always encouraged her to excel at school? This was the first time she realized education was only meant to increase her value in the marriage market. Her rosebud mouth purses a little, and a scent of orange blossom soothes the air.

My *hun* soul puts a shining arm around my shoulder. *Actually, I think it was the first time she realized it was possible for a child to hate her own father.*

⤜∽⤛

The next morning I went to Father's study, dragging my feet. He sat behind the huge ebony table he used as a desk. The table had belonged to my five-times-great-grandfather, and today the weight of all my ancestors' disapproval seemed to reside within its polished bulk. Without being told, I knelt in front of the table and bent my forehead to the floor, my hands outstretched on the fine Turkish carpet. I stared down at the deep blues and tobacco browns, patterns that twisted like my insides. But I was still angry.

"Third Daughter, your punishment is that you will not attend your convocation ceremonies tomorrow. Eldest Brother has already sent a note to the headmistress to say you are ill."

I willed myself to hold back my tears. I would not let Father see me cry.

He walked around the table. Shifting my eyes to the side, I

could see the tips of his shoes beside my head, bamboo leaves embroidered on their black canvas.

"Furthermore, Third Daughter, you will not leave the estate for the rest of the week."

He began pacing. "Eldest Brother and Second Sister asked me not to beat you or lock you in your room. They said missing your convocation would be punishment enough. Now sit up and listen to me."

I straightened and rested on my heels, my eyes still fixed on the rug.

"Third Daughter. You think you want to teach peasant children to read. Do you think they would come to a city school? You would need to go to them, live in remote villages. From this home to a cottage with dirt floors and vermin? An outhouse that's no more than a trench behind a wall? Daughter, you couldn't imagine such a life. Father knows this even if you don't. Go down to breakfast now and don't let me see you sulk."

He sounded almost tender, but I didn't raise my eyes to his face.

Downstairs, the silence at the breakfast table told me the extent of my disgrace. The servants avoided my eyes as they set down congee and poured bowls of chilled, sweet soy milk. Even Sueyin gave me a cold glare. It wasn't her fault I had ignored those kicks under the table.

Later, the newspapers arrived. The *Central Daily News* had printed one of Father's letters to the editor. In it, Father expressed mistrust of the young warlord Zhang Xueliang's motives for an armistice with the Nationalists. Father's mood improved considerably after that and we stopped walking on eggshells.

❧

I wasn't allowed any visitors, so Nanmei couldn't come to tell me about the convocation. I was also banned from attending our next salon, the final one of the season, but when the evening came I positioned myself behind the upstairs windows, hoping at least to catch a glimpse of Hanchin. He didn't appear. I comforted myself in the knowledge that when Father resumed his salons in the fall, Tongyin would be away at university in Shanghai and I would have opportunities to steal some time with Hanchin. But what did I have to offer him now except a dowry? I was only a high school graduate, unqualified to teach, useless for helping him in building a modern China.

All of this churned through my mind as I took daily walks with my elderly great-aunts and great-uncles around the lake in the Old Garden. I whiled away time playing with Fei-Fei and my little nieces. I explored the entire estate, something I hadn't done since I was a child. It was useless. Nothing could make me forget that all my plans had come to naught, like bright visions sunk into darkness. The library was my only refuge and that was where Tongyin found me.

"Here, take the latest issue. And you can borrow this."

He dropped a copy of *China Millennium* and his *Eugene Onegin* on the table beside me and walked out again, whistling. His uncharacteristically kind act told me my misery was so obvious that even Tongyin had noticed. The slip of pale blue onion skin was still in the book, proof that Tongyin hadn't even read it. I picked up the book and tried reading the first few pages. A week ago, I would have devoured it, but now all I wanted to do was cry.

I turned my attention to *China Millennium*, flipped through the magazine, and in minutes forgot I was in disgrace with my father, forgot I had missed my convocation, forgot I couldn't go to college:

QUESTIONS FROM READERS

In this issue, we inaugurate a new column. Unlike Letters to the Editor, where readers express their opinions, this feature answers questions from readers. We have many young readers who send in questions about our articles.

Our first question is from a young reader named Song who has concerns about proposals for simplifying our written language. Staff writer Yen Hanchin replies . . .

It was a secret correspondence, carried out in plain sight. What else could it mean except that he cared for me? He understood my situation and had shown the utmost delicacy by acknowledging my letter through his magazine.

❧

In our family, I tell my souls, there is a tale of a many-times-great-grandfather who fell in love with his bride before he had even seen her. As required by tradition, he never met the bride chosen for him until their wedding day. But they exchanged letters, for that was encouraged. They wrote to each other, composing verses so exquisite that when they finally met, they were already deeply in love.

Correspondence is a time-honored and entirely proper way for young people to get to know each other, my yang soul declares. *It allows a contemplation of each other's qualities far more meaningful than the distractions of dancing and films.*

How wonderful, my yin soul says. *To be in love with your husband before the wedding. And through poetry.* There is a sweet, musky scent in the winter air, amber and roses, and her face is rapt. *How happy they must have been.*

I shake my head. *Only for a while. The bride died in childbirth and her husband published their poems in a book dedicated to her memory. Father had a copy. I read them, but I was too young to truly understand.*

But you were enthralled by the notion of falling in love through letters, my hun soul suggests.

I knew it was possible to fall in love without ever meeting your heart's partner. It happened to our ancestor, it's not merely romantic fiction.

Questions about politics aren't romance, my yang soul points out, wagging his cane at me.

Oh, says my yin soul, rolling her brown eyes, *it's the fact that Hanchin devised a way for them to correspond in secret. You're all dry bones, yang, not a single soft spot.*

She skips to the edge of the terrace and turns to look up at the sky. It is still winter. Months of memories had flowed through my mind yet hardly any time at all had gone by in the real world.

Until you met Hanchin, all the obstacles in your life had been childish and trivial, hardly worth any distress. My yang soul strokes his gray goatee and squints at me in disapproval. *You couldn't imagine being thwarted. This clever correspondence only reinforced that belief.*

You still believed you could persuade your father, my *hun* soul says. *You still believed you would go to college.*

4

As soon as my house arrest was over, I went to see Nanmei and found her unhappy but philosophical. She wasn't going to Hangchow Women's after all, either. Nanmei's mother had made arrangements for her to attend Soochow University and to live with her aunt and uncle.

"My parents decided I shouldn't live in a dormitory when I could save them money by living with family." She groaned, and fell facedown on her bed. "Soochow is the only place with a university where we also have family, so Soochow it has to be."

Her news made mine slightly easier to share. She sat up and gave me a long hug.

"I promise to write to you every week; you'll know everything I'm doing. Promise you'll do the same, Leiyin."

"There won't be much to tell. I'll just be at home with my brain rotting away. Anyway, how can I write anything meaningful when Father reads all my letters?"

"Get a box at the post office, of course."

I shake my head.

"For goodness' sake, Leiyin. If you're worried about Nanny Qiu, just give her a little bribe to keep your secret." She rolls her eyes at my skeptical look. "Sometimes I don't understand how someone with your brains can be so naive. You could ask Hanchin to write to that post office box too."

She was right. "Nanmei, you're so practical and clever and I'm so . . ."

"You're so unaccustomed to deception, Leiyin."

I shrugged and pulled an envelope out of my purse. "I'll see about a mailbox. I'll find a way. But in the meantime, could you take this to the post office for me?"

⁓⁓⁓

The Questions from Readers column was proving popular. In every other issue of *China Millennium*, Hanchin replied to my questions and to others.' As I read his articles over and over, his words and opinions seeped into my thinking:

Basic arithmetic, writing, and some rudimentary science will pull peasants and small-town folk out of ignorance and superstition. Memorizing the Three Hundred Tang Poems will not. Young teachers and doctors, we urge you to find work in rural areas and to consider it a patriotic service to China. While you're young, the comforts of life matter less.

In one issue, he wrote movingly about a trip he had made to a little country school outside Soochow:

The poverty of their surroundings only made the pupils more determined to rise up out of destitution. The teacher spent his meager wages on chalk and pencils for his pupils. They shared lunches, for some of the students hadn't eaten all day. After my talk, the teacher asked me to join their little school and I must confess I was tempted. Their dedication was truly moving.

He ended each article with what had become his signature line: *You may lose all that you acquire, but knowledge and wisdom remain yours forever.*

Every word he wrote about education for the masses felt like a reproach. Unless I contributed to educating the poor and rural folk of China, how could I be worthy of Hanchin's love? I couldn't just accept Father's decision. There had to be a way.

Tongyin was now spending even more time at the journal's offices, but he didn't give up carousing with his friends completely. Sometimes they met at our house to smoke and drink on the terrace before setting out for the night. Cha Zhiming was part of that clique and whenever he caught my eye, he bowed in my direction, a patronizing smile on his face as though to remind me we shared a secret. But his manners were flawless, deferential.

Unlike some of the others, he never drank to excess or flipped his cigarette butts into the shrubbery.

"Second Son, your friend, that Cha, he seems a nice young man," Father remarked. "What are his career plans?"

We were at breakfast, and Tongyin, slurping down his congee, shrugged.

"I'm not sure, Father. Not completely. His father's a general, so he'll have a police or military career most likely."

"Military. Then why is he not attending Whampoa Military Academy?"

"He leaves for the academy this fall."

Stepmother put a slice of jellied pork on Father's side plate. "He seems thoughtful," she said. "He was kind to Fei-Fei."

"Really? When was that?" Father looked as surprised as I felt.

My stepmother paused to think. "When he was here last week. Fei-Fei was running through the garden and fell on the gravel path. He carried her to the terrace and she sat on his lap while Nanny Wong washed the blood from her knee."

"Hmmm." Father looked pensive. I couldn't tell what he was thinking, but I warmed up a bit to Cha Zhiming.

"By the way," said Tongyin, pushing back his chair from the table, "Cha Zhiming and his family will be at Sueyin's wedding. General Cha and Judge Liu are old friends."

～⌒～

In matching pink *qipao*s, Gaoyin and I walked on either side of Sueyin, each holding her by an elbow. Sueyin couldn't see out from behind the heavy red silk that veiled her face. Fortunately Gaoyin was in charge of the bride and knew exactly what the rituals required. As we walked, Gaoyin whispered and prodded us through the ceremonies so I really didn't have to pay much attention. I just bowed and knelt along with the rest of the wedding party.

The Liu estate was decorated to reflect the importance of the occasion. The main gates, built of massive wooden planks bound with studded iron bands, were wide open and red lanterns hung from the lintels. Carriages, sedan chairs, and motorcars thronged inside the enormous forecourt and circled out again. When we helped Sueyin out of our motorcar, the Liu gatekeeper began a shout that all the other servants took up: "The bride is here! The bride's family is here! The honorable Song family is here!"

Servants lit long red strings of firecrackers that exploded in percussive bangs, leaving behind the smell of flash powder. All through the gardens, red lanterns hung from tree branches. At the entrance to the grand banquet hall, guests signed their names on a long scroll of red paper flecked with gold. The hall would seat five hundred diners. Even with the doors and windows wide open, the air inside was muggy, warmed by mosquito incense, drifts of cigarette smoke, and the rich, fatty odors of roasted meats. The night was exceptionally hot and there was a faint stench of sweat.

The bride and groom sat at one end of the huge hall on a dais carpeted in red. Behind them hung a heavy banner of red silk embroidered with a huge gold double-happiness symbol. Tienzhen wore a long black silk gown patterned with gold dragons. A round black cap adorned with a single jade bead crowned his well-cut hair. The only Western items of his ensemble were his shoes, shiny black patent leather. His expression was placid, docile.

Sueyin wore robes of red, fine silk brocade embroidered with phoenixes. Although at this point in the evening she could have removed the red silk pinned to her headdress, Sueyin had chosen to stay veiled. When she entered the hall, the older guests had applauded their approval, pleased at such becoming modesty from the bride. Now she sat gracefully with her back pressed firmly against the ebony chair.

When it was time for the newlyweds to circulate through the hall to meet and thank all the guests, Gaoyin carefully detached the bride's veil from her headdress and Sueyin stood up. A low hum rose from the tables as the guests murmured their appreciation, my sister's lovely features revealed for the first time. Her expression was as veiled as it had been behind the red silk. There was none of her usual gentleness in the set of her lips, no sweetness in the fixed gaze of her dark eyes. She was as perfect as a wax image and as devoid of life.

The heavy air in the banquet hall felt like a shroud. I wasn't hungry at all, my pink *qipao* felt tight, and I was desperate for some fresh air and some time alone. I was still thinking about how to convince Father to change his mind. Or could I go to university without his consent? Perhaps I could speak to him again after the wedding. He would be in a good mood after the ceremony. I escaped from the banquet hall and wandered into the main garden, cooling myself with a gold paper fan.

The Lius' garden was huge, even bigger than our Old Garden. Its artificial lake contained not one but two islands. The larger one at the lake's far end held a pavilion and was connected to the shore by a zigzag bridge, a guarantee of safety from evil spirits, for they can't cross such bridges. On the smaller island beside me, red lanterns hung from willow trees. I spied a bench partially concealed beneath their branches and crossed wide stepping stones to reach it, stones so flat and carefully spaced they might as well have been a bridge.

Finally away from the din of the banquet, I closed my eyes and fanned myself. There wasn't even a whisper of a breeze. An orchestra played on the terrace outside the dining hall. Inside, the music had been barely noticeable above the clamor of conversation. I leaned back against the bench with relief and allowed myself the pleasure of listening to the plaintive tones of the *erhu* and *zhonghu* fiddles, the high notes of a *dizi* reed flute. The musicians, who were very fine, launched into "Spring Snow," a lively ancient tune.

Then something made me open my eyes: Hanchin stood before me.

Fortunately I was sitting or my knees would have buckled. Fortunately the musicians swung into the climax of the song or my gasp would have reverberated in the night air. Unfortunately I dropped my fan.

He bent down and handed it to me. I mumbled my thanks and fanned myself furiously.

"Aren't you hungry, Miss Song?"

"It's too hot to eat." And my too-tight dress was creasing across my stomach. I stood up and tugged the skirt down as discreetly as possible. "Are you a friend of the Liu family, Mr. Yen?"

"I'm just a poor distant cousin. However, on such a joyous occasion, even impoverished relations are invited to offer their good wishes to the newlyweds."

"You can't mean that. I'm sure the Liu family is honored to have such a famous poet-scholar in the family."

A white flash of teeth as he smiled. "If I hadn't run into Judge Liu at your sister's engagement party, I'm sure he would have left me off the guest list. This is a party for the city's elite."

He smelled so clean, a faint scent of sandalwood soap. The lanterns overhead cast shadows that made his cheekbones more pronounced, his face even leaner. His eyes were as intense as those of a bird of prey. He leaned against the trunk of the nearest willow tree, comfortable in the silence. I wasn't. Furthermore, the high collar of my pink dress was scratching my neck. My first opportunity to be truly alone with Hanchin and I looked like a pink satin sausage.

"Thank you for replying to my letters through the magazine," I said, desperate to fill the void. "You must think our family absolutely feudal, what with my father feeling entitled to read our personal letters."

"He probably continues his own father's practice out of habit. Don't resent it. He's allowed you other, more important freedoms. Your education, for example."

I wavered. I had to tell him I wouldn't be attending college. Better he should learn this from me than from Tongyin. It was only a matter of time before my brother let the news slip. But I held back as he continued talking.

"I hear from your friend Wang Nanmei that you received a scholarship to Hangchow Women's University. Well done."

"Nanmei told you this?" I had no idea that Nanmei had even met Hanchin. "How do you know her?"

"She came by the office a couple of times to drop off your

letters." He shrugged, and his next words drove all thoughts of Nanmei out of my head. "Will you write to me, Leiyin, when you're away in Hangchow?"

His eyes reflected back light from the lanterns, flecks of mica shining in the darkness.

"Yes, Hanchin. Oh, yes. Of course I will." My heart winced, a sharp stab of delight.

"You can write to me about anything once you're away from home."

Once I was away from home.

I could scarcely breathe. His hands on my shoulders steered me to the other side of the tree, into the darkness, out of the view of anyone who might be standing on the shore.

"You're every bit as beautiful as your sisters. You have the sort of beauty that springs from intelligence and courage." His lips brushed against my ear.

My face was hot, but it was nothing compared to the longing that seared through my body, a craving that softened my bones. Unresisting, I let him kiss my face and I tried not to gasp with the pleasure of feeling his lips brush against my cheeks, my eyelids, behind my ears. He loved me. Why was I in his arms unless he loved me? But when I lifted my face to him, he didn't kiss my mouth.

He shook his head and stepped back, teasing me with his smile.

"Your father would never allow this, you know."

"Oh, Hanchin. He admires your poetry so much. Times are changing. I'll be the first daughter to attend university. I'm going to teach."

I couldn't bear to break the spell by saying the words that acknowledged my dreams had been denied. Besides, I was going to change Father's mind.

"You're meant for grand alliances, like your sisters."

"Once I've finished college, my life will be my own. I can teach school and support myself. I won't need my father."

"You musn't alienate him, Leiyin." There was the smallest hint of warning in his voice.

A din of applause from the banquet hall told us the first speech of the evening had just finished. I leaned against the tree, unable to move.

"Come, we must get back to the banquet hall." He pulled me away from the tree. "Hold on, there are bits of bark on the back of your dress." Holding me by the shoulder with one hand, he brushed me down with the other, slowly, lingeringly.

"I'll leave first," he said. He made his way across the stepping stones, his movements casual and unhurried.

I crumpled onto the stone bench and watched Hanchin's retreating silhouette until it vanished through the doors of the banquet hall. I stretched out on the bench, its coolness a salve to my trembling body, its hard surface an anchor to reality, for I was almost floating from sheer happiness.

Once I was away from home.

But within minutes my problems brought me back to earth. After I had promised to write from college, after he had kissed me, how could I ever confess to Hanchin that I wouldn't be attending college after all?

cᴀᴏ

My *yang* soul's goatee shakes with disapproval as he gazes at my memory-self, a pink-clad body slumped over the bench. *That was disgraceful. Such behavior at such a young age.*

The sharp taste of raw ginger crosses the back of my throat.

You still believed you would find a way to get to Hangchow. A frown of distress creases my *yin* soul's baby-smooth skin.

You didn't have money for boarding fees, you depended entirely on your father, my *hun* soul says. Its visage is pure light, featureless, yet I imagine patient sorrow glimmering there. *Without your father's consent you had nothing.*

This was the night I knew beyond a doubt that Hanchin cared for me, I say. *All I could think of was finding a way to get to university. With or without Father's permission.*

Your sisters wouldn't defy your father. My *yin* soul, crouched at the edge of the island, reaches out to touch a water lily.

They had no career ambitions. I did.

Stupid girl! My *yang* soul's cane bashes the willow tree. The ginger is even stronger now. *Sueyin had more reason to defy your father. Yet here we are at her wedding to an opium user. Did you truly have no idea of how the world works?*

They fall silent. We watch my pink satin form sit up on the bench, then stand up resolutely.

There, says my *yin* soul. *That was when you made up your mind to get to Hangchow with or without your father's consent.*

I had to. I had made promises to Hanchin.

Have you noticed, says my *hun* soul, *that he hadn't actually made any promises to you?*

～～～

The rustle of duck wings in the reeds, the coolness of the stone seat, these were preferable to plunging back into the noise and heat of the wedding banquet. The applause was already more raucous; whistles and calls punctuated the clapping. I decided instead to look in on the smaller dining hall at the other end of the lake, where I had taken Fei-Fei and Changyin's little children earlier that day. There, away from the main celebrations, the youngest guests were served food more to their taste, and could make as much noise as they pleased.

The din from the main hall subsided as I brushed past shrubs and greenery, my footsteps silent on the hard dirt path around the lake. Closer to the pavilion, I heard murmuring voices, saw shadowy shapes partially hidden behind carved screens. The words grew more distinct as I neared.

"Have you never been kissed before, darling?" A man's voice, followed by an indistinct reply.

Another romantic tryst. With so much activity at a wedding, it was easy for guests and even servants to slip away for a few minutes of courtship. I closed my eyes with pleasure at the memory of Hanchin and slowed down to enjoy the scent of the honeysuckle growing beside the path. And to eavesdrop a little.

"Come, sit on my lap." That same voice, somehow familiar. "There, now you can kiss me, you pretty, pretty—"

"May I go now? Nanny said I was to keep an eye on the little ones."

I froze. I knew that confident young voice. Before I could speak, a small figure in pink tunic and trousers emerged from the pavilion. I didn't need to see her face as she skipped away over the zigzag bridge and onto the path toward the children's dining hall. I moved to follow, then ducked behind a rhododendron as a tall figure stepped out of the pavilion and tugged down his jacket. He strolled past me and disappeared in the direction of the main dining hall.

It was Cha Zhiming.

The zigzag bridge hadn't protected the pavilion from evil spirits.

∽∾∽

The small dining hall, despite the best efforts of the nannies, was chaotic, filled with those ear-splitting shrieks that only children of a certain age can produce. Amid the tables, there was a game of tag in progress, and one small boy bawled in his nanny's arms while she rubbed his knee.

"Was that you in the pavilion a few minutes ago, Fei-Fei?" I grabbed my half sister as she ran past.

She nodded, seemingly untroubled, fidgeting to get back to the chase. My heart resumed its normal beat.

"Fei-Fei, where's your Nanny Wong?"

"She wanted roast duck. She went to the kitchens."

"Who's looking after you and our nephews and nieces, then?"

"Nanny Wong said there're so many servants around, we'd be all right for a while."

"Well, I'll stay here with you until she comes back."

I smoothed her hair and straightened her tunic before she dashed away to rejoin the game. Then I settled in a chair to watch the unruly youngsters and wait for the delinquent Nanny Wong.

When I returned to the wedding, everyone's eyes were on the actress Li Minghui. She was Liu Tienzhen's favorite film star, we'd been told, and had been hired to sing at the wedding. Sueyin and Tienzhen were seated at a table beside the dais, which now served as a stage where Li Minghui was performing a *huangmei diao* from a traditional folk opera, accompanied by a two-stringed *erhu*. Tienzhen was holding Sueyin's hand and smiling with delight, his head swaying in time to the song. Gaoyin was at the same table.

"Where is Stepmother?" I whispered to her.

"At that table by the window. Why?" Then she saw my distress and followed me.

A few minutes later, we were all together, Stepmother sitting in a curved armchair of elm wood, while Gaoyin sank into a love-seat. We were in the dressing room where we had helped Sueyin adjust her heavy bridal clothing just hours ago.

I took a deep breath before speaking. "I have to tell you something, Stepmother. It's about Second Brother's friend, that Cha Zhiming."

"The young man who was so kind to Fei-Fei?"

"I went for a walk by the lake, to . . . to look in on the children. I overheard a man in the pavilion trying to seduce someone. It was Cha Zhiming."

Gaoyin yawned. "So you overheard a young man trying to steal a kiss."

"But he wasn't trying to seduce a woman. It was our Fei-Fei."

Gaoyin's eyes snapped wide open.

Stepmother stood up with a gasp. "What did he do to her?"

I shook my head. "I don't know, Stepmother. I don't think he had time to do much because she skipped out of the pavilion. You know how quickly Fei-Fei gets bored."

"Where was Nanny Wong?" Gaoyin asked, her expression grim.

"Scrounging for food in the Lius' kitchens. You can be sure I gave her a good speech when she returned. Enough to send her into tears."

I knelt beside Stepmother, who had sunk back down into the chair, and tried to reassure her.

"I'm sure he didn't do anything to Fei-Fei. When I found her in the children's dining hall, she looked fine. She just wanted to get back to playing with the others. I'm sure she didn't understand what was happening."

"Did Cha Zhiming see you, Third Sister?"

"No. When he came out, I hid behind a shrub. That's when I saw it was him." I tugged at Stepmother's hand. "We must tell Father. He would forbid Cha from ever coming to our home."

But she shook her head slowly.

"General Cha is a very powerful man," Stepmother said. "Powerful and vindictive, they say. We must not be perceived as hostile to him, or even let on we're privy to knowledge that might shame him—such as his son's despicable cravings. These are dangerous times and families are being ruined over lesser slights."

I had no idea Stepmother knew anything about General Cha or the political climate of the country. She never said anything when my father and brothers aired their opinions.

"You're right, Stepmother," Gaoyin said. "It would be easy to bring this family down now that Tongyin has fallen in with Yen Hanchin. Just a few rumors planted here and there."

"I think we're safe, thanks to your father's stature in this city," Stepmother said. "And now we also have the Liu family as in-laws. But in the future, who knows? The longer this civil war drags on, the more obsessed our Nationalist government grows about traitors. They see Communist spies behind every tree."

"But surely no one takes Tongyin seriously," I said, rolling my eyes. "Everyone knows he is lazy and without ambition. How could he be a threat?"

"Your brother lacks convictions of his own," Stepmother said. "So he embraces those of others with great fervor but without true understanding. That sort of fervor can be manipulated."

"He admires Yen Hanchin. Nothing more."

Stepmother looked at me as if to say something, then stopped. "Thank you for the warning, Leiyin. Please don't say anything to your father. You know how he is when he gets angry. He'd react impulsively, unwisely. This is a situation we women must handle delicately, from the inner courtyard."

"But, Stepmother—"

"Please, Third Stepdaughter. Fei-Fei is my daughter. Let me be the one to make this decision."

"I will abide by your decision, Stepmother," Gaoyin said, standing up to rejoin the party. "Leiyin, so will you."

5

*B*etween my concern about Fei-Fei and giddy memories of my time alone with Hanchin, it was nearly dawn by the time I fell asleep. Even though the dining room gong sounded an hour later than usual, I was late for breakfast, dawdling as I dressed and staring dreamily into the mirror. Would anyone be able to tell I was now a woman? That I knew how it felt to be embraced, to have my face caressed and kissed? It seemed as though bliss, and not blood, traveled through my veins.

Changyin and Shen were downing huge bowls of congee as though they hadn't eaten a fourteen-course banquet the night before. Since so many of the wedding preparations and activities were under Gaoyin's supervision, Shen and Gaoyin had received permission from his parents to stay with us on this visit instead of at his family's estate.

Stepmother and Gaoyin were at the second table. There were no children in sight.

"The children are still overexcited. They hardly slept at all," Stepmother answered when I asked after them.

Gaoyin greeted me with a nod from over her plate of toast and jam. I sat beside Stepmother and chewed on a corner of cold toast. Tongyin wandered in, hair disheveled and eyes half open. He sat beside Shen at the other table, his back to me.

"The Liu family spared no expense," Shen said. "Judge Liu told me Li Minghui and her staff traveled first class on the train from Shanghai."

"She was very charming." Gaoyin stifled a yawn. "Li Minghui told Tienzhen that Sueyin was more beautiful than all the leading ladies of Chinese cinema put together."

"Tienzhen told me he admires Father's literary salons," Changyin said. "He wants to hold salons too, but for the film industry. To encourage young actors and actresses."

Tongyin finally came to life after his third cup of tea. "Can you imagine calling a gathering of film actors a salon? Fortunately Hanchin said something very tactful. He suggested calling the events soirees instead."

"So Yen Hanchin is a friend of the Liu family?" Father asked.

"They're related, Father. Distantly, but of course the Lius are honored to have a well-known poet and scholar in their family circle."

I could have thrown my arms around Tongyin.

My brother spoke again. "There might be another betrothal in our family soon. Yes, very soon, possibly." Tongyin sat up to assess the impact of his statement, his expression smug.

Had Hanchin confessed his feelings for me to Tongyin? It

was too soon, Father wasn't ready yet to accept a poor poet into the family. I held my breath, the knot in my stomach struggling against the flutter of hope in my heart.

Father slapped his knee. "Tell me more, Second Son. Weddings beget weddings, they say."

"Father, yes. You're correct. I had a conversation last night with Cha Zhiming. You know his father is General Cha."

The knot was winning now. Had Cha Zhiming made a bid for my hand?

"General Cha?" Father sounded pleased.

"Yes, Father. Yes. Cha Zhiming is his eldest son, by his first wife. General Cha has younger sons by his second wife. Zhiming suggested matching his eleven-year-old half brother with Fei-Fei, and the General agreed. None of this is official until the matchmaker approaches you, of course. But we're good friends, so Zhiming told me. Informally, of course."

I opened my mouth, but Stepmother laid a warning hand on mine.

Father beamed at Stepmother. "Well, what do you think of little Fei-Fei marrying into the Cha family?"

Fei-Fei was only the daughter of a concubine, a younger daughter of minor stature. Any son of General Cha was highly eligible. She could do far worse in the matchmaking stakes.

"She's still quite young," Stepmother replied in an even, unruffled voice. "Isn't it unusual nowadays to make these approaches so early?"

"Stepmother," said Tongyin, "you're right. Quite right. But the General obeys his mother's every wish. Old Madame Cha wants the General to settle her grandsons' marriages before she dies. It would be unfilial of him to refuse."

"Hmmm." Father looked approving. Stepmother, merely thoughtful. She put some fruit on my plate and shot me another look.

"Father, there is one more thing," continued Tongyin. "A small thing. Zhiming tells me that the Cha family likes their future daughters-in-law to stay at their family home for a few weeks every year before the marriage."

Again, Stepmother had to put a restraining hand on my arm. Gaoyin frowned at me and mouthed the words "Keep quiet."

"But I thought Old Madame Cha was a very traditional lady," Stepmother said, her voice mild and steady. "Isn't she afraid her grandson and Fei-Fei will meet before the wedding?"

Tongyin nodded. "She is, definitely. She's very traditional. Fei-Fei won't meet the boy. Old Madame Cha just wants to get to know the girls because she's afraid she won't live long enough to see her younger grandsons' weddings."

The fear inside me rose higher. Fei-Fei couldn't be allowed near that family.

"Well, well," Father said. "Let's wait and see what happens. Plans made over wedding wine may come to nothing."

"What about Cha Zhiming?" I asked Tongyin. "Why is he still unmarried?"

"Unmarried, yes, but his fiancée has been staying with them for a month each year since she was a girl. When Zhiming graduates, they'll get married."

Then he tilted his chair back and leaned over to whisper in

my ear. "Don't worry, Little Sister, all isn't lost. I'll ask Zhiming to make you his concubine!"

I didn't bother telling him how badly he had misinterpreted my look, for now Stepmother rose from her seat.

"Please excuse me. I would like to take a stroll. After all that food last night, I think a long walk around the Old Garden is in order."

I stood up. "I'll walk with you. Gaoyin, why not come with us?"

⌘

The Old Garden had been designed as a retreat, with secluded spots where one could sit quietly to compose poetry or read. This we knew from a plan of the garden that had been drawn by the anonymous landscaper one of our ancestors had hired to create it. Halfway around the lake, an embankment of turf was planted with stands of oleander and pine that cast their shade onto the path. Together we ascended its ridge to where an ancient pine shaded a row of stone seats. A pungent resinous scent rose up to greet us as we walked over a layer of brittle needles.

"Tongyin has no idea what a monster that friend of his—" I began.

"Never mind Tongyin," Gaoyin interrupted. "The question is, how can we keep Fei-Fei away from the Cha family?"

"We could reject that once-a-year visit," I suggested.

"Not good enough. We'd have to tell Father why. And anyway, if Father agrees to even an afternoon visit, she would be in danger. The big question is how to avoid marriage to that family altogether."

"Let me figure out how to handle this," said Stepmother. "Old Madame Cha is very traditional." She took a deep breath and folded her hands in her lap. "As your father says, it may all come to nothing, so please, Leiyin, don't do or say anything. You've warned us, but hasty actions will only create more problems."

"But shouldn't we warn Father now?"

"Third Stepdaughter, please trust me in this."

"Don't fret, Leiyin," said Gaoyin. "Stepmother will find a way through this."

I nodded. We sat for a few minutes in solemn silence.

"Let's talk about something else," Stepmother said. "First Stepdaughter, when you were here for Sueyin's engagement party, you came to me for advice. How is your situation now?"

My sister's face flushed and she looked almost shy. "I did as you suggested, Stepmother. One of my servants has a sister who just had a baby girl. I hired the sister and she brings the baby with her. I spend a good part of each day with the baby. She's such a darling. I can hardly bear to be away from her."

"Good. Love the child as though she were your own."

"Why?" I asked. "Why have you taken in a servant's child?"

"Gaoyin is trying to conceive. I think her maternal essence needs help to flow more strongly. Sometimes fostering another's child invigorates a woman's essence."

Stepmother laughed at my skeptical look. "It's a cure passed down from my mother's family. Continue your walk, my dears. I need to get back to the house."

I held my tongue, but once Stepmother was well on her way around the lake, I shook my head. "That sounds like folklore, not science, Eldest Sister."

"We've exhausted science, both Western and Chinese. This is a bit of folklore that does no harm. I enjoy having a little one in our home."

"Is Shen so impatient for a son?"

She put her head in her hands. "It's Shen's mother. She wants him to take a concubine because we have been married three years already. She's impatient for a grandson."

"Shen adores you. He'd never take a concubine."

"I like to think we're a modern couple, but the truth is, he's still totally obedient to his family. He'd take a concubine if his mother insisted." Then her voice dropped to a whisper. "Oh, Leiyin. I can't bear the thought of him with anyone else."

"You're First Wife. You're allowed your say about concubines. Make Shen pick someone illiterate or ugly, someone he could never love."

"I'm hoping Stepmother's advice will let me avoid that. There. Now you know the truth. Your eldest sister is just a barren wife." She smiled and wiped her eyes.

Tears welled up in my own eyes to see my imperious older sister so insecure, so vulnerable. Hanchin would never take a concubine if I proved barren. We'd adopt orphans, perhaps even one of those Eurasian children nobody wanted. Just thinking about Hanchin gave me courage. I took a deep breath.

"There's something I want to tell you, Eldest Sister. A secret." She looked up with a small smile, prepared to hear a childish confidence.

"I've decided to go to Hangchow, even though it's against Father's wishes."

"Leiyin! You can't! You've only just regained Father's good-will." Exasperation replaced the smile on her face.

"All I need is money for room and board. And train fare. Will you help? I'm going to sell my jewelery but I'll need to borrow more."

"Third Sister! You can't do this! Think what it would mean if you disobeyed Father."

"It's the boarding fees that cost the most," I continued, as though she hadn't said anything. "I could never come up with that much."

"Leiyin, think what Father will do if you defy him like this."

"Once I get to Hangchow Women's, it'll be all right. We all know how impulsive he is when he gets angry, but I won't be around for him to punish. He'll forgive me eventually. You've said often enough that Father is as quick to forgive as he is to get angry. Will you help me?"

She held my wrist in a tight grip and shook her head.

"You'll be punished."

"What can he do except drag me home? Once I'm at school, he'd lose face if he had to do that. He'll have to go along with it or risk having people think he has no control over his children."

"Third Sister, listen to me. You've always been his favorite daughter. But such outright defiance would be unforgivable."

"Even if I get only one year at college, it would be better than none at all. Maybe Father will get used to the idea."

Again she shook her head. She stood to leave. I jumped up and caught her by the hand.

"Please, Gaoyin. This means more to me than you can possibly imagine. My entire future, my happiness depends on it, Eldest Sister. You must help me." For all my determination, I knew I could not do it on my own.

She saw my tears but didn't waver. "I can't, Little Sister. And I won't."

She clambered down the path and left me alone beneath the pines.

⌘

I suppose it was a good thing she left when she did, I tell my souls. *I was ready to break down and tell her about Hanchin and why everything depended on university.*

Gaoyin tried to warn you of the consequences. My *yin* soul chews on the end of a pigtail.

My *hun* soul hovers at the edge of the terrace, gleaming. *You overestimated Eldest Sister's capacity for defiance.*

No, I didn't. But I hoped. I had to try something, anything, I insist, still feeling the sting of desperate tears.

It's a good thing your first sister had the sense to refuse you, my *yang* soul says. He paces around the terrace, hands tucked into his wide sleeves. He glances up at the sky. *Ah, a full moon.*

We stand still, all four of us, and lift our eyes to watch the moonrise. I look for the rabbit in the moon, even though I know it's only a fairy tale. I remember Gaoyin reading me the story for the first time, when I was Fei-Fei's age.

She was always the bossy one with all the answers, I tell my souls. *I couldn't believe she was asking Stepmother for advice.*

You always did underestimate your stepmother, says my *hun* soul.

⌒∽⌒∽

When the newlyweds paid their respects to Father during their formal Third Day visit, Sueyin wore one of the new suits from her trousseau, pale blue, with a little blue straw hat. Tienzhen's striped necktie exactly matched the blue of her suit. We sat in the drawing room and a servant brought in refreshments served on our most expensive Limoges china, for now Sueyin was a guest, a member of the Liu family.

Changyin and Shen debated the success of the Nationalists' most recent attempts to disband the warlord armies, while Tienzhen smiled politely.

"How is your esteemed father?" Father asked Sueyin in a formal tone. Judge Liu was now her father. The Liu family now owned her loyalties.

"My father is well. His health couldn't be better."

Then she turned to our brothers. "There's a small theater at the estate. Mother doesn't like going out, so we watch films at home. We really enjoyed *Romance of the Western Chamber* the other evening."

"It's an excellent film," Tongyin was quick to say. "Most excellent. Hou Yao is the most talented director in Chinese cinema today. How do you find his films, Second Brother-in-Law?"

Tienzhen nodded, more animated now. "I didn't think he

could do better than A *String of Pearls* but this one is truly a masterpiece."

Sueyin stood up. "Please excuse me, Husband. I'd like to spend a little time with my sisters. When you're ready to leave, just send someone to get me."

Gaoyin and I followed her upstairs, where she opened the door of her old room and sat at the dressing table, now emptied of combs and creams. She gazed around at the walls, the panels painted in cream and gold, the leaf-patterned wallpaper, the pale blue drapes. We waited for her to speak.

"He's kind to me. And he says he's ashamed of his addiction. He's promised to try to give it up. But I don't believe he can. Let's say no more about it."

"All right then. What does he read?" I asked. "What do you enjoy in common?"

"He enjoys reading film magazines."

Gaoyin pursed her lips. In our family, that made Tienzhen practically illiterate.

"He confides in me, I think. He talks a lot when we're alone."

Gaoyin put her arm around Sueyin's shoulders. "That's good, isn't it?"

"He talks because I'm the only person who listens. His mother keeps to her rooms except when she plays *mah-jong*. For her, it's enough that he comes when she sends for him."

"But that estate is filled with family," I said. "There must have been a dozen households at your wedding, all those aunts and uncles and cousins."

"He doesn't like them. The entire family lives off the Judge's wealth. They flatter us and resent us."

"Oh, Second Sister, this is worse than we could have imagined," I said. "You'll find no true friends there."

"Second Sister, come to stay with me in Shanghai whenever you can," said Gaoyin. "Bring Tienzhen with you, if you have to."

A soft knock on the door, and we fell silent immediately. Stepmother entered.

"Your husband wishes to leave now, Second Stepdaughter."

Sueyin stood up and nodded. I could almost see her stiffen with the effort.

We escorted Tienzhen and Sueyin to the main gate. Lao Li and the Lius' chauffeur sprang to attention and the chauffeur pulled open the door of their motorcar with a white-gloved hand. Tienzhen held Sueyin's arm as she climbed in. The car horn tooted, and the vehicle pulled out onto the street. Through the rear window we saw Tienzhen lean over to kiss Sueyin's cheek. Then Lao Li pushed the gates closed again.

I turned back to the villa, but Gaoyin grabbed my hand.

"Let's go for a walk in the Old Garden." She put a finger to her lips as we turned away from the rest of the family.

Gaoyin marched at a pace more suited to leading an army, a grim set to her jaw. My leather pumps had low heels that dug awkwardly into the soft earth of the garden path, making it hard for me to keep up with her purposeful stride. She said nothing until we had climbed the path to the stone seats under the old pine tree.

Gaoyin paced before me, her expression unfathomable. I sat and waited.

"Little Sister, you deserve a better life. You must take the risk and follow your own destiny. Father gave me a bank account when I was married and I haven't spent any of it. Go to university. I'll help you."

"Oh, Eldest Sister!" I leaped up and threw my arms around her. But she didn't smile back.

"Do it for yourself, Leiyin. Do it for all of us."

6

A third cousin to General Cha arrived at our door with gifts and a proposal of marriage for Fei-Fei to the General's eleven-year-old son. The intermediary was a diminutive man of middle age who bowed more often than necessary. When he smiled, he showed more teeth than was natural. He was visibly relieved when Father accepted the canisters of fine tea and admired the teapot and matching cups, fired from the famous *yixing* purple clay.

"Fei-Fei is my concubine's daughter," Father said, patting Stepmother's hand. "She will deal with the rest of the formalities. In the meantime, please tell the General that we are honored by this offer."

"Very good, very good," the cousin said, this time bowing to Stepmother. "Old Madame Cha would like you to meet her fortune-teller, who will be casting horoscopes. Next week, perhaps?"

Stepmother bowed in return. "Next week."

After the cousin left, I followed Stepmother to her room, almost bursting with anxiety.

"Don't worry, Leiyin," she said. "This will come to nothing."

She looked very sure of herself. I had to trust whatever plan she had in mind. After all, Fei-Fei mattered more to Stepmother than anyone else.

⌒⌒⌒

Sueyin visited frequently, usually by herself and usually after lunch, when Tienzhen spent time with his pipe. She didn't seem bitter, just relieved at the opportunity to get away. These visits were all too short, but we took advantage of the quiet hour to walk around the Old Garden.

"Are your in-laws kind to you?" I asked.

"For now, everything is fine. We've only been married two months. If I'm not pregnant by winter, Tienzhen's mother will probably start feeding me fertility-enhancing soups. For the moment, she's happy enough showing me off to her friends. I'm her promise of beautiful grandchildren."

"What about the Judge?"

"He barely speaks to me. He vanishes into his study every evening. He just works all the time. But let's not talk about my in-laws. Are things back to normal between you and Father?"

"They are. For now."

Sueyin eyed me, her brow furrowed with anxiety. "Leiyin, what are you planning?"

I had to tell her.

"I'm surprised Eldest Sister agreed to help you," she said after hearing me out. "But you must have been quite persuasive. Shen's going to be very angry with her, not to mention Father. She's risking a lot for you. And, Leiyin, you know how Father gets when he's angry."

"Gaoyin and I are ready to face it. Second Sister, even if you don't approve, I know you understand. I must take control of my own destiny."

Sueyin gave me a long hug and a wistful smile. "Yes, you must. I don't want you ending up like me."

Then she stood, put her arm through mine, and said, "Come, I need to see Stepmother."

Stepmother wasn't in her room, so we went to the small sitting room that she used for receiving merchants. The door was shut. When we knocked, she called out for us to wait a few minutes.

When the door opened, a middle-aged woman emerged. She was stout and well-dressed, but not expensively so, in a short jacket of brown brocade over a brown *qipao*. Gold bangles clinked at her wrists and she greeted us with a nod that was at once friendly and appraising. We entered and Sueyin pulled the door closed again. The room was sparsely furnished, with a long polished table placed under the window so that merchants could display their goods under bright daylight. A black lacquered screen was the only ornament in the room.

"Who was that woman, Stepmother?" I had the feeling something important had just happened.

"That was Old Madame Cha's fortune-teller. She came about Fei-Fei's horoscope."

"Oh, Stepmother!" I wailed. "Why are you going ahead with

all these rituals? I thought you were going to prevent this marriage."

"Third Stepdaughter, please don't interrupt me. Old Madame Cha has asked her fortune-teller to cast the horoscopes, but of course she must also allow us to consult with the woman."

Sueyin began to laugh. "Oh, Stepmother, that's brilliant. How is the fortune-teller going to explain the nature of the conflict?"

"What's brilliant?" I was beginning to feel as though my stepmother and older sisters shared far more than I had suspected.

"Fei-Fei was born in the year of the Rat and the boy is a Goat, potentially a good match," Stepmother said. "But the fortune-teller looked more deeply into Fei-Fei's birth hour and found a strong risk of the five elements disrupting the three harmonies, all pointing to an unproductive union."

"So lots of quarreling and no babies," said Sueyin. "Was it an expensive bribe?"

"Not when you consider Fei-Fei's happiness. By the way, your father will never know."

Now I could give way to feelings of relief and admiration.

"How did you think of this ruse, Stepmother?" I asked.

"When you're a merchant's daughter, you know that everything and everyone has a price. Now then"—her tone became brisk—"why did you come to see me?"

Sueyin pulled a heavy leather pouch out of her handbag and put it on the table.

"Every week the Judge's concubines and I go to see him in his study," Sueyin said. "He hands us our weekly allowance and his secretary writes it all down in a ledger."

Stepmother didn't bother counting the coins, just held the pouch in her hand, testing its weight.

"How much does he give you?"

"I get twenty silver *yuan*. Nearly twice what the other women receive. I've spent nothing so far."

"So you've already saved nearly two hundred *yuan* in silver?"

"Yes."

A pause. Stepmother's look of sympathy, Sueyin's shrug.

"You should exchange these for gold, Second Stepdaughter."

"Stepmother, can you do the exchange and keep them for me?"

"Of course. We can review your accounts once a month. I'll keep a ledger and show you how much gold you own."

"But, Sueyin," I said, "why don't you deposit the money in the bank account Father gave you? Your wedding gift."

"Someone in that house might snoop and find my bank book. Anyway, I don't have a bank account. Father wasn't as generous with a second daughter as he was with Eldest Sister."

"That's not the only reason you don't have your own bank account, Second Stepdaughter. Your father's been buying property in other countries to get our assets out of China. The family's cash reserves aren't what they used to be."

❧

You know, I say to my souls, *the older servants, the ones whose families had been with ours for several generations, they looked down on Stepmother. Head Servant Lu, for example.*

My *yang* soul nods his head. *He served her reluctantly because her father was only a cloth merchant.*

But she was so well informed. So clever and ingenious.

And you seem so surprised at this. My *yin* soul's laughter tinkles.

Even more astounding, you managed to live nearly eighteen years in that home without realizing how much your older sisters relied on Stepmother's advice. My *hun* soul's words make me feel as foolish as I'd felt on that day in the small sitting room, with my new appreciation of Stepmother's intelligence and quiet competence.

Perhaps I should have asked Stepmother's advice about university and how best to persuade Father.

From my souls, I detect a similar regret.

◈

My escape plan began with a letter. I wrote to Hangchow Women's University declining their scholarship. I showed this to Father. Then I returned to my room, tore up the sheet of paper, and placed a different letter in the envelope. This one thanked the principal of the college for the scholarship and provided my arrival date. I sealed the envelope and placed it on the silver letter tray by the front door.

Next, Gaoyin invited me to stay with her in Shanghai. Her letter, written on beautiful cream stationery, proposed a visit of two weeks at the end of the summer. As we had expected, Father agreed, pleased I had gotten over my whim about attending university.

Now I felt I could meet Hanchin's eyes the next time I saw him, buoyed by the knowledge that I had kept up my end of our unspoken agreement. As for Nanmei, we agreed that I would write to her as soon as I was safely at university in Hangchow.

"But I don't think you should defy your father like this," she said, a crease in her forehead. "My father is ten times more lenient than yours but I'd never dare disobey him outright."

"What would you do, then?"

"Find some other way. I don't know what, but not this."

"My happiness depends on this. My career and my future with Hanchin. You know that, Nanmei."

∽∾∼

Father's salons were finished for the summer, but something new replaced them. Liu Tienzhen announced his first soiree, then threw himself enthusiastically into this new endeavor. A dozen at a time, he invited film directors, screenwriters, actors, and actresses. Since the film industry was based in Shanghai, his invitations included train fare to Changchow and accommodations at the city's finest hotel.

Sueyin organized the soirees. My dear Sueyin, who always tried to see the best in every situation, seemed genuinely relieved at this turn of events. It was an activity that kept her husband busy and gave them something to talk about. When my brothers and I attended the first soiree, we found Tienzhen effusive in his praise for my sister.

"My wife organized everything. The menu, the décor, even the special cocktails. She arranged it all so well." He lowered his voice. "And you should just hear how the directors plead with her to star in their films. Of course she is the most beautiful woman in the room."

"Your husband is very proud of you, Second Sister," said Changyin as Tienzhen turned away to greet another guest.

"He enjoyed the planning too. I don't think he's ever organized anything before. Come to the drawing room now. One of the directors has a new script and some of the actors have volunteered to do a dramatic reading."

Sueyin moved through the crowd like a swan. She wore a simple dress of pale green, a rope of pearls doubled around her neck. She was so elegant, cool as celadon porcelain. Around her, the starlets in their bright lipstick and showy dresses were like imitation cloisonné.

Looking over the collection of actors, I thought how louche and superficial they seemed when compared to Hanchin. I hadn't seen him since the wedding and wondered whether there was a way for me to give Nanny Qiu the slip one day while I was visiting Nanmei. After all, hadn't Anna Karenina employed ruses to tryst with Vronsky? I just had to see Hanchin again. Every time I thought of him, I could feel his arms around me, his lips brushing against my neck. His hand moving slowly down my back.

Then Tongyin remarked, "You know, Hanchin says that since so many people are illiterate, the film industry should take some responsibility for educating the masses. I'll ask Second Brother-in-Law to invite Hanchin to the next soiree."

～～～

Sueyin hosted the second soiree in the small dining hall that had been the children's dining room at her wedding. She had transformed it into a small theater with a low stage at one end where actors could perform short scenes. Café tables filled the rest of the room, giving it the look of an intimate restaurant. Servants threaded their way among the guests, offering food and refilling drinks. Overhead fans spun at full speed but did little to dispel the heat.

My only reason for being there was to see Hanchin. After exchanging with him the briefest of greetings at the start of the evening, I hadn't approached him, not once. I didn't trust myself to stand too close to him. I couldn't have my family suspect our attachment when I was so close to my goal of escaping from home. Yet it was pure bliss to glance in his direction and, occasionally, to see him glance back.

Tonight, most unusually, Tongyin wasn't attached to Hanchin like a limpet on a river rock. Half a dozen young actors surrounded my brother. From the admiring glances they cast at the table where Hanchin sat politely listening to the man next to him, I could tell that although Tongyin wasn't beside his idol, he was busy promoting Hanchin's accomplishments.

I made my way across the room toward Sueyin, passing through the eddies of conversation at each table, the voices louder than at Father's salons.

"If you ask me, there's only one reason that girl has any lines of dialogue in the new film Deng's directing." A young woman, her mascara already smudged, said this to her companion without any attempt to lower her voice. They were both staring in Hanchin's direction. The young man with him must have been Deng.

"I think you should worry about something else," said her companion. "Ever since Yin Mingzhou starred in *The Sea Oath*, directors have been trying to turn society ladies into actresses. Look at Chou over there, flattering Liu Tienzhen's wife. She's beautiful, of course, but can she act?"

"Liu Tienzhen would fund the production." The woman gave a resigned shrug of her padded shoulders. "So does it matter if she can't?"

At the next table, an intense exchange between two middle-aged men:

"If you're going to pitch a screenplay that features extramarital affairs or career women, don't bother going to Mingxing Studios. They only do family epics, the more Confucian, the better."

"But those are falling out of fashion. Mingxing is behind the times. I'll tell them this film could revive their popularity."

Sueyin and Tienzhen shared a small table with an older man who gestured dramatically as he spoke, undoubtedly yet another director or writer pleading with Sueyin to star in his next venture. I gave up any chance of quiet conversation with my sister. Soon the dramatic readings would begin.

Turning around for another look at Hanchin, I saw that the young director he'd been speaking with was gone. Hanchin now stood outside the open doors of the hall, under the wide overhang that shaded the veranda. He strolled to the end of the veranda and down the steps, vanishing along the path that led to the zigzag bridge and the pavilion on the little island.

The pavilion's carved shutters were partially open and the air was oppressively hot. But I had no desire to throw the panels farther open even though my linen dress was wilted, a damp panel against my back. Hanchin was sitting in the dim light, but stood up when I entered.

"Didn't you want to chat with those actors, Leiyin?"

"They're far more interested in meeting Sueyin."

"Not all. Some were talking to Tongyin."

"There was a director who asked him to point you out."

"Ah, yes. Deng Fuyang. He thought I was the author of *Anna Karenina*. He was most perturbed to discover I'm only the translator. But now he wants me to write the screenplay."

"Well, you could do that." My hands felt damp, too hot. "I'm sure you would do a wonderful job."

He smiled and moved closer. "So you think I should give up poetry and educational reform for a film career instead?"

"Oh, no, Hanchin. I didn't mean that at all, I'm sorry."

"I'm teasing, you know."

When would I ever learn to banter, to flirt with him?

"So do serious young women your age give educational reform much thought?"

"Oh, yes, Hanchin. Lots of my classmates share your convictions. Wang Nanmei, for example, plans to open a free school after she graduates from university. And I want to teach in a farming village . . ." I was babbling now.

"I was teasing you again, about being serious."

He moved even closer. The clean fragrance of sandalwood, the faintest odor of sweat. I could have stood there forever inhaling that scent. This time, he kissed my lips, but only lightly, brushing them with his own before kissing my cheeks, my forehead, the side of my neck. I stood tense and silent while his hands moved across my back and hips, caressed my buttocks. I locked my knees, fearing they might give way and cause me to collapse against him, for if I were to press my body to his, I would never let go.

I heard a low gasp as his tongue delicately touched my earlobe and realized it was my own breath. How could this be anything but true love, to render me so physically helpless and ecstatic at the same time? Inside the pavilion, only faint light from the house disturbed the darkness. He stepped away from me, holding on to my shoulders.

"We must be careful of your reputation. I'll leave first. Then you can go back to the party."

"No, Hanchin. Please, stay a little longer." My words were barely audible, my throat thick.

But he was gone. I stayed in the dark pavilion until my heartbeat finally calmed and the scent of sandalwood faded away.

❧

I felt like such a fool the next day, for I had forgotten to tell Hanchin I would be leaving for Hangchow the following week. I wrote him a brief letter, a very proper and formal one with no mention of our heated moments in the pavilion. It was just another letter from a student to the editor of the column:

> *I leave for Hangchow next week, to begin my training as a teacher. After graduation, I hope to put into action the principles you have written about so often and so eloquently. I will continue to read your column and send in questions.*

Nanmei, as usual, agreed to be my courier.

"It's no trouble at all, Leiyin. There's no excitement in my life. I'm living vicariously through your romance and daring escapades!" she teased.

"One day you'll meet someone who you just know is your soul mate," I assured her. "Perhaps when you get to Soochow."

We were in the small garden adjacent to the main courtyard of her home. These days I preferred to meet her at her home, for there we could speak more freely, without being overheard.

"Speaking of which, here's my aunt's address in Soochow," she said, passing me a sheet of notepaper. "I can't believe I'm leaving in two days. I'll write to you every week as soon as you write to me from Hangchow. Last night I dreamed your father let you stay at university, and I was so happy for you. When you're a headmistress, will you hire me as a lowly teacher?"

"Oh, Nanmei, I will make you at least an assistant headmistress!"

We burst into giggles, and suddenly I felt twelve years old, not seventeen. A wave of misgiving rippled through me uncomfortably. But the memory of Hanchin's kisses, his smile, his hands on my body, melted away my doubts.

❦

The day before I was supposed to leave for Shanghai, Stepmother came to my room, where Nanny Qiu was bustling about helping me pack. She glanced down at the clothes Nanny Qiu was laying out on my bed: plain blouses and pleated skirts, *qipao*s in solid colors with the barest hint of embroidery, flat-soled shoes and white socks, one blue jacket. They would barely fill my trunk, a monstrous leather-bound crate my father had used during his travels in Europe. The sort of trunk a young person of wealth would be expected to bring on a trip.

"Leiyin, these clothes are so plain. Why not bring that lovely blue gown with the sequined butterflies?"

"I don't need to bring any nice dresses," I lied. "Gaoyin is taking me to her dressmaker."

"She is so good to you. Can you do me a favor while you're there?"

"Of course."

She held out a slim package. "Just a few small gifts and a letter for my youngest sister in Shanghai. You don't need to take it yourself, just have one of Gaoyin's servants deliver it."

She had a younger sister. How little I knew of Stepmother. A brief sensation of remorse pulsed through my veins.

Father was pleased with the notion that I would return dressed in the latest fashions, for at dinner he pressed an envelope into my hand.

"For the dressmaker. There is no need for Gaoyin to take on the expense of turning you into a stylish young lady."

I hoped my smile didn't betray the twinge of guilt I felt.

⌒⌒⌒

Only a moment of remorse? Only a twinge of guilt? My *yang* soul says disparagingly, and my mouth fills with the taste of bitter tea. *What you were about to do was outright disobedient. In the old days, you would've been thrown into the street.*

She still believed her father would change his mind, my *yin* soul says. She rests on the stone wall at the edge of the terrace, swinging her legs so that her white socks flash from side to side. I catch only the faintest breath of chives, tinged with doubt and anxiety.

Father simply didn't realize how badly I wanted to go to university. I was certain once he understood I was willing to risk his disapproval, he'd give in.

My *yang* soul snorts again and stomps to the edge of the terrace to join my other souls.

It was too late anyway, my *hun* soul says. *By this time, too many balls were in motion.*

⌒∽⌒

I wouldn't be traveling alone. Nanny Qiu was to come with me on the train. She had never been out of Changchow, and alternated between excitement and trepidation. Tongyin had left for the *China Millennium* offices as usual that morning, but came by my room to wish me a pleasant journey. He was acting a lot friendlier these days. Father and Stepmother gave me their farewells at the door of the villa. Father was taking a business trip in a few days' time and was busy with preparations. Sueyin, the only one who knew my true destination, had promised to see me off.

Changyin took Nanny and me to the train station. "I have some business in Shanghai next week, Third Sister, so I'll stay with Gaoyin and Shen as usual. We can travel home together."

Since my plan was to spend only two days in Shanghai before

continuing south to Hangchow, by the time Changyin arrived, I would be long gone and my deception uncovered.

Sueyin and Tienzhen were already at the station when we arrived. Even on the busy platform, with travelers elbowing past one another and families shoving their way through the crowd, there was a circle of clear space around them, such a glamorous, beautiful pair. Tienzhen went with Changyin to find the conductor, Nanny sat on my trunk to fan herself, and I had a few moments alone with Sueyin.

"Good-bye, Little Sister," she whispered in my ear, the silk poppies on her hat brushing against my hair. "You can still change your mind."

"Don't worry, Second Sister. I'll write to you when I arrive in Hangchow."

Changyin waved at us from a passenger car to indicate he had found our compartment. Then I stepped onto the train, wading into the tides that would carry me away to unknown shores. I could hardly wait.

7

I barely looked out the window at the fields and farmhouses flashing by. I barely noticed the stops the train made. Now that I was on my way, there was no turning back, no avoiding the consequences. Father would be furious when my plans came to light. Would he travel to Hangchow to confront me? Would he send Changyin? Surely my tears and my sincere desire to become a teacher would move him.

My thoughts turned to matters that excited rather than worried me. What would they be like, my new classmates and new teachers? I would meet girls with the same ambitions, girls who, like me and Nanmei, had been inspired by Madame Sun Yat-sen.

Nanny Qiu proved a poor traveler and spent the entire trip lying on the lower bunk of our compartment, too miserable to pay attention to anything except her nausea. At lunchtime I brought her a steamed pork bun from the dining car, but she waved it away. Then her frugal nature asserted itself and she wrapped the bun in a napkin and stuffed it in her carpet bag in case, as she said, there wasn't anything worth eating in Shanghai.

Nanny dozed, moaning from time to time, and I daydreamed about Hanchin, about college, about my future. Finally we pulled into Shanghai as the late-afternoon sun cast long shadows that chased the train along its tracks. As the train slowed down, I lowered the window to look out as we entered the station. The smell of coal smoke wafted into the compartment, and I saw Gaoyin on the platform, waving madly and calling my name.

I was in Shanghai.

I was really on my way to university.

∽∾∽

"Lucky for us that Nanny Qiu isn't feeling well," Gaoyin said.

Delicately, she licked the cream out of an eclair. We were in the French Concession, in a café on Avenue Joffre, seated on little bentwood chairs facing the street. Lace curtains across the window created an illusion of privacy from passersby. "We'll tell her to sleep late tomorrow and rest. I'll have someone bring breakfast to her, and she won't notice you're gone until it's too late."

My train to Hangchow would leave at noon the next day. By the time Gaoyin and I left for the station, Shen would already be on his way to his family's tea warehouse. I'd thought of a number of ruses to keep Nanny from seeing my trunk being carried out of the apartment, from sending her on an errand to locking her in the servants' quarters. But now that she was ill and exhausted, it would be all too easy to persuade her to rest for another day.

Everything, I thought, must have been preordained. The gods were assisting me.

Gaoyin and I were enjoying a day of window-shopping along Nanking Road, where the buildings looked as though they had been lifted from a postcard of a European city, all stonework and porticoes, the sidewalks filled with shoppers dressed in the latest styles. The young women all had bobbed hair, and most were dressed in Western fashions. The few women in traditional *qipao*s didn't look traditional at all. If anything, they managed to look even more provocative than their friends in Western garb, for the dresses were tailored to cling tightly to their bodies from neck to hip. I didn't know how they managed to walk, even with the help of high slits up each side of their skirts.

I tried not to stare too openly at the foreigners, at their pale eyes, strangely colored hair, and oversize noses. Everywhere I looked, there were sailors with sunburned skin ogling the stylish women, bearded men in linen suits and panama hats, ladies with fluttering skirts, parasols lifted against the sun. They looked odd somehow, riding in rickshaws. At home, a European would have attracted a curious mob. In Shanghai, the locals prided themselves on being blasé about the foreign presence in their city.

"There are so many foreigners here!" I whispered to Gaoyin as we squeezed past a portly gentleman with a red face and red whiskers, perspiration beading his forehead.

"Twenty-five thousand of them," said Gaoyin. "And cruise ships bring travelers who want to see 'the Paris of the East,' so sometimes the promenade along the Bund hardly seems Chinese."

After Nanking Road, we had taken a rickshaw back to Avenue Joffre. Gaoyin had announced she was hungry again and we had settled ourselves at a café table, coffee and a plate of eclairs appearing almost as soon as my sister handed the menu back to the waiter.

"Perhaps I should go with you to Hangchow," she said thoughtfully. "It would seem more legitimate if you arrived accompanied by an older relative."

"Perhaps you should think about what you'll say to Shen. He'll be angry with you, Gaoyin. He'll lose face with Father for letting this happen while I'm staying in your home."

"Don't worry about Shen. I can take care of him." Her tone was firm and confident.

⌒⌒⌒

The skies were dark when we climbed out of the rickshaw, but the streets of Shanghai didn't concede to the night. Stores and restaurants cast light onto sidewalks, neon signs flashed, and automobile headlamps swung around corners, sudden and blinding. We entered the marble-tiled lobby of Gaoyin's apartment building, a box of pastries tied with red-and-white string swinging from my hand. We rode the lift to the sixth floor. When the doors opened, Nanny Qiu was in the corridor, her expression one of deep hurt.

"*Wah, wah,* Third Young Mistress. I was worried to find you gone."

"Oh, Nanny. We didn't want to disturb you. Come shopping with us tomorrow afternoon when you're feeling better." The lie slipped out so easily.

Shen's voice called, "Is that you, Wife? Is Leiyin with you?"

"Yes, Husband," Gaoyin said, unpinning her hat as she sauntered through the door. "We won't take more than five minutes to get ready for dinner. I'm starving."

We entered the apartment, into total silence.

"Third Sister." It was Changyin, his face granite, his voice my doom.

My first impulse was to run into the street, but Shen had closed the door and stood in front of it, looking as grim as my brother.

"I'm taking you home with me tomorrow," Changyin said.

Panic buzzed in my stomach like a nest of wasps.

"Please, Eldest Brother, don't take me back." Even as I pleaded, my daydreams were falling to dust.

"What's happened?" Gaoyin asked, still pretending innocence.

Changyin slammed his fist on the marble tabletop beside her, his determined composure shattered by her insouciance.

"First Sister, you should be ashamed of yourself!"

My eldest brother, normally so calm, so reasonable. I'd never heard him raise his voice before and I shrank away, pressing against Gaoyin.

"There's no way our little sister could have made these plans without your help, so stop play-acting. You want to know what's happened? What's happened is that yesterday a letter arrived for Third Sister from Hangchow Women's University with a receipt for payment of boarding fees. Father thought the college had made an error.

"Tongyin came home and proved it was no error. He saw a letter from Leiyin on Yen Hanchin's desk at *China Millennium*, promising to write from Hangchow. Father put two and two together, and I came to Shanghai on the morning train."

The pastries dangled from my hand, their movement stilled as though in sympathy with my heart.

"You stubborn, deceitful, spoiled little idiot! Do you ever think of anyone besides yourself? I've never seen Father in such a rage."

He looked weary all of a sudden, and the fury vanished from his face. My heart, so still a moment before, began to palpitate like that of a rabbit caught in a trap.

"What has happened, Third Sister, is that Father is furious with both of you. Tomorrow we return to Changchow. I can't defend your actions this time, Leiyin. I can't do anything for you."

Shen and Changyin locked me in my room. This, I thought, wasn't so bad.

Then I heard shouting. Shen's words were indistinct, dampened by the thick walls of the apartment, but his voice carried through, angry and accusing. I heard thumps, and a shriek of pain that made me run to the door, but my pounding fists brought no one to my rescue, or Gaoyin's.

"It was my fault, all mine," I screamed through the heavy wood. "Don't punish Gaoyin, it was all my idea!"

I slid to the floor and wept. My sister's marriage was truly in jeopardy now. She was suffering because she'd helped me. Exhausted, I finally fell asleep by the door, my cheek crushed against the damp pastry box.

Even if I had caught the train to Hangchow, she couldn't have avoided Shen's anger. I'm appalled, overwhelmed by guilt. Did

Gaoyin know this would happen when she agreed to help? Shen is such a quiet man.

The two of you were remarkably similar in many ways, my *yin* soul says. *She was certain she could manage Shen. You were certain you could persuade your father.* There is a scent in the air that makes me long for my sister: Shalimar.

She shouldn't have helped you, my *yang* soul says. *Although she no longer answered to your father, she had merely moved from being dependent on him to being dependent on her husband.* A sour flavor of red vinegar rises from my throat, overpowering the echo of Shalimar.

My *hun* soul pats me gently on the back. Its touch is cool. *Gaoyin is like everyone else in the Song family. She keeps her promises. Even if she had her doubts after promising you she would help, Gaoyin would have felt honor-bound to follow through.*

I wish she hadn't, I say, feeling dry, ghost tears slide down my cheeks. *I wish she had changed her mind. What if Shen takes a concubine because of this?*

⌒⌒⌒

In the morning, a house servant saw us out of the apartment. We took the morning train, a silent trio. Nanny Qiu was so terrified of being accused of taking part in the conspiracy she forgot to feel nauseated. It was early evening when we arrived back at Changchow station, where I had begun my journey only two days ago. When the motorcar brought us home, the street was quiet. Passersby were hurrying home to dinner and paid us no attention. Lao Li opened the gate to let us in, shaking his head as we drove past.

With steely fingers, Changyin steered me by the elbow to Father's study, where Tongyin sat, looking despondent. His expression changed immediately when he saw me, fury in his eyes and accusation on the tip of his tongue, but he said nothing. Then Father entered, followed by Stepmother.

I knelt, my forehead on the silk carpet, still hoping for a reprieve. To my surprise, Tongyin fell to his knees beside me. Then a quick whistling noise and a thud. I sensed Tongyin's body jerk slightly but he made no sound. I counted ten lashes of the cane for my brother and shuddered. What did Tongyin have to do with my misadventure? Surely Father couldn't blame him. First Gaoyin, now Tongyin, punished for my sins.

"Get up now, Second Son. Stay beside your sister, but sit up."

Trembling, but determined not to cry out, I waited for the beating to begin.

"In another household," my father said, in a voice I barely recognized, "a disobedient daughter would be beaten. But we are educated people."

I spent the next hour on my knees, eyes lowered to the ground, as my father lashed out with words instead of a bamboo cane.

For her role in my attempted escape, Father banned Gaoyin from our home.

He blamed Tongyin for taking me to that first lecture by Hanchin and bringing me into contact with bad influences. He forbade Tongyin from any further dealings with Hanchin, *China Millennium*, or any left-wing groups. If Tongyin disobeyed, it would cost him his allowance.

Then there were my letters to Hanchin. The mere fact that I had written letters to a man was damning proof of my infatuation.

"Did that man encourage your sister's affections, Tongyin? What do you know about this?"

"There is no such possibility, Father, none at all. Yen Hanchin only tolerated her letters out of courtesy and because of his friendship with me. He never wrote back."

Father berated me for taking advantage of the privileges he'd allowed me.

He said I had abused his broad-minded tolerance.

He accused me of being irresponsible, spoiled, stubborn, and deceitful.

He called me unfilial.

My father shouted all this and more, pacing on the carpet, his fury at high tide. The cane whistled through the air but never hit me. Finally, he ceased the stream of invective and sat down, almost panting.

"You must leave in the morning for your business trip." Stepmother spoke into the silence. "Please, sir, you must get some rest. Jiaxing is a long journey by riverboat."

"Yes, I have wasted enough time on this useless girl. Tongyin, go find Lu and have him assemble the house staff downstairs in the foyer."

Tongyin dashed out of the study. Our head servant must have been close by, for in moments, my brother returned to report that the servants were ready.

Father pulled me to my feet and out to the mezzanine by the staircase. Below us, the servants waited. I saw Nanny Qiu hiding behind our cook, a large man. My father's words to the staff made it perfectly clear I was no better than a prisoner.

"During my absence, Third Young Mistress will be confined

to her room. Bring her only two meals a day of the plainest food. Give her nothing to read and do not speak to her."

Then my father dragged me by the arm along the corridor, Stepmother and my brothers following. He threw open my bedroom door and flung me inside. The soles of my shoes slipped on the polished floorboards. I stumbled against the edge of a rug and fell forward, my hands outstretched. If I hadn't been wearing my travel jacket, there would have been bruises on my arm from where Father had gripped me.

I lay prone with my cheek on the floor, listening. The door slammed and there was a jingle of keys, a click of the lock. My father's departing footsteps were muffled, for he was wearing slippers, but the thump of his cane resounded like a battering ram as he retreated down the corridor. Slowly I sat up on the rug, rubbing my sore elbow.

I considered my situation. My being locked in my room meant Father still hadn't decided how to punish me. He'd have a week away to think about it. My hopes began to rise. Father always calmed down after an initial burst of fury.

Confined to my room, I had ample time to ponder my mistakes. I should have been more patient. I should have persuaded him to let me go to university, if not this year, then next. I shouldn't have raised the subject of a career. I should have said I just wanted the experience of living on campus, of being surrounded by other clever and educated girls. I could have won my battle in small, incremental stages. But in my eagerness to impress Hanchin, I'd been reckless and impetuous.

Father would return from his trip downriver with his temper quite restored, I decided. I would beg his forgiveness, and life would continue as usual—so long as I didn't mention university again.

Then there was Hanchin. He wouldn't be invited to our home ever again. With Nanmei gone, I wouldn't be able to get any letters to him. Perhaps I could bribe one of the maids to carry out that errand, but did I even want to burden him with the knowledge that I'd suffered my father's wrath for his sake?

But that was another problem, to be dealt with another day. I had to gather my wits and reflect on how to conduct myself when Father returned.

❧

Father hadn't inspected my room before he threw me inside. Under the bed was a stack of books I'd been meaning to read. I read during the daylight hours and spent the nights, before falling asleep, with my thoughts: romantic daydreams about Hanchin, tragic farewells, and ecstatic greetings at train stations.

By the third day, a certain routine had been established. First, one of the house servants arrived with a clean chamber pot and exchanged it for my used one. Another brought a fresh jug of hot water for the enamel washbasin. Then Nanny Qiu came to deliver breakfast and remove the previous night's supper tray. In the evening, Nanny and another servant came, Nanny with my supper on a tray, the servant with a fresh jug of water for the basin and a clean chamber pot. In between, silence.

At noon of the fourth day of my incarceration, I heard unexpected footsteps in the corridor. I tucked my novel under the mattress and lay down on the bed. When the door opened, it was

Tongyin. He closed the door and leaned against it, looking down at me in a way that made me sit up, instantly wary.

"You've ruined my life, you selfish little slut." A voice that could have sliced flesh.

I flinched at his words but didn't reply.

"I take you to one lecture and you thank me by causing all this trouble."

This was irrational and I didn't bother answering.

"You've been writing to Hanchin. How dare you bother him with your schoolgirl questions?"

He crossed the room in a rush and pinned me down to the bed by my wrists. I cried out, more shocked than afraid. I struggled, but my legs were wedged between his knees. I could only kick my feet helplessly at the air.

"Are you delusional? Do you actually think he cares about you? You've been pestering him!"

"I wasn't pestering him! He said I could write to him anytime."

"He was being polite, you idiot. Did you think he kept your letters tied up in a packet with pink ribbons? He doesn't care about you. If he pretended to, then like every other man in Changchow, it's only because of your dowry."

"No. He's not like that." Furious, I struggled some more.

This time, he let go of my wrists and stood up. He reached into the pocket of his trousers and pulled out a folded sheet of paper, thin and pale blue.

"Well, he has written you a note. I saw him this morning."

He flipped the paper onto the bed and I snatched it up. Although I was longing to read the note, I wouldn't, not in front of Tongyin. Undoubtedly he'd already read it.

"But you're not supposed to see him any more than I am."

"I can't help it if he walks into the noodle shop where I'm having lunch."

Tongyin didn't frequent noodle shops any more than he went to the public library. I looked at him sideways. He scowled and went to the door.

"I had to see him again, to tell him face-to-face that Father has forbidden me to associate with him. No more *China Millennium*, no more lecture schedules. I said Father didn't like you writing to him and that this has all been your fault."

"Did he ask about me? Did you tell him I tried to run away?"

"Why should I discuss our family scandals with an outsider? I told him you won't be going to university in Hangchow. Then he scribbled this for you."

"I'm truly sorry, Second Brother. I know how much working at the magazine meant to you."

His face twisted. "Damn the magazine." He slammed the door. A jingle of keys.

❧

Well, he managed to hide his feelings quite well. My *yin* soul sounds sarcastic. She sprinkles crushed star anise into the air, so strong I can taste it. She sits cross-legged on the terrace and pats the floor beside her. I join her there.

I don't see how I ruined his life. It was my future that was in tatters.

Oh dear, says my *hun* soul. *You didn't understand it then, but now do you really not see?*

Together we examine the memory again and this time I look more closely at my brother's face and at mine. Our expressions are identical, sorrow and loss barely hidden beneath anger and self-pity. Tongyin's eyes glisten in his handsome face. He had been close to tears before storming out of the room. Perhaps he'd stormed out in order to hide his tears.

Oh. How could I not have guessed? I say very slowly. *We were both in love with the same man.*

My *yang* soul opens his mouth as though to say something, then stops. Instead he ambles down the steps to the garden and vanishes into the bamboo grove. There is a taste of dry salt fish in my mouth, so intense it's almost bitter, and I understand that his apprehensions are as strong as my own. The reasons for our unease, however, are probably quite different.

Do you think Hanchin suspected Tongyin was in love with him? I ask my *yin* and *hun* souls.

What do you think? my *hun* soul asks, quite gently.

꩜

As soon as Tongyin slammed the door, I unfolded the pale blue notepaper:

Dear Miss Song,

I was sorry to learn you won't be attending university. Your spirit and intellect would have been equal to the challenge. You would have made a fine teacher. Please remember that

*school isn't your only avenue for education, for learning is
a lifelong endeavor.*

*You may lose all that you acquire, but knowledge and
wisdom remain yours forever.*

Sincerely, Yen Hanchin

I hadn't expected any open words of affection. After all, he
knew that Tongyin would read his message and that if Father
intercepted a love letter I would be disgraced even more. No, this
was as much as he could write and I was satisfied. I read the lines
over and over again, trying to divine a hidden message. He was
using *education* to represent our love. He was saying there could
be other avenues, other ways for us to be together sometime, and
then it would be for a lifetime. He was mine forever. I fell on the
bed, sobbing, consumed by my need to be in his arms. The ache
in my heart filled me with despair even as I thrilled to the words
in the brief note.

Sitting up, I wiped my eyes, pressed my lips to the paper, and
slid it carefully between the pages of a book. I had to practice vigi-
lance and obedience. The most important thing was to allay Father's
suspicions, bring life back to normal, and be allowed to leave the
house. Otherwise I wouldn't have any way to see Hanchin again.

Father had left instructions that I was to be fed nothing but congee
and pickled vegetables, but someone was disobeying orders. After

only a few days, fruit, pork buns, and sticky rice with chicken steamed in bamboo-leaf parcels began appearing on the tray. On the sixth day of my imprisonment, when Nanny Qiu brought me a tray and I lifted the cover off a bowl, I found my favorite dish: tiny river shrimp quick-fried with green peas.

The shrimp indicated to me that Stepmother had calmed down. If I could get her on my side, perhaps in time I would be able to see Hanchin again. I would ask Stepmother's advice.

Nanny Qiu left and locked the door. Outside she began scolding someone.

"*Wah, wah*, Ping, you lazy peasant, why this family ever took you in I'll never know. Where are those clean towels for Third Young Mistress's morning wash, you turtle egg?"

I knew from the sound of the footfalls that our young maid Ping was hurrying along the corridor as fast as she could to get away from Nanny Qiu.

Silence. Then Nanny's voice, muttering from the other side of the door.

"Now we'll see what happens to disobedient daughters. Now that the Master has sent a telegram."

Strictly speaking, Nanny Qiu wasn't addressing me. She would never dream of defying my father, but there was nothing to prevent her from talking out loud to herself. She was still angry with me, although no longer afraid of being blamed for my escapade. I knew this from other mutterings on other days.

I put my ear to the door. This was real news, not Nanny's usual diatribe. I spoke quietly into the keyhole. "Nanny, what was in that telegram?"

She continued as though she hadn't heard me. "Who knows what it said, but First Young Master shook his head and gave it to the master's concubine, who sighed and said, 'Poor Leiyin,' and sat down."

With that, she shuffled off. I would have to wait until my father came home to find out what was in that telegram. I couldn't concentrate on more than a sentence or two of a book before going back to speculating on the telegram's contents. Was Father sending me away to live with relatives, to get me away from Hanchin? My mother's family was in Hunan, quite far away from here. That didn't matter. I'd find a way to write to Hanchin at *China Millennium*. We'd find a way to be together, somehow.

The next evening, I stood at the window and watched Father return. He walked up the path from the main gate briskly, followed by his manservant and luggage. He didn't glance up in the direction of my window. He didn't send for me that night. He didn't send for me until the next morning.

༄

I knelt, forehead pressed to the Turkish carpet, palms stretched out in an attitude of supplication. Father sat behind his desk, reading a document of some kind. When I first walked into the study, only the tight set of his lips betrayed his emotions. Changyin, dressed to go out, stood by the door as if to prevent me from escaping. Beside Father stood my stepmother, holding the telegram. Tongyin wasn't there.

Finally, Father looked up.

"I had many things to say to you, Third Daughter. But you know why I'm angry with you. You knew my wishes, and yet you disobeyed them, deliberately."

He took the telegram from Stepmother.

"I have come to a decision." He tapped the telegram. "You're getting married. I have made all the arrangements."

I gasped, the only sound I could make, for a choking sensation clogged my throat. There had been no talk of marriage a week ago. Matchmaking between families such as ours was a time-consuming business. Father must have come to an arrangement with a family he knew well. There was no other way he could have struck an agreement so quickly.

My thoughts scrambled around in my brain. I was only seventeen. Father had always said his daughters wouldn't marry until we were at least twenty-one. I still had a few years to persuade Father to change his mind.

"Your husband's name is Lee Baizhen. I met his father on my trip. Their clan lives in Pinghu, a town south of Shanghai. It will be a very favorable situation for you. Lee Baizhen is an only son. Your wedding is in two weeks' time, in Pinghu."

Now I screamed.

"Please, Father, no! Don't send me away to a strange town and a strange family! Father, beat me and lock me up, but don't do this!"

"You're getting married. After that, there won't be any more nonsense from you."

"Father, no! Let me stay at home. Let me be the unmarried daughter who looks after you when you're old. Please, don't send me away!"

I crawled to his side, weeping. He jerked the edge of his gown away from my frantic hands.

"You've proved completely lacking in judgment. Impulsive. Disobedient. You're going to live in a small country town where no one ever goes and nothing ever happens."

He left the room, his footfalls soft and swift, merciless. When my cries subsided into sobs, Stepmother knelt down beside me.

"Your future husband is an only son, you're fortunate."

"I'd rather he beat me. I don't want to marry this Lee person! Eldest Brother, please, speak to Father."

"Little Sister, I warned you in Shanghai. I can't help you."

I met his eyes, then threw myself on the carpet and wailed in despair.

❦

Don't you have something to say about this? I address my *yang* soul, who is watching the scene with more than a trace of smugness.

I have nothing to add, he replies piously. He pulls a handkerchief from his sleeve. *Your father said it all. Disobedient, impulsive, lacking in judgment.*

He always favored you, my *yin* soul says. *But this time you pushed him too far. He had so many other worries on his mind.*

Memories come to me of Father seated at his table with Changyin leaning over his shoulder, looking at papers. Father pondering a map of China, marking boundary lines where the Communists held territories. Where the Nationalists had pushed through. Where warlords ruled. Where the Japanese occupied towns, whether it was official or not. Where we owned land and houses, quarries and mines, shares in railways and banks.

Five hundred years of wealth, built up by your ancestors, my *yang* soul points out. *All part of his legacy, all of it his duty to safe-guard. Why didn't you realize you were just adding to his worries?*

In a flash, memories of a photo album, pictures carefully tucked into the gold paper corners glued to its pages. Father as a student in Paris, looking jaunty with a tweed cap pushed back on his head, his arm around another young man, a classmate. Father in evening clothes, opera glasses in one hand, a champagne flute in the other.

Oh, come now, my *yang* soul says. *That was never your father, not really.*

My *hun* soul voices what I finally realized that day. *Those few years abroad were just a holiday before he took up his responsibilities as family patriarch. When he returned, no matter how much he admired Western culture, those few years could not compete with a thousand years of tradition.*

8

*T*here was no casting of horoscopes for my marriage, and no months of shopping for the dowry furniture I would bring to my husband's home. With only two weeks before the wedding, and given the utter lack of interest on my part, Stepmother did all the work. She ordered a set of rosewood furniture, factory made rather than hand-carved, and packed our second-best Limoges in straw to ship to Pinghu. Only Father, Stepmother, and my brothers would come for the wedding. Sueyin wanted to come, but Liu Tienzhen didn't want to make the long journey to a dusty little town. Gaoyin was not invited.

Father and Changyin went to Shanghai on business, but it was obvious they had left to avoid my tears. I was no longer confined to my room, but I wasn't allowed off the estate. Lao Li, the gatekeeper, had strict instructions.

I had no way of contacting Hanchin. The only telephone in the house was locked in Father's study. Nanmei couldn't help me. She'd left for Soochow the day before I ran away to Shanghai and had no idea of my predicament. I couldn't drag Sueyin into an escape plan, I knew better now. I had to do it on my own.

Sueyin brought me a wedding gift from Gaoyin. It was lovely, an English burr-walnut stationery cabinet no larger than a hat box. It opened to reveal vertical dividers filled with cream stationery and matching envelopes lined in navy tissue, the same as she had given Sueyin. There was also a heavy cardboard box with more of the luxurious envelopes and paper, enough to last for years.

"Gaoyin ordered this especially for us," Sueyin said. She pulled out an envelope and opened the triangular flap. With a slim finger, she lifted the navy tissue away from the paper. "The tissue lining isn't glued to the flap."

The deliberate steadiness of her voice caught my attention and I stopped caressing the polished golden walnut veneer.

"Between the tissue and the paper, Third Sister, there's a space, a pocket where you can hide a thin slip of paper. The letter you really want to write. Then glue the edges of the lining to the envelope. We'll do the same."

"Is this how you and Gaoyin . . ." Misery pressed into my chest like a fist, a foretelling of the loneliness I would face. That Sueyin already faced. "I won't marry this man, Second Sister! And this Pinghu, it's some dreary small town. I've never even heard of it. I won't go. I won't go!"

"The town isn't that far from Shanghai. You could visit Gaoyin if you get lonely."

We both knew it might be a while before Shen allowed me

into his home again. However, he had forgiven Gaoyin. She was pregnant.

"Shen will deny her nothing if she has a boy," said Sueyin. "Let's wait until the baby is born. Then we can make plans to meet in Shanghai."

"Second Sister, I'm not going to marry Lee Baizhen. You'll see." My words were defiant, but the escape plans I had conceived and discarded were as numerous as memorial stones in a graveyard. How could I get away this time?

∽∼∾

The Lee family sent a delegate to our home a week after Father's announcement. Madame Pao was middle-aged, a third cousin. When she bowed, her plump figure strained against a too-tight beige silk *qipao*. Her heavily powdered face beamed goodwill and excitement.

"I'm so honored to have the duty of telling the bride about her family. And to have the opportunity to travel to a big city."

Jeweled tassels dangled from her earlobes, old-fashioned earrings that swung in tiny flirtatious arcs when she nodded, much too youthful for a woman her age. Her voice reminded me of Nanny Qiu, loud and overeager. My determination to avoid the marriage was bolstered by the prospect of being related to Madame Pao.

She looked around the drawing room at its parquet floor and wallpaper. Her gaze swept out toward the terrace. The French doors were open to let breezes through, but the sheer silk draperies floating across the portals caught the sunlight, softening the harsh brightness of a hot summer morning. Outside on the terrace, urns overflowed with frothy late-blooming roses, white and pink.

"Your new home is just a traditional, old-fashioned house. But it's the largest of the properties owned by the Lee clan."

I knew that a bride must enter her husband's home with an understanding of the family hierarchy, its history, how its members are related. Madame Pao launched into a recitation of the names of the members of the Lee household. It was a short list. Lee Baizhen had no siblings, nor did his father. Then she moved on through the previous five generations of Lees, then the names and degrees of kinship of various third cousins living in the town of Pinghu.

I remained silent, my face in as bland a mask as I could muster. Sueyin and Stepmother kept the conversation running smoothly.

"Where do you live, Madame Pao?" Sueyin asked when the woman finally paused.

"*Ai-ya!* No need to be so polite. Call me Auntie. Are we not as good as kin already? Well, my home is very close to the Lee estate. In fact, our house used to be part of the larger main estate. My husband's family bought it the year we were married. It used to be Great-Uncle Lee Zhong's house, before he fell on hard times."

She caught herself, and leaned toward me reassuringly.

"But your father-in-law has no problems with money, oh no. He married well, very well. Your mother-in-law is from the wealthiest merchant clan in Hunan and brought a huge dowry with her, enough to keep the household in comfort for three generations, so it is said. And, of course, Lee Baizhen is the only son of an only son."

I knew what she meant. No spiteful unmarried sisters spying on you or gossiping about your every mistake. No brothers and their jealous families fluttering about, hoping to win favor from the patriarch. That was the life most women had to endure in the inner courtyard. But I'd had enough of being told how lucky I was to be marrying the only son of an only son.

"Auntie Pao, tell me more about Lee Baizhen," I said, in my most innocent voice. "Which university did he attend?"

Her face fell, her hands fluttered.

"He was tutored at home. He didn't have your brothers' advantages. But his tutor is the most respected in our town, a true scholar of the classics. Baizhen is an open-minded young man; he has the highest regard for education. He's delighted with you already. A scholarship to Hangchow Women's University, why that's almost as good as graduating from college . . ."

"Madame Pao, do you enjoy gardens?" With her sweet voice, Sueyin could interrupt without giving the slightest impression of disrespect.

Sueyin led the way, taking Madame Pao's arm. Stepmother and I followed, her hand firmly grasping my forearm. She gave me a stern look, which I ignored. Several paces ahead, Sueyin pointed out the different roses, saying their names in English and then in French: *Gloire de Dijon, Celestial, La Reine Victoria.*

Madame Pao clapped her hands in delight. "And you all speak foreign languages!"

"Very little, Auntie. Only some polite phrases." Sueyin picked a pink bloom and presented it to the beaming woman. "This one is called *Souvenir de la Malmaison*. It's the most fragrant of all the roses. Would you like to see our traditional garden?"

By the time Madame Pao had taken a walk through the Old Garden, it was time for late-morning tea. Stepmother insisted our guest try one of everything: the lotus-seed buns, the fruit tarts, the little squares of iced sponge cake. Madame Pao, already in raptures over our gardens, the houses, and the quality of our tea, twittered her praises even more forcefully.

"What a delightful visit this has been." Madame Pao bowed to us. She looked at me with a fond smile. "And what a beautiful, clever bride for young Baizhen. We're fortunate indeed to have you join our family."

Father's sedan chair and two chair bearers stood in the fore-court ready to take Madame Pao to the train station. The sedan chair departed. The gates shut. My sister and stepmother turned back toward the path that led to the villa. I hurried after them.

"I refuse to get married." The cry came out of me unbidden, words I had wanted to shout at Madame Pao, words I hadn't dared shout at my father.

They didn't seem to hear.

"You liked those little sponge cakes, didn't you, Second Stepdaughter? I'll put some in a box for you to take home."

How could they talk about cakes?

"Stepmother, Second Sister. You must help me."

They turned in unison, my stepmother stern, my sister troubled.

"We have been helping," Stepmother said. "No thanks to you, Madame Pao will return with favorable reports. Sueyin has been so charming she's managed to dazzle that woman into believing that you're capable of gracious manners as well."

"I don't care what they think of me."

Sueyin looked at me, anxiety and exasperation creasing her brow.

"But you must care, Third Sister. You'll be living with them for the rest of your life. Don't you understand?"

I ran ahead of them into the house and up to my room. I slammed the door. I did understand. To be treated well by one's in-laws was considered good enough. But a wife had to gain her in-laws' favor, otherwise, life could be unbearable. But it was all irrelevant because I wasn't going to marry Lee Baizhen. I wasn't going to forget what Madame Sun Yat-sen had said about the duty our generation's young women owed to China. I wasn't going to give up on my dream of a life with Hanchin.

I still had the money Father had given me before my journey to Shanghai. I opened my jewelery box and wondered how I could trade its contents for cash. If I went to a pawnshop, how much would that jade pendant fetch? Or my pearl necklace? I had no idea. How would I even find a pawnshop, one that wouldn't cheat me?

I stretched my hands out, inspecting the three jade bangles on my wrists. They were the most valuable things I owned, their color a pure, deep green like moss, their sound when tapped together a sweet chime. They had been my mother's and I would never sell them.

Tomorrow, when Father returned, I would beg him to cancel the betrothal. If he didn't, I would lean the gardener's ladder against the orchard wall and climb over. I would take a rickshaw to *China Millennium*'s offices. If Hanchin wasn't there, I'd wait all night. I'd beg or bribe his colleagues not to tell my family, to lie about my identity if anyone asked. This was the plan that had come to me since Madame Pao's visit, which had focused my thoughts and made me realize that my impending marriage was no idle threat.

But if I ran away again, Father would never take me back.

There was a knock on my door. It was Stepmother, her voice low.

"I'm taking you out."

"But I'm forbidden to leave the house."

"I'll wait outside while you get ready."

My heart beat wildly, hope stirring inside me. I rolled up some clothing and stowed it in the largest bag I owned. Money, jewelery, and my precious letter from Hanchin.

We left through the lane beside the orchard, Stepmother unlocking and then relocking the side door. At the top of the lane, she unlocked another door. This one opened out to the street around the corner from where Lao Li kept guard at the main gate. A rickshaw waited there and we squeezed onto the seat. I fought to keep eager questions from spilling out as hope and excitement pulsated through my veins.

"To Comb Alley Market," she said to the rickshaw puller. "But first, take us through the mill district."

The puller set off on callused bare feet, the knotted muscles of his thin brown calves bulging as he ran.

"Where are we going, Stepmother?"

"I want to show you something."

"Are you helping me escape?"

"After we go to the market, you can decide."

This was more help than I had hoped for from Stepmother.

The threat of Pinghu and the Lee family suddenly felt slightly less ominous. We left the streets I knew so well, the ones that were wide and smoothly paved, shaded by old sycamores and elms and lined with high whitewashed walls, a gatekeeper seated at every grand entrance. The rickshaw turned away from the canal and soon we were in a warren of narrow streets and dilapidated buildings that gave way to small, dirty storefronts. Ragged beggars, some with stumps instead of hands and feet, called out to us. Every corner and alcove seemed to shelter a vagrant. Our own street saw very few beggars, for the gatekeepers shooed them away.

A fetid stench assaulted my nostrils. Rotting food and worse filled the cracks between the paving stones. An oxcart ambled down the center of the street, probably after having delivered vegetables to the market. Some wilted cabbage leaves clinging to the side of the cart peeled off as I watched. An old woman, her back so crooked and bent she had to crane her neck to see ahead of her, picked her way quickly through the street, reached down, and stuffed the musty leaves into her mouth. I wanted to gag.

Stepmother tapped the rickshaw puller on the shoulder with the tip of her parasol, and pointed at a long, two-story building. "Stop there and wait for us."

The entrance to the building bore no sign, there were just the words TANG SHAN COTTON FACTORY painted in red on the dingy gray wall. A rank smell hung in the air. As soon as we entered the vestibule, the smell intensified and I could hardly think for the noise of machinery pounding behind the heavy double doors in front of us. An elderly clerk seated behind a battered desk stared at us with suspicion, squinting in the dim light. He stood up, a thin, short man in a faded blue tunic, his luxuriant gray hair out of place on his desiccated form. Then he broke into a smile, showing stained, broken teeth.

"Second Young Mistress, welcome, welcome!" He bowed to Stepmother. "I haven't seen you since the day you left home. What brings you here?"

"Good day, Ah Mao. I'm here to show my stepdaughter what a cotton mill is like. May I take her up to the observation floor?"

"Please, please. No need to ask. Your father and uncles are the owners! Please, up those stairs."

Stepmother and I ascended metal treads that clanked with every step. At the top she pushed open a door and the din grew louder. We emerged into a long gallery that ran the length of the building. A few lightbulbs hanging from wires criss-crossed the ceiling, so dim I felt as though I had walked into twilight. There were large windows near the ceiling, but they were so dirty they seemed to keep out rather than let in the light. The stagnant air stifled my lungs.

"This part of the factory is for weaving." Stepmother's voice was matter-of-fact.

There was barely enough space between the looms for work-ers to pass one another, and the machinery looked very danger-ous. Some of the workers were just girls.

"They work more than fourteen hours a day," said Stepmother, "and get nothing more than a bowl of millet gruel at noon to eat."

"What's that smell?"

"That comes from the other room, where the cotton is dyed. The dyes are cured with urine."

I counted about fifty women sweating behind looms, hair

bound tightly in kerchiefs, arms in constant motion, faces gray with exhaustion. I looked closer.

"Those are babies and small children down there! Sleeping between the machines!"

"Yes. The little ones look after the babies and try to keep out of the way."

"What about their husbands and fathers? Why do they allow this?"

"Some of the women are unmarried. Some are widowed or were abandoned by their husbands. Some have husbands but can't get by with one income. Some were sold into labor to pay off their families' debts."

A foreman carrying a thin bamboo cane patrolled the narrow aisles, his cane swinging from side to side while he shouted at the women. A boy ran to hide behind his mother and crossed the foreman's path. The cane shot out, slicing the boy's cheek. The foreman didn't pause in his stride, even as the child's shriek tore the air. No one bothered to pick up the child, not even his mother. The boy ran sobbing to wrap his arms around her knees.

"Stepmother! Do something. Your family owns this mill."

Moisture glistened in her eyes, but when she replied, her voice was brisk. "If I interfered, that woman would lose her job and another would simply take her place. Let's go now."

I threw a last glance at the little boy. When I told Hanchin, he would write about the disgraceful treatment of workers at this factory. No, I would write about it myself and send the letter to all the national newspapers.

We climbed back into the rickshaw, the sun scorching hot

now as morning gave way to noon. I didn't want to think about how the air inside the factory would grow even more oppressive.

"Stepmother, I thought your family owned a dry-goods store."

"They do. But since I became your father's concubine, my family has been able to secure credit more easily. They now own this cotton mill as well. My father and uncles have prospered."

"But why do they allow those women to be treated so badly? Maybe they don't realize what that foreman is doing. If those workers don't receive better conditions, they'll go elsewhere or organize a union. That would disrupt your family's business."

It was a good argument. It came straight out of *China Millennium*.

Under the shade of her parasol, my stepmother suddenly looked old. She was a plain woman. Her eyes were her one beauty, large and intelligent. Now there was tension around her mouth, too much color high on her cheeks.

"Those women consider themselves fortunate to have this work, Leiyin. It means the difference between living in squalor and not living at all. It means they can keep their daughters instead of selling them. They can't afford to care about workers' rights. They're just trying to survive day to day. China has an infinite supply of poor people and not enough work."

We continued in silence along the street; we were now in a neighborhood of cheap restaurants and dingy shops. Here were men and women in threadbare clothing. Children, some of them naked, stared at us with crafty, feral expressions. A middle-aged woman hobbled unsteadily on her crutch, moaning as she moved. When she leaned against a wall, I saw her bandaged feet were bloody, the rags wrapped around them oozing pus. I looked away.

"Some poor families still practice foot-binding even though it's banned," said Stepmother, seeing my reaction. "They hope to sell their girls to wealthy older men. Usually, the girls end up crippled and unsaleable, spurned. Without proper care, their feet rot away."

"Can't we help her?" I whispered, knowing the answer even as I spoke.

"She's dying already, of blood poisoning from gangrene."

The rickshaw entered a street of shabby homes whose ground floors were used as shops. Women sat outside the doorways, dressed too elaborately for this hour of the morning. They yawned and stared at us with dull curiosity. Some were combing each other's hair, others mending clothes. A few of the women laughed and struck poses when they saw us. Others simply sat there, limp and forlorn. I realized suddenly that the houses were brothels.

My shock must have been obvious, but when Stepmother spoke, it was as though she were pointing out the features of a garden.

"There was a girl from our neighborhood, from a respectable family. She didn't like her in-laws and ran away, returning to her family. But they refused to take her back. She had shamed them. I've heard she was seen working at a brothel somewhere on this very street."

"Stepmother, I know what you're trying to tell me. But I have an education. I can be a tutor. My life wouldn't come to this."

"Do you even know how much it costs to rent a room, Third Stepdaughter? How would you find pupils? How many hours of tutoring would keep a roof over your head and food in your belly?"

It was all true. I didn't know the answer to any of those questions. But surely Hanchin would help me.

The rickshaw rolled past more of the houses. One woman was dabbing a cloth at another's face, her thin blouse nearly slipping off her shoulder as she tended to her friend. The other woman turned to look at us and I saw she was young, a wasted figure with bruises around her eyes, rope burns around her wrists. I shuddered, not wanting to know the story behind those wounds.

Whenever I had read articles about poor workers, I had imagined sturdy men toiling away in factories full of shiny modern machines. I hadn't imagined women worked to death in stinking, stuffy buildings full of dangers, with babies underfoot. In the classic novels I knew, prostitutes were pretty young girls from poor families who entertained clients by strumming on the *pipa* lute. These were hovels, and none of the women looked young or pretty.

"The world is a cruel place for women, Leiyin," Stepmother said. "You've been raised in privilege. Don't mislead yourself into thinking you could live without three meals a day, a clean bed, and the protection of your family. Once you fall out of favor, it may be impossible to climb back into the fold. You've come perilously close and if your father didn't love you so much, he might have abandoned you already."

"Hasn't he done that?" I didn't bother biting back my bitterness. "He's married me off to a family in some miserable backwater town no one's ever heard of."

"No. He's entrusted you to the care of another family, a respectable family." Her voice, which had been so calm and reasonable, turned harsh. "The Lees value an alliance with our family.

If you're stubborn and rude, it will be hard to repair the damage later. You'll spend the rest of your life at odds with your in-laws. Treat them with deference and you'll gain their affection. You can find contentment, if not happiness."

I remained silent as the rickshaw carried us to Comb Alley Market. Stepmother got out to buy some dried fish and a few bundles of long string beans. When she came back, she pointed to the bag at my feet.

"I see you came prepared to run away. Now is your chance. I can leave you here in the market square, or you can come home again."

From the corner of my eye, I saw a plump woman at the edge of the square, an affable and artificial smile on her face, gold bangles on her arms. Beside her stood two young women, or perhaps they were just girls, it was difficult to tell under their thick, gaudy cosmetics. Their eyes were vacant, without hope.

And yet, when my thoughts turned to Hanchin, I knew I wouldn't end up like those girls. And I knew I could endure poverty as long as he was by my side.

I got out.

After parting from Stepmother, I hired a rickshaw. The ride from the market to the offices of *China Millennium* felt like a trip to the opposite end of the city. The rickshaw puller jogged along briskly, but my heart raced faster. Small stores and restaurants lined the sidewalks and when I spied the shop where Nanmei's mother had the family's shoes made, I knew I was nearly there.

The foyer smelled of cooking oil and garlic from the restaurant next door. I climbed up a rickety staircase to a landing with a sign that directed me up another flight of steps, and I pushed open a door bearing the magazine's name on a frosted-glass pane. Bells on the door jangled as I entered an office where a single electric fan beat the air with a quiet spinning sound. Behind a counter that marked out the small waiting area were four desks and a long bookcase untidily stacked with newspapers and magazines. Sunlight entered through large, clean windows, bare of curtains or blinds. There was a smell of ink and sweat. And sandalwood soap. I spied a sink in one corner. So this was where Hanchin worked.

There was only one man in the office. He put his magnifying glass down on the document he had been reading and came to the counter.

"How may I help you, miss?" We were downwind of the electric fan, and his body odor was strong.

"I'm looking for Yen Hanchin. Is he here?" Even though, clearly, he wasn't to be seen in the small office.

"Mr. Yen no longer works here, miss. May I be of assistance? I'm Lin Shaoyi, the editor of this journal."

"No longer here?" My voice rose, too shrill. I made myself calm down. "Then please, tell me where he's working now. I must speak with him."

"He left for Soochow yesterday. He's taken a new job as a teacher, a visiting instructor. He'll be going from village to village to train teachers."

I trudged down the stairs and collapsed on the bottom step, suddenly exhausted. Hanchin was gone. Was it because Tongyin told him I wouldn't be going to university? Had he heard about my marriage? Was it because he was no longer welcome in our home? Did he think our love was now impossible?

For a moment my vision turned black and I stared into darkness despite the bright sunshine streaming through the foyer's open door. Then my eyes cleared, but the colors of the world around me were shades of ash, bleak as winter fields. The smell of food from the restaurant next door, too strong a moment ago, now barely registered. I heard the calls of vendors out on the street with perfect clarity, but as though I were far away. The world was gray, my senses dulled. I wondered how my heart could beat so normally, compressed as it was to this leaden heaviness.

I thought of the young mother in the cotton mill, the noise, the smell. I saw again the dull-eyed prostitutes, their tawdry, brightly colored dresses, their painted mouths gaping in tired yawns. I tried to forget the hobbling beggar woman, her low moans of pain. I walked out to the street slowly, barely able to follow each step with the next.

I took a rickshaw home.

Part Two

Pinghu, 1935

We should tell you the story of your betrothal, my *hun* soul says. Its shining form settles down on the steps of the temple. Although it's early morning and the edges of the sky are barely streaked with light, looking at my *hun* soul is like trying to stare at a bird flying into the sun.

The circumstances of your betrothal to Lee Baizhen were so unusual they took on the status of legend in your husband's family, says my *yin* soul. She smooths down the pleats of her skirt and sits by my *hun* soul, knees drawn up, showing an inch of bare ankle above her white socks. There is a hint of crushed chrysanthemum petals in the air.

My *yang* soul looks bored. Rather than sit with the others, he chooses to lean against the temple door. I choose to ignore him.

Betrothals can take months of negotiation, my *hun* soul begins, as though reciting from memory, *especially when families like yours are involved. Your marriage arrangements were concluded so quickly and so strangely that by the time your bridal procession ar-*

rived in the town of Pinghu, the story had traveled alongside canals, over bridges, and into every small alley, as widely as the wanderings of a mendicant monk.

The story goes like this. An elderly relative had asked Lee Wenjing, patriarch of the Lee family, to handle the sale of some property in the town of Jiaxing. Lee traveled to Jiaxing to meet the prospective buyer, a wealthy man by the name of Song. Over the course of the day, the two men discovered they shared an interest in collecting rare books. They enjoyed each other's company so much that Song invited Lee for dinner aboard his private riverboat.

The boat was spacious and well equipped, more comfortable than most inns. There was a galley in the stern where Song's man-servant could prepare simple meals and boil water for tea. The two men sat on deck observing the comings and goings on the waterway. Under the influence of good wine, a bright moon, and the gentle rocking of waves, their conversation turned to family matters.

"My youngest daughter is seventeen and still unmatched," Song said. "If you could recommend a family with an unmarried son, I would be most grateful."

Lee pondered for a moment and said, "The Liangs are a good family, one of the great houses right here in Jiaxing. They're family friends and have yet to match their youngest son, about the same age as your daughter. Let me find out more tomorrow."

After another cup of wine, Lee cleared his throat.

"I'd like to ask the same favor of you," he said. "I have an only son. So far we haven't found anyone suitable in our little town of Pinghu. If you happen to know any families with unmarried daughters, I would appreciate an introduction."

To Lee's utter astonishment, Song dropped to his knees, banged his forehead three times on the teak deck, and cried out, "You have a son, I have a daughter, what more is there to say? Let us embrace and call each other kin!"

These lines are always uttered with great relish by the story's narrator, for Song had just made a very daring proposal and forced its outcome. Not only had the two men only just met, but Song was by far Lee's social superior. Thus Lee could hardly refuse when a man of Song's status knelt before him.

It was a match beyond Lee's wildest dreams. Telegrams were sent in both directions, and in the small town of Pinghu, Lee's wife, who was from a wealthy merchant family, could hardly contain her joy at this alliance with one of the great houses of Changchow.

There is a contemplative silence.

So that's how it happened. It was impulsive, an act of anger, wasn't it? I ask.

Can you blame him? My yang soul polishes his glasses with a worn handkerchief. *He had enough to worry about without your little dramas.*

This was done in anger, no doubt. My yin soul plays with the ribbons of her pigtail. *Oh, but there's no turning back from this one.*

Do you think he realized what he had done? I asked. *Is it too late now?*

He was terribly angry with you, my hun soul says. *But he loved you. He wanted to keep you safe. Marriage and a small town seemed like a good idea.*

9

Pinghu, 1928

The time leading up to my wedding day came to me in fragments as random as the passage of leaves carried by a stream. There were imprecise, jumbled images of a long journey by train, a small and dusty station at its end point. There was an old sedan chair that smelled of camphor wood and gloom, a bumpy ride down winding streets and over arched bridges that ended when the chair passed through a set of large entrance gates. Through a panel of red fabric I looked out of the sedan chair at a courtyard hung with lanterns and other swags of red cloth, at strangers who smiled and bowed.

There were no sisters by my side at the ceremony, only Stepmother and unfamiliar women who addressed me as "cousin" and "niece." At the banquet I sat as still as a wax doll, in the same red gown Sueyin had worn at her wedding, phoenixes embroidered on the bodice. Red silk veiled my face and a headdress decorated with jade and pearls weighed down my neck. The veil lifted a few times and I sipped from a cup of wine. I caught glimpses of a young man's face, a nervous forced smile, a sideways glance. Lee Baizhen. My husband.

Of my wedding night I remember only that same anxious face looking down at me, pink and shining with sweat. Then a sharp pain between my legs and a pleading voice, explaining it wouldn't hurt so much the next time. But it did, because the next time and the time after that followed far too soon, and it was day-break before my husband fell asleep. I didn't sleep at all. I didn't cry. I had been numb since the day I realized there was no escape from the fate my father had decreed for me.

☙❧

Why so few memories of that time? I see only moments here and there, erratic and unevenly spaced.

You only kept a very few memories from those days, so we only have a few to show you. A somewhat accusing tone from my *yang* soul. *You didn't like those weeks. You never were good at facing up to consequences.*

It was a nightmare for you, my *yin* soul says, *and it became worse once you understood it was no dream, but the rest of your life. In fact, there aren't any memories at all of your last week at home, the week leading up to your bridal journey.*

But your memories from the day after your wedding are all intact, my *hun* soul adds.

☙❧

The early-autumn afternoon was cool. Servants swept up the remains of the party, tattered red paper from firecrackers, dirt tracked into the halls. There was more than an hour to spare before my family's departure for the train station, and my new in-laws showed them around the estate. Lee Wenjing, the father-in-law I would now address as Gong Gong, led the tour.

Gong Gong was tall, nearly as tall as Changyin. His square jaw would have made him look stern if not for his drooping eyebrows, which gave him an indecisive air. He had an unusually large nose with a high bridge, almost like a foreigner's. He was distinguished rather than handsome, his height more impressive than his features.

Father strolled beside Gong Gong, and Changyin and Tongyin followed. Lee Baizhen—I couldn't yet think of him as my husband—walked between my brothers. He was a good six inches shorter than Changyin. I trailed behind, walking with Stepmother and my mother-in-law. I could hear Tongyin telling Baizhen all about university life in Shanghai.

"Our English professor is an Englishman," my Second Brother said. "He's very particular about pronunciation. Very particular. There's no pleasing him."

"What an advantage though, to learn from an actual foreigner." Baizhen's voice was wistful. "I've never seen one. Do they really have terribly large noses?"

Gong Gong's library contained some very fine paintings and works of calligraphy, many of them antiques. Father was clearly envious of the rare books my father-in-law had displayed in glass cases, which meant the collection was impressive. Then Gong Gong led us through the rest of the estate.

The main house, a sizable three-level mansion, stood against the back wall of a large courtyard. The center of the courtyard contained a formal rock garden planted with tall bamboos and plum trees; at its center was a clearing that held a large pavilion. I stumbled, catching my toe in a hole left by a missing paving stone. On one side of the main courtyard was a round moon gate set in a whitewashed wall. We passed through the moon gate and came to a path that led to another, smaller courtyard garden, which contained a small bamboo grove and a rock garden, and beyond them, a two-level house.

"This will be Baizhen and Leiyin's home," said Jia Po.

This was the first time my mother-in-law had spoken. Her voice was strong and confident, unexpected from such a tiny person. Her head barely reached my shoulder and to call her plain would have been a kindness. Her forehead was too wide and her chin jutted out. Her hands though, were beautifully shaped. A large pearl-and-coral ring showed off her long, slim fingers, and magnificent gold-and-jade bracelets adorned her wrist. Her clothing was otherwise very simple.

"Once all of Leiyin's belongings are unpacked, she and Baizhen can move in here. A young couple should have their own household." Jia Po hurried ahead to throw open the door to the house.

The walls inside had been freshly painted and the exterior looked clean and bright. But I saw Stepmother glance around and I followed her sharp-eyed gaze. Weeds clambered between flagstones and stagnant water filled a small pond by the rock garden. The walls of the house showed hints of dark patches that meant mildew and the carved shutters were cracked, their wood dry and in need of varnish.

Inside the house, my dowry furniture was already arranged in several of the rooms. A rosewood bedroom suite gleamed in one chamber, a table and chairs of lacquered wood inlaid with mother-of-pearl stood beside a window. In another room, another new bed, more tables and chairs, their shining surfaces a sharp contrast to the shabby wardrobe, original to the home, that was tucked in a corner.

"This is the newest house on the property, built in a more modern style." Jia Po had a brisk air about her, addressing me as though I were a buyer and not a new daughter-in-law. "This second-floor veranda is such a nice feature."

All the rooms on the second floor opened onto the veranda, which served as both balcony and corridor. She led us to a room at one end, small but bright, with a window that overlooked the courtyard and another that looked down into a small orchard. Empty bookcases lined one wall and two armchairs were positioned invitingly by the orchard window. Three wooden crates sat in the middle of the room. My books. Seeing them brought a pang of longing for home.

"A small library for your own use," said Jia Po. "This was Baizhen's idea."

It was a gesture of understanding, perhaps even compassion, that I had not expected. Baizhen smiled at me, shy and hopeful. I turned away, pretending to inspect the crates.

My husband was so ordinary I wouldn't have been able to pick him out from a crowd the next day. We were the same height, but his shoulders slumped, making him appear shorter. He squinted out at the world through wire-rimmed glasses with lenses as round as moons, which made his thin face look even thinner. His small mouth was habitually slightly pursed, as though he was chronically anxious.

"So thoughtful," said Stepmother, her smile genuine when she looked at Baizhen. "Leiyin enjoys reading more than anything."

We descended to the courtyard, and entered the orchard that stood behind the brick walls. Its broken wooden door was propped open with a paving stone. Inside, apple, plum, and peach trees had dropped the last of their fruit and wasps drunk on the juice staggered in confused circles on the ground. A small cottage sagged against the far orchard wall. The air smelled just the way it did under the fruit trees at home.

❧

All day long I compared Baizhen to Hanchin, I say to my souls. *All I could think of was how poor a bargain my father had made for me.*

It's a good thing Baizhen was so enamored of you, my yin soul says. She wags a reproving finger at me. *Yes, just look at him. He mistook your silence for shyness.*

Oh, he knew, my yang soul says. *Your husband knew you were disappointed in him, in this house, in this town. Believe me, he knew.*

So he knew I was disappointed. Did it matter?

It wasn't his fault your father forced this marriage, my hun soul points out, *and it's a good thing Baizhen didn't take offense at your cool behavior. You had a lifetime ahead of you with this man.*

Well, it ended up being rather a short lifetime, I say, a little testy.

❧❧❧

In the forecourt, a convoy of bicycle rickshaws and a donkey cart had assembled to take my family and their luggage to the train station. Changyin gave me an awkward farewell pat on the shoulder. Tongyin shook hands with Baizhen, nodded at me, and followed Changyin into a rickshaw. Stepmother hugged me, something she hadn't done since I was a girl.

"I'll write every month," she spoke softly into my ear. "Be agreeable, Leiyin. Be an obedient daughter and wife."

My father's hands held mine in a tight grip. "They'll be kind to you, Third Daughter, I know that," he whispered. "Write if you need anything."

I hadn't spoken to Father for a week; that much I could remember. I had no other form of protest and I wasn't going to say anything now. Baizhen and I bowed to him in farewell. The convoy departed and I turned toward the inner courtyard to begin my new life.

❧❧❧

In the dining hall of the main house, Jia Po introduced me to the servants. I met the cook, Old Kwan, and his wife, Mrs. Kwan, the head housekeeper. Little Ming, a girl of perhaps thirteen and granddaughter to Old Ming, the gatekeeper, was our housemaid. Then there was Dali, a thin and rather plain young woman who looked after the main house. There were more servants than family.

Although they were old-fashioned and a little dilapidated, the houses on the Lee property were well-built. Everywhere I looked, subtle details attested to the gracious lives of their past inhabitants. The slats of the wooden shutters interlocked with finely crafted joints that held tight even though they were badly in need of a coat of varnish. The plantings in the courtyard gardens were overgrown but showed evidence of thoughtful design. When I swept my hand over a cascade of winter creeper, I found beneath the leafy vines an exquisite marble plaque set into the wall, its polished surface carved with lines of poetry written by some long-dead Lee ancestor.

I was accustomed to a home where it was impossible to walk the length of a courtyard without stopping to exchange greetings with an aunt or tripping over a gaggle of small children. The Lee household felt hushed and dismal to me, as though it were awaiting news of a death.

Each morning, Baizhen and I offered greetings to my in-laws, kneeling before them in their matching mahogany chairs that sat side by side in the reception room. After a typically silent breakfast, I followed Jia Po while she discussed the day's meals with Old Kwan and inspected the house with Mrs. Kwan. I found it ridiculous that she clung to these formal routines with the servants when we were so few in number and entertained so little.

There was usually more conversation at lunchtime, when Baizhen returned with gossip from the town. Jia Po listened with interest, and Gong Gong listened while feigning indifference. After lunch, we took tea in the small parlor, perched on straight-backed ebony armchairs that had been part of Jia Po's dowry. That was when Gong Gong read all the household mail and the newspaper.

"This Northern Expedition against the warlords is in its third year." He gestured disdainfully and the newspaper crackled in his hands. "There's been nothing but war of one sort or another since they toppled the Qing Dynasty." My father-in-law made no secret of his longing for the days when the emperors ruled China.

After Gong Gong and Jia Po left to take their naps, Baizhen would offer me the newspapers. I never saw him pick them up after I finished, even though he appeared interested in whatever news Gong Gong read out loud to us. I would read quietly, one eye on the clock, hoping he'd leave the parlor to meet his friends at a teahouse and allow me some time on my own. Sometimes after I put down the paper, he'd shuffle nervously toward the door and look back at me over his shoulder, the way a cat does when it wants you to follow. Then we would return to our house.

Then an hour might go by before I could leave my bedroom, Baizhen still snoring in the bed, to wash myself in the narrow, tiled chamber next door. I'd get dressed and go upstairs to my little library.

Conversation at dinner was either nonexistent or gossipy, depending on whether we had hosted visitors in the afternoon. At half-past seven, Baizhen and I would bow to his parents and return across the courtyard and through the moon gate to our own house.

That was how my days passed.

⁓⌒⌒⌒

In the first few weeks after the wedding, guests arrived almost every day, curious to meet the newest member of the family. Second and third cousins, family friends, even merchants—anyone with the slightest connection to my in-laws—came to call. Evidently there had been much anticipation that I would provide fodder for gossip. I was from Changchow, a city even farther away than Shanghai, from a family tainted by foreign influences. To their disappointment, I didn't parade around in cocktail frocks or hold an ivory cigarette holder to my crimson-painted lips. I dressed each day in plain, modest gowns, my hair pulled back in a simple braid. I had very little to say to guests.

Actually, I never had to do much talking if Madame Pao was there. Her visit to our home, brief though it had been, made her an authority on my family. She came often during those first weeks and regaled our other guests with her descriptions of our villa, its rose gardens, the French furniture, the terraces of polished marble.

Other women peered at me critically, as though viewing an insufficiently exotic animal.

"Well then, do you speak any foreign languages?" one matron asked, eyeing me with bovine complacency.

"A little English," I said. "A few polite phrases."

The ladies squealed with excitement.

"Say something then," the bovine one cried. "Teach us English."

They sniggered as I pronounced for them the English words *thank you, good morning, good-bye.*

"*Gu bai, gu bai,*" they repeated after me, shrieking with laughter.

"There's one more phrase that's very important to learn," I said. "A greeting for honored guests."

They settled down. Then they carefully repeated after me, in English, *"You are stupid people."*

The ladies departed, trilling their farewells. *"Gu bai, gu bai."*

My mother-in-law was pleased.

⌘⌘⌘

Only when I was alone in my bedroom did I indulge in tears and longing for Hanchin. The sandalwood sachets Stepmother had tucked into my linens trunk scented my pillowcase and I dreamed of being enfolded in his caresses. I couldn't help but compare: Baizhen's moist mouth on my skin repulsed me as much as his odor, an intermingling of perspiration and mothballs.

My days were as repetitive as the devotions of monks over their prayer beads. Days went by when the courtyards and gardens seemed to shrink, when the whitewashed walls closed in on me, when even the sky pressed down, an airless blue ceiling. The future stretched ahead, day after tedious day into the distance, a dull and muddy slow-moving river.

Some days I survived by pretending to be inside a dream, an interminable nightmare that would end at daybreak. I willed myself to pass through it like a puppet playing the role of a young wife, obedient and unthinking.

"Of course, Mother," I would say when Jia Po asked me to help her with the household bookkeeping.

"Yes, Husband," when Baizhen suggested returning to the house for a nap.

"Right away, Father," when Gong Gong asked me to fetch him a book from his library.

I knew everything that was expected of a wife and daughter-in-law. I knew it in my bones the way I knew the brushstrokes that composed my name, the poetry I memorized to please my father, the lush scents of our rose garden in July. It was just that until now I had never believed this would actually define my life.

☙◦❧

I threw away the sandalwood sachets, you know. I realized there was no possibility I'd ever see Hanchin again.

A wise decision. My *hun* soul glows gently, sympathetic.

Yes, scent brings back memories more vividly than any other sense. My *yin* soul releases a hint of sandalwood before snatching it back with an embarrassed smile.

This house, Baizhen, this backwater town. They were all I had to look forward to for the rest of this life. I had to survive and I'd never manage that unless I forgot Hanchin.

It was time to discard all your thoughts of Hanchin, to quiet and not strengthen them, agrees my *yang* soul. *What could they do now except push shards of longing like broken glass into your heart?* For a moment his features look sympathetic, grandfatherly. He comforts me with the taste of sweet bean soup.

☙◦❧

One day Baizhen hired a bicycle rickshaw to give me a tour of Pinghu. He grew animated as he showed off the town's attractions. First we rode around the lake that gave Pinghu its name. At its shores, the families of fishermen lived in flat-bottomed boats, their nets spread out on the banks, their children spread out on the decks. Women worked beside wooden frames, rubbing salt on silvery fish drying in the sun.

The slow-running waters of the lake flowed into Big Canal, which divided the town into north and south. Pinghu's two main streets, Major Street and Minor Street, ran parallel on the two banks of Big Canal. Pedestrians idled beneath a canopy of elm, sycamore, and ginkgo trees, strolling along wide stone paths. Every few hundred yards or so, a smaller canal bisected Big Canal, with boatmen calling warnings whenever they neared the junctions.

"The teahouses beside Big Canal are very popular," Baizhen said. "Despite all the warning calls, boats still manage to collide. It's never anything serious, but the arguments can get very entertaining and the customers like to hang out the windows to listen." He shook his head and chuckled.

"You mentioned a film theater?" Listening to boatmen curse each other was not high on my list of entertainments.

"Yes, yes. Close to the temple and market square." He tapped the rickshaw puller's shoulder to get his attention.

The rickshaw carried us over arched stone bridges that spanned the canals. With their memorial plaques from the Ming Dynasty and intricately carved balustrades, the bridges were more interesting than the marketplace or the main temple, which was only a hundred years old. As for the tiny theater, it was showing a film that had played in Changchow at least four months ago.

"I've never been to Changchow," Baizhen said. "I suppose our town must seem very quiet to you."

"Small towns have their own charm." I said this to be polite, repeating what I had heard Gaoyin say to one of Father's guests a lifetime ago.

He beamed at me, his pride evident. "Oh, I agree. Pinghu is so beautifully positioned between hills and water. There can't be many towns as pretty as this one."

I stifled my impatience, but at the same time found myself strangely moved by his obvious love for this unremarkable little place.

Our ride around the market square had attracted attention, for this was my first appearance outside the family estate. I was the object of curious, guarded looks from the more polite passersby, of loud comments and even pointing from the lower classes. These yokels actually grinned when they saw me stare back defiantly, pleased that I had noticed them. Embarrassed, Baizhen cut short the tour and we hastened home.

❧❧❧

The little sightseeing trip seemed to put him more at ease with me.

"Wife, I'd enjoy it very much if you could read to me the article Father mentioned earlier, the one about the latest boycott of Japanese products."

Baizhen blurted this out one day after his parents had vacated the parlor. After speaking, he flushed crimson. I was able to hide my dismay by lowering my eyes to the newspaper in my lap. From then on, I spent an hour or more each afternoon reading the news to my husband. It allowed me to appear to be attentive to him while avoiding any actual conversation.

~~~

I was so angry with Father that day. Baizhen could barely read. About as much as a seven- or eight-year-old.

My souls rustle, echoing my remembered distress. And disgust.

Leiyin, your father-in-law collected rare copies of the classics. My *yin* soul picks at the edge of a handkerchief, her voice patient, as though explaining to a child. I smell iris. *How could your father have suspected that such a man could have a near-illiterate son?*

Do you mean he should have taken more time to investigate, as parents are supposed to, instead of marrying me off to the first stranger who came along?

I'm sure if he'd known — my *yin* soul begins.

No, not even if he had known, I interrupt. *He didn't cancel Sueyin's engagement even after we discovered Liu Tienzhen was an opium addict. So I'm sure even if he'd known about Baizhen, he wouldn't have called off the wedding.*

My *yang* soul clears his throat uneasily. *That is your family's hallmark. You have a reputation for keeping your word.* All the same, I can tell the old man is hard pressed to defend my father. Turnips flavor my tongue.

You no longer lived at home and didn't have to face your father, my *hun* soul says. It shimmers along the periphery of the terrace. *Baizhen, however, you saw every day. I hope you weren't obvious in your scorn.*

I suppose we'll know soon enough whether I was kind or cruel to him.

*W*hat I lived for were letters from my sisters.

The first time one of the creamy envelopes arrived, carried in on a tray with the newspaper and other correspondence, I felt sick with anxiety at the sight of the familiar stationery.

"Ah, a letter for Leiyin," Gong Gong said, reading the address. "From your sister in Shanghai."

He held it out and I rose from my seat to take it. I returned to my chair and felt his eyes on me as I slid a brass paper knife under the wax seal. I pulled out the letter, two stiff pages, and he held out his hand again. I stood and passed them to him, keeping the envelope on the small table beside my chair. He didn't ask for it.

"This is good news indeed," he said, scanning the letter. "Your sister says the doctor assures her the baby will be a boy. Her husband is in banking, is he not?"

"The Zhao family owns tea plantations in three provinces. My brother-in-law manages their warehouses and the export business." All I wanted was for everyone to go take their naps. But I couldn't show impatience.

Baizhen picked up the empty envelope from the table and stroked it. "This is such beautiful paper. Is it foreign?"

"It's from England," I said, resisting the urge to slap his hand. "I have a large supply of the same stationery. You're welcome to use it, Husband."

"No, there's no need. I was just admiring the paper."

The afternoon felt like eternity. When Jia Po and Gong Gong finally left for their rooms, I read the newspaper to Baizhen.

"There's an article about tensions in Tibet over territories ruled by warlords. Are you interested?" I struggled to remove the irritation from my voice.

"Thank you, Wife, but no. Let's return to our house now."

I tucked Gaoyin's letter into my tunic, stifled my terse reply.

It was midafternoon by the time Baizhen fell asleep. I got up from the bed and dressed quietly. I slipped out the door, taking the softest of steps as I climbed the staircase to the veranda. In my little library, I hurried to the desk and pulled a letter opener out of the drawer. Sliding the thin blade carefully along the envelope's flap, I separated the blue tissue from the small dabs of glue holding it down, then pulled out a small sheet of paper almost as thin as the tissue:

Dearest Third Sister,

Shen is so happy about my pregnancy he has completely forgotten about my role in your escape. I think Father has forgiven me too, because Stepmother writes that he is very

excited about becoming a grandfather again. How are you?
Our brothers told Sueyin all about your wedding. She told
me Father seemed distressed by the state of the Lees' home
and disappointed by your husband's lack of interest in the
classics. I miss you. Write soon.

I smoothed out the paper and read her words again and again,
imagining her quick and confident voice speaking those words to
me. I didn't dare keep the secret letter, however. I made a trip to
the outhouse and ripped up the thin paper, watched the shreds
flutter down the dark pit.

A day later, another letter arrived, this time from Sueyin. She
described the latest soiree she and Tienzhen had hosted, naming
a few starlets and directors:

My husband is very pleased. His evenings are gaining
a reputation for bringing talented young actors to the
attention of directors and producers. The director Zhang
Xichuan has invited us to the Shanghai premiere of his
latest film, The Girl Detective.

Gong Gong grunted when he handed me the letter. He didn't
approve of film stars.

Alone, I read Sueyin's secret letter:

Tienzhen is only interested in two things: the films and
his opium pipe. Now he joins the actors when they read
scripts. He'd like to be an actor but the Judge would never
allow anyone in his family to pursue the cinema.

*Since he returned from your wedding I've seen Second
Brother only once. He's rather critical of your husband. But
your husband's appearance and education don't matter to
me as long as he's kind to you, Little Sister. Father is very
reserved when I ask about your in-laws. I sense he regrets a
hasty decision made in anger.*

My father might be feeling regret but I was the one who had
to live with the consequences. When I wrote back, I described for
my sisters the Lee property, Gong Gong's collection of rare books,
and the town:

*There is a temple with a thirteen-story pagoda called the
Temple of Soul's Enlightenment. The Buddha in this temple
is supposed to be especially sympathetic to the spirits of the
newly dead.*

Then I cut a thin sheet of paper in half and wrote to my sisters,
two identical letters in the tiniest script possible:

*I'm trying to get used to a quiet life. Here the dining table
is set for four, nothing like the boisterous meals at home.
My husband, it turns out, is nearly illiterate. Which of
us has the worse bargain? Second Sister with her opium
addict or me with an uneducated dunce? Tell Father that.*

After lunch the next day, I placed the unsealed envelopes
on the red lacquer tray that was used for the mail. Gong Gong

flipped them open and read my letters. He nodded his approval before placing them back for Old Ming to post.

There was no point in telling my sisters about Hanchin. I didn't want them to know how naive I had been. There was no need for deception, just omission. If only I'd confided in them sooner, they might have warned me.

But do you think you would have listened to them? my *hun* soul asks. *Why didn't you tell your sisters about Hanchin when you were still at home? You're dead now, be honest with yourself. You have nothing to lose by it.*

Everything seemed so complicated then. I pause before answering. *If they'd thought Hanchin was encouraging me, that I'd been alone with him, they would have seen that as bad for my reputation. They would have told Father.*

My *yin* soul kneels on the stone steps to pet a stray cat, a calico who rubs up against her small hand. *Tongyin probably guessed you were infatuated with Hanchin. But he didn't raise the alarm.*

Tongyin was in love with Hanchin and didn't want him banned from our home any more than I did. Anyway, he never believed Hanchin cared about me.

Hanchin made advances to you when he knew he didn't stand a chance of marrying you. My *yang* soul thumps his cane on the ground and the calico cat leaps away, startled. *Didn't that tell you something about his character?*

Leiyin never would have kissed anyone unless she was in love, my *yin* soul says. She tries to coax the cat back. *She assumed it was the same for him.*

∽∼∾∾

I received one letter from Nanmei, forwarded to me by Stepmother. My friend's words were awkward, formal congratulations on my marriage and a stilted account of her life at university in Soochow. I imagined the difficulty Nanmei must have had trying to write it. She knew how her descriptions of classes and new friends would only hurt me. She knew better than anyone how this marriage had ruined my dreams. Thankfully, she didn't mention Hanchin. I didn't know whether this was out of consideration for my feelings or a suspicion that my letters were not private.

I read her letter only once. It stirred too many emotions in me, envy so sharp I could taste its iron tang, regrets as abundant as autumn rains. I couldn't bear the memories of the two of us giggling together over my audacious plans, blithely ignorant of the ruin I was about to inflict upon my life. I couldn't bear the thought of her pity. Nor could I risk her accidentally giving away my secrets in a letter. My married life was unbearable enough already.

Dear Wang Nanmei,

Thank you for your letter. It brings back memories of when we used to do homework together, our discussions about the

Russian novels, and our arguments about Anna Karenina. *You took the position that Anna was foolish to write letters that could be used against her.*

Now that I'm married, Changchow and all my friends seem very far away, and those days so very long ago. My husband and in-laws are very kind to me, I couldn't ask for more. I wish you every success at university.

Song Leiyin

And with that, I cut myself off from another reminder of Hanchin. I hoped Nanmei would understand. I believed she would.

To my surprise, I received the latest issue of *China Millennium* in the mail from Tongyin. There was also a note, a few untidy, scrawled lines:

Greetings, Little Sister,

Sometimes I take the editor out for a meal and he gives me a couple of free copies. I'll try to send you an issue every so often. No promises.

I examined the brown paper wrapper. The address wasn't in Tongyin's handwriting. He must have tossed the journal to a servant with instructions to mail it.

Gong Gong scanned the journal, his lips tight with disapproval.

"This is a leftist publication. I'm surprised your brother sends you such magazines to read."

I kept my voice calm and reasonable.

"My father encourages us to read all points of view. He believes that understanding an ideology, no matter how flawed it is, helps us appreciate the virtues of our Nationalist system even more."

Gong Gong grumbled under his breath but gave the magazine back to me. The issue's feature article was by Hanchin:

DISPATCHES FROM THE FRONT LINES OF RURAL EDUCATION

Readers will recall how often I have praised the efforts of schoolteachers in rural districts. After all those lofty words, it was time for me to put my beliefs to the test. Although many of my assignments will take me to remote towns, I'll endeavor to send essays to this journal whenever possible.

I couldn't even begin to guess why Tongyin would send me copies of the magazine. Was he taunting me, keeping my wounds fresh? Or was he being sympathetic in his own perverse way, sending news of the world without realizing that I had no chance of escaping this dull country town? I decided not to reply. Instead I wrote to Gaoyin and asked her to send me magazines or newspapers she had finished reading. Gong Gong subscribed exclusively to the *Central Daily News*, a staunchly Nationalist paper.

⌒⌒⌒

A few months after the wedding, my life changed again.

I bent over the porcelain chamber pot every morning, pale and heaving. I didn't know which made me feel worse, the symptoms of pregnancy or the realization that a child would bind me inescapably to this house, to this town, to this husband. I tried to be discreet in case I was mistaken and just suffering from poor digestion.

But Little Ming reported to Mrs. Kwan that I spent my mornings vomiting and Mrs. Kwan reported the news to Jia Po. There was a flurry of activity, and Old Ming was sent around the corner to alert the doctor that I would be visiting. A rickshaw was called to the door even though the clinic was less than a ten-minute stroll away.

When I returned from the clinic with Jia Po, she was radiant with smiles, as excited as a little girl. Old Ming rushed out to help me down from the rickshaw. He grinned at us, delighted to be the first to receive confirmation of the news.

"Oh, my dear," said my mother-in-law, "a baby in August! We must take very good care of you."

She gave me a hurried hug and rushed toward the main house, calling for Mrs. Kwan. It was the first time she had addressed me with true affection. I knew her concern was for her unborn grandchild, not really for me, but I hadn't realized until then how much I craved warmth. I had been living for months in perpetual twilight.

In my little library, I opened my photograph album and

turned to pictures of Fei-Fei and my little nieces and nephews. They laughed at the camera, chubby and squinting. Fei-Fei's hair was bunched up in two small pigtails. I remembered their hands reaching up for mine so trustingly, their chiming laughter and voices as sweet as the clink of jade bangles. If I had my own baby, I thought, life could be bearable.

The next morning, I opened my eyes and the world was once again awash in color.

11

The entire household's attention now bent to my well-being. I was as pampered as a spoiled child, as cosseted as an invalid. Jia Po had Old Kwan purchase a stewing hen each week to simmer into broth, and while everyone else ate plain congee for breakfast, mine was boiled in broth, garnished with shreds of cooked chicken, an egg beaten in for extra nourishment. When I confessed to a fondness for dried kumquats, Jia Po immediately sent a note to the shop at the top of Minor Street and within the hour a large glass jar of orange sweets appeared in my little library.

Baizhen's plain face had broken into a delighted grin when Jia Po announced my pregnancy and the smile rarely left his face now. He even walked differently, shoulders square, and back straighter than before. He went out less and spent more time with me, but he no longer came to my bed, for which I was grateful. He visited me each morning to inquire whether I had slept well.

"I'll have Little Ming bring your breakfast on a tray," he would say if I looked tired. "I'll tell my parents you need to rest a little more today."

The doctor had suggested regular walks to promote good circulation. Baizhen accompanied me, one hand carefully holding my elbow. Our daily promenade meandered through our courtyard and the orchard, out through the moon gate to the main courtyard, then around the forecourt, where Old Ming kept sentry by the gate, and back again to our courtyard.

During these walks I learned more about Baizhen's childhood. He pointed out a low cave in the rock garden, his favorite hiding spot, and the old chicken coop in the orchard where he once kept rabbits. He pointed out the small cottage at the far end of the orchard. An elderly, impoverished great-uncle had once lived there. Since his death, the cottage had fallen into disrepair.

A side door in the orchard wall opened out to a private lane leading up to Jade Belt Road, where the main gates to the house stood.

"I used to sneak out through that side door because Old Ming couldn't see and wouldn't be able to tell on me," he said. His grin gave me a glimpse of the boy he had been, a little naughtier than I had imagined.

"Where did you go when you sneaked out?"

He shrugged. "I used to wander along Jade Belt Road, go around the corner, and watch the boats on the canal. Sometimes I tied string to a bamboo pole and pretended to fish. Or I'd buy something to eat from a street vendor and chat with him."

But he didn't mention friends. Did he even have any? Where would my child find friends in this town?

⌘⌘⌘

They were kind to you, my *yin* soul remarks. She is still coaxing the calico cat to play, and has pulled the ribbon off her pigtail to tempt it. *I think they would have been kind even if you weren't pregnant. Baizhen and Jia Po, anyway.*

Now I know why cats pounce at nothing, I remark. The cat leaps at the ribbon and my *yin* soul laughs, a gleeful child.

But I never felt they were being kind to me for my own sake. Baizhen yes, but my in-laws only because of the baby.

My *yang* soul strokes his goatee. He looks troubled. *You don't give others enough credit.*

Maybe they felt uncertain about you, what would please you. Pregnancy finally gave them an excuse to show affection. My *hun* soul taps my cheek with a bright, cool finger.

We watch Baizhen take me into the orchard, the tree branches tipped with green-and-white buds. Already there is a scent of blossom in the air.

⌘⌘⌘

I wrote to Father about my pregnancy. It was my duty.

I wrote to my sisters with real joy. If all went well, Gaoyin's baby would only be a few months older than mine.

Father sent a generous gift of cash for my personal use, which Gong Gong "put away" for me. Stepmother sent packets of herbs and warm flannel cloth for baby garments. Sueyin sent expensive maternity clothes and Gaoyin a crocheted button-up sweater and matching red hat—her own rather lopsided effort. It amused me to think of my glamorous sister struggling with a crochet needle. She wrote to me:

Impending motherhood has had a peculiar effect on me. I'm more interested in knitting patterns for baby clothes than fashion magazines.

Her secret letter wasn't quite so sunny and maternal:

Tongyin called on us last week and brought his friend Cha Zhiming, who has dropped out of Whampoa Military Academy. But that doesn't matter because Cha will be given an important position in the police force, thanks to his father's connections. No battles on the front lines for him. I hear gossip that Cha and his friends frequent the disreputable nightclubs in Shanghai. I don't want to worry Father, but I think Tongyin is one of those friends.

Sueyin's letter came only a day later:

I'm so happy for you. You've always loved little children. Now that you will have one of your own, how fulfilling your life will be.

Sueyin's letter hinted delicately at her hope that I would find real and not feigned contentment. From her secret letters I knew that the longer she lived with the Liu family, the less hopeful she felt about her own marriage:

Judge Liu is too busy to bother with reading my letters. However, this doesn't stop Tienzhen's aunts or his cousins' wives from pawing through my belongings. They think I don't notice. My mother-in-law isn't as old as she seems, she's only just turned forty. I feel sorry for her and try to be kind. The Liu family is a cold-blooded lot. I wonder if she began taking opium to ease her loneliness.

⤛⤜

Now that I was with child, Jia Po seemed to fold aside a screen that had stood between us, revealing a talkative and friendly woman. We discussed how to arrange the nursery and interviewed potential wet nurses. We cut patterns for baby clothing and devoted entire days to sewing, making the most of the daylight. I laughed along with her as she told stories of her ignorance as a young wife, and listened attentively to what she shared about her own pregnancy. Children, her family's health, domestic chores. This was the world she preferred to inhabit, I learned. She confessed that when Gong Gong read the news, she only pretended to listen.

My sewing skills improved from dismal to adequate. I used to be impatient with the needle, but now I had nothing but time. I wanted every stitch small and even, well-placed so the thread wouldn't chafe my baby's soft skin.

"I learned to take care of the household like this, you know, by following my mother-in-law on her rounds," Jia Po said to me one day. It was spring now, and we were on our daily inspection of the house and kitchen. "My mother-in-law had bound feet, so she rode a chair mounted on rails and carried by two male servants."

She sounded wistful, and glanced up at the wooden shutters of her house, beautifully carved but weather-beaten. "Those servants also did a little gardening, and the carpentry work. They kept the houses in repair."

"This once was a beautiful estate." I forgot myself and spoke in the past tense. But Jia Po didn't seem to mind.

"Yes, it's shabby now, but in the old days we kept to very high standards. This house and its amenities, the gardens and the kitchens, all compared favorably to my family home in Hunan."

This was the first time she had mentioned anything about her own family. I wondered whether she missed them the way I missed mine.

∾∾∾

Most of the houses along the perimeter of the Lee estate had been sold off piecemeal as one generation after another fell on hard times. With each sale, walls went up to separate the new owners from the sections that still belonged to the Lee clan. Gong Gong's portion of the estate, which we entered through the imposing double gates that faced Jade Belt Road, was the largest and most complete of the surviving properties. At one point, Gong Gong's father had been close to selling off even more land and houses. But like a gift from the gods, Jia Po came to marry Gong

Gong and her stupendous dowry had staunched the outflow of property and cash.

"The wedding procession was the longest I ever saw in this town." Old Kwan whacked a thick knob of ginger with the flat of his cleaver. My in-laws had told me about the eminent ancestors of the Lee clan, but not very much about recent generations. Old Kwan filled in the gaps with gusto, sensing in me an attentive audience.

I was a constant presence in the kitchen these days, helping him string beans or de-vein shrimp, skills I had never learned while living in Changchow. On my lap, a basket of pea pods rested against my round belly and on the brick floor, live river shrimps waved their whiskery feelers in a bucket of water. I had been craving shrimp sautéed with peas.

"Rumor had it the Mistress brought a dowry rich enough to last three generations. Her family is one of the wealthiest in Hunan province, you see, but they started out as rice farmers. So they bought themselves a bit more status marrying into an old and famous lineage."

He removed the ends from a bunch of green onions, then chopped the onions and a small wedge of pork belly into tiny shreds.

"The Mistress came off the boat in a sedan chair hung with bells, the same one you rode on your wedding day. The procession went on forever, twenty mules loaded with luggage, and five oxcarts of furniture, porcelain, and rolls of silk. One cart held a metal-bound chest with the lid open to show off a pile of silver bars."

Old Kwan was warming up to his story now.

"That silver was only for show, though, because all those

silver and gold coins, plus cash and deeds to property, had already been deposited with a bank in Shanghai."

"But how did the Lees manage to spend so much money in such a short time?" I asked.

Kwan laid a shrimp on the cutting board, and with a smooth swipe of his knife opened the shell along its back, stuck the tip of the knife in and dug out the vein.

"Well, there were debts going back a generation or two that had to be paid off, you see. When your husband, the Young Master, was born, the Old Master ordered three days of feasting, with gifts of silk and tea for all the guests. Then the Old Master died, so the Master rebuilt the family mausoleums to honor his departed father. And the Master loves his rare books and paintings."

He poured oil into the iron wok to heat, threw in the ginger and some salt. Ginger neutralized seafood poisons, according to Old Kwan. He mixed water and cornstarch into the bowl of shrimp, just barely coating their surfaces. His flat nose flared: he could tell by smell the moment when the oil was just hot enough to absorb the flavor of the ginger. He tossed the chopped onions and pork belly into the wok. It spattered and hissed, the shrimps went in, Kwan's spatula turned and flipped. The smell was divine.

"But why didn't Jia Po stop him?" I couldn't imagine watching so much wealth melt away without protesting.

"He's the patriarch, Young Mistress." As though this explained it all.

Old Kwan threw in a handful of peas, gave them a stir, then added a few drops of sesame oil. My stomach gurgled. He lifted the metal pan as though it was as light as a porcelain cup, spooned the shrimp into a bowl, and set it in front of me.

"Here. Do you want rice?"

I shook my head, picked up some chopsticks, and shoveled shrimp and peas into my mouth as though I hadn't eaten lunch just a few hours ago. He took off his apron, washed his hands, and leaned against the doorway to look out at his kitchen garden.

"And now, Young Mistress, it's your dowry that keeps us fed."

∽∼∾

Gong Gong paid more attention to me now too. He invited me to his study and said I could borrow any book I wished, except for a few of the rarest antiques.

"During pregnancy," he intoned, "a woman should avoid stories of war and tragedy. Choose stories about filial piety and books that promote peaceful thoughts. Read poetry or novels about family life. If you do, your child will be assured of an obedient temperament."

He pointed at a long table bearing stacks of books and scrolls.

"You can borrow some of the books from that table too. I take them out to show friends," he said. "But I'm not very good at putting them away."

"I can put these away for you, Father. I used to help my father organize his collection and I'm familiar with the classics."

For the next hour, I gave in to the enjoyment of handling the wonderful volumes.

"Was this inherited from one of your scholarly ancestors, Gong Gong?" I nearly gasped out loud when I saw the last book on the table, a single tome containing three volumes of poetry by Zhou Bi of the Song Dynasty. It was only a copy of the original, but still valuable because it had been printed during the Ming Dynasty. What made it even more precious were the annotations in the margins, couplets inspired by the original poems as well as brief essays and critiques. These had been added by the book's previous owners, a few of whom were famous poets in their own right. My father had agonized over buying such a book once. Reading it, he said, would have been like a conversation with literary connoisseurs from another era. But he couldn't justify the expense of buying it.

"No, no. I bought that one myself on a special trip to Hangchow." Gong Gong looked pleased. "It took quite a lot to persuade the previous owner to part with it."

"It must give you such pleasure to read the notations from previous owners," I exclaimed, carefully turning the pages.

To my surprise, he just shrugged.

~~~

He didn't even read those rare books. He just wanted to look like a wealthy gentleman scholar. I shake my head, watching Gong Gong lock the glass doors of the bookcase where he kept the finest items in his collection.

My yang *soul looks a little uncomfortable.*

After that, I tell my souls, *there was no need to ask whether my dowry would be used for repairing the broken paving on the terrace, the creaky stair treads, or the wobbling handrails. What was the point? Jia Po didn't even raise the subject.*

You looked down on Jia Po for not standing up to Gong Gong and his spendthrift ways, my *yin* soul remarks.

Your mother-in-law was raised in a very traditional family, my yang soul hastens to say. *Her father was the supreme authority. It never occurred to her that she could criticize her husband.*

Are you saying Gong Gong was right to squander her fortune like that?

A pause, and then a nervous cough. *He was entitled. He was the patriarch. But he could have shown some restraint,* my yang soul admits.

Do you remember the other thing that happened that afternoon? my yin soul asks. She had managed to coax the calico back onto the terrace and it rested on its side, chin blissfully raised to accept her stroking.

Yes. Yes, I do. That was the moment I vowed that no child of mine would ever depend on dowries or the generosity of in-laws.

That was when your ambitions began to stir again, a spark of purpose awakening. My hun soul gave me a prod. *You had ambitions for your child.*

12

W hat's the next generational name for the family?" I asked Baizhen one day. He had come to the door of my library. It was now June and the windows were open. Fresh green scents from the garden drifted in, smells of damp earth and white peonies.

"*Wei*, 'strength.' And the generational name is the middle name." He had come to see what I was doing.

A stack of blank cardboard squares lay on the table. I wet my brush on the slick dark surface of the ink stone, then carefully wrote the character *wei* on one of the squares. It was a good word, one that lent itself easily to pairing with a given name.

Baizhen picked up a card. "Wife, what are these?"

"They're for teaching children how to read. It's how I learned."

I couldn't help but feel excited when I spread out the cards I had already made, simple words such as *mountain, water, big, small, person*. And of course, *mother* and *father*. On the reverse were images to go with the words, pictures cut out from magazines or simple sketches I had drawn and colored. I imagined how my child would play with them, picture side up at first, and then poring over the written characters.

"They're not as beautiful as the printed cards we have at home in Changchow," I said, "but I like making them." I surveyed the results with pride.

"Our tutor used to have us play games using word cards," I continued. "By the time I went to middle school, I had a better reading vocabulary than any of my classmates." Except Nanmei, I remembered, with a small ache in my heart.

"You played games to learn how to read?" Baizhen's eyebrows lifted.

"I don't remember exactly how, but somehow everything fell into place and it became easier and easier to recognize the characters. We were surrounded by books," I said, thinking longingly of Changchow.

I remembered following Gaoyin's slim finger as it moved along the lines of text in a book of folk tales. She read me the stories so often I had memorized many of them. One day, she was reading the tale of how the rabbit went to live in the moon; then the next day I found myself running my own finger beneath the lines and sounding out the ancient tale word by word. I was suddenly ablaze with understanding, with the realization that each character held a meaning of its own. After that, I couldn't learn new words fast enough.

The look on Baizhen's face, the emotions I saw struggling there, startled me. He picked up the card with the character for *wei* and studied it carefully. When he finally spoke, he was looking down at the card, a red flush on his cheeks.

"My tutor didn't believe in these modern methods. Do you think word cards would help me learn?" I could barely hear him, and hardly knew how to reply.

He looked away, toward the bookshelves, his eyes those of a child peering into a candy-shop window.

"We can begin now, if you like." The words sprang from my heart, the first genuine impulse of kindness I had felt for him since arriving in Pinghu.

He hesitated. "It sounds like a lot of work. Perhaps we should wait a few years. When you're teaching our child, I can just sit in."

"It's no trouble," I said reassuringly. "I have so little to do all day. I'd welcome the distraction."

I waited for his response, for the anxious pucker between his brows to soften.

"But please, Wife, don't let my parents know."

Dearest Second Sister,

Although I didn't manage to train as a teacher, I'm teaching now, every day. After talking over the meals and chores for the day with Jia Po, I return to my library and teach Baizhen. Please don't mention these lessons in your "open" letters.

Dear Eldest Sister,

*Don't laugh, but I'm inventing new ways to teach Baizhen
how to read. To teach him the same way as children would
be insulting, so I've devised a different sort of word card.
Instead of a single word, I've written a phrase that uses that
word. Seeing how one character is used in many different
ways has been very helpful for him.*

◦◦◦

"When you were young, Husband, why did you find it so hard to
read? You're memorizing words at a very good rate now."

We had just finished a lesson and it was nearly time for lunch.
I sharpened some pencils and Baizhen put away his notebooks.
Over the weeks he had filled their pages, copying each new word
a hundred times. It was a repetitive task, but necessary if he was
to commit them to memory.

"I don't know. Teacher Liao never actually explained anything. He just made me memorize poems. Then he'd beat me for
not being able to recite them perfectly."

Baizhen didn't sound resentful but the more he told me, the
more indignant I grew.

Teacher Liao was a sixty-something gentleman from an impoverished family, a failed scholar of the sort every small town possesses. Before the Qing Dynasty fell, Liao had gone to Hangchow
no less than twelve times to take the Imperial Examinations, until
his family's funds and his own hopes ran dry. Some of the towns-

folk actually took a perverse pride in how many times he had failed. His was by no means the record for our province; there was an elderly scholar in Ningbo who had failed the Examinations for twenty years. But as far as Gong Gong was concerned, Liao was the closest the town had to a classical scholar and so he engaged the bitter old man as a tutor.

When Baizhen turned twelve, Teacher Liao declared that Baizhen had received all the tutoring he needed and was ready for school. Baizhen enrolled in the village school, only to discover that Teacher Liao's efforts had left him far behind the rest of the class.

Rather than lose face, Gong Gong pulled his son out of the classroom.

"Did your parents find you another tutor?" I asked in my mildest voice.

"No, Father said we couldn't afford it. We would have had to hire someone from out of town, and then house him and feed him."

But Gong Gong could afford rare books and antique snuff bottles.

"Oh. Then did your parents tutor you themselves?" I busied myself putting away some magazines so he couldn't see my face.

"Father tried, but he didn't have the patience, and Mother said what I knew was good enough. She doesn't read that well herself." He gave me an embarassed smile, but it was for his own shortcomings, not theirs.

Thus my husband could recite a few classical poems, use the abacus to do a little arithmetic, and write just enough to add a greeting at the end of my letters to Father. He always wrote the same sentence, laboriously, I had noticed: *Honored Father-in-Law, I hope you are well.* If Baizhen had been raised in our family, how different a person he might have been.

I looked up and realized he was speaking to me.

"I'm sorry, Husband. What did you say?"

Standing at the door, he repeated in a low, self-conscious voice, "You had a scholarship to university, Wife. Do you ever regret not going?"

He didn't wait for my answer, just ducked his head and left the room. I heard his footsteps creak away on the warped planks of the veranda floor.

⌒⌒⌒

He knew, my *yang* soul declares. He paces, jabbing a finger in my direction. *I always said he knew you better than you thought. He knew you were ashamed of him.*

Mostly, I was angry with Gong Gong and Jia Po for not taking more care with his education.

Jia Po, I can understand, my *yin* soul says thoughtfully. A faint odor of something green and leafy. *Some merchant families are like that. As long as you can work an abacus, what other education do you need? But Gong Gong, I agree, had been negligent.*

Negligent? I have a harsher word for him right now. I'm outraged, even as my heart softens toward Baizhen. Despite it all, he had grown into a good person, kind and unpretentious.

Baizhen isn't much to look at, but he's very considerate, says my *yin* soul, reading my thoughts.

Yes. Yes, he is, I agree. *But it hadn't been enough.*

Were you still longing for Hanchin even though you were pregnant? My *hun* soul gets straight to the point.

I sigh. *It was easier to forget Hanchin once I became pregnant, but I still dreamed about him. I couldn't help wondering what it would have been like to have Hanchin in my bed instead of Baizhen.*

My *yang* soul stops pacing, horror and disapproval so plain on his wrinkled face I have to laugh. So do my *yin* and *hun* souls, one a sweet giggle, the other a tinkling like wind chimes.

I thought you said there was no need for shame now that I'm dead. I can't help the little jab.

⌒⌒⌒

Each month I wrote to Father, my words carefully formal and distant. It was duty, no more. Father didn't write back, not real letters. He never did more than add a few jotted lines at the end of Stepmother's letters, polite greetings to my in-laws. I imagined my name on Stepmother's list of chores for the month, her letters to me just another task to cross off. She wrote to me of domestic matters and family news, and of course always included a report on my father's health. There was usually a recipe or a list of ingredients for a nourishing herbal soup that would balance my body's elements. After a while, Gong Gong barely read past the first page of Stepmother's letters, and just handed them to me without a word.

Unlike my sisters' secret notes, which plainly stated their

fears, Stepmother's letters spoke guardedly of the problems our
family faced as China's fate grew more uncertain:

> *Gaoyin returned to Changchow for the birth of her son.*
> *Little Zhao Yang is beautiful and healthy. The Zhao*
> *family is already planning the hundredth-day celebration*
> *but it will be a modest affair. These days it is best to avoid*
> *displays of wealth.*
>
> *You may have heard that Changyin's wife is pregnant*
> *again. Geeling seems happiest when she's expecting, and*
> *it is a good thing right now because Changyin is away*
> *in Shanghai most of the time. Your father has him reno-*
> *vating an old apartment building in Shanghai, one they*
> *bought ten years ago. The foreign presence in Shanghai*
> *makes it the only city safe from the civil war and Japanese*
> *aggression, so that's where we shall relocate if we must. Yet*
> *Shanghai has its own dangers, so I'm not anxious to move*
> *there until it is absolutely necessary.*

Gaoyin's next letter was about motherhood, but it was also
filled with worry:

> *I'm so relieved to be back in Shanghai. Shen's mother prac-*
> *tically lived in our quarters while we were in Changchow.*
> *Besides the baby, there was a lot of talk about family fi-*
> *nances. Both our families are moving more cash to Hong*
> *Kong and Singapore, away from the uncertainties of our*
> *civil war. Tongyin spends a lot of time in Shanghai now,*

where he has rented rooms. All his friends have rented apartments and mistresses. At least he doesn't have a mistress.

When Sueyin wrote, it was about her family's new living arrangements, for the Judge had given in to Tienzhen's requests for a second home in Shanghai:

We have leased an apartment in Shanghai, not far from Gaoyin and Shen. To placate my in-laws we spend half the month in Shanghai and half in Changchow. My husband's obsession with the film world grows every day. The producers flatter him, hoping he will fund their next film. I think the Judge hopes Tienzhen's fascination with the films will come to a halt when he realizes the producers are only interested in his money. But I fear Tienzhen also moved us here because opium is easier to find. His habit disgusts me. But when he smokes, he falls into such a stupor that he does not come to my bed.

I read the newspapers Gaoyin sent, looking for articles written by Hanchin, or any mention of his name. I looked for him out of curiosity, that was all, I told myself. He was no more than a scar on my heart now, and the occasional need to scratch at the memory waned each week as my child grew larger in my belly. He had no place in my life anymore.

To judge from the newspapers, the outside world had gone insane. In Shanghai, the Nationalist secret police were arresting scores of people suspected of being Communist spies on the flimsiest of evidence. The Shanghai gangs, once merely common criminals, had found profitable new enterprises, sanctioned by a government desperate to stay in control. It only took a sliver of a rumor for a man to vanish, pushed into a waiting motorcar.

The journalists wrote about a government in constant internal turmoil. Battles between Nationalist and Communist armies carved China into regions where boundaries and loyalties shifted every week, and the Northern Expedition had finally taken Peking from the warlords. In our town, though, there was more talk of the lantern contest and the price of winter melons than news about the front lines. On the streets of Pinghu, the daily rhythms of life flowed on, complacent as the waters of the town's canals, its good folk living each day as unsuspecting as tiny crustaceans in a tidal pool.

13

*A*t eighteen, I became a mother.

Gong Gong named my daughter Weilan, a name that pleased me, for I hoped my daughter would be as strong as the generational name *Wei* signified and as beautiful as an orchid, the elegant flower he had chosen as her given name.

My father-in-law managed to hide his disappointment at having to wait for a grandson, but only just barely. Jia Po was content for the moment, for she regarded little Weilan as proof that I could carry a healthy baby to term. Baizhen was nearly incoherent with joy.

I hadn't known it was possible to love so deeply.

The days that once ran through my fingers as predictably as prayer beads now flew by like abacus counters beneath a shop-keeper's nimble fingers. The hours seemed too short, every change in Weilan too fleeting to enjoy properly, each moment a fresh enchantment. I spent every waking hour with my daugh-ter, delighting in her tiny hands and feet, the way she turned her head, ever alert to the sounds and sights of her little world. I loved having her sleep in my bed, her small weight pressed against me, her quiet breathing, and the way she rubbed her eyes while asleep. I was glad she was "only" a girl; otherwise Jia Po would have taken over.

Our wet nurse was a distant relative of Old Ming by the name of Wu. She was delighted to have this coveted position, to be called Amah Wu, to sleep on a cot in the nursery, and, above all, to eat as much as she liked. She assured me that her own baby girl was well cared for, nursed by a younger sister.

"I eat better here than at home, earn cash, and I don't have to work in the fields." Her strong white teeth flashed in a happy smile and her big hands gripped a bowl of steamed rice topped with Old Kwan's savory pork stew. There was no chance her milk would be soured by discontent.

Baizhen was the only one in the household who was as besotted with Weilan as I was. I could say the most foolishly fond things about her to him, and he always agreed.

"Look how she loves to play with that writing brush," I would say. "She's a little scholar." Or, "See how she toddles along, you can tell she'll be graceful when she is grown, our little Sesame Seed." Or, "Such a fine curve to her eyebrows, like my mother's, have I ever shown you my mother's picture, Husband?"

Baizhen marveled at her along with me. We discussed our child's many charms in private, for my in-laws and the servants didn't approve of such conspicuous fondness lavished on a child. Baizhen and I were not superstitious but our servants scolded us for tempting evil spirits by making Weilan sound exceptional.

"*Wah, wah*, Young Mistress," Amah Wu would say. "This

baby is stupid, you can tell. Look at those dull eyes." And she would raise her eyebrows and glance sideways in my direction to let me know she was saying this for the benefit of any evil spirits hovering about.

"She'll be difficult to marry off," Little Ming would add. "Look at that coarse and unruly hair and her clumsy movements. Who would want such a girl?"

Jia Po also disapproved of our doting words but for different reasons.

"You musn't spoil the child with praise," she admonished. "If she grows up vain and headstrong, it will take a large dowry to offset that sort of reputation."

❦

Baizhen and I talked far more easily now. I hadn't realized before how much I had taken my family for granted, especially my sisters. Baizhen didn't have any cousins in Pinghu, for Gong Gong was an only son. I couldn't remember my childhood without hearing laughter, shrieks when we ran circles around the lake in the Old Garden, the affectionate scolding of aunts and nannies as we raced our way through the courtyards. The gentle tug of my sisters' hands braiding my hair.

"I hope I get to see your home in Changchow one day. How lucky you were to grow up in a household with so many playmates," my husband said to me one day.

"We could visit Changchow when Weilan is older," I said, pulling another diaper out of the basket to fold. "I want her to meet her cousins. Gaoyin could bring her little Zhao Yang at the same time. And she should meet my sisters; they'll adore her."

Baizhen had distant cousins, but they were all at least a decade older than him. He had no school friends, for he hadn't attended school. As for the company he kept at teahouses, these weren't truly friends, more like fellow idlers he shared little with except time to waste. Baizhen's closest ally during his childhood had been Old Kwan, who was a repository of stories and dished out rough affection like chunks of roasted yam.

"I hope we have another daughter someday," Baizhen said, his voice decisive. "Of course I want a son next, but Weilan should have sisters to love, the way you do. And I promise to treat all our children equally, as your father did."

"My father didn't treat us all equally," I said evenly. "He allowed his daughters many liberties but he still favored his sons."

"Your father is exceptionally liberal for the older generation, Wife. But you can't expect him to jettison all the traditions that shaped him." When he looked at me, his eyes were kind.

⚭

I don't know about you, my yin soul remarks, *but Baizhen seems deserving of more affection. You'd have to travel far to find another man who'd ask for a second daughter.*

A son next, my yang soul says firmly, *and your duty is done. Two sons, even better.*

I ignore them, still riveted by the sight of Weilan as a baby. The shock of joy I felt each time I saw Weilan never diminished, never failed to swell my heart until it felt too large inside my rib cage. That feeling had been more glorious than anything in the world. My Small Bird.

It was as though I finally understood love, I tell my souls. *The world became a wondrous place. Wondrous, yet dangerous. Suddenly I was alive to all that could befall my child.*

Think how your father must have felt, my *hun* soul replies, *trying to protect five children.*

Fathers don't feel as deeply as mothers, I snap.

༶

When Weilan caught the measles, we didn't trust Amah Wu to be sufficiently vigilant. Baizhen and I took turns during the night keeping watch over Weilan, making sure her little hands didn't scratch the red scabs and leave pockmarks on her perfect skin. My husband responded to Weilan's wailing and petulance with unswerving patience, even when I felt ready to bury my head beneath pillows to muffle the sound of her cries.

Gong Gong didn't approve.

"It's a woman's responsibility," he said to Baizhen. "Let your wife and the servants handle the girl."

I could imagine my father saying the same thing. But Baizhen and I continued to share the nighttime vigil. We simply refrained from mentioning it to Gong Gong. After all, who would report on us? Certainly not Amah Wu, who was happy to let us take over so that she could sleep undisturbed.

One afternoon I entered the nursery and found Weilan asleep under a bright quilt, Baizhen beside her, sprawled at the edge of the bed. His blanket had fallen to the floor. I picked it up and tucked it around him, taking care to fold one end over his bare feet. Straightening up, I realized I was smiling fondly at both of them.

⟳⟲

Since Weilan's birth, my open letters to Gaoyin and the ones I received in return were filled with domestic life, newly interesting to me. Gong Gong did no more than scan through my mail these days. All he found in our letters were pages solidly dedicated to rhapsodizing over our children, sometimes composed specifically to dissuade him from intruding on my correspondence:

> *Last week Weilan caught a bad cold. My goodness, Eldest Sister, I didn't believe one small child could produce so much snot. Fortunately it was only a head cold and didn't go into her bowels. You'll remember last year when she had diarrhea along with a cold, we practically had to hang her over the chamber pot for three days. This time, we managed to make her drink an infusion of hibiscus petals and ginger, sweetened with rock sugar. It was extremely effective.*

Sueyin wrote less frequently than Gaoyin:

> *Motherhood has made you more accepting of your situation. If I had a baby, that would be true for me as well. But I don't want to be accepting, so I'm taking measures to pre-*

vent pregnancy. The Judge is getting impatient. He wants Tienzhen to take a concubine, which would be a relief to me and no shame. Tienzhen refuses because he wants to be "modern," which means only one wife at a time. The Judge has too much respect for Father and won't consider a divorce. Not when a second wife or concubine would do the job. Thus they are at a standoff.

Gaoyin's second child was another boy, Zhao Rong. My sister was as beautiful as ever in the photograph she sent. Her eyes shone with radiant serenity, a woman certain of her worth. She held the baby on her lap and little Zhao Yang stood at her side, a sturdy toddler in shirt and bow tie, legs planted wide apart. Shen stood behind the chair, a proprietary hand on her shoulder. My sister's face was more rounded now, and the boldness of her eyebrows still gave her an imperious look, but her jaw was softer, less determined. She had sent a note too:

A baby brings back such happy memories of the days when you, and later Fei-Fei, were just tiny. I played with you as though you were dolls. It's a wonder I never dropped you by accident. Tongyin came by yesterday with an issue of China Millennium *and a box of chocolates. I asked whether he still goes to the* China Millennium *offices when he's in Changchow. He just smirked and said, "Of course not. Father has forbidden it." But you know how his eyelids blink rapidly when he lies. He bragged about having friends in high places and hinted that he was involved in political intrigues. Then he boasted that he mixes with both left and right, because his friendship with Cha Zhiming means the Nationalists can't touch him. I don't understand it all but I worry about our brother. And he ate all the chocolates he brought. But enough about our worrisome brother—I've already had a marriage inquiry for baby Zhao Rong!*

Marriage. I wanted Weilan to get away from this dusty town, whose cultural highlights consisted of the annual watermelon contest and performances by itinerant folk opera singers. To my shame, I remembered scoffing at my aunts and older cousins for their seemingly inexhaustible interest in matchmaking. Their conversations around the *mah-jong* table used to make me yawn.

"I'm thinking about little San-San," Second Aunt might say, bringing her daughter into the discussion. "The Chen family has a son the perfect age, five years older."

"They're related to the Qu clan, it's true," Fourth Cousin would have replied. "But they're not that well off."

Then Second Aunt would play her winning hand. "Well, my sister just told me that the Chens' eldest son has been promoted to manage a branch of the Kincheng Bank. Not just any branch—the Shanghai Nanking Street branch."

And the women would all exclaim over this nugget of news and rearrange the eminence of the Chen family in their hierarchy of suitable alliances.

Now I would have joined in such discussions willingly, storing away bits of intelligence about good families, examining the information, and drawing up a list of suitable candidates. Now I understood this planning for what it was: cold calculation born out of love, conducted with more urgent concern for a daughter than for a son.

If I matched Weilan to a kind husband and courteous in-laws, she would grow to care for them. She would be bound to them once she had a child, just the way I had come to accept my marriage. How could I regret the path that had led me to my beautiful daughter? I'd find Weilan a better match, though, with someone educated, in a family where she could easily find contentment. Romantic love was fleeting compared to essentials such as a daughter's security.

◦◦◦

Ah! my *yang* soul exclaims. *Do I hear echoes of your own father's words? Do I sense forgiveness and understanding now that you have a child of your own?*

I hadn't forgiven Father. Not yet. But I was getting closer to it. I did understand him better. More than anything I wanted Weilan to be safe, under the protection of a family with wealth, connections, and a position in society.

Of course, says my *yang* soul, not bothering to hide his sarcasm. A dash of capsicum crosses my tongue. *That's all any parent could ask for.*

What about happiness? my *yin* soul asks quietly. *Didn't you want Weilan to choose her own husband and her own destiny?*

I would choose for her carefully. After all, Gaoyin is happy with Shen, I point out. *If I hadn't run away, Father would've been quite lenient with me, I'm sure. He would have allowed me some say in a choice of husband.*

My *hun* soul is silent, but it's a silence that speaks volumes. *But you wouldn't have been able to choose Hanchin.*

I'm quite aware of that, I say, irritated. *But that's not the point. The point is, I would only match Weilan to a husband and a family who would treat her well.*

As your father did for you. My *hun* soul liked having the last word.

14

*A*s the civil war grew more heated and the Japanese more hostile, Gong Gong began reading the newspapers Gaoyin sent me as carefully as I did. Each time a packet arrived we sat in the parlor to compare the different newspapers' accounts, sharing a pot of tea and a plate of fruit while we read snatches of news out loud to Jia Po and Baizhen. The tumultuous politics that surrounded the war sparked clashes that were fought in words as well as on battlefields.

The newspapers said that Madame Sun Yat-sen, who had gone to Moscow after falling out with the Nationalist leaders, had come back to Shanghai. At this point in my life, I could hardly remember the essay that had inspired me so much.

Tongyin sent copies of *China Millennium* now and then. It was still in circulation, though many magazines had sprung up and failed; most managed to stay in print for only a few months before their editors and staff ran out of money and idealism. A writer with the pen name Nobody Special gained attention for publishing thought-provoking essays and fine poems that made their way into various magazines. An editorial claimed that Nobody Special was actually a number of poets and writers who used a single pen name to denote solidarity:

> *What does it matter who does the oppressing?*
> *To the one-legged beggar, the aging singsong girl, the*
>   *dull-eyed kitchen drudge,*
> *Four thousand years, and turmoil never changes.*
> *Changed are the colors of soldiers' uniforms,*
> *Changed are the names of their tormentors,*
> *Their lives have not changed.*
> *How can I compare my sorrows to theirs? But I do.*
> *Colors of uniforms have separated us,*
> *The springtime scent of your laughter is gone.*
> *When shall I hear your step at my study door again?*
> *My life has changed.*
> *Childhood friends and our love, years pass and they*
>   *change not,*
> *Like a cherished secret, when released, they return us to joy.*

There were many such new poets, writing in the vernacular, abandoning the high-brow classical language of earlier generations to craft verses whose sentiments felt fresh and unaffected.

I dreamed about Hanchin after reading one such poem. I was standing at the train station in Changchow. It was winter, and my hands were bare, bitterly cold. A train arrived and emptied out its passengers. When the last compartment door opened, Hanchin stepped out and smiled at me. I felt weak from the scent of sandalwood, hungry for the curve of his lips. He kissed my cold hands, and in my dream I cried out with happiness, "Oh, Hanchin, I knew you would come back to me!"

The emotions were so intense I woke up, the memory of sandalwood still lingering at the verge of my consciousness.

◦◦◦◦

For a few befuddled moments I thought the dream was a premonition that Hanchin would enter my life again, I tell my souls. We watch my memory-self sob into her pillow. *Despite my better judgment, I was crying for all my lost dreams. How could I have wanted him still so badly, after all that time?*

They say nothing, but I sense my *yang* soul's exasperation in the lift of his gray eyebrows, the taste of raw onion, and I sense my *yin* soul's pity in the melancholy fragrance of lilac.

It's possible, she ventures finally, *that, even knowing he was only toying with you, you'll be in love with Hanchin until the day you die.*

At least that day won't be too long in coming, I say. She bites her lip and blushes, realizing what she has just said.

◦◦◦◦

The years went by, but to Jia Po's dismay I didn't conceive. Each month my menses reddened the strips of rags between my legs, and each month the herbalist delivered concoctions to prevent stagnation of my *qi*. The herbalist had declared this was my problem, since *qi* stagnation exhibits itself in tense muscles, restrained anger, and digestive problems. But Jia Po wasn't relying on medicine alone.

"Make offerings to the Goddess of Mercy at the Temple of the City God," she instructed. "That particular Goddess of Mercy is sympathetic to women with no sons."

So I went to the temple each week, sometimes by myself, sometimes with Baizhen at my side. The Goddess's altar was covered in layers of heavy silk, altar cloths embroidered with images of a hundred baby boys, offerings made by desperate women. Those visits did nothing except depress me.

I wanted a second child, of course, and so did Baizhen. He came to my bedroom almost every night. I wanted a son too, partly so that my in-laws wouldn't lose patience with me and force Baizhen to take a concubine. I didn't want Weilan displaced in the family hierarchy by a younger half brother. If I couldn't bear a son, she'd have no champions except for me, a sonless mother. How powerless I'd be then to help my daughter.

For the hundredth time I thought bitterly that my education held no value in this family, where dead ancestors meant more than the needs of the living. If Weilan was to marry into a modern, enlightened family, perhaps one that had sent sons abroad for Western schooling, she needed a good education herself. The local primary school was a one-room building tucked behind the Temple of the City God, staffed by a few sincere but woefully inadequate teachers.

When she was old enough I would send Weilan to a good boarding school. I would beg money from my sisters, even from Father, if necessary. I hoped Baizhen would find the backbone to stand up to his parents when that day came. But I had learned the folly of impatience. For Weilan's sake, I had to move with care and deliberation.

"She's so bright," I said to Baizhen. "We must marry her to someone equally intelligent, a well-educated young man who values a modern, educated wife."

Baizhen and I were on the second-floor veranda watching Weilan play on the terrace below. She and Little Ming were drawing a hopscotch court on the stones.

"I can tutor her until she is ten or twelve," I continued casually. "I'm capable of that. If she does well, we can send her to boarding school."

Baizhen lifted his eyes from Weilan to beam at me. "Leiyin, your education is superior to that of most of the men in this town. How could she do better than to follow your fine example?"

♋︎∾♋︎

Weilan wanted to read all by herself. At three years old, she sat on my lap, insisting that my finger follow the words as I read to her out loud. I taught her simple words, making a game of it. I brought out the word cards I had made before she was born.

"Look, here is the character for *big*," I said. "It looks like a man with his arms spread out wide. And see how the character for *small* is like a man also, but with his arms held close together."

Baizhen, now more than able to teach her simple words, also joined in.

"What's this word, Small Bird? Read it for Papa."

"*Fish!* Papa, it's *fish!*" she shouted in triumph, miming the four waving fins at the bottom of the matching pictogram.

"*Cat!*" she said for the next one, gently touching with one small finger the character that looked like a pair of eyes above a tabby-striped body.

She copied words in gridded notebooks over and over, her small tongue licking her top lip with the effort of keeping the strokes of each character neatly within its square, her small fingers cramped around the yellow pencil.

I included Little Ming in our lessons. She was growing into a young woman, although her exact birthdate was unknown, for who bothered recording the birth of a poor girl? She had lived at the Lee residence since childhood and was as naive as Weilan, as superstitious as Amah Wu. Little Ming put together sentences using my homemade word cards and read out aloud from simple textbooks, laughing good-naturedly when she made mistakes. With Little Ming for a classmate, lessons were more interesting for Weilan, but that wasn't my only reason for recruiting our maid. If Little Ming could master some simple writing and arithmetic, she would find better employment when she was older. She deserved better.

Weilan loved learning so much she could hardly tell the difference between doing her lessons and playing games. I had told her about my student days in Changchow, rows and rows of girls in uniform giving their full attention to the teacher. She wanted to play school and when we did, she was always the teacher— Baizhen, Little Ming, and I her students.

"And what is this word?" she would say, holding up a vocabulary card with utter seriousness.

"Is it . . . *sky?*" Little Ming would pretend not to know.

"Really, Miss Ming, you learned this word only yesterday."

Such a stern tone from her child's voice made it hard for us to keep our faces straight. "Try again."

"I don't know. Young Master, you try." Little Ming was dangerously close to breaking into giggles.

"I think . . . it must be . . . *tree!*" said Baizhen, biting his lips with the effort of suppressing a smile.

"Very good, Papa! Yes, it's *tree!*" She gave him a wide and happy smile.

At such moments, I couldn't imagine how life could be more fulfilling.

⌒⌒⌒

Weilan had taken to reading and writing very naturally, and was devouring all the children's books on our shelves. Whenever my sisters or Stepmother sent us a new book, Weilan could hardly be persuaded to put it down to eat or play outside — even if it was too advanced for her.

I was terribly proud of her, but in secret, I considered Baizhen my greatest success. He had abandoned school texts and worked from newspapers now, asking for my help only with especially difficult or unfamiliar vocabulary.

"It looks very bad, Wife." His newspaper was spread out on the library table, the dictionary beside him. I listened to him read it out loud, pausing between sentences. When he concentrated, he licked his top lip with the effort, just like Weilan:

> Between the warlords, the attempt to restore Manchu rule,
> President Yuan Shikai trying to crown himself emperor,

*and now the Nationalists and Communists, there have
been civil wars of one sort or another since before the fall
of the Qing Dynasty. The Japanese have taken advantage
of our domestic conflicts by marching into Manchuria, all
the while insisting that they are protecting Japanese com-
mercial interests. What does it take for our own armies to
unite against this threat to China?*

"We can't do a thing," I said, a fist clenching in my chest.
"The other nations won't intervene. The newspapers spout out-
rage, but we're helpless."

❧

The year 1932 had begun badly for China, with Shanghai's
merchants initiatiating a boycott of Japanese goods. We learned
that a mob in Shanghai had attacked a Japanese monk. When
the monk died of his injuries, Japan took advantage of the incident and dropped retaliatory bombs on the city. Thus began the
January 28 Incident, fought beside the banks of Soochow Creek
in Chinese-held Shanghai.

I knew my sisters were safe, for their homes were in the
French Concession. Japanese airplanes wouldn't attack there,
nor the International Settlement, for that would amount to de-
claring war on the British, French, and American governments
whose citizens occupied those zones.

So from the safety of luxurious hotel rooms and apartments
overlooking Soochow Creek, Europeans and Americans in the
foreign concessions watched our armies battle the Japanese.

According to one newspaper, the foreigners exhibited no more concern over the slaughter than if they'd been watching dog races at the Canidrome. Finally, in March, Western powers stepped in and officially ended the battle, but at a high cost to China.

"This proposed cease-fire agreement between China and Japan is humiliating," Baizhen said. He sounded sad rather than angry as he took his glasses off to rub his eyes. "It makes Shanghai a demilitarized zone. Our own troops can't enter the city anymore. And Japanese troops have been allowed to occupy the cities of Soochow and Kunshan."

But there was worse to come. In April, when the wisteria vines around the pavilion began uncurling in tender green shoots, Gong Gong opened the newspaper and gave a startled cry.

"The Communists have invaded Changchow!"

I jumped from my chair, knocking a cup to the floor, and jerked the paper out of his hands, not caring about my breach of protocol. Gong Gong said nothing and Jia Po quietly pressed a rag over the puddle of tea beside my chair. Baizhen stood behind me anxiously, peering over my shoulder while I scanned the story.

"I must send a telegram to Father," I said, dropping the paper. "I must know how they are. It says the Communists have taken over the central city."

Baizhen and I took a rickshaw to the post office.

"Changchow is under attack. Your telegram won't get through," said the clerk, a thin, perspiring man. "Who's there to deliver it? You'll have to wait till the fighting's over."

"Then I must send a telegram to my sister in Shanghai."

My hands trembled as I wrote it out. Gaoyin and Shen had a telephone. She might have managed to call Father. I wanted to wait for a reply, but Baizhen persuaded me to return home. A reply could take hours.

When we returned, Old Ming took control. He sent for one of his many grandchildren and within a half hour a skinny twelve-year-old arrived at our gate. He was dispatched to the post office with a steamed bun and strict instructions to stay there until the clerk put the reply telegram in his hands.

I spent the next few hours walking through the gardens, unable to sit still. I even snapped at Weilan when she tugged at my skirts. Jia Po bundled her away with promises of sweets from Old Kwan. Baizhen kept his distance, but I could sense him at the periphery of my vision while I paced through the courtyard, anxious and inarticulate.

Perhaps this was one of the weeks Sueyin and Tienzhen had stayed in their Shanghai apartment. Perhaps my father and Changyin were away on business. Stepmother, however, never had reason to leave Changchow. What about little Fei-Fei, Changyin's wife, Geeling, my nieces and nephews? I even hoped Tongyin was in Shanghai, drunk but safe in some seedy nightclub.

"Come in for supper, Wife. You must eat something," Baizhen pleaded, his hand on my arm.

"But a telegram might arrive." I pulled away from him irrationally.

"If it does, whether you read it right away or two minutes later, it won't change what's already happened. Please."

I didn't know what the chopsticks lifted to my mouth, for it all tasted of ashes. Then we sat silently in the parlor. The moon was just a sliver overhead when we heard the cries from the main gate at last.

"The telegram is here, the telegram is here!"

The boy's voice carried clearly through the night air and brought us all to our feet. I ran for the entrance courtyard, where Old Ming stood beneath the dim lightbulb that hung in the gatehouse. His grandson was perched on the tall stool beside him, panting and gulping down cold tea from an enamel mug. The old man held out an envelope, his hands shaking as much as my own. I ripped it open:

Tongyin and Sueyin are in Shanghai. Everyone else in Changchow. Telephones out. Will send news as soon as we know more.

I sagged against Baizhen.

⌇⌇

I had always imagined the front lines as far away, in distant regions where no one lived. I thought that soldiers died instantly, felled by a single bullet through the heart. When we read about Japanese planes attacking Shanghai, I pictured them flying in disciplined formations over the city, dropping bombs that landed in unfortunate neighborhoods, nowhere near my sisters' fashionable apartments.

Now I saw our beautiful villa ransacked, its gardens trampled, the great front gates smashed open. Our family had always believed ourselves safe in our estate, sheltered behind white walls topped with broken glass, guarded by loyal servants. But in fact we had been sheltered by privilege. The men who fought in the streets now knew nothing of privilege, cared nothing for our name or status.

The daily newspapers told us about the battles in lurid detail. The photographs accompanying the reports were suddenly far too real. Dead and maimed soldiers and citizens sprawled obscenely on the streets, in places I recognized. Bodies piled up against the doorway of a café. Others sought the inadequate protection of a crammed arched passageway. A child's embroidered shoe lay abandoned by the curb.

All I wanted was to see my father again.

Then, abruptly, it was over. "THE COMMUNISTS HAVE RETREATED," the headlines proclaimed. I smoothed a broadsheet out on the table with nervous hands, heedless of the ink smudging my sleeves:

After three weeks of bitter fighting, Nationalist forces have taken back Changchow, driving away the guerrilla army led by Mao Zedong. Our brave soldiers were aided by Western gunboats in Xiamen Bay, which prevented Russian arms shipments from sailing up the Jiulong River to resupply Mao's forces.

Relieved, I handed the newspaper to Gong Gong. Surely it wouldn't be long before Changchow's telegraphs and telephones were working again. There would be news from home.

A day later, news did arrive. It was a telegram from my eldest brother, Changyin.

Father was dead.

I return to the roof beams of the temple. Three red sparks join me there, hovering silently before my eyes. Below, the temple doors stand partially open, holding back the muted light of dawn.

My *yang* soul speaks first, a lament. *Too late now, too late. Too late to reconcile with your father. You will regret this until the day you die.* Bitter gentian root washes over my tongue.

I'm past the day of my death and I regret it. I'm numb with disbelief. How could I have lost all memory of Father's death? *I forgave him everything when Changchow was invaded. All I wanted was to see him and all my family safe and unharmed. I was going to write him a real letter once the battles were over.*

That's the trouble when you're young, my *hun* soul says. *You think you have all the time in the world. You think the world will wait until you're ready.*

A new thought comes to me. *Father's dead, but so am I. Will I be able to meet him?*

Perhaps. My *hun* soul sounds doubtful. *If you're able to make amends quickly enough you might catch up with your father in the afterlife before he moves on.*

Moves on where?

To his next reincarnation, my *yin* soul replies.

Of course.

15

*B*aizhen went with me to Changchow. Gong Gong wanted to come too, but war disrupts everything, even gestures of respect. The estate had been vandalized and many of the servants were missing. Changyin's telegram explained that they couldn't entertain house guests.

The retreating Communist army had looted its way out of the city. The men who invaded our home might have been soldiers from either army, or local thugs taking advantage of the chaos. It was hard to tell, for the Communists couldn't afford to supply all their recruits with uniforms.

I learned that Father and Changyin had tried to reason with the horde that pounded at our gates with rifles and threats. The looters kicked Changyin to the ground and when Father tried to intervene, one of the men struck him with a rifle butt.

"Only a single blow, according to Stepmother," Sueyin said. "But it was to the head, and he collapsed. He was unconscious, and by the time Stepmother found a doctor, it was too late."

The courtyard of our ancestral temple should have been over-flowing with mourners, packed tightly as fermented black beans in a stoneware jar. Instead, Father's funeral was small and hurried, attended only by family, not at all befitting his status. There were so many funeral processions filing through Changchow's shattered neighborhoods that week that we nearly tripped over one another on our way to the cemetery.

Members of the family capable of making the walk trudged silently behind the coffin, our white mourning robes like scraps of rice paper against the hillside as we ascended to the clan's burial grounds, trampling pine needles and fallen plum blossoms as we went.

In front of the grave, Baizhen and I dropped to our knees. My sisters and their husbands knelt to our left, Stepmother and Fei-Fei to our right. Geeling, who had insisted on walking with us on her deformed feet, knelt at the end of the row. In front of us were Changyin, Tongyin, and our uncles, Father's younger brothers. They bowed in unison, bundles of incense in their hands. We followed suit, touching our foreheads and palms to hard dirt. I said farewell to my father, mute anguish striking at my heart. Even the sharp, resinous scent of pine felt like a reproach.

❧

The morning after the funeral was the first opportunity for time alone with my sisters. I had been the last to arrive home, only just in time for the funeral. Now my sisters and I climbed the embankment in the Old Garden and sank down on the carved stone seats under the pine trees.

"I hoped so much we would sit here together one day," Gaoyin said, dabbing her eyes, "but not like this."

Sueyin said nothing, just squeezed my hand.

"If it weren't for Stepmother," Gaoyin said, gazing at the lake, "our family would have lost much, much more."

The moment word came of armies marching toward Changchow, Stepmother had sent away all but the most trusted servants. Then she and Head Servant Lu had organized each family to collect its most precious treasures — antique porcelains, jewelery, gold, and jade. They packed the valuables into crates, baskets, and canvas sacks. The servants dragged the valuables into the middle of the lake, where they vanished from view, covered by a film of duckweed and lily pads. Then Stepmother had wrapped Father's most treasured books and paintings in layers of oilskin and hid them in the servants' outhouses. What remained on display was more than enough to convince the peasant army that they were rifling through our very best possessions.

I almost couldn't bear to look at the villa. All the smashed glass had been removed from the windows but there were holes in the wallpaper where crystal sconces used to shine, and my mother's chandeliers had been torn from their fittings. The Old Garden, natural in its contours and artlessly wild, had lost nothing more than some plantings of irises, run over by the gardeners' wheelbarrows, which the looters had used to carry away their spoils, but the rose garden, with its pergolas and carefully trimmed hedges, had been flattened.

"How are things with Shen's family?" I asked Gaoyin.

"The armies didn't pass through their street, thank the gods."

The Liu estate had fared worst of all. The Judge tried to

lecture the looters, invoking Confucius and shaking his cane at them while they plundered the property. The soldiers laughed at the old man and, before they left, threw burning torches into the houses. The aging wooden mansions sparked like twigs held over a bonfire. Madame Liu, emaciated and deprived of her opium supply during the three weeks of battle, died the day after the fire.

"The Judge has told us that life is precarious and he wants a grandson. Now that Father's gone, he may allow Tienzhen to divorce me." Sueyin paused. "In his own way, Tienzhen tries to be loyal. He says he needs someone who can be hostess at his soirees. He'll only marry someone as beautiful as I am."

"They'll need to search long and hard then," I said. "Do you really want a divorce?"

My sisters exchanged glances.

"Now that Father's gone," Sueyin said, "I feel as though a great burden has been lifted from my heart."

"What on earth do you mean?"

"Don't look so shocked, Little Sister. Of course I wish Father were still alive. All I mean is that I don't need to worry about shaming him anymore."

"So you're leaving Tienzhen, then?" Gaoyin asked gently.

Sueyin nodded. "With or without a divorce."

"Good." Just one firm nod of the head from Gaoyin.

"Why didn't you tell me you were leaving your husband?" I knew I sounded sulky. "Obviously this isn't a surprise to Eldest Sister."

"There wasn't anything *to* tell. When Father was alive, I could only dream about leaving Tienzhen. Now, I can actually do it."

"Do you expect Changyin to let you live at home?" I asked, worriedly.

"I'm not coming back to our family." She smiled at me ruefully.

"But where will you go? What will you do?"

"Remember my weekly allowance from the Judge, Little Sister? I've saved nearly all of it. And I'll wait to see whether Father left me anything in his will." She paused. "I've been offered a contract to act in a film. In Hong Kong. I'm leaving Tienzhen for Ma Fong, the director."

I could only gape. Gaoyin didn't seem surprised at this bit of news either.

"I met him last year at a film premiere in Shanghai," said Sueyin. "Then Ma Fong came to one of our soirees. When the time came for actors to read scenes from a script, Ma insisted I be part of it."

"I was there that night," Gaoyin said. "The actor they paired with her did a respectable job, but Sueyin was mesmerizing. Absolutely and believably tragic. My handkerchief was soaked in tears. At the end, Ma Fong asked Sueyin to audition for his film."

"How did Tienzhen take it?" I asked, dubiously.

"He was proud and pleased," said Sueyin with more than a hint of wryness. "Pleased in the manner of a child whose dog has performed a clever trick. Of course I couldn't audition. But from then on, Ma kept coming to our parties."

"So you're leaving because you're in love with Ma Fong?" I asked.

"You mean, am I alienating my family for love?" She

shrugged. "This isn't love, Little Sister, it's a business transaction. Unlike the other men, Ma Fong didn't flatter or flirt with me. He offered me a contract and a salary."

There was a hard edge to her voice I hadn't heard before. Yet I was glad of it.

"Couldn't you do something else? Must you become an actress?" The consequences of her decision had dawned on me.

"I'm not qualified for any respectable jobs like teaching or nursing. What do I have besides my face?" She smiled as though she was amused, but it was heartbreaking.

"But our families will make us shun you! I'll have to write to you in secret." I nearly wailed.

"Is that so different from what we do now?"

∽∾∾

The next morning I began setting the library to rights. I gathered up the books and scrolls and sorted them for reshelving. I was almost glad Father wasn't there to see his beloved library in such a state. Several fine watercolors lay on the floor, torn and trampled beyond repair, long strips of landscape paintings mixed with fragments of blue-black iris flowers.

"Good idea." Stepmother smiled at me from the doorway of the library. Her eyes were weary, ringed with dark circles. "You're the best one for this job. You know how your father organized his books."

"You look tired, Stepmother. Sit down and talk while I work."

A low cough interrupted us. Geeling, Changyin's wife. Her hands fluttered nervously.

"Third Sister-in-Law. You're a guest. You don't need to do this." Her whispery voice was barely audible and she bit her lip. But there was a new air of authority, even insistence, about her. I saw a jade brooch pinned to her silk jacket, a rare piece, deep green on one side and pale as a cabbage leaf on the other. It had been my mother's.

"I'm happy to get Father's library organized again," I countered.

"Really, you don't have to. We're moving in here next week, you know." Suddenly, despite her breathy voice, she looked like an aggressive little hen. I glanced over at Stepmother.

"Fei-Fei and I will move into our own little house," Stepmother said, smoothly and naturally, before any awkward pause could develop. "The one in the fifth courtyard. Please excuse me, I must go to the kitchens and see how they plan to feed our guests tonight."

Geeling blinked and whispered, "No, no. That's my responsibility now. I'll go."

We watched her shuffle away.

"Do you mind moving out of the villa, Stepmother?" I was a bit worried about Geeling's newfound assertiveness.

"It was my idea. Your First Sister-in-Law is now Mistress. She takes her matriarch role very seriously; it's how she was raised. She should take her rightful position."

Another discreet cough from the library door. This time, it was Head Servant Lu. He bowed deeply. It took a moment for me to realize he was bowing to Stepmother.

"Madame should rest now. It's been a difficult time and she has done more than enough. "

"I will, Lu. But first I need to speak to you about all the broken furniture."

"I have some ideas, Madame." Then he turned to me and bowed almost as deeply.

"Third Young Mistress, the Master wishes to see you." The Master. Changyin now, not Father. My chest tightened up again.

On my way out I glanced back. They were deep in conversation, Lu nodding his head deferentially while Stepmother spoke. Geeling wouldn't be a problem for her.

಼ೲ

Father's study door was open and Changyin sat at the long table. His face was still bruised, and he winced when he leaned across to pick up some papers. He looked much older than thirty-one.

"Third Sister. It's good to have you home again." He gave me a sad smile and pulled out a handkerchief to polish his glasses. "It's about Father's will. How would you like to receive your inheritance?"

"I wasn't expecting anything," I said in surprise. Father had no reason to leave me an inheritance. He'd been disappointed with me and I had all but ignored him these past few years.

"Father left you twenty thousand *yin yuan*." A small fortune in silver coins. I gasped.

Changyin tapped the paper lying in front of him. "That's what's written in the will, Little Sister. But very recently he expressed the hope that you would let me invest it for you, so that you could receive an income every year instead of one lump sum."

He looked up at me. "He worried about you and your daughter."

He sat in silence while I struggled to control tears. There was no hope of tempering the guilt that was wrenching me apart.

"What would you like me to do, Third Sister?" he asked again, gently. "Would you like a few days to think things over?"

I shook my head. "Please. Invest it as Father would have wished. But don't give me an income. Let it accumulate. I'll need it for sending my children to boarding school and university."

"All right, then. I'll send you a statement every three months."

"Eldest Brother, please don't. I trust you." I paused, then added, "I'm going to tell my husband it's an education fund. If we really need the money, I'll write to you."

Another silence.

"I see. So Father was right to be worried."

I nodded and hurried out of the study, waiting until I was on the curved staircase and out of sight before wiping my eyes.

❧

The sadness in his voice I could bear. His pity I could not. But this was not the real reason for my tears.

I can tell the night is cold. There isn't a single rustle from animals on the prowl to disturb the quiet, and a film of frost whitens the paving stones of the terrace. Even my *hun* soul shines with a chilly, unforgiving light.

My *yang* soul tucks his hands into the wide sleeves of his padded jacket, out of habit more than any real need to keep warm. My *yin* soul stands balanced on the rail that surrounds the terrace, arms outstretched, pretending to be an acrobat, a tightrope walker. Despite her game, her gaze is as sorrowful as my own.

I was a terrible daughter, yet my father still left me money. I'd give anything to see him again, to beg his forgiveness.

Then you must hurry, my yang soul says. *If you can get through the portal to the afterlife before your father goes to his next reincarnation, you might see him.*

But years have passed since he died, objects my yin soul. *Would he still be there? Surely he's been reincarnated already.*

Years have passed only in the real world, my hun soul reminds her. *In the afterlife, time means nothing. Perhaps Leiyin's father waits for her even now. One never knows.*

I sink to my knees and bury my face in my hands. If my father has been waiting for me, delaying his own reincarnation, it's a grace I don't deserve. In the natural order of things, my souls and I must leave this world. No matter how much I love Weilan, how can I do anything to help her? I'm only a ghost; I can't even bend a twig. The restless pull of the afterlife reminds me of this, relentlessly. And now, if I stubbornly stay here and keep my father waiting in the afterlife, I'll only add another act of ingratitude to my slate.

✑✑✑

At the landing, I paused to look out the window. Tongyin and Baizhen sat on the marble balustrades at the edge of the terrace, facing out to the garden. The wicker chairs were gone, broken beyond repair. From the way Tongyin was gesturing, I could tell he was explaining how the rose garden used to look. I went down and joined them, hiking up my skirt to swing my legs over the stone railing. On this visit Tongyin had been considerate. Perhaps it was our shared grief. Perhaps we had both grown up. He was making an effort to be friendly to Baizhen, and I felt a rush of gratitude. Life was precarious indeed, and I needed to make more of an effort to get along with Tongyin.

A light wind rustled the branches of cassia above and for a moment I closed my eyes and imagined being a girl again, ready to jump off the marble barrier and race for the rose arbor.

"What will you do with your inheritance, Little Sister?" Tongyin's voice was casual.

I chose my words carefully. "Father has left an education fund for our children, which Eldest Brother will manage."

"That's wonderful!" Baizhen beamed.

"And you, Second Brother?" I wanted to change the subject.

"I'm going to invest some of mine in a nightclub," Tongyin said. He seemed very cheerful. "Do you remember my friend Cha Zhiming? He knows a club that would do very nicely after some refurbishing. He's looking for friends willing to join in."

"You're sure it's a sound investment?" I knew that Father wouldn't have liked anything to do with nightclubs. And I didn't like anything that had to do with Cha Zhiming.

Tongyin waved his hand carelessly. "Shanghai is full of wealthy foreigners. Yes, full of them. They're making money by cheating China, why shouldn't I make money by cheating them?"

"Does Cha know anything about the nightclub business?" I tried again.

"Little Sister, there's nothing to worry about. Nothing at all. The whole reason this enterprise will be profitable is *because* of Cha." He looked very pleased with himself. "With his position in the Shanghai Police and his father's connections, we're guaranteed to do well. We'll have good customers and we won't need to pay out bribes for police protection."

I couldn't imagine what Father would have said about Tongyin going into such a business. But now that Father was gone, there was no one to hold him back.

16

We returned to Pinghu the next day on the early train. It was a long and tiring trip in third class, the only seats available. The train overflowed with refugees, some continuing eastward, most getting off in Shanghai to try their luck in the foreign concessions. We sat on hard benches, legs hanging over our luggage protectively, as did our neighbors in the compartment, who eyed us as suspiciously as we did them. Baizhen and I said very little to each other. I was still overwhelmed by Father's death and dozed fitfully against my husband's shoulder, thinking that all I wanted was to see my daughter.

At the station, Old Ming's grandson, the rickshaw puller, met us on the platform. It was just before suppertime and the streets were noisy with vendors hawking their food and wares before the last shoppers returned home. I leaned back in my seat and moved closer to Baizhen. He gave my hand a comforting squeeze and then cleared his throat.

"I never realized, I mean, now that I've seen your home—it's grander than anything I ever imagined. And you're so close to your sisters. You must miss them terribly. If you ever want to visit . . ."

"It's all right. I'm quite content living in Pinghu." I found I meant those words.

"Pinghu is such a small, backward place compared to Changchow."

"Husband, this is my home now." I clasped his hand tightly. "But please, don't say anything to your parents about the education fund. Not yet."

"Why not?" he asked, puzzled.

I leaned closer to him, suddenly exhausted from the past several weeks, Father's death, the sight of my home. Sueyin.

"I don't want your father to know. If we really need money, I'll write to Changyin. But our children's education matters more than anything. If they can't earn their own living, they won't have a future. Please. Promise me."

I saw that I didn't need to say anything more.

He gave me a sad smile. "You're right as always, Wife."

⌒⌒⌒

"Weilan wanted to stay up," Little Ming said. "But she was so excited she ran around the gardens all day and fell asleep before dinner."

As soon as we paid our respects to Gong Gong and Jia Po, we went to the nursery. I removed Weilan's thumb from her mouth and put my head down on the pillow beside hers. The scent of her clean skin and hair, which usually filled me with contentment, made me shudder at what might have happened if we had been living in Changchow. What if she'd been forced to hide somewhere, terrified, or to watch her grandfather being beaten to death? At least she was safe in Pinghu, a place that mattered to neither side. I'd never long for the excitement of a big city again. My daughter's well-being outweighed all else.

⚭⚭

The final consequence of Father's death came several weeks after our return. Changyin mailed us a terse note to say that Sueyin was no longer a daughter of either the Liu or the Song family. He gave no reason, but in families such as ours, when it comes to shame, it's possible to gauge with exquisite precision its depth and degree by the surrounding silence. In Sueyin's case, the silence was absolute, her disgrace unredeemable.

Gong Gong didn't press me for details.

⚭⚭

Weeks later, a letter from Gaoyin arrived, tucked in her monthly package of newspapers and magazines. There was good news in her open letter—she was pregnant again—but it was her secret letter that gave me news of Sueyin:

> *You will see why I've sent you a gossipy film magazine, Little Sister. Changyin is furious and says Sueyin has shamed Father's memory. Liu Tienzhen is divorcing her.*

It's been three weeks since she left with Ma Fong. She's signed on with the Hong Kong branch of Lianhua Studios and taken a stage name to protect our family. Look on page 42.

On page 42 of *China Film World Weekly*, a publicity shot of Sueyin filled a quarter of the page. She gazed out from a black-and-white photo, unsmiling, heartbreakingly beautiful, a tragic and knowing quality in her eyes. The article beside it was written in the typically breathless prose of fan magazines:

Lianhua's latest discovery, the beautiful Chen Dai, keeps her origins a secret but it is rumored she is a socialite who has broken with her family in order to pursue an acting career. Already in great demand by directors and leading men alike, her first role will be in Ma Fong's upcoming film, A Song of Orchids. *The young director has been escorting Miss Chen around the most fashionable night spots in Hong Kong, and there is talk of a relationship that transcends business. How can anyone blame Ma for seeing stars?*

I showed the magazine to Baizhen.

"Please don't mention to your parents that Chen Dai is my sister. If Gong Gong forbids me to read these magazines or watch her films, I'll never see her face again."

"Don't worry. There's no danger he'll ever find out. Unless he suddenly starts reading those magazines or goes to see a film." He laughed.

"There's no danger at all, then." I couldn't help but smile at the thought of Gong Gong reading about starlets.

"I'm just sorry you're cut off from your Second Sister." He was so sincere.

"I'm glad for her, you know. I'm glad she found a way to leave her useless husband," I replied, then bit my lip and added quickly, "Tienzhen takes opium, have I ever mentioned that?"

Amazing, says my *yang* soul. He sits down heavily on the stone steps and straightens the skirts of his long scholar's gown. His round glasses reflect the setting sun, masking his eyes.

What do you mean, amazing?

Amazing, he says, *that Sueyin should be the one who discredits her upbringing. I didn't think she would follow through. She outdid your escapade, Leiyin.*

I'm not the least bit ashamed of my sister. Think of what she was trying to escape.

It's exciting to have a film star in the family, says my *yin* soul, twirling around the terrace, pretending to dance with an invisible partner. She stops. *If only Sueyin's reasons for becoming an actress were not so sad.*

She joins my *yang* soul on the steps and leans against his shoulder. He pats her hand.

Life isn't always black and white, is it? my *hun* soul says, standing beside me.

In the fall, all the film magazines featured promotional stills from *A Song of Orchids*. Although Chen Dai had only a minor role, she appeared in as many photographs as the leading lady. Sueyin had already been signed to three more films.

Finally, four months after her departure from our family, a letter from Sueyin arrived, enclosed in one from Gaoyin:

Tienzhen is angry, but not because of Ma Fong. He is jealous of my film career, such as it is. Only the prospect of being cut off without any income prevents him from moving to Hong Kong to join me. I hear the Judge has found him a new wife.

I receive offers every day from wealthy businessmen to be their mistress. One from an American. Occasionally I receive marriage proposals that might even be sincere. By film-world standards I'm very dull, for even when Ma Fong strays, I don't. Am I happier? Perhaps. But at least I'm responsible for myself and bearing the consequences of my own decisions.

The critics gave *A Song of Orchids* mediocre reviews, criticizing its weak plot. But Sueyin dazzled them. It would be several months before the film finished its run in the big cities and meandered its way to the theaters of small towns like Pinghu.

Little Ming waited eagerly for the film magazines. She turned immediately to the photographs of her favorite actresses and I helped her decipher the captions beneath. We read about films and society parties, the fashions, the gossip, and the romances.

There was no doubt that films spurred her to read more than the books in my library did.

"You look a bit like Chen Dai, Young Mistress." She pointed at the latest photo of Sueyin, in high-heeled boots with a fedora angled over her brow.

"Little Ming, there are such important things happening in China and the rest of the world," I chided. "Wouldn't you like to read the newspaper to understand more about what is going on between the Communists and the Nationalists?"

She looked over at me, puzzled. "Mao and Chiang are the two biggest warlords, Young Mistress. That's how it looks to me."

I couldn't blame her for preferring the glamor of the film world. How could I expect her to make sense of the chaos that was Chinese politics?

⌘

"You're doing very well, Husband. What's your vocabulary count up to now?"

"A few words over three thousand five hundred."

To read the newspapers, Baizhen needed to know at least four thousand of the most common words.

"You've made good progress."

"It's purely memory work, I know that." He sighed. "To think your father and brothers studied French and English too. How did they do it?"

"If your father knew how hard you've been working, he'd be proud."

Baizhen shook his head.

"I think he'd berate me. Why couldn't I have found such diligence fifteen years ago?"

"That wasn't your fault," I said fiercely. "He should be pleased with you. I'm pleased." I patted his shoulder. He looked up, his face earnest.

"I don't want our daughter to be ashamed of me."

Our daughter.

How could I deny that I was bound to this man?

⁂

Copies of *China Millennium* continued to arrive from Tongyin. I still read every issue, but since coming home from Changchow, I no longer looked for mention of Hanchin. I hadn't seen his name on any articles in almost two years. It was amazing that *China Millennium* still managed to put out issues, I thought. The Nationalist government censored all journalism heavily, and although the magazine's writers conveyed their Communist sympathies carefully and subtly, they were dancing on the edge.

But the latest issue of *China Millennium* broke all the rules. The editor, Lin Shaoyi, expressed disgust with the Nationalists for starting a civil war and fighting our own countrymen instead of uniting with the Communists to fight against the Japanese:

Generalissimo Chiang has placed naive and touching faith in the Western powers for aid against Japanese aggression. Foreigners have no stake in Chinese sovereignty; they only care about our goods and trade. The Nationalists must face reality. Only another Chinese army can help us repel the Japanese invaders.

On the next page, Nobody Special openly accused the Nationalist government of corruption:

Western dollars have never disappeared so quickly. Generalissimo Chiang could have a unified Republic of China if even half the money sent by our American allies— millions of dollars, rumor has it—had been used for weapons and military training to defeat Mao's army. Nationalist leaders have so little faith in their own future they are planning their escape routes and lining their own pockets in anticipation. If so, then the Communists have already won.

In the absence of the Qing Dynasty, Gong Gong backed the Nationalists.

"The Chinese Soviet Republic? Don't make me laugh!" he snorted.

We were entertaining Old Master Chou, Pinghu's last remaining Qing Dynasty scholar. Master Chou had attained the rank of *juren* in the Imperial Examinations more than fifty years ago. If Gong Gong was gruff and old-fashioned, Master Chou was even more calcified in his outlook.

"The Communists are fighting behind wooden barricades and in trenches," said Master Chou. "They can't hold out. The Nationalists are well funded by the West."

American, British, or French—it was "the West" to these old men. I longed to say that the Communists were funded by the

West also, by the Russians. But my role was to sit quietly beside Jia Po on a carved rosewood chair, rising occasionally to pass around the almond biscuits.

"And this peasant, Mao," Gong Gong continued. "The Communist Party used to be run by educated men. Educated in the West—that's how they got these barbaric ideas—but at least they were educated boys. From good families. They should have known better. And now we have an army of peasants. What do peasants know about governing? Finance? Foreign policy? And who will plant the fields now?"

"What about you, Baizhen?" Old Master Chou pointed his cane at my husband. "What do you think of all this?"

I could tell Gong Gong was about to say something un-complimentary about his son's lack of interest in politics, but Baizhen spoke up.

"My hope, sir, is that both sides unite against the Japanese threat. If Mao or Chiang wins, we still have Chinese ruling China. If the Japanese invade and win, we lose our sovereignty."

Gong Gong nearly dropped his almond biscuit.

"Well spoken, my boy, well spoken!" Old Master Chou thumped his cane in approval.

For the rest of the visit, Baizhen sat as silent as a mouse, trying to remain invisible to a hawk, startled at his own boldness. When I poured another round of tea, our fingers touched. I smiled at him and winked. He blushed, then grinned.

After Old Master Chou's departure, Gong Gong asked Baizhen how he had acquired an understanding of the news. When Baizhen confessed that I had been teaching him how to read, Gong Gong demanded a demonstration.

Nervous but steady, Baizhen read out loud the opening of an article about modernizing banking practices:

The nation's banks would do well to eliminate the practice of lending money based on personal relationships. They should follow the Western practice of approving loans based on objective measurements of creditworthiness.

"Stop," Gong Gong said. "Enough. I am pleased."

He included me in his gaze. "From now on, my son, you can travel with me on business. I can teach you something about the business world."

I bit my tongue.

⌒⌒⌒

As soon as *A Song of Orchids* reached Pinghu, we rushed to see it. I sat in the darkened theater with Baizhen, barely able to wait for Sueyin to make her entrance. According to the reviews, the story was about a Ming Dynasty princess who offers to take her older sister's place in marriage to a barbarian king, so that the older princess can continue her love affair with a court poet. Sueyin played the older princess, a minor role, for the tale centered on the feisty younger sister.

When Sueyin first appeared onscreen, her features were modestly hidden behind a fan, shielded from the dark eyes of the barbarian delegation. The emperor ordered her to show her face and slowly, reluctantly, the princess lowered the fan. The camera lingered on Sueyin's face. For a moment, there was silence. There wasn't a single crack of peanut shells, not a murmur of conversation in the entire theater. Only an audible intake of breath.

The sisters' farewell, minutes later, was Sueyin's final scene. From that point onward, the story followed the younger princess and her life at the barbarian court. Again, the camera focused in on Sueyin's lovely face as she waved at the departing caravan, a long procession that snaked away from the palace, taking the younger princess with it.

To my right, a middle-aged woman bawled into her sleeve and on my left, Baizhen sniffled. I cried and cried. I couldn't stop, even after we left the theater. I cried for the princesses, for Sueyin, for myself. I cried because I knew I would never see her face again except in a film theater, shared with a crowd in the dark.

❦

In the spring of 1934, just before my twenty-third birthday, Jia Po and I studied our household finances and came to the conclusion that we had to send Amah Wu back to her family farm. Between Little Ming, Baizhen, and me, Weilan received plenty of attention. She didn't need a nanny who did nothing except follow her around and snore on a cot in the nursery.

"It's not just her wages. Amah Wu eats enough for three people," my mother-in-law said. "Even though she's not nursing anymore."

The next morning, Amah Wu, sniffling and red-eyed, left for home with our promise that she would be called upon if we needed a nursemaid again. That afternoon, in response to a note from Jia Po, Jeweler Mah came to the house. He left with Jia Po's second-best gold-and-jade bracelets and a silver-filigree box that contained a huge Burmese ruby brooch. He also took a few pieces of the Limoges china that had been part of my dowry. He would show it to his other customers. If he could sell the whole set, Jia Po and I would part happily with it, for we never used it. We could eat for another year if we were frugal.

"I wanted to give you that brooch one day." She looked apologetic. "It was a wedding gift from my grandmother."

"Can't you speak to Gong Gong?" I asked, thinking of the rare books in the library. "There must be something he can sell."

She didn't reply, just counted ten silver coins into my hand and stacked the rest inside her metal cash box.

"Take Little Ming with you to see a film," she said. "It's not your fault money flows out of this house like water."

❧

You could have offered to take money out of your inheritance, my *yang* soul says. His glasses flash and I taste strong black tea. *What was the use of saving money for Weilan's education if she starved in the meantime?*

I would have written to Changyin once all our other means were exhausted. I didn't want Gong Gong to think there was any hope of getting his hands on my inheritance. Not until our situation became desperate.

Greedy, says my *yin* soul, her sweet face scornful. *A greedy man.*

No, I disagree. *Just weak. Vain and weak. His own father was probably not much better when it came to money.*

Fortunately Baizhen was content with a frugal life, my *hun* soul says. *He could have been a far worse husband. It's amazing he wasn't.*

⟡

Baizhen organized an outing to celebrate my twenty-third birthday. Old Kwan packed a lunch for us, and we piled into a hired donkey cart driven by yet another of Old Ming's grandchildren. This one turned out to be Little Ming's brother, a young man of nineteen. Baizhen sat in front beside the driver, Weilan on his lap, while Little Ming and I rode in the cart, facing backward, legs dangling over the side.

"No, no, I won't tell you where we're going," I heard Baizhen say. Weilan had been pestering him with questions. "All I'll say is that our family owns a very interesting property on the outskirts of Pinghu."

"Be patient, My Only Heart," I called from the back of the cart. "Papa wants this to be a surprise."

The paved streets of Pinghu rolled away from us and turned into hard-packed dirt roads. The old quilts folded under our buttocks did little to cushion us as the cart bumped and jolted over ruts, but I didn't care. A clear blue sky with a few clouds like handfuls of ruined lace, small farmhouses, and tidy fields: it all filled me with a sense of well-being.

When the cart stopped and Little Ming helped me slide off my seat, I wasn't prepared for what I saw when I turned around. A hill rose up from an otherwise rocky, flat landscape. It was smoothly rounded and resembled a huge burial mound covered in flowering shrubs.

"It's called Infant Mountain because it's just a baby of a mountain." Baizhen looked proud. "We'll climb to the top for the view and eat lunch there."

I must have looked unsure. He added, "It's a gentle climb. I used to do it as a boy."

Little Ming lifted the wicker basket of food and balanced it easily on her head. Her brother unhitched the donkey to let it graze, and settled himself under the shade of a large bayberry tree. I carried old quilts to spread on the ground and Baizhen swung Weilan onto his shoulders, making her squeal with glee.

He trampled over weeds to a small, derelict cottage at the foot of the hill, paused by a broken-down fence of bamboo slats, and pointed to a path, overgrown and barely visible. The path led us up the hill in a slow spiral between dense growths of azaleas and rhododendrons, the shining smooth leaves of camellias and their red-and-white blooms, and the fragrant branches of lilacs.

Pines, maples, and elms grew tall, shading the path. We brushed past masses of orange and yellow azaleas, stepped on woody stems that gave off a fragrance like incense. A thick mat of pine needles cushioned the path and birdsong shrilled above the sound of birch leaves fluttering in the breeze. Branches of flowering cherry trees that hadn't been pruned in years dropped the last of their pink and white petals.

"*Wah, waaah!*" Weilan shouted with delight each time her upraised hands brought down a shower of blooms.

"My seven-times-great-grandfather built this hill when our family was at the height of its prosperity," Baizhen said. "I remember coming for picnics when my grandfather was still alive. Now

Father wants to sell Infant Mountain. I wanted you to see it before it goes."

Dappled light opened up on the summit, where we found a small pavilion, no more than a thatched roof atop four posts. Baizhen set Weilan down on the trail and she immediately scrambled to the peak. He pulled me up the final incline.

I found myself looking down on Pinghu and the surrounding countryside. Amid a glaze of green fields, the lake that gave Pinghu its name gleamed like polished amethyst. I could see the town, the pagoda by the lake, and the monastery beside it. I could even see the dusty faraway hills that marked the boundaries of the next town.

"Oh, it's so beautiful," I exclaimed. And I meant it.

All at once it came to me that Pinghu had given me the serenity of ordinary days, a quiet pond set in the chaotic landscape that was China. For as long as it could hold back the inevitable intrusion of war, I would cherish its simple pleasures.

Weilan scampered around the clearing, urging Little Ming to unpack our lunch. I knelt down to hug my daughter, and pointed to the north, where I could see a distant locomotive approaching the town, its plume of black smoke a contrast to the bright landscape all around.

❧

My souls and I watch, enjoying the memory.

My memory-self is relaxed and laughing, teasing Baizhen and Little Ming. My face almost glows, radiant with newfound appreciation for my little world.

This town, this marriage, they were not what I had imagined for myself, I tell them. *But I had a husband who loved me with great devotion and a daughter we both adored. It was enough. I was content.*

At last, my *yang* soul grumbles. *You took long enough to realize it.* But he sounds pleased and sweet honey coats my tongue.

That was a very happy day. My *yin* soul stands at the summit, where a light wind makes her hair ribbons flutter. Lilacs scent the air.

It was certainly the day I realized I could be truly happy.

Look, says my *hun* soul. *The train has pulled in to the station.*

17

*T*he package from Gaoyin contained only a few newspapers and film magazines. Her open letter amused me: it detailed at length the challenges of toilet-training her youngest. Her secret letter made my heart sink:

My Dearest Sister,

I don't dare continue our secret correspondence any longer. Read the news and you'll understand why I'm sending only government-approved newspapers and journals from now on. The secret police are far more thorough than our families when it comes to searching for hidden notes. If ours are discovered, just the fact that we write in secret will implicate us.

Many of the writers and poets Father used to invite to his salons have gone over to the left. Tongyin is mixed up with the Communists in some way and I'm worried for him. Tell your husband to stay away from politics.

So this would be our last secret letter. Gaoyin had her children to consider. She was a more cautious person now than the sister who had agreed to help me run away. I hadn't felt this lonely since my first year as a wife, before Weilan was born. As for Gaoyin's warning, there wasn't much danger of anyone in Pinghu getting caught up in politics, I thought. For one thing, politics would first have to find this town.

I turned to the newspapers and began to read. On the second page of the *Shanghai News* I saw it:

CHINA MILLENNIUM *SHUT DOWN BY POLICE*

Police have raided the offices of China Millennium, *citing treasonous writing as the reason for arresting the editor, Lin Shaoyi. Yen Hanchin, poet and translator of Russian novels, who has been identified as the anonymous writer Nobody Special, is still at large. Staff at the journal were burning documents when police arrived, including a list of subscribers to the magazine. Police, however, already had a copy of the list and are making further arrests.*

Like everyone else, I had believed Nobody Special was a collective of poets and writers, but it had been Hanchin all along. His name in print no longer made me catch my breath, but this news made me wonder where he was hiding.

❧

"Ah, here's something interesting," said Gong Gong.

We were in the parlor. I was sewing a tunic for Weilan in her favorite shade of turquoise, and Jia Po was making a pair of cloth shoes for Gong Gong.

He handed me an invitation to the opening of a new bookstore on Southern Harmony Street. I recognized the name of the proprietor, Wang Duchen, the son of Bookseller Wang, who used to find rare books for Gong Gong.

"I'll ask Bookseller Wang about this," said Gong Gong. "If his son has opened the store with his blessing, then I'll attend the opening to show my support."

"He's selling books by contemporary authors," I noticed with interest. "He won't be competing with his father's business."

GRAND OPENING
*Thousand Wisdoms Bookstore, 24 Southern Harmony
Street*

We specialize in contemporary works of prose and poetry, and literary-arts journals. Our publications come from Peking, Shanghai, and Nanking. Please honor us by attending our opening-day celebrations, to be held at noon on the sixth day of the sixth month.

Wang Duchen, Proprietor

Gong Gong went to Bookseller Wang's shop that very after-noon and returned with assurances from Wang that his son had opened the new shop on behalf of the Wang family.

"Wang wants to see whether modern literature will sell," Gong Gong reported. "But he doesn't want any young radicals mixing with his own customers, so they opened a separate store, which his son will manage. Bookseller Wang is very considerate, for a shopkeeper. But then, he does sell books."

On the sixth day of the sixth month, my father-in-law set off to inspect the new store. When Gong Gong returned, I was in the main house with Jia Po, adding knot buttons to Weilan's blouse, struggling to keep the stitches hidden. He carried a small package of books. The store, he reported, wasn't hanging its hopes solely on modern literature. There was a small selection of classics as well as some children's books.

"I made a small purchase. Just to show support for young Wang."

He placed the books on the table beside his chair. Jia Po brought his slippers and I poured out fresh tea for him.

"The clerk who helped me said these authors are the most popular right now. Lu Hsün, Hu Shih, and some poet called Yu Dafu. Never heard of them."

I picked up one and then the next, greedy for the prospect of something new.

"Which one will you read first, Gong Gong?"

Gong Gong waved his hand. "Take them all, take your time. I'm not interested in modern literature. Oh, and there's some-thing for you. For Weilan, actually."

He pointed at a cheap copy of *The Children's History of Twenty-Four Exemplars of Filial Piety.* "The clerk gave it to me for free. For my granddaughter, he said, although I don't remember telling him about our family." He paused, then continued. "Well, I'm sure Bookseller Wang briefed the staff on his most important clients."

I finished my struggle with the blue buttons, folded the little blouse into my sewing basket, and picked up the new books. Jia Po was engrossed in the gossip Gong Gong had brought back from town, and the two were oblivious to my presence when I stood up to leave. There was time for an hour of peaceful reading, and I decided to do it in the pavilion. A light breeze had come up and with it the promise of one of the brief but powerful summer showers that blow in from the sea. I could smell it in the air and I hurried through the bamboo grove to the shelter of the pavilion. Like everything else on the estate, it looked a bit forlorn: the ancient wisteria vine planted at its base hadn't been pruned in a decade. Any day now the roof would come free from its moorings, prodded off by the wisteria's creeping tendrils.

I sat on one of the curved stone benches in the pavilion and skimmed the first pages of each book, unable to choose between them. I opened the children's book and flipped through the familiar stories. A slip of blue notepaper was tucked in the middle, a bookmark or a price tag, I thought. Idly, I drew it out.

There was a faraway rumble of thunder and raindrops began flicking off the wisteria leaves. But I barely noticed. The pale blue onion skin was as familiar to me as the handwriting on it:

Come to the Thousand Wisdoms Bookstore on Thursdays.
Special prices for old friends.
You may lose all that you acquire, but knowledge and
wisdom remain yours forever.

I tucked the slip of paper back in the book, closed my eyes, and felt my body shiver, but not because of my wet clothing. No, it simply wasn't possible.

❧

The following Thursday, with a list of things I didn't really need tucked in my tunic pocket, I went shopping. I bought dried shrimps and straw mushrooms, a jar of bean paste, and a spool of black thread. I looked modest and matronly in a high-collared tunic of deep blue and a matching skirt, but with every step my heart pounded as loudly as the drumbeats of a dragon dance, my thoughts were clotted and confused, my body drawn forward by a nameless compulsion that was both pleasurable and frightening.

Eventually I stood at the threshold of the Thousand Wisdoms Bookstore. I loitered outside, pretended to read the notices pasted on the whitewashed wall, lists of books that had just arrived. Finally when I could delay it no longer, I pushed open the door to a harsh jangle of brass bells.

At first I couldn't see anything. Then my eyes adjusted from the bright sun outside to the store's gentle light, filtered as it was through paper shades. A young man faced the counter, a customer.

Behind the counter was Hanchin.

He didn't look like a simple store clerk, not to my eyes. Even with round glasses perched on his nose and wearing an old-fashioned *changshan* gown of dark gray, he carried himself with too much confidence. He nodded at me and resumed wrapping the customer's package, so I lingered in the far corner of the store beside a case of children's books. I stole glances at him while thumbing through a picture book.

"You'll enjoy those books, sir," Hanchin said, as he opened the door and bowed to the customer. "This author used to write for *New Youth* and other magazines."

He stood outside the shop entrance for a moment, polishing his glasses with a handkerchief of faded green plaid. He held the glasses up to the light, squinted, and put them back on. He was thinner than when I'd last seen him, his cheekbones standing out in sharp ridges. Reluctantly, I realized he was also far handsomer than I remembered, more forceful and enigmatic than the romantic figure from my faded daydreams.

He looked up and down the street. Then he came back in, pulling the door shut.

I spoke into the silence, hoping my voice wouldn't tremble.

"Do you really need those glasses, or are they a disguise?"

"Really, Leiyin. We haven't seen each other in years and you ask about my glasses?" The same amused, intimate smile. "Yes, I've grown a little nearsighted. And you. You're a mother now, I understand."

"Six years. We haven't seen each other in six years." I steadied my voice. "Yes, I have a daughter, almost five years old. What are you doing here, Hanchin?"

"I'm in hiding." As calmly as if he were talking about the

weather. He took the picture book out of my hands, replaced it on the shelf. His movement stirred the stale air of the bookshop, spread the faintest trace of sandalwood.

"But why here? This town is a backwater."

"That's why it's perfect. Who'd ever think of coming to a town such as this?"

"Did you know I lived here?"

"Yes, I knew. I've always known."

Against my will, my heart raced. I'd stopped looking for his name in the newspapers but he had somehow kept track of me.

"What if I hadn't seen that note in the book you gave my father-in-law? I wouldn't be here today, on a Thursday."

"Well, the book was meant for your daughter, so there was a good chance you'd see it. And even if you weren't sure what the note meant, you'd know who it was from." Oh, he was so sure of himself.

"What if I hadn't seen the note at all?"

"A new bookstore, Leiyin. How could you resist? You would have come through these doors before long. But Thursdays are convenient. Young Wang usually helps his father at the other store on Thursdays."

"Why did you contact me, Hanchin? You're a political criminal. Why would I endanger myself for you? I hardly know you."

I was speaking the truth. I knew nothing about his childhood or what he'd been doing these past few years.

"And yet you came." The scent of sandalwood grew stronger as he moved closer, took my hand.

"I have to get back." I pulled my hand away. "Just tell me why you contacted me."

"I need you to hide something for me. Then I need you to give it to someone when the time is right."

"What's the 'something'?" I could almost see the lure he was placing before me, drawing me in with curiosity.

"A document. I'm still writing it." He smiled. "It's a Communist manifesto for China."

"A what?"

"A manifesto is a declaration of principles and objectives." As if I didn't know that, but I wanted to hear his voice. His eyes were mysterious, those glints of light in dark pupils. "Our history and beliefs aren't the same as those of Western nations. Our manifesto must build on the foundation stones of our own culture, not theirs."

I leaned back against a tall bookcase. "But why hide it? Why not take it with you?"

"I can't risk that. I may be captured. The manifesto is more important than I am, Leiyin. If the Party approves, it'll be distributed all over the country to inspire and guide people, to allow all Chinese to move forward as one." His eyes shone in the dim light of the store, and his voice was husky, fervent.

"Surely there are others who can do this. Young Wang, for instance."

"If the Nationalists come looking and find out I worked here, he'll be the first one arrested. But there's nothing to link you and me. That's one of the reasons I chose to hide in Pinghu."

"I see." He was here because there was nothing between us.

"After I leave Pinghu, a courier will come to get it from you. Will you hide it for me?" He took my hand again and put both of his around it.

Part of me, the part that remembered being seventeen and insane with love, longed to say I would do anything for him. Another part realized I had been too naive about Pinghu. It might be a boring small town, but if Wang, the bookseller's son, was a Communist sympathizer, then the civil war had found its way here long ago. And now Hanchin was asking me to risk my family's safety.

"How can you ask me to do this? I have a husband, a child . . ."

"Leiyin, I'm only asking you to do what you feel is right. Once, you wanted to make a difference to our country. You should know that even in small towns such as this all over China, men and women are taking a stand."

In my new life, in this town, there was no point holding on to my convictions. Or so I had told myself. I felt ashamed for losing sight of Madame Sun Yat-sen's vision for a new China, one where women had a voice. But that vision didn't include helping a wanted criminal.

"Leiyin, you understand better than anyone else what this work means to me. There's no one else I would trust with this document. As for the other reason why I came to this town . . ."

He lifted my chin with a long finger and I pulled my eyes away from his. I shook my head, but he pulled me toward him, pressed his lips against my forehead. I willed myself to resist the feelings his touch aroused in me but then his lips met mine. He bent down farther and his mouth moved behind my ear, below the tortoiseshell combs in my hair, down to my neck.

"How did you end up married so quickly?" he said, his breath warm beside my neck. "One day you were a pretty schoolgirl and the next day you were gone."

I felt my knees soften, a slow melting that threatened my ability to stand upright.

"My father wouldn't allow me to go to college, so I ran away. But I failed. Father married me off as punishment for my disobedience." I hated that I couldn't control my breathing, short panting gasps that I tried to keep quiet.

"You're not in love with your husband, then?" He said this teasingly.

"He's a kind husband and a good father." I pushed myself away from his embrace.

"I'm glad to hear that." The playful tone was gone.

Suddenly I thought of Gaoyin's last letter, her concern for Tongyin.

"Hanchin, what's been going on with my second brother? Is he mixed up with you and the Communist Party?"

"What do you think? Is Tongyin capable of political intrigue?" His eyes narrowed.

"My brother's capable of boasting, that's all. But he could get into a lot of trouble that way."

"You're right to worry, Leiyin. Tongyin talks too much." His voice grew serious. "For your own sake as well as his, Tongyin must never know I was here. The less either of you know about my situation, the safer it is for you."

The brass bells rang and a young man pushed open the door. He stood for a moment outlined against the sun, blinking while his eyes adjusted to the muted light. Hanchin moved to a display shelf beside me and pulled out a magazine.

"On page sixteen there are some verses by that poet who interests you, Madame. Please accept this magazine with our compliments. Come by the shop again next Thursday. The book should be here by then. There's no charge if you change your mind."

He turned to the new arrival. "Welcome, welcome. How may I assist you?"

A SONG OF PURE HAPPINESS IV
by Nobody Special, after a poem by Li Bai

Her face like moonlight brightens his heart to springtime.
He yearns for her voice in the echoes of morning birdcalls.
He sets aside his pen and recalls her loveliness,
Promises they have yet to keep, the place where they last
    joined hands.

It wasn't his best poem.

But it didn't matter because I knew what the verses signified. Once again, Hanchin had declared his feelings, both secretly and openly, and in print. Alone in my library, I pulled out a copy of *The Complete Tang Poems*, a volume Father had given me years ago. I read the referenced quatrain over and over again even though it was one I knew well, one I had memorized to please my father.

A SONG OF PURE HAPPINESS III
by Li Bai
Tang Poem Number 319

The beauty of his lady amidst his flowers
Brings eternal pleasure to the emperor's eye

On a railing in the Aloe Pavilion she leans
As he listens to the distant spring wind sigh.

The pavilion. Where we last joined hands. I felt my hard-won contentment washing away, swirling downstream in trails of indigo, dye that had never set properly in the fabric of my life.

⌘

My souls flutter in distress, making a noise that mimics rainfall on green bamboo.

I was never in love with Baizhen, I tell my souls. *You know that.*

But you were fond of Baizhen, weren't you? My yin soul gazes at me, her brown eyes reproachful. *He was a kind husband and a good father.*

More than fond. Baizhen was my family.

But you never lusted after him. Humph. My yang soul stomps away across the garden, taking a swipe at a row of oleander shrubs with his cane. *It wasn't enough for you to have a kind husband who didn't blame you for only giving him a daughter.*

I hang my head, unable to counter his accusation.

You knew when your memories began unfurling that Hanchin would return to your life, didn't you? My yin soul. I smell the damp freshness of rain on moss, a hint of camellia growing nearby.

At the far end of the garden, my yang soul pulls out his hand-kerchief. The calico cat has returned and he flaps it at her. She springs at it, playful rather than frightened.

When will I die, and how? I wonder. But my souls shake their heads, no wiser than I am about what the past has yet to reveal.

The moment I saw the slip of blue paper in the book, I knew Hanchin had something to do with my death. I don't have much longer, do I?

No, not much longer, says my *hun* soul, stroking my hair. *Your life is nearly over.*

⌒⌒⌒

Waiting for Thursday was like a life sentence. My senses felt vividly alive, but a blur of emotions distracted me every moment. Hanchin's words and his touch rolled back the years, reminding me of my ambitions: to teach, to help educate the poor, to make a difference to my country. I felt the walls of the Lee estate close in on me again. I avoided Baizhen as much as possible, certain that my shifting moods, my anxiety and anticipation, would betray me and tell him how I longed for someone else's company. The veneer of courtesy that concealed my true thoughts was so thin I didn't trust myself to maintain it.

So I busied myself with household finances, sat for hours in Jia Po's small office, and riffled through years of bills and scribbled budgets. I reviewed our expenses, rewrote menus and seasonal shopping lists to economize on food. I went into the storerooms, pulling out trunks that hadn't been opened in years, searching for fabric to sew new clothes for Weilan, who was growing so quickly her ankles already stuck out past the hems of trousers I had made for her a few months earlier.

When Thursday finally came, I went to purchase thread and buttons for the new trousers I was making for my daughter. My errand at the dry-goods store didn't take very long, and left me only a short walk from the Thousand Wisdoms Bookstore. Again I loitered outside, pretending to read handbills pasted to the wall. It was early afternoon, the time of day when young mothers settled children down to naps, when elderly gentlemen rode in the privacy of sedan chairs to visit old friends or favorite courtesans. Cooks and housewives had long since finished at the markets and returned home, their arms laden with green cabbages or shiny freshwater eels still twitching in tightly woven baskets. The street was empty when I stepped inside the shop.

Hanchin looked up when the door opened. He was alone. He had only to look at me to know my decision.

"Thank you, Leiyin," was all he said, but his smile said much more.

Then he took my hand and I followed him to the back of the store, where a curtained doorway led into a storeroom. It was lined with stacks of books and wooden crates. There was an old cot pushed against one wall and, beside it, a washbasin on a wooden chair. A wide plank set across some crates served as a desk.

"This is where I live, work, and write. Room, board, and wages." He was still holding my hand, still smiling.

I pointed to a stack of paper on the plank, weighed down by an ink stone. "Is that your manifesto?"

"Drafts. The fifteenth or twentieth—I've lost track. I'll need another week or two."

"I read the poem," I blurted out. This was what I really wanted to ask him. "Were you thinking of me when you composed it?"

In reply, he pulled me into his arms. His lips brushed across

my forehead, eyelids, cheeks, and, finally, my mouth. The desire
I had felt when I was seventeen didn't compare to this. Now I was
married and understood the urgent needs of a man's body, understood more about my own. I wanted to satisfy his hunger. I helped
him undo the buttons of my tunic, felt his fingers stroke the silk
undershirt beneath and lift it away from my skin, felt his hands
slide up over my breasts and then down my back to unfasten the
hook at the top of my skirt, felt the fabric drop to the ground. Felt
his hands explore between my thighs.

I gasped. This wasn't anything like the intimacies I shared
with Baizhen, for Hanchin's touch was slow and lingering, a lei-
surely appreciation.

"All those lost years," he whispered. He guided me to the cot,
where I collapsed, unable to take my eyes away from him. At that
moment, I was willing to risk everything, ignore all my fears, put
aside all shame. Desire pulsed through my veins. He pulled up
the skirts of his *changshan* and prepared to mount me.

Then we heard the clanking of bells as the door to the shop
opened, and a rough voice called out, "*Eh*, Shopkeeper!"

"Wait here," he said in a low voice, straightening his gown.

I sat up on the cot, pulled my clothing off the floor, and got
dressed quickly, reeling as much from disbelief as from his caresses. *All those lost years*, he had said. He had loved me all these
years after all. What were we to do, now that we had declared our
feelings, a married woman and a wanted political enemy?

After what seemed like hours, another jangle of bells indicated the customer had left. Hanchin returned to the storeroom,
knelt by the cot, and held me. I shuddered, fearful yet hopeful,
still willing for him to take me. But he shook his head.

"This is no place to meet. And you shouldn't come here again if you can help it. You might be seen. Wang mustn't know about our relationship, or that we even know each other."

"But he should know that I'm on your side, that he has an ally here."

He shook his head again. "If he doesn't know about you, he can't give you away. You should go now."

I clung to him. "But how can we see each other? You need to get your manifesto to me."

"I come and go as I please. Wang knows I have business more important than this bookstore. You sort it out, Leiyin. Find a way for us to be . . . together."

∽∾∾

I still can't believe my foolishness. I had wanted excitement and Hanchin had rekindled my cravings for a different life.

Hanchin made me feel seventeen again. It was so potent, the rush of passion, my remembered longings, impatience to make up for all those lost years.

You were lonely, my *yin* soul says, her voice soothing. *Your sisters couldn't write to you anymore, you had no other contact with your old life in Changchow. You were vulnerable.* The fragrance of steamed rice, the most comforting scent in the world, rises around me.

He says nothing, but the sour, unripe plums in my mouth tell me my *yang* soul isn't so forgiving.

We watch my memory-self fumble through farewell kisses, her flushed face and parted lips, the feral shine of her eyes. Hanchin, expert and restrained, gives me a final caress and a gentle push out the bookshop door.

And now? my *hun* soul asks. *What do you feel now?*

Now I'd give anything just to be alive again, passing each day in quiet contentment with my child and my husband.

∽∾∾

My small world was entirely contained within walls and court-yards, where any change in routine was noticed and any departure from ordinary behavior cause for concern. Now I had to deceive my husband and family to be with Hanchin. Spots of fever rose on my cheeks whenever I remembered his touch. I wanted to inhabit a world only large enough to contain the two of us, and then return to my normal life. But how could I do this without losing my daughter or hurting Baizhen? I wavered, all the while stumbling closer to a fork in the road from which there would be no turning back.

When Baizhen came to my bed at night, I clutched at him urgently. Although he expressed surprise and pleasure at my ardor, his body couldn't fulfill my needs. The darkness obscured my grimaces of frustration at his clumsy caresses, his too-moist lips, his limbs that always seemed to jab me in all the wrong places. When he left my room, I lay awake in despair, desperate to find a time and place to be alone with Hanchin.

Over the next few days, I floated through the hours lost in my scheming, devising and discarding one ruse after another. There were times when I was irritable, impossible to please. On those days, I snapped at the most innocuous of comments.

"For women, an even temper is evidence of good breeding," Jia Po said sternly, after I had reduced Little Ming to tears. She was upset with me, for she was fond of Little Ming. "It's difficult to sleep in such hot weather, Daughter, but don't allow your tiredness to affect your conduct, especially with the servants."

"I'm sorry, Mother. But you're right. I've hardly slept in days." I was relieved that she attributed my erratic mood to insomnia.

"I'll have Mrs. Kwan make some sweet-date syrup for us after supper. It will help us all sleep better."

～～～

Then the gods cleared my path.

"It's time to sell Infant Mountain," Gong Gong announced. "We'll go to Shanghai and place an advertisement in the newspaper. We'll stay for two weeks, or until a buyer contacts us. It's easier to have a first meeting right there in Shanghai."

By "we," he meant himself and Baizhen. I couldn't have cared less about Infant Mountain. All I knew was that with two members of the family away, there would be fewer people to deceive.

I copied down Gaoyin's address in Shanghai for Gong Gong and begged him and Baizhen to pay my sister a visit. I knew Gaoyin and Shen would invite them to stay at their spacious apartment. With expenses reduced, it was more likely that Gong Gong would linger in Shanghai.

A day later, Little Ming came to see me, twisting her handkerchief. Her mother was very ill.

"Please, Young Mistress, I'd like to go home at night to take care of my mother. I'm her only daughter and my brothers all work at night with their rickshaws. It's their busiest time—that's when the drunken gentlemen need to be taken home."

"As long as you come back in the mornings before Weilan gets up." I tried to sound sympathetic, not jubilant. I would have sent her away for a month if it were possible. Now, except for Weilan, my house would be empty each night for at least a week, perhaps two, if Little Ming's mother was slow to recover.

I blessed the fact that no one in the main house could see or hear anything beyond the moon gate of our courtyard. I thanked the gods for the unfortunate circumstances that had left the cottage in the orchard abandoned and empty. It was destiny, I thought. Fate had finally rewarded me. My love for Hanchin, so long unrequited, had been sanctioned by the gods.

At the train station, I bade farewell to Baizhen and Gong Gong, my face cheerful as I wished them luck selling Infant Mountain. Weilan and I stood on the platform for a long time. She insisted on waving until the train was out of sight. Then we went home and I waited for the afternoon, when Jia Po and Weilan took their naps.

I stole into Old Ming's storage room with an empty Tiger Balm tin and came out with the small red container full of heavy grease. I looked in on Weilan, who was fast asleep. Little Ming would be in the kitchen helping with the servants' meal while Old Kwan prepared ours. I hurried through the orchard, where the leafy branches hung low, heavy with near-ripe fruit and scented with peach and pear, hints of the sweetness to come.

The orchard's eastern wall held a heavy wooden door that squealed when I pushed it open. I smeared the latch and hinges with grease, then tested the door a few times to work the lubricant deeper into the rusty metal joints. This side door was the one Baizhen had used when he was a boy, to slip in and out of the house unnoticed. Then I turned my attention to the old cottage, greasing its door as well.

When I had finished, I wiped my hands on a rag, then hid it with the Tiger Balm tin behind some hydrangea shrubs. I left the orchard and went into the tiled bathing room, washed my hands, scrubbed the black grease from under my fingernails, and smoothed down my hair.

◠◡◠

The thought of seeing Hanchin again carried my feet skimming over the walkways and bridges. A string bag slung over my arm held a few paper twists filled with dried herbs, my excuse for the outing. A heavy key wrapped in a sheet of notepaper weighed down one of my skirt pockets.

I pushed open the shop door. Hanchin sat behind the desk that served as a sales counter, facing two young men in long, loose gowns. They looked up as the door opened, caution on their faces. Hanchin smiled and nodded his head to greet me. I was just another customer. He continued talking to the young men while I feigned interest in the children's books at the front of the shop.

Finally I heard Hanchin say in an exaggerated voice, "I'll send you a note, sir, as soon as the next issue of *Analects*

Fortnightly arrives. Please, look around the shop while I assist this lady."

But the men murmured their good-byes, the brass bells jangled, and in the silence my breathing quickened.

"Do you need help?" A young man in a pressed white shirt came out from the storeroom.

"No, Manager Wang," replied Hanchin. "There's only one customer here now. Please don't trouble yourself."

Young Wang bowed slightly in my direction. I nodded. He vanished through the curtains, back into the storeroom.

"Alas, the store is busy today." Hanchin touched my face with one finger and grinned. I pressed his hand to my cheek and then kissed his palm. There was a smudge of blue ink on one of his knuckles and I kissed that as well.

"It doesn't matter," I said, breathless with daring. "I've found a way for us to be together. My husband and father-in-law are in Shanghai for two weeks. Here. I've explained what to do. Tonight. Please."

I pressed the key and the note into his hand.

The bells rang noisily on my way out, but they were not half as loud as the ringing in my heart.

❧

My brisk walk to the shops and back should have been exhausting in such hot weather, but I was exhilarated and alert. My mind spun like a water wheel through a cascade of possibilities. Weilan slumbered soundly every night, the sweet, undisturbed sleep of a happy child. Jia Po used a chamber pot, so she had no reason to leave her room, let alone her house, at night. Nonetheless, I had to minimize my risk of being caught. I brewed red-date syrup for Jia Po and Weilan to drink after supper, adding some herbs.

"It's been hard trying to sleep in this heat," I said. "We can all use some help."

I forced myself to wait beside Weilan's bed until her breathing grew deep and regular. Then I returned to my own room and sat in front of my dressing-table mirror. I fussed with my hair, combing out my long tresses and wishing I had a short, stylish cut with a permanent wave. I dabbed orange blossom water behind my ears and, brazenly, I thought, between my breasts. My cheeks needed no extra color.

Then I waited in the dark for the streets outside to grow quiet, listened to the last drunkard singing his way home, the rasping of gates being pulled shut. I became aware for the first time of the animal sounds that filled the night: the sudden, soft thud of moths when they careened into a window, the scuffling of small creatures traveling through shrubbery.

Finally I heard what I had been waiting for, footsteps that would have been inaudible to anyone not listening for them, then a quiet scraping sound.

I threw a deep blue robe over my white nightclothes and hurried along the veranda. I stepped down to the courtyard and followed the path toward the outhouse. The courtyard was flooded by moonlight, empty and silent but for the singing of a lone cicada. A row of pink and white oleanders, their leaves dense and vibrant, screened the small building. From there it was only a few steps to the orchard door, all hidden from view, only a second or two when I could be seen.

I stayed close to the sheltering orchard wall, then ducked through, into the quiet welcome of fruit trees and Hanchin's embrace.

"What now, Leiyin?" His voice was teasing. "Do I make love to you under the pears and peaches?"

"I've made ready the cottage," I said, inwardly afraid of abandoning all restraint, of crying out my need for him to the night sky.

Inside, I reached into the drawer of the old table, found matches, and lit a small stub of candle, which I set down on a broken tile. He never took his eyes off me. He smiled, candlelight flickering over his face, his eyes glinting.

"I would've taken you under the trees outside, under the moonlight. How beautiful you look with your hair down."

Suddenly I felt shy. "I have a quilt for the floor. And a sheet. I'm sorry but the bed's too old."

I pulled out the rolled-up bedding from where I'd hidden it at the back of the ancient wardrobe amid a jumble of moth-eaten pillows and blankets. We spread it out on the floor. I sat down and looked up at Hanchin. Then he knelt beside me.

I was a married woman. My husband came often to my bed for the game of clouds and rain. But that night I realized that what I knew about the pleasures of the bedchamber wouldn't have filled a thimble.

I'd been prepared to endure Hanchin's weight on my body, his hands groping my breasts and buttocks, the sharp thrusts of his manhood. The only pleasure I expected for myself was the closeness of his body to mine, knowing that I had satisfied him. I wasn't ready for the satisfaction of my own needs, for the skillful caresses that made my body arch against his.

"Does this please you, Leiyin? And what about this, how does *this* please you?" he whispered. I could only gasp in reply.

Until a beggar eats her fill she doesn't realize how hungry she's been all her life.

∽∂◠∾

Immoral. Utterly immoral and shameful, my *yang* soul mutters. He stalks away to the far end of the terrace. But I smile because my mouth fills with the seductive taste of ripe fruits: sweet plums and cherries.

Hanchin was so desirable. My *yin* soul stretches, arching her back—a bit voluptuously for one so young, I think.

And so experienced, I say, suddenly recognizing what I had witnessed. *Why didn't I ask myself how he knew so much about giving pleasure?*

Because you believed it was love that made the difference, says my *hun* soul. *You thought it was love that made your bodies so pleasing to each other. It's understandable because sometimes it's true.* It gives me a patronizing tap on the head.

In this case, was it true? Did he love me? He must have loved me, to risk a rendezvous when there was so much at stake. Not just us, but also his manuscript.

My souls don't reply and the memories flow on.

∽∂◠∾

"I loved you the moment I saw you, Hanchin. How did you feel about me?"

"I couldn't stop thinking about you." Again, a mischievous note.

I covered his face with kisses. "Even though we barely had any time alone, every time we met, I felt more certain you cared. Why did you leave Changchow? I ran away from home to find you and you were gone."

"Your brother told me about your marriage the day I got the offer to teach. I left because I had the chance to make a difference. Directly, not just through my writing."

"I would have gone with you," I insisted, filled with regrets. "I wanted to be a teacher, to be worthy of your love. To be a partner who could work with you to transform China. I would have used my dowry to help you set up schools for peasants."

"A nice dream." Condescending. As though teasing a child.

"Yes, a dream, because my father never would have let me marry you," I said, somewhat annoyed at his tone. "So why did you flirt with me?"

He kissed me again, caressed my thighs. "Let's just say I couldn't help myself. You were so . . . irresistible." His low laughter, my helpless need for his touch.

I rested my head against his chest, tucked myself under his chin.

"Tell me everything, from the time you left Changchow."

I learned that for a year he had lived in Soochow, using it as a base for traveling to small towns and rural communities in Jiangsu province. Then for a while he ran a school in Jiangxi province, where he and an assistant taught adult peasants how to read.

"I could have been of use," I said, envious of the person who had worked alongside him. "I've devised ways to teach my . . . to teach adults how to read. With methods more suitable than lessons designed for children."

"Alas, that school is no more," he said lightly. "We ran out of funds. But I'm not surprised you found a way to put your ambitions to work."

I glowed from his approval. "Do you remember the last letter you sent me? You wrote that the most important thing was to keep seeking knowledge. Even here, in this small town, I read everything I can find."

"The written word endures longer than anyone realizes. Words are a powerful tool for winning the war."

I felt like I was in heaven, sitting there on a pile of old blankets, musty pillows between our backs and the wall. I rested my cheek against his shoulder.

"You always wrote your articles so carefully, never any direct criticism. Why did you write such a blunt piece in that final issue of *China Millennium*?" I had to ask. "Now you're on the run."

"We knew it was only a matter of time before we were arrested. There was a spy in our midst. We all decided that we might as well print a final issue that spoke without equivocation."

"A spy!" I shivered. "Did you know who it was?"

"Yes. I knew him and used him to our advantage for a while. But I played his game too long and now so many people will suffer because of my overconfidence." Even in the wavering candlelight, I could see the troubled lines on his face.

"You mustn't feel that way, Hanchin. You can't foresee every danger."

Almost absentmindedly he reached over to stroke my naked breasts and I shivered again, this time with delicious anticipation.

⌀⌀⌀

Hanchin couldn't come to me every night, of course. He and Young Wang organized clandestine meetings where Hanchin spoke to sympathizers about what the Communist Party would do for ordinary people.

"If you don't hear me in the alley by midnight, I won't be coming," he had told me one night. "Some of these meetings continue until dawn. We're recruiting for the Party."

"Let me attend your meetings," I begged. "I want to know more."

He propped himself on one elbow to look down at me and laughed.

"Leiyin, you of all people can't come. You must be my secret. How else can you hide my manuscript?"

"But you're taking a risk by speaking at these gatherings at all. You're a wanted man."

"I'm not using my own name. No one in Pinghu knows what Yen Hanchin looks like. They won't associate the clerk at the bookstore with the Yen Hanchin who writes political editorials." He seemed confident, but I had my doubts.

"Then don't leave Pinghu, Hanchin. Please, stay where no one knows who you are. Stay with me."

He didn't reply, but instead lowered his face to my belly, lips parted.

On the nights I couldn't be with Hanchin, sleep eluded me. I wanted him by my side, remembered his hands on my body until I was ready to cry with frustration. Once or twice, hearing sounds in the alley, I ran out to the orchard to find the cottage empty and the side door locked. When we did meet, the dusty cottage was our haven, but an hour or two was all that I dared.

After lovemaking, he would doze sweetly. I held the candle over him and moved the light along his folded limbs to learn every inch of his face and body. When he awoke, we talked. I wanted to know everything about him, to make up for all the time we had lost.

His life could have been so much easier. His family had ties to the Liu clan, albeit a connection so slight it was tenuous even in the extended hierarchy of Chinese families. Hanchin's grandfather had shared a tutor with Judge Liu's father, making the two elderly gentlemen classmates and friends as well as distant cousins.

"While Judge Liu's father lived, we were invited to Liu family gatherings," he said, a hard glitter in his eyes. "We sat at the edge of the dining hall, arrived and departed with the other poor relatives through side doors, never the main gates."

Old Master Liu had promised Hanchin's grandfather a loan to pay for Hanchin's education. But then Old Master Liu and Hanchin's grandfather died in the same year, just before Hanchin finished high school. The invitations ceased and along with them, any mention of a loan.

"Why didn't your father remind the Judge of this promise?"

"My father said we were poor but we didn't need charity. And I wanted none of their money either."

Moonlight shone through the empty windowpanes, a cold radiance that matched the expression on his face. I imagined how he must have felt as a boy, his glimpses into the opulent lives of the Liu family, and returning to a home where poverty hid behind a brittle facade of genteel sophistication.

"The Liu estate burned down two years ago, you know, when the Communist army invaded Changchow."

"Yes, I heard." He smiled and it frightened me, something scornful and knowing in his face. Then his features smoothed out and he pulled me closer.

"Men like Judge Liu are the reason we need to build a new China, Leiyin. A country that the rest of the world will respect. You could make a difference to that new China."

I nodded, remembering how I had felt as a teenager, the intoxication of discovering a purpose greater than my own blinkered life. I remembered reading Madame Sun Yat-sen's essay out loud with Nanmei, her words lending us courage and stoking our ambitions. It was a bright and hopeful horizon I had thought forever lost to me. I gathered my courage and sat up to face him.

"Hanchin, when you leave Pinghu, I want to go with you."

∽∾∾

My *yang* soul shakes his head, his judgment clear. He doesn't need to speak—a rancid taste saturates my mouth, making me want to retch. The sickly sweet smell of rotting fruit fills the air, my *yin* soul equally unhappy with what we're seeing.

I'm astonished at my rash words. At the same time, I remember how absorbed I had been in the small world of the dilapidated cottage, my compulsive need to be with him, my endless desire, and the bright horizon of a life outside this small town.

It was like an illness, a form of insanity that came over me, I tell my souls. *Each waking minute was an exercise in restraint, for I wanted nothing more than to run over the bridges and canals to the bookstore. Our need for secrecy only added to the excitement, doubled my desperation to be with him. I couldn't give him up, I just couldn't.*

To the point where you were willing to leave your daughter behind? Those words from my *hun* soul are gently spoken, but they make me flinch.

No, no. I can't believe I would have done that. I would have come to my senses.

⚭

Each day I watched for signs that I'd been seen during my midnight outings, but Dali's plain face never changed, Mrs. Kwan gave me no curious glances, and Weilan never voiced any awkward questions. I bathed carefully every morning to remove the traces of lovemaking. When Little Ming brought the bucket of hot water for the wooden tub, I would complain that the heat made me perspire uncomfortably at night.

"Yes, Young Mistress. I can hardly sleep either in this heat wave." She looked tired, but her smile was joyful.

"How is your mother?"

"She's recovering slowly, Young Mistress."

"There's no need to rush back," I said, trying not to sound too eager. "Stay with her until you're sure."

I was torn between taking Weilan with me when I left with Hanchin, and leaving her in a place I knew would be safe. One moment I couldn't imagine being separated from Weilan; she simply had to come with me. Then I'd worry. It was too dangerous. I had to leave her here and hope that she'd understand and forgive me someday, when the war was over, when she was older and we saw each other again. But always, I wavered. I spread clothes across my bed, hers and mine, picking out the best ones for travel, the most rugged, the lightest and warmest, for what I knew would be an arduous journey. Little Ming thought I was inspecting them for moth holes.

I was frantic knowing that Hanchin was almost ready to leave our town. He hadn't yet agreed to let me travel with him.

"I can endure anything if we're together," I told him. "I'm not the schoolgirl you knew in Changchow."

"Leiyin, I'm on the run. If I'm caught, you'll be arrested with me."

"They won't be looking for a couple. They're looking for a single man." A young family would be an even better disguise, but I didn't mention Weilan. One step at a time.

"We love each other, Hanchin. So many wasted years, you said so yourself. We can't ever be apart now."

My hand slid down between his legs and I felt his heartbeat quicken.

"You can't wander all over the province with me, Leiyin. I won't be taking a direct route. Besides, who will look after the manifesto?"

He was right. I had made a promise to safeguard something he valued more than his own life.

"Then send for me when you're safely behind the front lines. Promise me."

I sat up and straddled him, lifted his hands to cup my breasts. His breathing grew heavier.

"All right. I'll send for you. But promise you'll stay here and keep the manuscript until the courier comes."

He handled me roughly, but I didn't mind.

∽∼∾

Gong Gong and Baizhen sent a telegram letting us know their return date. Old Ming's grandson would meet them at the train station with the donkey cart. My stolen hours were coming to an end for another reason: Hanchin had completed his manifesto and was preparing to move on.

On our last night together, Hanchin brought me an envelope sealed with red wax.

"Please, don't open it. If the seal is broken, our agents will think the network has been compromised." All the lightness and teasing were gone from his voice, his expression severe.

"I won't. I promise. And I've thought of some places where I can hide it."

"Now listen carefully, Leiyin. When I get to my next hiding place, I'll arrange for a courier to come get the manifesto. After I reach Chinese Soviet territory, I'll send another courier. He'll bring you to join me. It could take a few weeks. In the meantime, be patient and trust me."

"I do trust you," I said, kissing his neck. "I'll keep your document safe. But how will I know who the courier is?"

"The courier will know you. It's better if you don't know."

"What route will you take to the front lines? I want to know," I begged.

"It's better if you don't know," he repeated. "Even my train tickets were purchased by other people."

We made love for the last time. My hands ran over his body voraciously, I coaxed and kissed him wherever my mouth could reach. Afterward, I was exhausted, but could not fall asleep. I gazed at him as he slept, thinking that if only I knew the route he would be taking, I could pay attention to news from those places, reports of unrest or fighting. I needed to know.

I hesitated for only a moment before reaching for the clothing on the floor. The candle sputtered, its wick nearly spent. In the faltering light I looked through the contents of his pockets and found train tickets in his vest. They indicated a circuitous route, and I memorized dates and names of cities. I returned them to his vest just as the candle burned out.

When Hanchin awoke, we got dressed and together we stuffed the bedding back into the armoire. We emerged to a waning moon and rustling leaves. Gently he pushed open the orchard door.

"I'll send for you. Take care of my manifesto."

I clung to him, weeping silent tears that darkened the front of his tunic. He wiped my eyes with his handkerchief and pressed it into my hand.

"I'll send for you," he repeated. "Be patient."

≈

If my betrothal to Baizhen had been a knot of dread that choked my heart, then parting from Hanchin was a knife wound that wouldn't close. I cried all night and tried to get my emotions under control in the morning. When Gong Gong and Baizhen came home from the train station at noon, I was still in bed.

"I'm unwell. I've been sleeping poorly in this heat," I said in a cross voice to Baizhen. Then I turned my back to him. He retreated, a bit puzzled, to his own room to unpack his luggage.

I got up for dinner and made an effort to appear interested in Gong Gong's account of their trip. Infant Mountain hadn't attracted a buyer.

"These days, only gangsters have money to spare," said Gong Gong bitterly. "And they're too busy trading profits for power to pay any attention to a pleasure garden out in some provincial town."

"Did you enjoy your time with my sister and her husband?" I asked.

My husband and father-in-law grew animated and praised Gaoyin and Shen's hospitality. For the rest of the meal, I didn't need to say anything.

That night, despite his long journey, Baizhen brought me chrysanthemum tea to cool my *qi* and damp towels for my forehead. Thankfully he didn't stay in my room after delivering them. The next night, however, he did. I tried not to think about Hanchin as my husband moaned and thrust into me, pulling my buttocks up toward his hips.

❧

The household returned to normal. Weilan once again shared her room with Little Ming, whose mother had recovered and no longer needed her constant care. I did the weekly shopping as usual, but never went close to the Thousand Wisdoms Bookstore.

In August we celebrated Weilan's fifth birthday with a box of chocolates, a gift from Gaoyin. At the end of August Old Ming carried ladders into the orchard and we picked fruit. We filled baskets with apricots and peaches, stored away apples and pears, boiled misshapen and undersize fruit into syrups.

Baizhen and I went to see Sueyin's latest film, another costume drama set in the Han Dynasty, another tragic role. My sister had chosen her own path and soon I would take mine and be with the man I loved.

I waited and waited for word from Hanchin. In my wardrobe, two small canvas sacks of clothing were hidden beneath folded blankets, ready to be carried off at a moment's notice. Next to them was a handbag with money, a sewing kit, and a small box of essential medicines. I still agonized over whether to bring Weilan.

There would be two contacts, Hanchin had explained. The first courier would come for the manifesto. The next one would come for me. I didn't expect the second courier before September, when Hanchin would be using his final train ticket to reach Wenzhou. I didn't know how he'd slip into Communist-occupied territory from there. But the first courier should have contacted me by now.

Autumn arrived with no word from Hanchin. I read about

the Encirclement Campaigns being fought in the south, worried for Hanchin, wondered whether he had reached his destination safely. The newspapers didn't mention his name, so I guessed he had managed to evade capture. There was news that Mao's army was losing ground and retreating in order to set up a new base. Perhaps Hanchin had needed to find a different route to cross through the contested territory. I had to be patient.

18

*T*he moment I was certain of my pregnancy, I told Baizhen. Not because it would make him happy, but because the news would allow me to sleep undisturbed, free to dream and worry about Hanchin alone. The news raised cries of joy in the main house. Again my mother-in-law took me around the corner to the clinic. After the doctor had placed his fingers on my various pulse points and consulted some charts, he proclaimed my second pregnancy easier to read than the first.

"There are very strong indications that you're carrying a boy," he said, nodding.

When we returned home, Jia Po closed the door to Gong Gong's study and remained in there for a while. Dali reported to Little Ming, who reported to me, that after a long argument, Jia Po had come out of the room looking victorious.

The next day, Bookseller Wang paid a visit to Gong Gong. They disappeared into the library and, after an hour, Wang left with several volumes tucked in his shoulder bag. A week later,

Wang visited us again. He had gone to Hangchow, a city known for its love of literature. There, Gong Gong's rare books had sold for more than Jia Po's gold-and-jade bracelets. Gong Gong grumbled that they hadn't fetched anywhere near as much as what he had paid originally, but in the face of Jia Po's new determination, he appeared resigned to the eventual loss of his library.

The prospect of a grandson cheered him up considerably, however, and he teased Baizhen with good humor.

"Had we known that a period of absence was all it took to make you potent, we would have sent you away to Shanghai years ago!"

Baizhen looked at me, pleased and embarrassed. I looked away, an exasperated expression on my face that I didn't bother to conceal. Once more I had become the most pampered member of the household, and if I was irritable or morose, even Jia Po excused my behavior.

"By this time of the year it should be cooler. No wonder you're out of sorts. I'd bring you more chrysanthemum tea, but you mustn't have more than three cups a day. Too much of its cooling properties might affect the balance of *qi* for the baby."

I didn't want chrysanthemum tea. I wanted news of Hanchin.

I wanted him to know I was carrying his child.

Hanchin's child?

But where's my baby? Did I die in childbirth? Is that how it happened?

We can't tell you. In any case, we don't know everything, not yet, my *yin* soul murmurs.

But dying in childbirth doesn't seem right, I muse. *Surely I would remember giving birth again. And I haven't heard any sounds to suggest there's a baby in this house. Weilan was the only child at my funeral.*

Hush, just wait, says my *yang* soul. *Let your memories unfold and we can all find out what happened.*

There aren't many more memories left, my *hun* soul says. There is a hint of melancholy in its shimmering light.

Then my souls guide me back to the stream of memories, which now flow thick and dense, more quickly than before.

∽✦∽

Once I left to join Hanchin, I'd be cut off from my family. Even Gaoyin would disown me. But I was more impatient than ever to get away, to be with Hanchin when our child was born. Would I bring Weilan with me?

I wrote to Gaoyin to say I was expecting again. This was the first letter I'd written her in weeks. In careful, proud brushstrokes, Baizhen wrote a short letter to Changyin: *Soon, you will have a new nephew.*

Stepmother, as considerate as ever, sent a package of flannel fabric for baby clothes.

We received a telegram from Tongyin. My second brother was coming to Pinghu on behalf of the family to offer gifts and congratulations. This was very odd. If Changyin didn't trust the postal system, all he had to do was send one of the servants by train. Tongyin must have volunteered. But Pinghu was bereft of nightlife and fashionable society, so I couldn't fathom why he would do this.

On the day Tongyin arrived I was feeling particularly irritable and refused to get out of bed. "I'll get up for supper. I can see him then," I said, rolling over and turning my back to Baizhen.

"Of course, Wife," he said, stroking my hair. "Your brother understands your condition. I'll return to the main house and chat with him."

"Mama, should I bring a cold towel for your forehead?" Weilan had appointed herself my nurse, though her performance was erratic.

"No, Small Bird. Just let Mama get some sleep this afternoon. Ask Little Ming to take you with her when she goes out to the market."

"Little Ming has a bad tummy again. Dali's going to market instead."

"Then go out with Dali. Go get some fresh air."

The house and small courtyard emptied of people and noise. I knew the rest of the family and servants were doing their best to stay away from our house, keeping as quiet as possible while I slept, the way we did whenever Gong Gong and Jia Po took their naps. The shuttered windows sent bright bars of sunlight onto the wide-planked floors and my pillowcase held the soothing fragrance of English lavender, but I remained wide awake, my mind busy, my heart in turmoil.

I couldn't stop thinking about Hanchin. I turned my face in to my pillow and fingered its crocheted edges, then reached deep inside the pillowcase and pulled out a green plaid handkerchief, all I had of my beloved.

But now I also had his child. I wanted it to be his child.

What choice did I have but to be patient?

∽∼∾

I hadn't seen Tongyin since Father's funeral two years ago. His face had filled out, as had his slim frame. Instead of his usual three-piece suit, he wore a traditional *changshan* gown over gray flannel trousers, no doubt in deference to Gong Gong and Baizhen, both of whom still dressed traditionally. At dinner I said almost nothing to him.

Tongyin was at his most charming. He admired our table, for Jia Po had brought out the fine porcelain from her dowry, delicately patterned with a lotus motif. He praised Old Kwan's cooking and ate heartily: tiny river shrimp sautéed with peas, a thick fish soup, cabbage braised with shreds of dried scallops, an entire chicken stuffed with sticky rice and baked in lotus leaves. We would eat nothing but rice and vegetables for a month after this. Our wine cups were filled with French cognac my brother had brought as a gift to Gong Gong and Baizhen.

"You're blooming, Third Sister," he said, lifting his cup in my direction. "The impertinent schoolgirl is now a beautiful mother."

"She still keeps up with world events," Baizhen said. "Your eldest sister sends us newspapers every month and Leiyin reads them all."

Gong Gong interjected, "We all read and benefit from your

family's knowledge of current events. Tell us what you think of the Encirclement Campaigns, honored kin."

"You're speaking to the least informed member of the family." Tongyin inclined his head modestly. "If you're reading all the news, you already know more than I."

"You're too modest." I could see Gong Gong was pleased with Tongyin's self-deprecating reply. "You would hear more news just standing on the street corners of Shanghai than we'd get from a month of reading the papers. Is there any consensus on the out-come of the battles in Jiangxi province?"

"The news is good, very good. By all accounts our Nationalist forces are winning the Fifth Encirclement Campaign. Soon Mao's army will be in a noose they can't escape. We hear that large numbers of Communist agents and agitators are going into hiding, unsure of what to do next or where to take their orders from. It will be a rout, an absolute rout."

Tongyin was being a perfect guest, but I could tell that be-neath the pleasantries he was impatient, on edge.

After dinner, Jia Po proposed a game of *mah-jong*. It pleased her to have someone new at the table. Gong Gong excused him-self; he never enjoyed playing. The rest of us sat down at the felt-topped table and opened the case of ivory tiles. We played for toothpicks because Jia Po refused to gamble with real cash. Tongyin kept the conversation lively with gossip about Shanghai society matrons who ran high-stakes *mah-jong* games.

"Mrs. Goh always won. But then her *mah-jong* partners began to notice things," he said, of one prominent hostess. "In particular, how the maid offering snacks would circle the table and place a few sunflower seeds or dried plums beside Mrs. Goh's teacup every now and then. Unlike the other ladies, Mrs. Goh never helped herself to any snacks. Her maid always put something down for her."

"So did her friends accuse her of cheating?" asked Jia Po, fascinated.

"No, not at all. They couldn't, not without causing her to lose face. Eventually they said it was unfair for her to host all the *mah-jong* parties and that they should rotate among their homes. She knew she'd been caught but since no one had accused her openly, everyone managed to save face. When it was Mrs. Goh's turn to host again, the maid no longer hovered over the game."

By the end of four hands, Jia Po was giggling. A little more wine and Tongyin had talked her into another round. Baizhen, who had been cheerful since the announcement of my pregnancy, needed no encouragement to down more cognac. It didn't worry me to see Baizhen drink. It meant he would fall into his own bed tipsy and happy, to sleep soundly until late morning. He wouldn't come to my room to fuss or make sure I was comfortable before going to his own room for the night.

At the end of the second round, Jia Po stood up.

"That's as much excitement as I can take. It's already ten o'clock. What a night, what a night! Ah, if only we entertained such amiable company more often!"

Tongyin bowed to her. "If only my commitments allowed me to visit more often."

She tapped his arm playfully with her folded fan. "No need to be polite, there's nothing in this town to bring you here except duty and affection for your sister."

She turned to leave, a little unsteady on her feet. Baizhen sprang up.

"Ma, let me help you to your room." Together, they made their way out in slow, deliberate steps.

Alone at last, Tongyin and I looked at each other. My guard remained up.

"Well, Little Sister. Motherhood suits you well, yes, very well."

"Thank you for being so kind to my mother-in-law. I'm sorry to be unsociable, but I'm having rather a difficult pregnancy and I'm tired. Good night."

"Wait, Sister. We must talk. In private."

"Anything you want to say to me, you can say in front of my husband tomorrow."

"You wouldn't want your husband to hear this. Meet me at the pavilion at one o'clock. It's about Yen Hanchin."

He turned on his heel, not waiting for my answer.

Was it possible that Tongyin was the courier for the manifesto? After all, he'd been friends with Hanchin, had once given his support to Hanchin's work. But he was also in business with Cha Zhiming. I couldn't figure it out.

I lay awake, my eyes fixed on the wall clock. At a few minutes before one, I pulled a woolen coat over my nightgown. The sky was clear and the moon so bright I didn't need a lamp to find my way to the main courtyard. A light wind rattled through the bamboo stalks, but the trembling in my hands had nothing to do with the chilly air. When I emerged from the bamboo grove the smell of cigarette smoke told me that Tongyin was already at the pavilion. He was leaning against a post, his face tilted toward the moon. He had changed into Western clothes, a pullover and corduroy trousers.

"I thought that could be our excuse, if we are discovered," he said, pointing his cigarette at the bright circle overhead. "I'd say I came to admire the moon and found you here, a fellow insomniac."

"What do you want to talk about, Second Brother?" I didn't have to pretend much to sound annoyed. "I'm pregnant and sleepy."

"Let's come straight to it then. I need to know where Hanchin has gone."

"How would I know?" I was startled by this question, and the surprise in my voice was genuine.

"You read the papers, Leiyin. You know he's on the run. He was hiding in Pinghu."

"In *this* backwater town?" I filled my words with doubt and scorn.

Tongyin nodded. "Yes, but by the time I realized it, he'd moved on. Where did he go?"

"Why are you asking me? The last time I had anything to do with Hanchin was when I lived at home."

His hand gripped the railing. "Are you still in love with him? Is that why you won't tell me?"

Feigned apathy was my best ally. "Second Brother, I'm married and a mother."

"Hanchin asked about you not so long ago, Third Sister, about where you lived. That's how I guessed he'd found his way here, to this town."

"Well, if he came here, it wasn't to see me." Facing away from the moonlight, it was easier to hide my true reaction.

"Hanchin was here, Third Sister." My brother's voice was low and urgent. "He needed someone he could count on, but who wasn't a known supporter of the Communist cause. A place to hide, someone to help him buy train tickets. I don't care what you did for him, just tell me where he is now."

"I don't know anything except for what I've read in the papers. And why are you mixed up in any of this anyway?" I snapped.

"I want to protect you, Third Sister. When they told me to get on Hanchin's trail, I realized he might be here because of you. But I never said anything to them about you. I let them assume he had other contacts here."

"Who is 'them'?" I asked, exasperated.

"The Nationalist secret police."

My breath stopped. "And how are you mixed up with them?"

He gripped my shoulders. His handsome features were taut, anxious.

"Father used to invite Hanchin to our home, so now our family's under suspicion. The Nationalists can make a case for us being Communist sympathizers. But I told Cha Zhiming I would find Hanchin. If I can help them find Hanchin, nothing happens to us. I'm protecting you. And our family."

He blinked rapidly. The liar.

I pulled away and sat down on a stone bench, mulling over Tongyin's words. I shook my head.

"If Cha Zhiming knew you were in Pinghu looking for Hanchin, his secret police would be here already. He has no idea what you're doing. You're up to something because you're the one who's in trouble, not me or our family."

He put his head in his hands. His shoulders drooped. It was several moments before he spoke again.

"You're the cleverest of us, Third Sister," he said wearily. "You're right. I'm the one who is in trouble. If I don't find Hanchin or at least help find him, Cha Zhiming might throw me to the secret police."

"I thought you were great friends with Cha?"

"I'm more than that. I spy for him." He lifted his head, defiant. A little proud.

I almost laughed. "Why you?"

"When Hanchin came back to Changchow, Zhiming asked me to . . . well, Hanchin and I renewed our friendship. Cha gave me money to invest in *China Millennium* to keep him working in Changchow. They kept the magazine in business, as bait to attract left-wing journalists and writers."

Hanchin had said nothing of this, had denied any recent connection with my brother. But he was just trying to protect me. The less I knew, the safer it was for me.

"Hanchin used my Shanghai apartment whenever he was there. That made it easier for us to keep an eye on him. Cha gave me false intelligence to pass on to Hanchin and I tried to pass information back."

"What went wrong?"

"Hanchin knew all along that I was working for Cha. The bits of information I found out were true, but always too late to be useful. Then Hanchin gave me false information that landed Cha Zhiming in a lot of trouble. Zhiming is furious. If he withdraws his protection . . ." He shuddered. I almost felt sorry for him.

"So to prove you're innocent, you have to find Hanchin and turn him in?"

"I thought I could keep him safe, Leiyin." His cigarette trembled, and he stabbed it out on the bench, lit another. "I persuaded Cha Zhiming he was more useful out of jail. But Hanchin used me."

He sat down beside me, an unhappy gleam in his eyes.

"He never would have married you, Third Sister. No, never. He didn't love you."

I shrugged, angered by my brother's attempt to shake my faith in Hanchin. He was just trying to goad me.

❧

I turn to my souls. *Hanchin didn't tell me very much about his life, did he?*

My *yang* soul scowls. *He seduced you, a married woman. That should have warned you he couldn't be trusted to tell you the whole truth.*

My *yin* soul says, a little doubtfully, *It was to protect you. The less you knew, the safer you were, remember?*

But look at Tongyin. We study my brother's face. He was truly afraid of being thrown in jail. My poor Second Brother.

There's something else too, my *hun* soul says.

I look again at Tongyin. His handsome face is strained, his eyes bleak. Even in moonlight, I can see worry lines around his mouth.

He's heartbroken, isn't he? He's been in love with Hanchin all this time.

My *hun* soul's voice is gentle and it slips its shining arm through mine. *And now, to save himself from arrest, your brother must betray his lover.*

No! They couldn't have been!

Oh, Leiyin, my *yin* soul says, equally gentle. *The hun soul is right. How could your brother have stayed in love with Hanchin for all these years without encouragement?*

◌⌒◌⌒◌

"Did Hanchin tell you about his wife?"

"You're lying!" The words leaped out of my throat, even as I realized that Tongyin would say anything to unsettle me.

"He's married, yes, he is. To a fellow Communist. They met while they were teaching together at a village school. She was his assistant."

"That's impossible!"

"They've been married five years. Not everyone knows because she travels so much. She sets up schools for the Party in its rural outposts. The love poems he wrote under the name Nobody Special were for her."

I could hardly breathe. Each heartbeat was a hammer blow of pain. My face burned with humiliation and I hoped the moonlight had washed all the color from my cheeks. I told myself Tongyin was desperate. He would say anything, tell any lie to confuse me, damage my trust in Hanchin.

"Little Sister, try to let go of your infatuation with a man who

only ever saw you as a harmless flirtation. Why protect him? I'm
your brother, your own family. Help me."

He sounded so gentle, so concerned. If I didn't know him so
well, I might have been convinced. Now that I knew what was
going on, I wasn't worried about Tongyin. If Cha Zhiming were
truly suspicious, my brother would be in jail already. Tongyin
always did have an inflated sense of drama.

"I don't know anything, Second Brother. I can't help you."

I left him sitting in the pavilion.

∽∽∾

Against my will, Tongyin's words pounded in my head all night,
cluttering my memories of Hanchin. The pavilion poem, his
regret about all the wasted years, his insistence that he couldn't
stop thinking about me from the moment we met. Those kisses,
the ardent lovemaking, the confidences about his childhood. He
simply couldn't have shared intimacies like that with another
woman. He was only reluctant to have me follow him because he
feared for my safety, I told myself.

By the time dim morning light seeped through the blinds, I
had regained a measure of calm. I pretended to be asleep when
Baizhen tiptoed into my room. He left without disturbing me and
I heard him outside the door.

"Play by yourself and don't disturb your mother, Weilan.
Grandfather and I are taking Second Uncle out for breakfast."

An hour later, I rose and got dressed. I had been caught off
guard last night and Tongyin knew I had seen Hanchin. But as

long as I claimed to be ignorant of his whereabouts, my brother couldn't push me into any further indiscretion.

Despite Baizhen's orders, Weilan came to find me. She'd made herself ill gorging on dessert the night before. I'd just finished feeding her a concoction of ginger and mint when Dali came to the nursery. She was puffing slightly, as though she'd been running, and her thin braid had come loose from its bun.

"The Mistress wants to see you in her room, Young Mistress. And she says to leave the little one behind."

"Don't worry, Weilan is on the chamber pot and isn't going anywhere. Where on earth is Little Ming?"

"She's with the Mistress." Dali looked apprehensive. "I'll look after the Little Miss."

When I arrived at Jia Po's chambers, she greeted me with a face like thunder. Despite the coolness of the autumn day, she was waving a sandalwood fan vigorously. Little Ming crouched in front of her, forehead touching the polished floorboards, shoulders heaving with sobs.

"Mother, what's the matter?"

Jia Po just pointed at the young woman. "This, this . . . all those nights she was away, she wasn't caring for a sick mother. She was with a man!"

Little Ming's words were choked with her tears. "Have mercy, Mistress, have mercy!"

From the look on my mother-in-law's face, she wasn't inclined to mercy just now.

"She's lived in this house since she was a girl. We've fed her and clothed her. And now she has a big belly, no husband, and no dowry!"

I sat down on one of Jia Po's beautiful rosewood chairs.

"Little Ming, how far along are you?"

She sniffed. "Nearly three months. Same as you."

Jia Po brought her folded fan down on the poor girl's head.

"How dare you compare yourself to my virtuous daughter-in-law! To the mother of my grandchildren!"

"Mother, please," I said, trying to bring calm to the room. "Little Ming, who's the father? Will he marry you?"

This brought more wailing and incoherent sobs from Little Ming. She shook her head.

"Is he a married man?" I asked, as gently as I could.

She wiped her eyes and nose with her sleeve.

"No, Young Mistress. He's not married."

"Then we need to find him and make him marry you."

"He's gone. Left town. He was the clerk at the Thousand Wisdoms Bookstore and he left town two months ago."

My heart stopped. I pushed away visions of Hanchin, naked, Little Ming arching her back beneath him. The giggling and fondling afterward.

"How did you get mixed up with a store clerk?" It took everything I had not to scream at her.

She fell forward into a crouch and began sobbing again.

"He was standing outside the bookshop talking to my brother, the one with the donkey cart. So I stopped to chat. He asked me if I wanted to hear him give a lecture that night. I went. It was so exciting the way he talked about politics."

Jia Po was even more furious now. "What! Politics too?"

She struck Little Ming again with her fan. If it had been in my hands I would have beaten Little Ming until it broke.

"I don't understand anything about politics, Mistress. I went because he was so handsome. I went to all his lectures. I'd meet him afterward. But only a few times."

"Did you think he'd marry you?" Jia Po was calming down now, even as I burned.

She burst into a fresh flood of tears. "No, Mistress. Never. I knew he was leaving because he asked me to buy his train tickets. I knew I couldn't matter to someone like him, not really."

I couldn't listen anymore. I could imagine all too well what had happened. Little Ming had been sport for Hanchin, a pretty distraction. And Hanchin had never actually said he loved me. He'd only said, in his bantering way, that I was irresistible. I was the one who had said we loved each other; he simply hadn't bothered contradicting me.

We were both fools, Little Ming and I. But she was a simple servant girl. I should have known better. A courier would come for the manifesto, but no one would come for me. Hanchin was on his way to the front lines, perhaps to his wife. He wrote his poetry for her, out of true love. Seducing me had been his duty, necessary to keep his document safe. A duty, and entertainment to while away his days in hiding.

"Well," said Jia Po, finally sitting down. "You're a stupid, stupid girl."

Little Ming nodded her head, her face wretched. The front of her green tunic was damp with tears. I could see Jia Po's anger fading, her affection for Little Ming reasserting itself. Jia Po put down her fan. "This isn't the first time a maid has given in to temptation, and unfortunately it won't be the last. Have your baby. But give it to your mother to raise. Or take it to an orphanage. In the meantime, keep working here. Go to your parents when you're too big to be useful. Come back after the baby's born."

"Oh, thank you, Mistress, thank you." Little Ming pressed her forehead to the ground.

"No." My voice was harsh. "She goes now."

They both looked at me.

"She's a slut and a liar. I won't have her around my daughter or in this house."

It was going to be difficult enough trying to forget Hanchin, but with Little Ming's growing belly to remind me of my humiliation, it would be intolerable. Both of us, carrying his child.

"Daughter—" Jia Po began in a soothing voice.

"No! I want this creature out!" I screamed, and Little Ming's sobs turned into terrified hiccups. My mother-in-law looked alarmed, and then frowned. I was the Young Mistress, pregnant with a son. My desires were paramount. Little Ming was only a maid.

~~∽∽~~

Little Ming left an hour later, back to live with parents she hardly knew. Old Kwan, Mrs. Kwan, and Dali peered at me, their judgment silent. Old Ming looked woeful and Jia Po regretful. But I didn't care.

I was waiting for Baizhen and Tongyin by the moon gate when they returned.

"Weilan's in bed with an upset stomach, Husband. Can you sit with her and let me spend a little time with my brother?"

Suspecting nothing, Baizhen went to the nursery to comfort Weilan.

The look on my face told Tongyin all he needed to know.

"He had train tickets, Second Brother. He was on his way to the front near Jiangxi. First Ningbo, then to Wenzhou. Wenzhou would have been his last destination before he tried to slip across the front lines. That's all I know."

I watched him leave through the moon gate, back to the main house. He didn't press me for more. He could tell I'd given him everything.

I refused dinner and stayed in bed for most of the next morning, consumed by anger and jealousy. What sort of woman had Hanchin married? My imagination conjured a paragon of intelligence and beauty. Someone sophisticated, with a university degree, perhaps an accomplished poet. A revolutionary. A woman who was everything I wasn't.

I'd become dull and domesticated, so starved for excitement I'd been heedless to common sense and willing to throw away my future for a man who was loyal only to his politics. At least I was the only witness to my sorry, sordid tale. So long as I kept it to myself, my humiliation would remain a secret. It was small comfort.

By the time I rose to get ready for lunch, Tongyin had left for the train station. In the afternoon, Baizhen took Weilan to the herbalist to buy some ginger candies to soothe her upset stomach. I pulled out the canvas bags I'd hidden in the wardrobe and returned our travel clothes to their drawers. I removed the plaid handkerchief from my pillowcase and folded it in the bottom of a trunk. It would remain there, a hidden reminder of a reckless, foolhardy time, silent admonishment of my poor judgment.

❧

Was there anything in Hanchin's behavior that should have warned me? I ask my souls. *Why didn't I see the signs?*

You didn't see because you wanted so badly to believe he loved you, as deeply as you loved him. My *yang* soul is being uncharacteristically kind. He turns away to look out at the garden, trying to conceal the expression on his face, but on my tongue there is dried kumquat.

He used you. There is saltpeter in the air, my *yin* soul's anger. She shakes out her pigtails and begins braiding them again. *He had it all planned.*

He despised me. And Tongyin. I see that now. To him we were just rich children prattling on about things we didn't understand or believe.

❧

I didn't think a person could live with such pain every hour of the day. Before my eyes opened in the morning, before I could even remember my name, I felt the nagging, dull pain in my chest. Some days I woke cold with anger at Hanchin's casual manipulation of my feelings. I was even upset on Tongyin's behalf. Were we nothing to him but a pack of playing cards? Angry or aching, my blood boiled with humiliation over my stupidity. Had it been love or obsession?

It took great effort to be amiable and I didn't always succeed, but everyone just assumed I was having a difficult pregnancy. No one commented on my melancholy state or my desire to be left alone. My family's genuine affection only made me feel worse about what I had done.

Had I actually planned to abandon my daughter, or take her away from a loving father? What sort of insanity had come over me? Had I really been willing to put my innocent child through such grief? Ready to devastate a kind, decent man like Baizhen, who in all these years had never raised his voice or hand to me?

I vowed to be a better wife, one who deserved a husband like Baizhen.What harm was there in letting everyone believe this baby was his? My adultery and its consequences would never come to light as long as Baizhen believed I had been faithful. And who was to say the baby wasn't his?

But I had had my revenge, I reminded myself. I had betrayed Hanchin. He would be caught and jailed.

こうのか

Baizhen and I went to the theater to see the latest Chen Dai romance. Sueyin was famous now for playing tragic heroines in costume dramas. Her fans didn't want her in cheerful musical roles or comic romps; they wanted to see her face, a single tear coursing down her perfect cheekbone, her mournful gaze as it lingered on a departing lover. The magazines reported Lianhua Studios was planning a Chinese version of *Anna Karenina*, starring Chen Dai as Anna.

Jia Po and I inspected the estate, shaking our heads at the state of the shutters and woodwork, once so beautiful. The stairs creaked, and many of the railings suffered from dry rot. Weeds had taken over the courtyards and the fruit trees needed pruning. Tiles had come loose from the roof of the main house.

"We will send for Old Fong just before spring planting to clean up the gardens," Jia Po said. "It will give him some extra cash to buy seeds for his crop."

"Will you speak to Gong Gong about hiring a carpenter?" I asked. The houses needed repairs that couldn't be delayed any longer. "It's not safe. I'm always telling Weilan not to lean against the railings and banisters; I'm so afraid she'll fall."

"Yes, we've put off calling in a carpenter for too long. Let's do it in the spring."

⤳⤳

It was January, but the afternoon was warm enough that I couldn't resist settling on the second-floor veranda to read. Baizhen put soft cushions on the wicker seats and filled the enamel bowl on the table with dried fruit.

My heart was still torn between sorrow and anger, but I resolved to forget Hanchin. I was only three months away from my due date, larger and more awkward than I'd been during my first pregnancy. A boy would bring great happiness to Baizhen, and this mattered very much to me now. I longed to hold a newborn in my arms again, to show Weilan the wondrous perfection of tiny hands and feet. I only hoped the baby wouldn't resemble Hanchin.

Baizhen came up to my library to deliver the *Central Daily News*. It was three days old: the mail from Shanghai arrived erratically these days.

"Let's read this out on the veranda," I said to Baizhen. "Natural light is so much better for the eyes. Let me make some tea, and then come sit with me. Dali just brought in a kettle of boiled water."

Baizhen waved me aside, indicating he would prepare the tea.

"Sit and read, Wife. Will you be cold?"

"I'll put on a warm vest. Where's Weilan?"

"Mother has gone to visit Old Lady Bao and took Weilan with her. She says our daughter needs to practice good manners." He chuckled and went in to make the tea.

I unfolded the newspaper and scanned the front page. The news was depressingly similar day after day, transcripts of speeches by Generalissimo Chiang, the latest glib pronouncements from the Americans and British about their solid support for the Nationalists.

On the second page, I saw his name:

It has been confirmed that Yen Hanchin, Communist agent and agitator, Russian scholar, journalist, and poet, was executed by firing squad on January 5, 1935, in Ningbo. He had been in custody for several months, but under a false identity. A witness who knew him came forward and

Yen confessed his real name. He was given the opportunity to renounce the Communist cause, but refused.

I sprang to my feet with a cry. I never thought Hanchin would be executed, only jailed. Baizhen came running when he heard me call out, but before he could reach my side, I collapsed against the veranda railing.

Fifty years of dry rot and neglect gave way beneath my weight. My body fell through the air.

Below, the gray stones of the courtyard.

Part Three

Pinghu, 1935

Stop now. Please. No more, I say to my souls. *I need to walk.*
I was desperate to get away from the frantic efforts to save
my life, the murmured exchanges between the village doctor
and the midwife, their ministrations over my still, unresponsive
form. To get away from the sight of blood, the glimpse of an infant
whose souls winked away the moment he came into this world.
Away from Baizhen's grief; Weilan's small, shocked face; Jia Po
keening in the corner over a tiny bundle. *My son is dead. He was
my guilty secret, but he would have brought us such joy.*

My souls trail behind as I leave the temple. Moonlight passes
through us and casts no shadows. We enter the bamboo grove,
where stiff green leaves flutter in a light wind that bends their tall,
hollow stalks. I climb the few steps up to the pavilion while my
hun soul makes a slow circuit around it before coming to rest on a
bench. My *yin* soul joins it and turns her face up to the moon. My
yang soul sits across from them, leaning forward with his hands
folded on his cane.

So there were two deaths. The baby's and mine. But where is he now, my child? Why isn't my son here with me?

My *hun* soul gestures upward. *Your child was blameless. His souls went immediately into the afterlife. Perhaps he's been reincarnated already.*

Those tiny feet. The sweet scent of clean baby skin. Gone. I would never know them. I feel the sensation of tears but when my fingers brush my face, there is nothing.

All my memories are back and I still don't understand. How is Hanchin the reason I'm trapped on this earth?

Isn't it obvious? Hanchin died because you betrayed him, my *yang* soul says, and there is a sharp taste of tamarind on the tip of my tongue. *You told Tongyin how to track him down. You must make amends for his death before we can ascend to the afterlife.*

But Tongyin also betrayed him. Doesn't he share the guilt?

Tongyin will atone for his sins when it's his time. Right now it's yours. My *hun* soul pats me on the arm but I move away, my mind still rippling.

But how am I supposed to make amends?

There is silence.

We don't know, my *yin* soul admits. Her young face is anxious and there is an odor of mildew and old books. *It's up to you to find out. We're all counting on you, Leiyin.*

19

I'm not a ghost, at least not the sort people notice. I call out greetings when Dali sweeps the temple floors each morning, but she just continues with her broom, paying more attention to cobwebs than she does to me. I can find no way to reveal my presence: not through the creaking of ancient door hinges, not in cold breezes that raise goose bumps on her arm and lift the fine hairs at the nape of her neck.

How can I atone for Hanchin's death when I can't even make myself heard, or seen, or felt? When I don't even know what the gods consider proper penance?

When I was alive, I had been slightly nearsighted. Now when I gaze at the ginkgo tree, its leaves are sharp outlines against the sky. Each feather on a flycatcher's wing glistens blue as it skims past. Even from inside the temple I can hear the daily rituals of town life: washerwomen scrubbing clothes on the banks of the canal, water lapping as flat-bottomed boats are poled on their way along the banks, cries of greeting and gossip. And the scents. The fragrance of early-blooming clematis in the next courtyard fills my nostrils as though I'm standing beneath its rustling vines. The smell of garlic wafting over from the kitchen is so strong I can taste it.

I worry about Weilan. She sits by herself in what was my library, copying characters into her exercise book: *Mother. Mother. Mother.* Over and over. And in the margins: *Please come back.* She is like a small ghost herself, silent and pale. She hardly eats. At night, Jia Po lets Weilan sleep in her room. She comforts my daughter whenever she wakes up crying in the big bed.

"Mama, I want Mama!"

"Po Po is here, my precious, Po Po is here."

"No, no! I want my mama!"

I can't bear to be in the room when Weilan cries. She's so unhappy and I'm so helpless. But even if I hide myself in the farthest corners of the estate, I can still hear her heart-rending wails.

❧

Weeks go by and there comes a morning that begins with weeping and harsh words, a quarrel between my in-laws. Curiosity pulls me away from the temple and to the main house, where Mrs. Kwan dawdles by the door and Dali is sweeping steps that are already clean. Old Kwan and Old Ming loiter in the main courtyard, within earshot of the house.

"It's your fault she's dead, our daughter-in-law, and the grandson she was carrying!"

"Be reasonable, Wife." I can tell Gong Gong is nonplussed, and so am I. Jia Po has never raised her voice to him.

"I've been reasonable for thirty years! I've been reasonable while you frittered away my dowry on monuments to your dead ancestors. Reasonable when you couldn't spare a thought for the living!"

"It was an accident—" he protests.

"It was your negligence! That railing broke because it should have been replaced ten years ago, no, twenty years ago! Instead you wasted a fortune on books and snuff bottles, on useless, useless things!"

More shouting, and a door slams. Heavy footsteps sound on the staircase, and the servants scatter as Gong Gong storms out the door, Baizhen at his heels. My husband looks embarrassed more than anxious.

"Son, pack me a suitcase and send it to the Eight Willows Guest House. Ming! Old Ming! Call me a rickshaw! At once!"

✿

"*Wah, wah*, I've never heard the Mistress shout at the Master." The day after the excitement, Old Ming is comparing notes with Mrs. Kwan and Dali. "No wonder he refuses to come home, he's never been treated this way before."

"You say the Master's hired your son to fix up the cottage on Infant Mountain?" Dali asks. "If the Master moves to the cottage, will they divorce?"

Mrs. Kwan says in disdain, "They're not Shanghai society, Dali. They're too old for such nonsense. When will the Master move into the cottage, Ming?"

"In a few weeks, as soon as it's ready," says Old Ming, stroking his goatee. "My sixth grandson has agreed to live there with the Master, to do his cooking and housekeeping."

"Hmmm." Mrs. Kwan sounds doubtful. "Tell your sixth grandson to stop by whenever he's in town. Old Kwan will cook up a few of the Master's favorites for him."

Dali picks up her basket and sets out for the market, ready to share her new stock of gossip. In a few hours all Pinghu will know that the patriarch of the Lee family has fallen out with his wife and moved out of the family home.

While Old Ming's son works on the cottage, Gong Gong shuttles between the Eight Willows Guest House and our home on a daily basis. Sometimes it's to fetch an extra pair of trousers, or because he has letters to write. Sometimes he slips a few of his antique books in a satchel to take away. When he passes Jia Po in the courtyard, he speaks to her courteously, hope barely disguised on his face. But she remains cold to him. She spends her days in her room and emerges one afternoon with a stack of letters for Old Ming to post. They're addressed to members of her family in far-off Hunan.

Baizhen pleads with his mother to reconcile with Gong Gong.

"It looks bad for the family if you and Father live apart. What will people think?"

"Let your father worry about what people think. He cares more about keeping up appearances than our family's welfare." Her words are tinged with bitterness.

"Mother, you can't blame him for everything," Baizhen says, trying to reason with her.

"He thinks only of himself!" she snaps. "Do you know what

it's costing to fix up that cottage? We can barely feed ourselves
and now we have to maintain two households."

"Father said he's sold more of his books."

"He spent a fortune on those books! But not on your education, so that you could earn a living. He should have found you a
better tutor, sent you to boarding school. Look how quickly you
learned to read and write after Leiyin arrived." She bursts into
tears. "My beautiful, clever daughter-in-law. My grandson!"

"Ma, please, Weilan will hear us."

Baizhen cries every night too. I wish he loved me less.

⌒⌒⌒

Do I need to atone for being unfaithful to my husband?

I don't think so, my yin soul says, pushing back her bangs.
*Baizhen never knew about your affair. There was no actual harm
to his life from that.*

Oh, what's the use in speculating on how I can do penance? I
kick at a pebble, but it doesn't move. *I thought ghosts had powers. I
can't haunt the living, let alone find out how to atone for Hanchin's
death. Can't you tell me what to do?*

We would, but we don't know, says my yang soul. *We truly
don't. And it's extremely important for all of us that you find a way
to ascend to the afterlife.* He sounds glum, and a peppery tang
lingers on my tongue.

Test the limits of your existence, my hun soul advises. *Explore.
There is a way, we do know that much. Perhaps more than one way.*

Don't forget your father, my yang soul reminds me. *You wanted
to get to the afterlife to apologize to him.*

Yes, but what if I don't want to ascend to the afterlife? I know I sound childish and petulant. *If I stay here, I can watch over Weilan.*

There is a collective intake of breath, if such a thing is possible from souls.

There will be times when reincarnation seems less important than staying on this earth, my *hun* soul says, its words careful and deliberate. *But as the weeks and months go by, you'll feel the pull of that golden light and you'll find that it grows stronger, more insistent.*

If you don't find a way to ascend, says my *yin* soul, her girlish voice edged with panic, *you'll feel as though you're being pulled apart.*

Pulled toward the portal, but weighted down to this earth, says my *yang* soul. *We'll feel it too. We'll begin to fade. And then you'll become a hungry ghost. Insane. Doomed to roam this earth without the comfort of your souls.*

His words reverberate in my head like a gong, shattering and painful. I retreat into the temple and refuse to speak. I shut out the world. It's too much.

❧

Several weeks after Gong Gong's stormy departure from the estate, Baizhen makes an early morning visit to the shrine. Today his clumsy hands are even less certain than usual. They flutter and fuss over a plate of steamed buns, a tidy pyramid of preserved kumquats arranged next to them. It is all on one of my Limoges platters. He lights twice the normal number of incense sticks. He weeps as I haven't seen him weep since the first days after my funeral, then he stands up and wipes his eyes. When he pushes the temple door open, he draws a deep breath, then squares his shoulders to step outside.

The incense has just burned down when Gong Gong and Jia Po arrive together, carrying more food and incense. Are they reconciled?

Jia Po sweeps the fine ash off the altar with a hand broom while Gong Gong gets out a feather duster and flicks it over the carved wooden tablets. They bow before the ancestral portraits on the wall. Then they stand before my name tablet, light fresh incense sticks, and bow deeply. Three times.

How can they not hear my shocked gasp? They're my elders. They're not supposed to be venerating me. Why do they feel the need to placate the spirit of a daughter-in-law, one who didn't even give them a grandson?

"Daughter-in-Law, our son's first wife, give us your understanding and blessings," Jia Po murmurs. "Forgive us, we couldn't wait. It's for the good of the family."

Wait for what? I must find out.

I follow them outside into the pale sunshine of early spring. The flowering plums are just showing their buds and they fill the courtyard with the thinnest haze of green and white.

"How many for dinner tonight?" Gong Gong asks, his breath visible in the cold air.

"Thirty-six, including children," Jia Po replies in a neutral tone. "Just family and our closest friends."

He looks at her wistfully. "Do you remember when Baizhen was born? We had a feast for two hundred in the large hall and gave gifts of tea and silk to everyone."

"I must go see Old Kwan." Jia Po's voice is curt. Not reconciled then.

∽∾∾

I've been dead for two months and now it seems there's some cause for celebration. I follow my mother-in-law through the courtyards and the reception hall. Only a few months ago I had been the one making the rounds, helping to manage the household, going through the accounts, deciding how to economize on food and clothing.

The reception hall is decorated with branches of flowering plum, arranged in tall celadon vases on rosewood stands. It strikes me as a nice way to bring some freshness inside, but I pause when I realize the exquisite paintings that once graced the niches where the vases sit are gone. The fresh-cut blossoms are there to fill the gaps.

The doorways of the large dining hall are swathed in red fabric. Red-and-gold lanterns hang from ceiling beams, red draperies wrap the wooden pillars. Everywhere, red.

Red is for weddings.

Another wife, another dowry. Another chance for an heir.

There's no other explanation for Baizhen's tears or my in-laws' behavior. He's getting remarried before the customary one hundred days of mourning are complete. For a good dowry, they're willing to risk my wrath and the wrath of their ancestors.

And why not? There's not much risk in angering me now. I'm as dead as any of their ancestors and I lack the power to damn or bless anyone. Only the living can inflict suffering on each other, I've learned.

My daughter will have a stepmother. I suppress a pang of fear.

I hurry after Jia Po and find her in the kitchen giving instructions to Old Kwan and Mrs. Kwan.

"When you serve the chicken and duck, cut them into small pieces that are easy to pick up," Jia Po says. "And slice the ham very thin, we must have enough for three platters."

She walks out of the kitchen, her back straight.

"One hundred days of mourning less forty." Mrs. Kwan counts out loud. "I wonder how much they had to give the fortune-teller to tell them this was the most auspicious date for a wedding, mourning or not."

"Probably less than they gave to the Temple of Soul's Enlightenment to hurry along the Young Mistress's reincarnation." Old Kwan snorts. "Those priests will promise anything for a fat donation, you know, but if it makes the Master and Mistress feel better about cutting short the mourning period, why not."

Whatever they paid the priests to do, it hasn't worked. I'm still here, not yet even in the true afterlife, and nowhere close to reincarnation.

In what was my house, Gong Gong and Jia Po are gathered in Baizhen's room. He stands before the wardrobe mirror, buttoning a fur-lined vest over a gown of black silk brocade. His cloth shoes are new, his black silk cap topped with a jade bead. I've never seen these clothes before. The sleeves hang nearly to his knuckles, so I guess they are from Gong Gong's wardrobe. After

Baizhen finishes with his vest, Jia Po adjusts his round cap. He sits down on a chair and grips the ends of the armrests. He stares straight ahead, avoiding his parents' eyes. No one speaks.

Dali comes in, holding Weilan by the hand. My daughter is wearing pink, a flowered tunic and matching trousers, pink ribbons tied to her pigtails. I remember buying the fabric. Jia Po must have sewn the clothes for her.

Weilan runs straight to Baizhen, who lifts her onto his lap. She buries her face in his chest and begins to cry, her silent tears absorbed by the black silk. Jia Po opens her mouth to protest, then stops.

I watch from the veranda as my in-laws leave through the courtyard. At the moon gate, Jia Po pauses to look back at Gong Gong, her voice cold once more.

"My brother has found a family willing to marry their daughter to our unlucky son. This dowry will get us through the next ten years if we're careful. If you squander it, we'll have to sell off this estate. Our son and grandchildren will end up living in the servants' quarters, if not on the streets."

"You didn't need to remind me again, Wife," Gong Gong says peevishly. "We will buy only necessities from now on. But don't forget we still have an income from Old Fong." This was the tenant farmer.

"That income is so insignificant we may as well sell the land—if anyone wants to buy that rocky plot of dirt."

"Old Fong and his family have worked that farm for generations," my father-in-law says. "I'm responsible for them. What would they do?"

"They'd find another farm. You just don't want to sell it because then you won't be able to call yourself a landowner any-more. What vanity."

No, it doesn't appear as though they've reconciled.

⌒⌒⌒

The bride is the eldest daughter of a family that owns a distillery. She's young, of course, and as short and squat as a jar of cook-ing wine. The family is from Haiyang, a seaside town south of Pinghu, not too far away. They're in awe of the Lee family's lin-eage, impressed by their supposed connections in Shanghai, and eager to please Jia Po's oldest brother, a long-time customer who has recently invested in their distillery.

Her name is Meichiu. Autumn Beauty. It's an unfortunate name, because it draws attention to attributes she will never pos-sess. Beneath her red veil, I see a moon face and heavy brows. My daughter will address this woman as Stepmother, and my in-laws will treat her with as much respect as her dowry and a potential future inheritance command.

Meichiu's father brings all his children and both his wives to the wedding. The bride's two brothers and four sisters resemble their father, square and solid. While Meichiu's mother fusses over her in a dressing room, her siblings swarm through the estate, marveling at the mansion's fine architectural details, the rocks in the garden, the courtyard walls, and the graceful moon gates. They're cheerful and uncritical, boisterous as schoolchildren. A flock of relatives follows behind them, uncles and aunts, cousins, and a deaf grandmother. They flit through the courtyards like brightly colored parrots, filling the air with cries of discovery.

"Look at this wonderful rock shaped like a bear!"

"Read the name on this pavilion: *Reflections of the New Moon*. How beautiful!"

"Oh, look, this must be the house where Meichiu will live, two levels with verandas. Don't you wish we had verandas?"

My family hadn't behaved like this during my wedding. Meichiu's family is exuberant and joyous, completely unself-conscious.

During the banquet, one of Meichiu's uncles indulges too liberally in the family product and explains that the bride's child-hood nickname had been *Shao Chiu*, Little Autumn.

"But it also sounds like Little Ball," he slurs, "so this was what we called her because she was a little ball of a child. A round head on top of a chubby round body."

I feel sorry for Meichiu. Her family's laughter is affectionate, but I see embarrassment radiating from her, her cheeks nearly as red as the veil over her face.

After lunch, the guests file out of the dining hall and into the forecourt. Out on the street, hired rickshaws and donkey carts wait to carry the bride's family to the train station for the journey home. It's been an abbreviated celebration, because the bride's family must return to their home and business.

During the farewell rituals, the bride weeps sincerely, tears streaking her heavy rice-powder makeup. She falls on the slate flagstones and wraps her arms around her mother's knees. Then she shuffles over to her father, who pats her on the head. The winemaker gives Baizhen's thin shoulder blades a jovial thump.

"Son-in-law, I'll bring more wine on our next visit. On the occasion of Meichiu's first pregnancy."

Baizhen lowers his head and smiles uneasily.

Relatives circle Meichiu for a final round of embraces, words of farewell, and promises to write every week. They depart in a flurry of waving hands. Then out on Jade Belt Road, it is quiet once more.

༄༅

My house has a fresh coat of paint. The railings on the veranda and along the staircase are new. My bedchamber is almost bare of furniture: only an old trunk and an armoire remain. Some of my dowry furniture is in Meichiu's bedroom, a small chamber that is nonetheless infinitely preferable to the one where I died. Weilan is out of the nursery now, her little bed moved to one of the second-floor rooms.

The bride spends the rest of the afternoon in her bedroom. With Dali's help she changes out of her wedding finery, then sits on the bed while Dali unpacks her trunk.

"I'm your house servant and also part-time nanny to your stepdaughter," Dali says, folding clothes into drawers. I can tell the servant is trying not to be too obvious about running her hand over the clothing to judge its quality. "Young Mistress will like Weilan, she's very bright. She can read already."

Meichiu doesn't reply.

"The Mistress will show you the whole estate tomorrow. You'll find this house very comfortable, Young Mistress. It's the newest one on the property. There's even a small library upstairs."

Meichiu stands up. "Where's the toilet?"

She hasn't spoken in a normal voice before; I've only heard

murmured replies and teary farewells. Beneath her weary tone, there's a no-nonsense quality to her voice.

The wedding day ends with a light supper. Jia Po serves the newlyweds a soup of dates and lotus seeds. After they spoon up the hot, sweet liquid, Baizhen and Meichiu bow to Jia Po and Gong Gong. Then Meichiu follows Baizhen through the court-yard and up the shallow steps to the lower floor of the house.

I don't follow. I return to the temple, welcoming the dim si-lence. But my sharpened hearing still detects a quick, stifled cry followed by a low moan.

ᴄᴏᴄᴏ

The next morning, Jia Po takes the bride on a tour of the estate, through the courtyards, each of the houses, and the kitchen. It seems only a few short years ago that I went on this same walk, as apprehensive as Meichiu. I see what Meichiu must be seeing, water stains seeping down the walls, shutters that need replacing, unmistakable signs of encroaching poverty. I find myself hoping she can look past the shabbiness and appreciate the estate's ele-gant proportions and thoughtful design. When she's lived here longer she'll see how the bamboos in the courtyard sway in the slightest breeze to make a hot day cooler, how the deep veranda roof provides comfortable shelter from the summer rains. How the lazy afternoon light shimmers over the rock garden, washing the tall stones with gold.

Meichiu quickly settles into the daily routine. She helps with housework, tidying the main house and sweeping cobwebs from the ceilings. She's much stricter with Dali than I used to be, for I had known nothing about proper housekeeping.

"The new Young Mistress is very particular," says Dali to Mrs. Kwan with grudging approval. "And she's not above doing some of the work herself."

"Our first Young Mistress was far too well-bred," says Mrs. Kwan. "Too much education, all of it the wrong sort for a small household."

Meichiu is deferential to Jia Po and shows her respect in ways that had never occurred to me: blowing on the surface of a hot cup of tea before serving it, kneeling to rub the old woman's feet at the end of a long day.

And I can't complain about how Meichiu treats Weilan. She doesn't go out of her way to make a fuss over my daughter, but neither is she unkind. It's as much as anyone could expect. Weilan avoids her stepmother, but I can't tell whether it's out of hostility or shyness.

ᷛᷓ᷒᷍

Jia Po says there's only enough dowry money for another ten years. How is everyone supposed to eat after that? I must find a way to tell Baizhen to contact Eldest Brother about my inheritance. Why hasn't he written to Changyin?

He's probably waiting until the situation gets desperate, my *yin* soul says. *He's respecting your wishes.*

Find a way to talk to your husband, then. But stop wasting time, says my *yang* soul. He stands at the center of the pavilion, his hands joined inside the cuffs of his jacket. He seems older and frailer somehow.

It's more important to find a way to make amends, says my *hun* soul.

I'd rather find a way to talk to Baizhen, I snap. *The most important thing is to ensure he makes good decisions for my daughter. There's plenty of time for making amends, however I'm supposed to accomplish that.*

My *yin* soul looks distressed and dried lemongrass fills the air. *I don't know exactly how much time you have, but it's probably less than you think.*

I think, my *hun* soul says, *that if you manage to communicate with the living, it will lead you to an understanding of how to make amends.*

20

*I*t's becoming clear that I can't deny the pull of the afterlife, an elusive tugging so subtle it could be my imagination. But each day it grows stronger, the sensation of being stretched, each tendon of my ghost body elongated to the point of mild discomfort. At night, when the household is asleep and nothing distracts me, I am restless. I roam through the estate haunting family and servants alike, avoiding Meichiu's room if Baizhen is there.

Watching Weilan sleep calms me. I can fall into a peaceful state when I'm beside her and feel as though I'm about to doze off myself, my mind passive, wandering pleasantly toward a void. The afterlife's pull recedes when I'm with her, waiting for her eyelashes to still and her breathing to grow soft and regular.

"Small Bird," I whisper. "Sesame Seed. My Only Heart."

One day, Baizhen takes Weilan to the market square to see a troupe of traveling acrobats. This is the first time since my death that Weilan has gone out with her father, and she fairly skips along. They return just before suppertime, Weilan so tired and excited she can't finish her meal. She chatters away while Dali bathes her in the wooden tub, washing the sticky remnants of candy and fruit juice from her small hands.

"There were acrobats, Dali, six of them." She squints as she submits her small face to the soapy washcloth. "They climbed up on each other's shoulders until they were a tower, three, then two, then the last one on top."

"Close your eyes again, I'm going to pour water on your face."

Weilan does as she's told. "And there was a girl, about my age, she was so pretty. She was all in blue, a beautiful tunic and trousers, with pink ribbons in her hair. She climbed up and stood on the shoulders of the man at the top. Everyone was clapping and cheering."

She sighs with happiness. Once she's out of the tub and tucked into her blankets, she's asleep before Dali even shuts the door.

The full moon shines through the window, its cold radiance softened by rice-paper shades. I sit beside Weilan, ready to settle down for the night. Something causes me to blink once, and then once more. Surrounding Weilan's little head is a second, hazy outline against the pillow. This, I think, is a trick of the moonlight. Or my vision has blurred in this drowsy state.

Then my *hun* soul prods me.

Look, it says, pointing, and I do. The bed casts no second silhouette, nor does the wardrobe, which stands in sharp focus against the far wall.

That outline, that second silhouette, is only around Weilan's head, my *yin* soul exclaims. She is excited, hopping from foot to foot, her pigtails bouncing.

Take a closer look, my *yang* soul urges, almost as excited.

Tentatively, I reach out to touch the blurry shape above Weilan's head, expecting my hand to pass through it, as it does with all things in the earthly world. Instead, my fingers make contact with the edge of the shape. It's as insubstantial as a fine silk thread, but it's there and I can feel it.

Startled, I snatch my hand away, but the edge of the shape clings to my fingers, sticky as a cobweb. As I draw back from the bed, the edge remains attached to my hand, stretching out the shape above Weilan's head as I pull away. Its hazy outline balloons into a shimmering oval that hangs in the air just above the ground. Shadows move across the oval, figures from the other side.

My souls murmur in wonder, in hope.

Is this another portal to the afterlife? my *yin* soul asks, eager but fearful. A scent like fermented rice.

It can't be. You haven't made amends yet, says my *yang* soul. This gives us pause.

What's the worst that could happen? I say, finally. *I'm already dead.*

And I step through the shimmering oval.

Immediately, a hollow sensation in the pit of my stomach tells me my souls haven't followed. I'm alone, but I must go on.

⌘

The scene before me is disappointingly familiar. It's the courtyard of our house, the rock garden at one end, the bamboo grove shading the other, the moon gate separating our garden from the main courtyard. I hear giggling from the bamboo grove and turn to see three children race out toward the rock garden, Weilan in the lead.

I recognize the other two, a boy and a girl, both in rags. For a while they had wandered about on Jade Belt Road. It troubled Weilan's tender heart to see them. Once I gave her a coin to offer to the little girl. The child had snatched it away and put it in her mouth, her face hostile. After a few months, we no longer saw the two little beggars, but we never knew what had become of them.

What are they doing in our garden? What kind of place is this?

An instant later Weilan stands on the path among the rocks, and the urchins are gone. Baizhen is beside her now. I call out, but they neither hear nor see me. He takes her hand and together they drift, rather than walk, through the moon gate. I hurry to follow.

Beyond the moon gate is a busy street that resembles Minor Street, but not quite. The trees are taller, the canal wider, the ancient arched bridges steeper. Baizhen and Weilan cross the canal. Colored paper lanterns hang from the sycamore trees and a festive feeling is in the air. The street is busy with pedestrians but when I look closely I cannot recognize any of them: their faces are blurs.

We enter the market square to the shouts of stall keepers and the nasal, high-pitched wailing of the folk-opera singers. Baizhen pushes his way through a crowd gathered around a small outdoor stage. Acrobats in bright blue tunics, lithe and muscular, walk through the air as though balanced on invisible stair treads.

This is no afterlife. I'm in Weilan's dream.

Three muscular male acrobats lock arms and stand as immovable as blocks of granite while two others leap up onto their shoulders. One more man climbs to the top of the pyramid. Then a little girl dances her way up to stand on his shoulders. It's Weilan. She smiles and waves to the crowd, the sequins on her blue tunic winking back sunlight.

Then she leaps off the pyramid and swims through the air toward her father, wafting down as gently as a leaf to settle in his arms. She laughs at his delight and her own prowess.

"How did you learn to do that, Little One?" he exclaims.

"Oh, I've been practicing with the acrobats," she says, nonchalant but proud.

"I wish your mother could've seen you."

Immediately, Weilan's face loses its animation.

A misty figure at the edge of the crowd catches my eye, coming into focus as it walks toward my daughter. As it draws closer, I realize it looks like me. It's even wearing my favorite green velvet skirt. My daughter has conjured me in her sleep.

"But she did see me!" Weilan cries out, running toward the figure. "Mama, were you watching?"

Without hesitation, I step into my dream image. My body tingles, stings, and suddenly the uneven paving stones of the market square are beneath my feet, my shoulders bumping against other people as I push through the crowd. The tingling stops and I kneel down to throw my arms around my daughter. Finally I can hug Weilan's small body. I nearly weep with joy at the softness of her cheek against mine, knowing that she can feel my arms around her thin shoulders. She presses against me, squirming with delight.

"Oh, Mama! I knew you would come back to me!"

But her emotions are so intense, her happiness so powerful, the flimsy threads enclosing her dream snap apart.

She wakes up.

I am jolted out of the dream and find myself back in Weilan's bedroom, still kneeling on the floor, arms outstretched.

Weilan jumps out of bed, and then runs out the door into the gray morning light. She sprints to the little library, calling for me. She runs along the veranda and down the stairs screaming, "Mama! Mama!" as she pushes through the door of my empty bedroom.

Baizhen stumbles out of Meichiu's room, groggy and alarmed.

"Little One, what is it? Why are you out of bed?"

"It's Mama! She's back! I saw her!" Weilan runs toward the main courtyard.

In no time at all, she's woken up the entire household. She calls for me and looks in the kitchen, the reception hall, her grandfather's study. She's hysterical when Baizhen catches up with her.

"Where's Mama?" she sobs into his shoulder. "Where is she?"

"Mama's gone, Small Bird. She's not here."

"No! No!" Her shrieks pierce my heart. "She was here with us just now, watching me perform with the acrobats!"

"You were dreaming," he says, lifting her off the cold floor. "I dream about her too, but it's not real."

"No! She was real. I could feel her!" She beats her fists in frustration against Baizhen's chest as he carries her back toward the main courtyard.

"What's going on? Baizhen, why is your daughter screaming?" Jia Po comes out of her house, a blanket draped over her shoulders, gray hair in a loose braid.

"She had a bad dream, Mother."

"It wasn't a dream!" My daughter's face reddens in frustration. "Mama came back. I saw her."

Jia Po's papery skin turns slightly paler.

"Baizhen, take her back to bed. I'll send Mrs. Kwan over with date syrup to calm her nerves. She must make offerings to her mother later."

ᑦᐧᑌᐧᑏ

When I was alive, my dreams were so vivid they remained with me for days. In one of my dreams about Hanchin, we were together at a train station; he was dressed in a tweed suit and a heavy coat. He pulled me into his arms as snow fell around us, a Russian winter. He smelled of sandalwood. It felt so real. I woke up wildly happy, believing the dream was a message, a premonition, before common sense intervened.

But common sense isn't always much help for a little girl who has lost her mother. My actions were thoughtless; her grief had been renewed, as fresh now as it was on the day of my burial.

Just before supper that day, Baizhen takes Weilan to the family temple. They light incense in front of my name tablet and fill a dish with dried red plums. Weilan appears calm. Only the reddened rims of her eyes betray the turmoil of emotion she's lived through today.

ᑦᐧᑌᐧᑏ

I'll never interfere with her dreams again, never even enter them. It's better for her to forget all about me than to spend any more of her childhood grieving.

The real question is, of what use is this ability to enter others' dreams? Something spicy scorches my lips. My *yang* soul is excited by this development. They all are. They circle, red sparks like fireflies dancing around the altar.

You must find out more, says my *yin* soul. *Can you enter anyone's dreams? Can you make yourself seen and heard in any dream?*

I'm not barging into anyone else's dreams. Look what happened with Weilan, the damage I caused.

It seems to me that until you enter a dream-person, you have no effect at all, my *hun* soul says thoughtfully.

You must try again, urges my *yin* soul. *Not Weilan's dreams. But there must be a reason ghosts can enter dreams.* A scent like peppercorns. Or white freesias.

⌒⌒⌒

The next night, I go into the servants' quarters, an area I rarely entered while living. Two long brick buildings face each other across a wide stone walkway. The buildings are separated from the kitchen by a courtyard, where Old Kwan grows vegetables and the ginger, garlic, and green onions a cook always needs. The area is ruled by an ancient rooster, and a dozen hens peck assiduously at the ground, looking for insects between the newly planted rows.

Old Kwan had told me that when Baizhen's grandfather was still alive, fourteen servants had lived in these quarters. Now only one of the buildings is in use, and its roof sags so much the two middle rooms are open to wind and rain. Old Kwan and Mrs. Kwan live in the two best rooms, closest to the courtyard, using one as a bedroom and the other as a sitting room. Dali occupies a single chamber at the far end. The second building contains a jumble of broken pottery and some old furniture, meant to be repaired someday but more likely to end up chopped for firewood.

Dali's bed is made of carved elm. Once a finely crafted piece of furniture, it has lost its legs and now rests on a low platform of bricks. A cheap mirror lies facedown on a table by the window, along with a wooden comb, a jar of cold cream, and a dish of hairpins.

Dali combs out her hair before braiding it again loosely. She hums "Purple Bamboo Melody" off-key, rubbing cold cream on her face until it's covered in an oily sheen. Still humming, she lies down and stretches her legs under the covers until her feet touch the hot, flannel-covered brick stowed underneath. With a sigh of contentment she shuts her eyes.

We wait, my souls and I.

Dali snores with a stuttering snuffle. This time, knowing what to look for, I watch a soft dim shape form over her head. My fingers reach to touch it, but I can feel nothing. Disappointed, I pull back.

Wait, my *hun* soul advises. *Wait a bit.*

Dali's snoring grows regular, and I can hear a slight whining each time she exhales. The silhouette grows more defined, its edges like light shining from under a door. This time when I reach toward it, my ghost fingers touch its edge and it clings to me. I pull at it carefully, as though lifting a delicate curtain. As I step away from Dali, the shape balloons out. I glance back to see my souls peering anxiously at the portal as I step through and into Dali's dream.

I'm in a theater and onstage is Dali, in bright satin robes and face paint. She stands opposite a tall, handsome actor, on a floor painted with a river of clouds. It's the tale of the Heavenly Weaver Maid and the Oxherd. Behind them cymbals clash and wooden flutes trill plaintively. Then the musicians quiet down and the hollow tok-tok-tok of drumsticks tapping on wooden fish signals a solo, the Weaver Maid's lament to her lover. A musician pulls a bow across the strings of his *erhu,* and Dali begins:

I once wove garments of stars for the Great Empress
Who favored me with the peaches of immortality.
But I would throw my loom and all the fruit in those trees
To the furnaces of hell, ai, ai, ai!
For they keep me away from your love!
For they keep me away from your love!

Her voice is thrilling and the audience of well dressed older men surges to its feet to applaud as Dali gives them a stylized bow. The decorations on her headdress bob and she smiles coyly. She is Dali, yet not Dali. Her thin lips are plump and inviting, her bony hips now padded and swaying.

I hurry over to the stage and approach her leading man. I try to step into his figure, as I did with my own image in Weilan's dream, but instead I walk right through him. I try the same maneuver, more cautiously, with Dali's dream-self and find I can't enter her shape either. Even though I know what the result will be, I stroll around the theater touching members of the audience just in case I am able to inhabit one of their figures.

Then the theater melts around me and I'm back in Dali's room. She sits up drowsily and reaches over the side of the bed to pull out her chamber pot.

༄

The Kwans are sound asleep. A dim aura fans out from both their heads. This time I don't hesitate; I reach toward Mrs. Kwan. Threads from the silhouette cling to my fingers and as I step away it swells out. I can see shapes moving on the other side of the threshold. My souls watch me step over it.

Mrs. Kwan walks down the hard dirt road of a tiny farming village, her destination a small house at the end of the road. A fence of thin bamboo slats, more to keep the chickens in than people out, encloses the front yard, where a small girl is playing.

"Mama, Mama," she calls out when she sees Mrs. Kwan. The little girl runs toward her, her gait awkward. She moves with a limp.

Mrs. Kwan drops her canvas sack and squats down to hug the child. I hadn't known the Kwans had a daughter. A woman comes to the fence, her hair tied in a kerchief, a bowl of rice in her hand. Two half-naked toddlers hide behind the woman's knees.

"Second Cousin," she says. Her features shimmer and won't hold still, but I catch an impression of slyness, large teeth, a lined face.

"We gave you money to look after her," says Mrs. Kwan, anguish in her voice. She gets up to face the woman. "Enough to feed her and your own children. Now look at her."

The girl droops in Mrs. Kwan's arms, gray skin gleaming with sweat.

"We did our best," says the woman dismissively. "She was feeble, she couldn't do her share of the work."

"You stupid, greedy peasant," Mrs. Kwan screams, the child in her arms now no bigger than a doll. "You starved her to feed your own brats. Now she's dead and you'll get no more money for her keep."

Tears roll down my cheeks. I can't bear to watch so much pain. I raise my hand to wipe my eyes and feel something on my fingers. My fist clutches at threads, thin filaments that stretch across the road where a view of fields billows gently like a stage backdrop. I follow the threads and pull aside the edge of the dream. I step back into the real world. Mrs. Kwan moans in her sleep.

❧

Old Kwan dreams of tea shops and pretty serving girls, of stealing an extra bit of ham to barter for tobacco. Astonishment and pleasure light up his face when a young man enters the kitchen. I realize that only in his dreams does Old Kwan have the son he longs for.

"We must find you a wife," says Old Kwan, pushing a bowl of hot soy milk across the kitchen table toward his dream-son, who looks like a younger version of Kwan. "I'm getting the matchmaker to look into it, you know, to find a maidservant with the wealthy Mah clan. You could pick up seasonal work there from time to time."

"Is she one of Old Ming's granddaughters?" The young man's white teeth flash. "We'll end up related to half the town."

They both laugh, more like brothers than father and son. I've never seen Old Kwan this happy in real life. I wish he could have a son instead of a dead daughter.

⌒⌒⌒

My souls don't speak about my evident restlessness, but as the weeks go by they quiver with increasing agitation. My *yin* soul's smiles are strained and there are dark shadows under her young eyes. My *yang* soul looks fatigued, no longer a vigorous older man, just old. Only my *hun* soul seems unchanged, but unless its radiance dims altogether, it would be difficult to detect any change in its bright shape.

I can no longer tell myself that boredom is what drives me to explore the world of dreams. The restless, pulling sensation is relentless. Was it only a few weeks ago that I said I would stay on the other side of dreams, to respect the living and their secrets? And now here I am, trying to journey into their sleep-lives every night. But I can't help myself.

⌒⌒⌒

It doesn't seem as though there's anything I can do to make a differ-ence in this world, to help my daughter or anyone else. I'm so frus-

trated. The sparks that are my souls circle the pavilion, bobbing like fireflies. *How am I supposed to make amends for Hanchin's death?*

Continue exploring the land of dreams, says my *yang* soul. *There must be a reason why it's open to you.*

The real world hasn't given you a way to communicate with the living, my *yin* soul agrees. *You should continue to travel through the household's dreams; we may learn something.*

Leiyin, you seem reluctant to enter Baizhen's dreams, my *hun* soul observes.

I don't want to know what they contain. If I don't learn anything useful from spying on the servants, I'll enter his sleep-world. But not just yet.

The truth is I feel strangely envious when I watch him with his new wife. I'm reluctant to learn what his true feelings are for her.

∽∾⌣

Baizhen is unfailingly courteous to Meichiu. For one thing, he never mentions me. He shows her nothing but consideration. There's never a trace of displeasure in his attitude, in the words he uses, or in his tone of voice. It's not in him to be unkind and he would never let Meichiu feel unwanted. She's lucky to be married to him. I wish I'd shown him more affection.

"Be careful, the bowl is quite hot," Baizhen says, handing her some hot soy milk sweetened with cane syrup.

They're in the parlor of the main house. Jia Po is upstairs taking her afternoon nap. Meichiu spends more time at the mansion than I ever did. She waits on Jia Po, fetches her reading glasses, reads out loud to her. If the old woman wants to go for a stroll in the garden, Meichiu kneels down at Jia Po's feet to change her house slippers for shoes. Evidently Meichiu received better training in domestic rituals than I did. Was this how Jia Po had expected me to behave? What a disappointment I must have been.

"Thank you, Husband, for remembering how much I like sweet soy milk." She seems genuinely grateful.

"Are you lonely here?" He sits down beside her. "You can invite one of your sisters for a visit. I know Pinghu is a dull place."

To my surprise and Baizhen's, she rises from her chair and sinks to her knees before him. She places her hands over his and looks into his face.

"I'm quite content living here, Husband. Your kindness is far greater than I expected. The matchmaker told us about your first wife. I can never be as beautiful or as learned, and my family isn't from a great and wealthy clan, but I can be useful."

Baizhen looks astonished.

Her next words come out in a rush.

"My parents say I'm *nen-gan* and it's true. I'm a competent person and I'm not afraid of hard work. In time, I'll find a way to make our family prosper."

Her eyes betray anxiety at having spoken so directly, but her hands on Baizhen's are firm and steady. I doubt she would have alluded to the family's dwindling fortunes had Jia Po been in the room. A look passes between them. Baizhen's expression is one I have never seen before. Is it relief? Hope?

Then Meichiu gives a businesslike nod and returns to her chair.

❦

One morning, Dali hurries straight from Meichiu's room to Jia Po, nearly bursting with excitement. Jia Po, in turn, bustles over to the house, followed by Dali and Mrs. Kwan. In the bedroom, Baizhen is holding Meichiu's head over the chamber pot. Jia Po beams and helps Meichiu back into bed.

Baizhen tucks the covers around Meichiu and carefully wipes her pale lips. "For the past week she's been queasy, Ma."

"Good, good. Stay in bed, Daughter, and rest for an hour until the doctor's office opens." Jia Po spoons leaf tea into a pot. "I'll have Dali bring breakfast to your room."

Meichiu sinks down into the pillows and nods, an obedient smile fixed on her face. She looks different, something new in her smile, an awareness of her increased value. The household rouses to a new day, Meichiu at its center.

21

*T*hat quilt is useless lying on an empty bed," says Jia Po. "Bring it to my room, Dali. You can keep the old cover for yourself if you like."

The quilt I had brought with me from Changchow still lies on my bed. Filled with goose down, light and warm, it's the best quilt in the house and Jia Po has decided to take it for herself. Its removable cover is made of soft cotton sheeting stitched to a warm flannel underside. I can sense Dali's desire for a warmer cover tussling with her fear of using a dead woman's belongings. She enters my room and tugs the cover off the quilt. But instead of taking the cover to her room she folds it neatly on the foot of my bed, then takes the quilt to Jia Po.

That night, Dali dreams of me.

She's out doing errands, bundles dangling from her hands. Dali hurries down the Street of Lantern Makers and through the door of the Three Lanterns Pastry Shop, the bakery with the best moon cakes in town. It's Mid-Autumn Moon Festival time and the shop's glass display case overflows with the different varieties: lotus-seed paste, sweet black-bean paste, red-bean paste, sesame paste, and with or without savory egg fillings. She turns to one side, uncertain, and my dream-image appears beside her, inspecting the pastries.

"Young Mistress, I forget which kind of cake the Mistress wanted me to buy."

"The kind with egg yolks, Dali," my image says. "Both the Mistress and the Young Master like those best."

"But do you think the Mistress wants red-bean paste or lotus paste?"

My image wavers, fading out as Dali turns her attention back to the pastries. I step quickly into my dream-image and feel a sensation of pins and needles throughout my body. My form grows solid. When another customer bumps against me, I stagger a little to recover my balance.

"Let's get a dozen, half red-bean and half lotus," I suggest.

She nods and we leave the shop with a box tied with red string. The Street of Lantern Makers melts away. Now we're in a rickshaw, jouncing over potholes and heading toward the Temple of the City God. Dali doesn't seem surprised to find me still beside her. On impulse, I put my hand on her forearm.

"Dali, don't worry about the quilt cover. Please take it, with my blessings."

She looks surprised, and then smiles. "Thank you, Young Mistress."

"Will you remember this when you wake up?" I ask.

"Wake up?" She looks puzzled.

I slip off the rickshaw and follow the threads from my fingers to the edge of the dream.

In the morning, Dali goes to my room. She opens the door as though expecting to see someone inside. She steps over the threshold, removes the cover from the bed, and takes it to her room, where she slips it over her own thin quilt.

⌁

I can enter anyone's dreams, but I have to enter my own dream-image to be seen and heard. I can only make myself known if people dream about me. Otherwise, I'm as invisible as I am in the real world.

My *yin* soul perches on the railing of the pavilion. My *yang* soul is gazing into the bamboo grove, hands on top of his cane. My *hun* soul is hovering near the roof of the pavilion.

It could've been a coincidence. We don't know whether or not Dali remembered your words, it says. *Perhaps she just woke up feeling reassured about using your quilt cover.*

We need to find out whether you can communicate with the living, says my *yang* soul. *In a way that they can remember.*

And what words do I need to say? Please help me make amends for Hanchin's death? Burn paper money for him?

One step at a time, says my *hun* soul. *We don't know what use dreams can be to a ghost who needs to get to the afterlife. But perhaps they can be of use to a mother who wants something for her child.*

But first Baizhen must dream about me. I guess I can't put it off any longer.

‿◠‿◠‿

I enter his sleep every night that month. He dreams of Weilan, of playing word games with her in the library, of taking her for strolls along the banks of the canal to watch old men play *go* on stone tables inlaid with black-and-white squares. He dreams of window-shopping in Shanghai, of streets where one block of stores contains more flashing neon signs than all of Pinghu. Finally, on a night when the full moon casts leafy shadows across his bedroom floor, my husband dreams about me.

He's at school, the elementary school in Pinghu he attended for a few humiliating months. He's a small boy again, close to tears, cowering at a low desk. A middle-aged man in well-worn tunic and trousers stands over him, slapping a ruler in the palm of one hand.

"I'll smack your hands again if you don't get it right," the teacher shouts. "Can't you see that the symbol for wood, *mu*, when written twice side by side, means *ling*, forest?"

Now Baizhen is no longer at his desk. The cracked walls of the classroom fade away, replaced by a room lined with bookshelves. He's in the library at home, with Teacher Liao pointing a long fingernail at characters on a sheet of rice paper. Although the paper is covered in writing, not a single character represents a real word.

"Yes," says Baizhen, now a grown man. "That's exactly how Leiyin explained it to me, Teacher. I do remember."

Teacher Liao looks up toward my dream-image, which stands across the table, watching.

"How dare you interfere with my lessons! You're behaving in a most unseemly way for a woman."

"Please, Teacher Liao," Baizhen says placatingly. "My wife comes from a very learned family."

I waste no time walking into my dream-image. I ignore the pins and needles that prick me all over as I enter my shape and I ignore Teacher Liao.

"Baizhen, we must talk about our daughter. You must find her a tutor so she can continue her lessons."

"But you're tutoring her," he says, looking puzzled.

"My husband, it's your responsibility now to make sure she receives a good education. Please, it's the most important thing you can do for our child."

"Yes, I know. You're right, you always are." His face brightens. "I know it's only a dream, Wife, but it's so good to see you again. I think of you all the time."

"Can you tell this is only a dream?" Hope rises in me, perhaps he will remember.

"Yes. How can I forget you've died? This must be a dream."

"Then please, remember my words when you wake up. Find Weilan a tutor. Please."

I hasten to the edge of the room and step out. It seems best to leave before I do any damage.

∽∾∽

Over the next few days I stay close to Baizhen, watching for signs that the dream has left an impression. He seems thoughtful, and on a number of occasions he opens his mouth to speak to Jia Po when they are alone, but he never says what I'm waiting for. Nor does he dream about me again.

Then one afternoon he ventures into his mother's sitting room, where Jia Po and Meichiu are sewing by the window, talking together softly. Meichiu is embroidering tigers onto a pattern for baby shoes, and Jia Po is basting long strips of soft cloth into night diapers. Meichiu's needlework is impeccable.

"Ma, I've been thinking." He clears his throat. "Weilan should go to school."

She looks amazed, then scandalized.

"The women in this family do not attend the public school."

"Then I'd like Weilan to have a tutor."

"Teacher Liao is retired," says Jia Po. Like the rest of the town, she maintains this fiction to save face for Teacher Liao, who now spends all his waking hours at wine shops. "Anyway, we can't afford to waste money educating a girl."

"When it's time to find a match for her, we'll have a better chance with a good family, for they would value an educated daughter," he continues, determined.

Meichiu listens to all this silently, her needle bobbing in and out.

"My son, this is a futile discussion," Jia Po says impatiently. "We can hardly provide a dowry for her as it is. An education will just give her expectations we can't meet."

There it was. The problem I had refused to face since the day Weilan was born. No matter how pretty and talented she might be, a woman's true value is measured by the size of her dowry. Even though the groom's family has to pay the girl's family a bride-price, it's a token amount. It's the size of the dowry the bride's family provides that secures her position in her husband's family. Jia Po knows this better than anyone.

I used to write letters to Gaoyin and Sueyin, asking about good families with promising sons, but I had been deluding myself. Without a dowry, who would want my beautiful girl? She would probably marry into another proud and poor Pinghu family, a family who needed a daughter-in-law able to cook meals frugally and mend tunics so cleverly they could be worn another few years. Russian novels, the Tang classics, and knowledge of English would be worthless.

"Ma." Baizhen's voice is gentle but firm. "By the time Weilan is a young woman, she may need to support herself. There are women working in banks and offices, there are schoolteachers and nurses. If she can earn her way, a dowry will matter less."

I can hardly believe my docile husband is talking back to his mother. He's dared to bring up the unmentionable: that her granddaughter may have to earn a living. Baizhen has reasoned his way through Weilan's options in a way I never had. Despite my fantasies of attending university and helping Hanchin set up village schools, I had never actually considered the prospect of a real career. I had pictured living with Hanchin in a lovely house of our own, holding salons for artists, writers, and poets. With what income would we have paid the rent?

"There's one more thing, Ma. Leiyin's father left a fund for Weilan's education, so she could attend boarding school and university. But she'll never get into a good school if she doesn't have a tutor to prepare her."

"He did? But too much education for a girl is a waste." I can tell Jia Po is wavering. My father, patriarch of the Song clan, had felt that it mattered for his granddaughter.

Meichiu is soft and respectful when she speaks.

"My mother reads a little. She's very good with arithmetic. She helps my father in his business."

"Your mother married into a family of merchants." Jia Po speaks sharply, always a little defensive about her own background, despite her family's tremendous wealth. "The Lee clan does not trade."

"My mother's dowry was small, but my father always says he wouldn't have been as successful without her." That undertone of steel I'd heard before in Meichiu's voice. "He couldn't afford a bookkeeper at first and she kept track of their money. If Weilan can read, write, and do her sums, it won't hurt her prospects. And if she doesn't marry, she'll be able to work and help support our family."

I can't believe Jia Po is just sitting there allowing her son and daughter-in-law to offer contrary opinions after she has stated hers so firmly. Then I look at her again, an old woman in a household kept afloat by dowries. Her own huge fortune, so quickly depleted, then my dowry, and now Meichiu's too.

"Find someone cheap," she says.

∽∾∽

With the help of a dictionary, Baizhen composes a letter, copying it out four times before he finally puts his pen to a sheet of fine cream-colored stationery.

Esteemed Brother-in-Law:

I hope all is well with you and your honored family. How fondly I recall your last visit to Pinghu.

I'll keep this letter brief so as not to insult you with my poor calligraphy.

Your dear sister was teaching Weilan to read and write. I'd like our daughter's education to continue. Can you recommend a tutor who isn't very expensive? We can't offer much more than room and board, and no more than two silver yuan per month in wages. Your good opinion is all I require to have confidence in any tutor you recommend.

This isn't quite what I had hoped for. Baizhen has made it plain that so long as Tongyin endorses the tutor, formal credentials don't matter. An unqualified tutor costs far less than one with proper training. But will my brother be helpful or will he ignore the request? Does Tongyin even know such a person?

⌘

"Where's Old Fong?" Mrs. Kwan demands, eyeing the newcomer up and down.

He's a solid young man of medium height, legs sturdy as tree trunks. His bushy eyebrows arch above an impertinent smile. A rolled cloth bundle under one arm indicates he's prepared to stay for a few days.

It's now summer and in the courtyards the flagstones are still buried under drifts of fallen leaves from the previous year.

Normally Old Fong, our last remaining tenant farmer, arrives in early spring, leaving his small plot for a few days so he can earn a little extra by tidying up the fall debris. But my funeral and then the wedding disrupted that routine, and then came spring planting. Now that planting time is finished, Jia Po has sent word to Old Fong, asking him to come. But the young man at the door isn't Old Fong.

"Old Fong is my father. He's getting too old to walk all the way into town. He says that from now on I'm to do the seasonal gardening."

"You know what the chores are?"

"Sweep leaves, take them to the compost pile to burn. Pull weeds from all the gardens, take them to the compost pile to burn. Gather fallen branches, break them up for kindling, take them to the kitchen woodpile." He recites the list of tasks as though he's memorized it.

"All right. You can sleep where your father sleeps when he's here."

Mrs. Kwan points toward a room in the servants' quarters and tells Dali to give the young man a blanket. Then she alerts Old Kwan that there will be an extra person to feed for the next few days.

"There's a hole in the roof," says Dali, handing Fong the blanket. "But as long as it doesn't rain, you'll only be cold, not wet. And if you want to burn leaves or twigs in that stove to keep warm, go ahead."

"Where do you sleep?" he asks, flashing that insolent smile, white, wolfish teeth showing.

At this, Dali turns to leave the room, indignant, but just then Mrs. Kwan returns from the kitchen.

"Dali, show the boy where everything is. The garden shed, all the gardens, the orchard."

"I'm too busy, Mrs. Kwan," says Dali, her lower lip sticking out.

But after a while, I can tell she likes playing the grand lady to a peasant, enjoys pointing out the features of the houses and gardens. Fong saunters beside her, grinning and amiable.

When Fong gets to work, he's efficient and doesn't dawdle. He stops only to mop his forehead with a dirty kerchief. He repairs a loose handle on the wheelbarrow without being asked. He doesn't look up when Mrs. Kwan walks past, but smiles from under those eyebrows at Dali.

❦

How can you tell the difference between a dream that is only a dream, and one where the dreamer has real intent?

In Fong's dream, I see green fields, stacks of harvested wheat, and a small cottage, its walls streaked with soot. I smell manure, urine, and vinegar: odors of despair and desperate poverty. I see an old man and three grown sons. There's a woman of indeterminate age with callused, knotted hands, the oldest son's wife. On the dirt floor, several children squabble and scream, naked and runny-nosed.

Then silence. Fong is standing in the doorway of a room in the servants' quarters, looking at a sleeping woman. He pushes his way into her bed, and the woman's face is the tired face of his brother's wife. Her strong legs wrap around his back as he plunges into her again and again.

I move to the edges of the dream, not wanting to see any more.

Then a cry of pain and I look back. The woman turns her head and Dali's face looks out from behind Fong's shoulder. She resists, struggling fruitlessly because her hands and feet are tied to the bed, her screams choked by the filthy kerchief stuffed in her mouth. Fong strikes her face, then continues pumping between her legs. When he is finished, he pulls up his trousers and gives her ribs a kick. He picks up his cloth bundle, slips out of the servants' quarters, and steals past Old Ming's gatehouse. Fong opens the wicket gate and steps over the threshold into the silent dark street. He is whistling.

I stand in the first rays of morning light, shuddering from the violence of the dream. On the bed, Fong grunts, half awake. His hand moves rhythmically under the thin blanket.

❧

Around the servants' table in the kitchen, Fong brags openly of abandoning his family's farm. Our servants, who have no intention of leaving the Lee household while they can still get three square meals here, listen skeptically.

"I'm going to join the Communist army in Shaanxi. Once they take over, every farmer will plow his own fields. No more landlords." He nods knowingly.

"What about your father?" This from Old Kwan. "Won't he

need your help on the farm? The Lees aren't bad landlords compared to many."

Fong waves a brawny hand.

"My father has two other sons. They can farm your master's
land. After I've finished with the gardens and been paid, I'll be
leaving on the first train out of here."

He won't be caught once he's boarded the train; he is uncon-
cerned about being punished for the crime he'll commit. I visit
the servants in turn that night and the next. But they only dream
of their own, circumscribed lives. How can I warn Dali? How can
I warn any of them? It took nearly a month for Baizhen to dream
about me so that I could speak to him. I don't have that much
time to help Dali.

When I try my luck with Baizhen, he's dreaming of his favorite tea house, gently waving a cup beneath his nose to inhale
the first-harvest *huang shan*. Outside, the elm trees that line the
canal are clothed in the pale tender green of new leaves. The
proprietor's wife brings him a bowl of rice and lifts the lid from
a bamboo steamer. Inside, a small carp, covered in thinly sliced
green onion and ginger, swims in a fragrant mixture of hot oil
and soy.

"Wonderful, wonderful!" says Baizhen, sniffing the fish.

"Your wife enjoys this dish," says the woman, although there
is no way she could know this. "Lightly steamed, with bubbling
hot oil and soy poured over."

At the mention of my name, my dream-image appears and
the restaurant walls blur. Now Baizhen and I are seated in our
dining room with Gong Gong and Jia Po, who seem oblivious of
our presence.

"Will you take some fish?" Baizhen offers the steamer basket to my likeness.

"Thank you," says my dream-image, just as I enter it. There's a tingling sensation as I settle in and then my hand raises chopsticks to my lips. I swallow. The wonderful flavor of tender fish fills my mouth. But I must make the most of this opportunity.

"Baizhen, please listen to me." I tug at his arm urgently. "There's something very important I need to tell you."

He lifts his chopsticks and smiles at me.

"That gardener, Baizhen—that Fong. He's planning to do something horrible to Dali."

"Who? What's going on with Dali?"

"The gardener, Old Fong's son." I shake his arm again. "He's leaving in two days and I think he's going to rape Dali before he runs away from Pinghu."

"Come, have some more fish. It's your favorite."

"You must stop him," I say in despair. "Husband, send him on his way now."

"Yes, yes. Of course."

I have to be content with that.

❧

The next day, the only evidence that Baizhen has remembered the dream is his breakfast-time request for fish for supper. Steamed with ginger and green onion, with hot oil and soy. In the afternoon, Baizhen stops by the kitchen to see whether Old Kwan has managed to buy a good fish.

"Here, Young Master. Come have a look." Old Kwan shows Baizhen a basin where a small carp twitches, half submerged in water. "I'll add a little bit of sugar to the hot-oil-and-soy mixture, Shanghai-style, the way our first Young Mistress liked it, you know. This was her favorite way to cook fish, elegantly simple."

"I dreamed about this dish all night, Kwan. When I woke up, all I could think about was fish for supper."

Baizhen hasn't remembered anything but the fish.

❧

That night I try again, this time visiting Old Kwan. He's in the kitchen preparing a huge carp, scaling it skillfully with a huge knife. Beside him on the chopping block is a chipped bowl full of sliced ginger and green onions. Dali is at the sink washing pots and pans.

"I need that skillet cleaner than clean, Dali. No hint of the pork skins we fried up earlier, you know, that taints the flavor of the fish."

"I prefer fish to pork," says Dali.

Her image wavers, fades, and when it grows solid again, it's my dream-image at the sink, rinsing a pan. Wasting no time, I step inside it, accustomed now to the brief stinging sensation. I drop the pan into the sink and approach Old Kwan.

"I need to warn you about something, Old Kwan."

"Yes, Young Mistress." He continues to work on the fish.

"That gardener, Fong. He's up to no good."

"Ah, I knew it!" He puts down the knife and turns to me with a satisfied shake of the head. "That sly smile, that boastful talk. He's always trying to flirt with Dali, you know."

"Old Kwan, please listen. It's about Dali. Tomorrow night Fong's going to try to assault her. You must do something to get rid of him before nightfall tomorrow."

"Young Mistress." He falls silent, troubled. "Is this a message from the grave?"

I don't want to frighten him, or start any tales of haunting, but I must make him pay attention to my words. I put my hand on his shoulder.

"You feel it in your belly, Kwan. You know that man is no good. That's why you dream about me, so that I can tell you what you already know." I have to give warning, but still sound reassuring. "Please, just get rid of Fong before nightfall. Please remember my words."

I leave the kitchen and Old Kwan's dream.

I continue to circle through the sleeping household, but no one else dreams of me. Old Kwan is the only one I've managed to warn. Will he remember in the morning?

⌒⌒⌒

"You, gardener!" Mrs. Kwan's voice rings across the kitchen garden. "I hear you've finished."

It's after supper. Fong is shirtless, washing from a bucket of cold water. He turns to her, puzzled.

"Here's your pay from the Mistress." She hands over a small bag of coins. "You wanted to stay one more night, didn't you?"

He nods, tossing the burlap pouch from hand to hand.

"Well, since you're leaving first thing in the morning, you can share Old Ming's room in the gatehouse. We can't have you stumbling through the estate waking up the family on your way out."

Fong looks nonchalant as he puts his shirt back on. Later, he leaves the servants' quarters with his belongings rolled up in his cloth bundle, a thin blanket thrown over his shoulders. He whistles on his way to the gatehouse. He seems calm, not angry as I thought he might be. Perhaps he wasn't planning to attack Dali. Perhaps it was only a dream after all. But I'm on edge until the first streaks of sunrise mark the horizon and the roosters start their crowing. Old Ming shuffles out and opens the wicket gate, stretching and yawning. Fong, cloth bundle tied to his back, steps onto Jade Belt Road and saunters away, whistling "Purple Bamboo Melody."

His whistling fades as he crosses the bridge over the canal, and in that moment my souls rise. It's as though a tether has been lengthened, a sensation of relief, as though I had been a ball held under water and then suddenly set free to shoot up to the surface. Somehow I know I've moved closer to that shining portal to the afterlife.

Then, in the next moment, I see Dali in my mind's eye. She's bound to her bed, naked and brutalized, gagging on a kerchief, blood running down her face. Outside, Mrs. Kwan calls her name and when she enters the room, horror fills her eyes. Dali weeps in shame and pain. Then I see Dali again, now middle-aged, a cowering and fearful woman with a long purple scar across her cheekbone, afraid to sleep in the dark.

I'm seeing the fate that would have been hers. The fate I've averted.

Now I understand how to atone for Hanchin's death. Now I know what I must do for release from this world.

∽∾∾

My souls swirl around the altar, incandescent.

At last, at last. My *yin* soul dances, her red spark so frenzied that it flashes with excitement.

My *yang* soul slows his spinning and once again he is an elderly gentleman. His face is thoughtful and he voices what I have realized.

They will all die someday, all those who knew you, he says. *So you must succeed in making amends before there's no one left to dream about you.* Something pungent and herbal sits on my tongue.

Weilan's still a little girl, I say. *Baizhen's barely thirty. There's lots of time to right the balance.* But something else nibbles at the edge of my thoughts.

As time goes by, they may dream about you less and less, says my *hun* soul. Its voice is distant and regretful. *After a while, perhaps not at all. Once your family forgets about you, stops dreaming about you . . .*

I hadn't considered this.

My *yin* soul comes down to earth, blouse untucked and face flushed. Her exuberance has wilted. She says nothing, but her brown eyes are wide with anxiety and there is a smell of mothballs in the air.

If I don't ascend to the afterlife before everyone I knew dies, I'll be trapped forever in this in-between world. As I fade from living memory, as people dream about me less and less, I'll have fewer chances to enter my dream image and communicate with the living. My time for making amends is even shorter than I first thought.

22

*A*mah Wu has returned, with hopes of being engaged as nanny to the child Meichiu is carrying. Uninvited and of her own accord, she made the two-hour walk to the estate to stake a claim for her former position. She arrives just in time to join the servants for lunch in the kitchen. Then, with a contented sigh, she wipes her mouth on her sleeve and follows Mrs. Kwan to the small parlor, where Meichiu and Jia Po are sewing baby clothes.

Jia Po is agreeable to hiring Amah Wu again, but Meichiu, normally so deferential to her mother-in-law, puts her foot down. After only a few minutes she has taken a strong dislike to our former nanny.

Amah Wu wails all the way from the mansion to the kitchen, where Old Kwan puts some sesame cakes and steamed buns into her cloth bag to quiet her down.

"The first Young Mistress promised me the job." She sniffles. "The next baby should be my charge."

"Well, the new Young Mistress isn't obliged to keep that

promise," says Mrs. Kwan with a glare. "She hasn't even started looking for a wet nurse. Don't come again unless you're sent for."

Still whining, Amah Wu shrugs her bag over her shoulder and leaves our home. Mrs. Kwan watches by the gate with Old Ming as the peasant woman's sturdy figure plods down the street. Old Ming shakes his head.

"What was she thinking, coming here to demand a job when the Young Mistress is only three months pregnant?"

"This was the best life she ever had," says Mrs. Kwan. "She got too eager. Her smile was too greedy."

"She's sharp, our new Young Mistress. She'll sort out this family. The money will last longer."

"How's Little Ming? And your new great-grandson?" Mrs. Kwan's interest is genuine.

"Both in good health. But who knows what she'll do next. Her parents don't want her and they don't want her bastard either."

☙❦❧

So Little Ming has had her baby. Hanchin's son. My *yang* soul sighs as he sits on a rickety stool by the door of the family shrine.

How do you feel? my *hun* soul gently asks. Its radiant shape lights up the shrine and reveals cobwebs and dust that Dali doesn't bother to clean.

I was just as foolish as Little Ming. Worse, in fact. She never expected anything of Hanchin, while I fantasized about a future with him.

I feel sorry for her, my *yin* soul says. *And for her poor baby. What will they do now? Can we do something for Little Ming?*

⌒⌒⌒

Usually I avoid Jia Po's dreams. They're uncomfortable, suffused with bitterness, overcast with a tint of sulphuric yellow. Anger, loneliness, and despair fill her nights. I don't know how she wakes up rested. All her anger is directed at Gong Gong.

She dreams of going to the cottage at Infant Mountain, raging at him, harsh words she should have spoken sooner. She regrets her decades of submissiveness, feels complicit in Gong Gong's extravagant spending. She dreams of occasions when she should have stopped him from buying certain high-priced antiques and rare books. She worries endlessly in her sleep about making ends meet, selling more property to buy rice, dipping into the meager funds she had set aside for a grandson's education.

She dreams of her childhood. I wander behind her through an enormous estate, awed by its grandeur. There is a private theater and the park is bigger than Judge Liu's in Changchow. But even here she is lonely, for the figures that pass through the houses and gardens never stop to talk to her, never materialize into anyone she recognizes. She's a little girl again, her plain face lit up with eagerness as she runs to find her playmates, following the sound of laughter and games always just one more courtyard away, one more threshold to cross.

Suddenly she stops before a moon gate. A young Gong Gong, tall and clean-shaven, slouches against the wall. He wears the same clothes Baizhen had dressed in for his wedding to Meichiu.

"Here you are, Wife." It's the smooth, clear voice of a young man. "When are you coming home?"

She bursts into tears and I see that she loved that young man, loves him still, in spite of all. Unsettled by seeing her so vulnerable, I want to slip out of her dream. But I steel myself and go to her room every night.

A week after Amah Wu's visit, Jia Po finally dreams about me. She is sitting at her desk, sorting through ledgers.

"Here you are, Daughter," she says, turning in her chair. "What do you know about these expenses?"

She appears no older than thirty but looks weary. We used to sit in this room together, in despair, staring at all the bills. I want to hug her thin shoulders, but I hold back.

"Let's talk of something else, Mother. Come, let's sit in the pavilion and catch a breath of fresh air."

I take her by the elbow and guide her outside, through the bamboo grove. We mount the steps to the pavilion. With a sigh, she sinks down on the stone bench that rings its interior. She is in a summer-weight gown with short sleeves but the air is cold, the trees bare. The wisteria, however, is in bloom, its flowers hanging in pink cascades.

"What do you want to talk about, Daughter?" She looks older now.

"Mother, since Meichiu doesn't want Amah Wu to look after her baby, I have a suggestion."

Jia Po looks up, astonished.

"Little Ming has had her baby. Bring her back to be wet nurse and nanny. Let her bring her son. Meichiu's child will need a playmate."

"But you're the one who sent Little Ming back to her family! You threw her out for getting pregnant."

"I was wrong, Mother, very wrong. Please, bring her back. She's lived with this family since she was a child. We're responsible for her."

I take her hands between mine. They are smooth, dry and soft as rice paper. Jia Po looks down at our hands.

"Are you speaking to me from the afterlife, Daughter-in-Law? Tell me, what's it like?" Her voice is low and wistful. I squeeze her hands again, reassuringly.

"This is just a dream, Mother. You know that bringing Little Ming back to our home is the right thing to do, and you have dreamed about me so that I can tell you this. Will you please remember when you wake up?"

I leave her sitting beneath the wisteria.

⤫

A few days later, Little Ming arrives at the estate, her son in a sling across her chest and a change of clothing in her bag. She washes in the servants' quarters before going to see Jia Po and Meichiu. Dali and Mrs. Kwan fuss over the baby while she bathes.

"You look older," Dali says, but not in an unkind way. "You've lost weight."

"You must take some food home with you," says Mrs. Kwan. "You'll never have enough milk for your son if you don't eat well yourself."

Little Ming smiles at them, a sad curve to her lips. She looks as if she'll never giggle again. "Then I'd better eat it here. My father will take anything I bring back as payment for the food I eat at his table."

"Even with a grandson!" Dali is indignant.

"Ah Jiao is a bastard," Little Ming says quietly.

Ah Jiao. What a common, graceless name for the son of a poet.

"But he's a boy!" Mrs. Kwan exclaims. "A girl in my village gave birth out of wedlock to a boy. Her parents were overjoyed to have a grandson finally, even a bastard."

"My parents have four sons already. This one is just another mouth to feed."

Hanchin's son sleeps quietly in his bundle, his fists close to his chin. I peer at his face, looking for any resemblance to his father. So far he is more Little Ming than Hanchin. When Little Ming looks at her baby, I recognize in her eyes the same adoration I felt when Weilan had just been born.

Little Ming sighs deeply and straightens her shoulders.

"Here I go," she says. "You don't need to show me the way."

Meichiu inspects Little Ming's hands and nails. Little Ming's tunic and trousers are wrinkled but clean, a plain green set she had sewn for herself the year before. I remember giving her the fabric.

Jia Po clears her throat. "How is your milk?"

"I have enough for two babies, Mistress. And in any case, by the time the Young Mistress has hers, mine will be ready to eat congee."

"You'll be expected to wet nurse and nanny at the same time," says Meichiu. "Weilan hasn't had a nanny since you left."

"I'd be happy to look after the Little Mistress again."

"Did you bring your baby with you?" asks Meichiu.

"Yes, he's in the kitchen with Mrs. Kwan. He's very good, no trouble at all."

"How are your parents treating you and the baby?" Jia Po asks with real concern.

"They're very angry with me," Little Ming says softly, not looking up. Tears glimmer in the corners of her eyes. "I've shamed them. Please, Mistress. I'll do anything to come back."

She drops to her knees on the floor, hands outstretched toward the older women. Her body shakes with silent sobs.

Jia Po looks at Meichu. Meichiu clears her throat.

"Mother, have you any objection to Little Ming coming back right away, to her former position of house servant and nanny? That way we'll have time to observe her and be certain she's healthy and free of illness before she begins as wet nurse."

Jia Po doesn't hesitate. "Yes, and she must be well-fed in advance so her milk is as nourishing as possible. Little Ming, come back in the morning with your things. And bring your son to live here also."

Little Ming is nearly incoherent with gratitude. She backs out the door bowing repeatedly, mumbling her thanks. The two women watch from the window as Little Ming makes her way in a near-skip to the servants' quarters. Jia Po sighs, relieved.

"I can see you care about her, Mother," says Meichiu, picking up her sewing. "And she's loyal to this family. She won't be foolish again. In time, we may find her a husband."

I hardly have a chance to feel grateful to Meichiu, for in that moment I am unburdened of a great weight, lifted closer to the portal. A glowing outline appears in the sky, brighter than ever. My souls circle toward it, exultant sparks springing higher.

Then my mind's eye sees Little Ming's future as it would have been, had I not intervened. She is tired and haggard, the only servant in a large house, in another town. She cleans the house and scrubs dishes, washes all the laundry, peels and chops vegetables for the cook, empties chamber pots. Little Ah Jiao is tied in a sling across her aching back as she works.

I see her on a narrow bed in a windowless room, struggling against a man who presses down on her, swearing while he forces open her legs. I see the man's wife, the mistress of the house, screaming at her. I see Little Ming pushed out the door, clutching her cloth bag and her son. I see her sink down, exhausted, in a shop doorway, a cold winter wind blowing dead leaves toward her. She bends over Ah Jiao to shelter him from the cold.

I see another face now, a boy in his early teens who looks like Little Ming but with Hanchin's glinting eyes. He throws a few coins into the bowl of a beggar, a woman with a vacant expression. His sleeve flaps when he tosses the coins, revealing elaborate gang tattoos on his forearm.

"I'm running errands for the big boss tomorrow," he says to her. "Don't go wandering if you want money from me. I had a hell of a time finding you today, Ma." Words of exasperation and frustrated love.

This is the future I have averted for Little Ming and Ah Jiao.

∽∾∾

The buoyant feeling stays with me all day. I glow with a sense of accomplishment. My *yang* soul looks stronger, a man in the prime of old age. My *yin* soul's cheeks are rosy again, her eyes bright and lively. My *hun* soul shines brighter. My good deed has revived them.

But the next day, although the sensation of being pulled between heaven and earth has lessened, my emotions are restless, and I sense that my souls are in turmoil too.

How many good deeds does it take to atone for a betrayal that cost a man his life? I ask them. *Do I have other sins that need to be balanced out with good deeds?*

There is silence as my souls consider this.

It doesn't matter, my *yang* soul says finally, tapping the handle of his cane. *We can't know all the sins the gods considered worth recording in their ledger. You'll just have to perform good deeds until we're freed from this world.*

But do it soon, says my *hun* soul.

Dear Brother-in-Law,

I'm honored to be of assistance to you in the matter of my niece's education. I can recommend a young woman by the name of Wang Limou, and am enclosing a reference letter from her former employer. She has finished high school and was partway through college when the war put an end to her education. She is more than qualified to teach primary school. Since she lacks formal qualifications, she is willing to work for very little. I have paid her train fare to Pinghu.

Sincerely,
Song Tongyin

"Miss Wang was educated in Soochow," Baizhen says, reading out loud to Jia Po. "Then she was a teacher's assistant with a private girls' school, but the school has been closed. She's capable of teaching up to the middle-school level."

"Soochow? The women of Soochow are immodest." Jia Po sniffs. "Flirtatious. They can't help it, with that accent. They sound like singsong girls even when they're reciting the times tables."

"We should respect my brother-in-law's recommendation. In any case, he has bought the teacher a train ticket and she's on her way. Miss Wang Limou is arriving at the end of the month."

∽∾∾

I tag along when Baizhen and Weilan go to the train station to meet the new tutor. The platform is crowded and chaotic, as usual. Departing travelers shove their way onto the train, ignoring the shouts of the station master imploring them to let the arriving passengers get off first. Baizhen can't get near the train and stands on his toes to scan the crowd. Finally, with a belch and a whistle, the train rumbles away. The vendors sit down again to gossip, setting aside their trays of cigarettes and candies until the next train pulls in. The platform clears.

The only person left there is a young woman who's being pestered by rickshaw drivers.

"Miss, miss, where are you going? I know every street in this town."

"If you're in a hurry, I can get you there faster than any of these louts."

"That must be her, my teacher," says Weilan excitedly. "Miss

Wang Limou." She has been oscillating between eagerness and anxiety all morning.

The young woman is my age, fragile and thin as a stalk of rice, her face framed by a straight, short bob. She carries a cloth suitcase and stands beside a cardboard box bound tightly with rope. From her haggard face and the way her clothing hangs, it's evident she's lost a great deal of weight at some point. Despite its age, her coat is well tailored and made from good cloth. Its deep blue makes her skin look sallow and draws attention to the dark circles around her eyes.

I would recognize those eyes anywhere.

It's my old friend Wang Nanmei.

"I'm Wang Limou," she says, bowing to Baizhen.

"Miss Wang, we're very pleased to welcome you."

She bows again, deeply. "Mr. Lee."

There are strands of gray in her hair.

"I brought some books," she adds, indicating the box. "I hope this isn't too much luggage."

"No, not at all. We'll get a big bicycle rickshaw."

A young man sidles up to Baizhen. "Mr. Lee, I'm Old Ming's fifth grandson. I know exactly where you live."

"But do you have a bicycle rickshaw?"

"Better. My cousin's donkey cart is outside. I'll take the young lady's luggage."

Baizhen makes small talk on the ride home, pointing out the town's landmarks: temples, marketplace, the two main streets that run parallel to the canal. Nanmei says very little but glances from time to time at Weilan, who is wedged between her father and the new teacher. Finally their eyes meet and they exchange shy smiles.

"I hear you already know how to read," Nanmei says.

Weilan nods, still shy.

"You're very pretty, Weilan. You look like . . . like someone I used to know. And if you're as clever too, it will be a joy to teach you." The clatter of donkey hooves almost drowns out her quiet voice, but my sharp ghost ears catch its tremor, my eyes see the tears glinting in the corners of her eyes as she gazes at my daughter.

I know Nanmei will be kind to Weilan. She'll appreciate my daughter's quick mind. But what has happened? Her family was almost as wealthy as mine. And of all the tutors Tongyin could have found, how did he end up sending Nanmei?

∽∾∾

Baizhen shows Nanmei upstairs to a small room beside the library. A chest of drawers and an old desk are the only furniture in the room besides the bed, which is merely a cot made up with a thin mattress and a quilt. Nanmei unpacks her few belongings, listening all the while to Weilan's chatter.

"Do you want to put away your books, Teacher Wang? We have a library. Then we should wash our hands and go to dinner."

"You have your own library?"

"Yes. It's also the schoolroom."

Nanmei follows Weilan next door into the library, toting the heavy box. She sets it down on the long table and looks around the room. Almost immediately she spies a framed photograph on the wall above the table and moves closer to look.

"That is my mother," Weilan says eagerly. "And that's me on her lap, when I was a baby."

"Your mother was beautiful," Nanmei says quietly.

"My father says she was the most beautiful woman in all of Pinghu. She taught me how to read. She taught Papa too. And she taught Little Ming, my nanny."

"It sounds as though she was born to be a teacher." Nanmei is close to tears but Weilan doesn't notice.

Little Ming calls from below, "Little Mistress, come down and wash your hands. It's nearly dinnertime."

"I'm coming, I'm coming. I'm just showing Teacher Wang our schoolroom!"

∽∾∾

Do you remember the letter Nanmei sent me when I was first married? I ask my souls. *I replied to her so brusquely.*

My *yin* soul, sitting at the library table, gives me a sideways glance and smooths out the pleats of her navy blue skirt. *It did read like a brush-off.*

I had no way to warn her that Gong Gong felt entitled to read all of our letters, coming or going.

There was more to it than that, don't you think? My *yang* soul gives me a stern look.

I had prattled on to her about Hanchin and I was mortified that all my plans had unraveled and come to nothing, I admit. She was going to college and I wasn't.

You didn't want any reminders of the life and the dreams you had left behind, my *hun* soul says. Its glow casts shadows the living can't see. *Now that seems so petty, doesn't it?*

I look at Nanmei's shabby coat and tired features, evidence of a life more difficult than mine had been.

I could have been a better friend.

⌒⌒⌒

Nanmei watches Weilan run down the staircase, then returns to gazing once more at my photograph. Will she reveal to my family that she was my classmate and friend?

"I've missed you so much, Leiyin," she says. "I can't believe you're gone. Please forgive me."

Forgive her for what? I'm the one who should ask her forgiveness. I had made no effort to learn where life had taken her.

She rubs her eyes and I realize she's crying. She glances at the door and whispers, "When Tongyin said your daughter needed a tutor, I couldn't believe it. It was as though you were helping me from beyond the grave. Leiyin, I'm leaving as soon as I've succeeded in this mission, but I promise you, no matter how much or how little time I spend here, I'll teach your daughter with all the dedication you would have."

She's here on a mission? Her tutoring position is a ruse? What sort of confidences has she shared with Tongyin? I will her to say more, but Weilan's footsteps clatter up the staircase.

"Teacher Wang, I've finished washing my hands and face. We must go to dinner."

⌒⌒⌒

Nanmei waits until all of the family members have helped them-selves before putting any food into her own bowl. She eats her rice with neat, scooping movements, spilling nothing on the table. She eats everything and doesn't mention likes or dislikes for any kind of food.

"Your Soochow accent isn't very strong, Teacher Wang," Jia Po says casually, but I can tell she is curious.

"No, Madame Lee. I went to college in Soochow and also worked there for a few years, but I'm not from Soochow."

"Where does your family come from?"

There is the slightest pause, and then Nanmei says, "My family is from Hangchow."

She's not going to reveal any connection with Changchow. Perhaps it's embarrassing for her to have come down so much in the world.

"What's your father's business?" Jia Po continues her interro-gation.

"My father . . . he owned a cloth store. But my parents are both gone."

My poor friend. Orphaned, and somehow penniless.

Meichiu speaks for the first time, a friendly and pleased look on her face. "We're both merchants' daughters then."

I feel a small twinge of jealousy.

After dinner, in the privacy of the small parlor, Jia Po admits to Baizhen that she can find no fault with the new tutor's demeanor.

Whatever she's up to, she doesn't want them to know she comes from Changchow or that she knew me. If she's lying about that, how do I even know her parents are really dead?

The household is getting ready to retire for the night. Little Ming and her baby are in the nursery. Weilan likes to chat with Little Ming until Ah Jiao falls asleep. Then Little Ming gives Weilan a bath and puts her to bed. Weilan is much happier now that Little Ming is back.

～∾∽～

Maybe she thinks it would be awkward for them to know you were once friends, my *yin* soul says. She runs her finger along the spines of the books Nanmei has arranged on a shelf. *It could be as simple as that.*

She could tell the truth about being from Changchow without revealing that she knew you, my *yang* soul says, leaning on his cane. *We know there's more to this. A tutoring job isn't why she's here.*

Perhaps you could learn the truth from her dreams. My *hun* soul stands by the window, looking down into the orchard.

Dreams aren't the same as memories, I say. *What I see happening in dreams could be anything, real memories and imagined events all mixed up. The dreamer has no control.*

The only way you can find out is to ask her yourself, my *hun* soul says, *and hope her dream-self speaks the truth.*

～∾∽～

There's so much to find out. Nanmei has a secret motive, but I also want to know what's become of her family. Then there's Tongyin. Knowing my brother, there must be a self-serving reason for his sending Nanmei to us. He's on the Nationalist side, but bragged to me about being a double agent. Has he sent her to spy on the Lee family? Yet even Tongyin must realize that Baizhen and Gong Gong have less than no interest in getting involved in politics, so that can't be the reason.

Did he recognize Nanmei as the school friend who used to come to our house to study with me? It's true he ignored us back then. To him we were just two schoolgirls, as absorbed in our world as he was in his.

Why is she here? Only Nanmei can tell me.

But Nanmei does not dream.

Each night I wait for the hazy outlines of a dream shape to form around her, but nothing that materializes is substantial enough to touch. So troubled is her slumber, there's never more than a pale gray aura. She dozes, halfway between sleep and consciousness, tossing constantly, restless as a sick child. Sometimes she lies with eyes wide open, staring into the darkness, her breathing heavy and strained. No wonder she's so bony, her eyes so cavernous. Until she manages to settle down into restful sleep, I won't learn anything.

Nanmei is pleased with the library, with where I had hung the old chalkboard, with the plentiful supply of paper and pencils, with the room's large windows. The only change she makes is to move the table right beneath the window that faces the orchard so that sunlight falls bright and unobstructed across its surface.

"It's important to read in good natural light," she says. "You have such pretty eyes, Weilan. We don't want you to become nearsighted."

My daughter nods, already charmed. The two of them unfold a world map and Weilan points to all the countries whose names she knows. Then Nanmei hands her a textbook.

"Please read this page for me."

"Oh, I know this story." And she reads out loud from *The Children's History of Twenty-Four Exemplars of Filial Piety*, the story of the little boy who slept naked on hot summer nights so mosquitoes would bite his tender flesh and leave his parents alone.

Nanmei claps her hands and holds out another book. "Excellent! Try this one."

My daughter reads two more stories, the texts increasing in difficulty. She's showing off, but how can anyone blame her for enjoying the attention? I'm envious of Nanmei, sorry I can't join them, my daughter and my best friend.

"Now let me hear you recite your times tables."

"I can go up to the nines, Teacher Wang."

When Weilan is partway through chanting the fives, Meichiu enters the library. Weilan pauses, but Meichiu waves at her to continue. She is nearly six months pregnant, her belly prominent and her face rounder than ever. She leans against the door, her head bobbing in time to Weilan's lilting recitation. At the end of the nines, both Meichiu and Nanmei clap. I join in even though they can't hear me. Weilan blushes.

"Would you like me to recite a Tang poem for you, Teacher Wang?" she asks.

"No, but get some writing paper and copy out this page for me. Let me see how well you can write."

With Weilan busy at her task, Nanmei turns her attention to Meichiu.

"Young Mistress, did you want me for anything?"

"Actually I came to see whether *you* needed anything, Teacher Wang."

"No, no. We have all the books and supplies we need."

"I hope you teach a lot of arithmetic? That would be a more useful skill than reciting Tang poetry." Meichiu rolls her eyes but smiles to show she means it kindly.

Nanmei smiles back. "Don't worry. As you said, I'm a merchant's daughter."

Meichiu returns to the veranda to knit. She pulls yarn from a basket on the wicker table beside her. Baizhen joins her to read a newspaper. A gentle gust of wind blows through the bamboo trees, filling the courtyard with a light flicking sound. It's October, but the afternoon is warm and the sun stretches across the rock garden, staining its surfaces with a rosy gold light. The murmur of Weilan's and Nanmei's voices drifts out from the open door of the library.

I lean against the door, pretending that I'm part of this world, that my daughter is simply too absorbed in her studies to notice me.

༄༅

Meichiu is making friends with my best friend.

My *yang* soul raises his eyebrows and I realize how petty this sounds. I try to explain myself. *Nanmei is only a hired tutor. Meichiu is a mistress of the house.*

I don't think Meichiu is very strict with protocols, says my *yin* soul. *After all, a teacher is a respected figure.*

Yes, *and they have so much in common*, I snap. *Nanmei is no mere merchant's daughter. Her father owns the biggest cotton mills in the province.*

First Nanmei is only a hired tutor, now she's too good for Meichiu, my *yin* soul remarks, yawning, showing her tongue, as pink as a cat's.

They're both lonely and they're of a similar age, says my *hun* soul. *You should be happy that they're getting along. And didn't you hope Meichiu would be kind to Weilan? I think she's being very nice, and Nanmei's presence helps bring them closer.*

If she delivers a son, who knows how she'll treat my daughter? That's when we'll see her true colors. I can't help my grumbling, even though I know how unreasonable I sound.

23

Old Kwan is speechless at the sight of three huge air-dried hams from Jinhua, the finest he's ever seen. Meichiu's mother has sent two servants to Pinghu, laden with food and herbal tonics to nourish Meichiu during her final months of pregnancy. There are also gifts for Baizhen and my in-laws: European cookies filled with cream and nuts, chocolate candies, and, of course, several jars of strong rice wine. There's even something for Weilan. It's only a length of fabric, blue cotton woven with pink blossoms, but since Meichiu's family isn't obliged to give my daughter anything at all, I'm immensely pleased by this gesture.

Meichiu's family had swarmed all over our houses and gardens at the wedding. It had really been too cold to sit outside in the pavilion, but they did so anyway, delighting in the rock garden, the bamboo grove, the orchard. I had been envious of Meichiu's brisk and sensible mother, her amiable father, her high-spirited siblings. I hope the gift of fabric is a hint from Meichiu's mother that she should be kind to her little stepdaughter.

To Weilan's delight, the servants have also brought ten black silkie hens and one black rooster. Six of the hens are meant for the pot; broth simmered from these birds is extremely nutritious. The rest are to be raised for their eggs, and for chicks to increase the flock. Apart from a stray calico cat, who didn't stay long, and some goldfish we kept in a stone urn by the rock garden, Weilan has never had any pets. She has always loved animals, though, and the silkies fascinate her, for they are gentle birds with soft, fluffy plumage.

Old Kwan, however, isn't pleased. The day after the silkies arrive, he stomps into the dining room, upset. The chicken coop in the kitchen garden isn't large enough to hold the silkies as well as the hens we already have. Old Kwan refuses to unsettle his tried-and-true egg-layers by bringing new birds into an established flock.

"Furthermore," says Old Kwan to Jia Po, arms crossed, "we can't raise them. Those silkies are too meek to be part of a mixed flock. By tomorrow, you know, our old rooster will have pecked that little black male to death. We should cook them all."

"But, Kwan, can't we just separate the two flocks?" Meichiu asks.

She's the Young Mistress, but Old Kwan rules the kitchen and its gardens.

"Where would you run the fence, Young Mistress? Through my spinach patch? And we'd need a second coop."

Little Ming, who is feeding Ah Jiao at the next table, speaks up.

"There's an old chicken coop in the orchard. My grandfather could mend it and we could raise them in there, away from the chickens in the kitchen garden."

"I am not," says Old Kwan, glaring at her, "going to walk every day all the way to the orchard to feed those chickens and shoo them in and out of the coop."

"I'll do it! I will!" Weilan leaves Little Ming's side and runs up to Old Kwan. "I'll look after them. The small orchard is just beside our house, I can do it easily."

"Children are forgetful." Old Kwan scowls down at her. "They'll die. We should just cook them all."

"We can take care of them together," says Nanmei. "We won't forget, will we, Weilan?"

Meichiu claps her hands. "So kind of you, Teacher Wang."

Old Kwan stomps away, appeased but still muttering.

Old Ming mends the orchard coop as promised and that evening the silkies are safely enclosed within its walls.

Each morning Weilan and Nanmei open the coop door to a symphony of crooning and clucking as they scatter grain for the mild-mannered chickens. In the evening, Weilan hunts for eggs in the coop and around the orchard, carefully tucking them in a basket to give to Old Kwan.

"Who lived here?" Nanmei asks one afternoon. She pushes the cottage door open wide and steps inside.

"I don't know," Weilan says. She comes in with her basket. "Papa says if he'd had a younger brother, his brother would've lived in this little house. Or, if we had an elderly aunt or uncle, they would've lived here, where it's quiet."

I can't bear to follow them inside. The rolled-up old bedding is still there, the stub of melted candle on the broken tile. The open door reveals a space even more decrepit than I remember, this room that was once my haven, but it's humiliation that washes over me. And memories, now unwanted, of delirious lovemaking.

"I suppose you were a much bigger family once," says Nanmei, shutting the door. "Look, two eggs under that hydrangea shrub."

Weilan kneels to reach into the leafy stalks, and when she scrambles up she adds two pale eggs to the basket.

"It's so peaceful here, like another world," Nanmei says, gazing toward the branches overhead, now nearly bare of leaves. "It must be beautiful when the fruit trees are in bloom."

They round up the silkies and shut them in the coop.

After they leave, I drift over to the cottage door. Traces of grease still cling to the latch. I hope Nanmei didn't see this clue to my affair. I'm just a ghost now, but somehow I still don't want her to know.

∽∾∾∽

Nanmei. How I waver between gratitude and jealousy. She's a good teacher, patient and observant, always mindful of Weilan's needs and interests, ready to fan curiosity into knowledge. She's reserved and respectful with adults, but when she and Weilan are alone she's as merry as a child. Her eyes shine with as much pleasure as Weilan's when the two of them turn the pages of the books my sisters sent us years ago.

She explains each lesson instead of having Weilan just memorize the words, and takes her questions as seriously as though they come from an adult. Weilan would stay in the schoolroom all day but Nanmei insists on naps.

"You need to be rested so that what you learn can settle into your brain. Besides"—she laughs—"I need a rest too, just to keep up with you."

Nanmei tells Baizhen that Weilan is quite possibly the cleverest little girl she has ever taught.

"Her mother was well-educated, and tutored her," says Baizhen, beaming. "My first wife came from a fine family, a long line of scholars. But of course, you know that if you know her brother."

"He's the friend of a friend. I can't claim the honor of calling him my own friend." She is courteous, but guarded.

❧

When Weilan naps in the afternoon, Nanmei stays in the library. She seems to have set herself the task of examining all the books there. She pulls each one out in turn, flipping through pages but rarely seeming to read. She marks her day's progress with a slip of paper tucked between two volumes and, at the next opportunity, starts her inspection again from there. She even looks through the used exercise books I could never bring myself to throw out: they contain Weilan's earliest efforts at writing.

I must find a way to enter her dream life. I wait each night beside her bed, watching for a sign that she has finally settled into a sleep deep enough to hold dreams.

On a night when the moon is full, I visit Nanmei as I often do, but this time she doesn't sleep at all. She pulls her coat on over her nightclothes. Her cloth shoes slide silently along the veranda and down the stairs, which are repaired now and don't creak. Her trembling fingers press the latch of my bedroom door and she slips inside. The door closes behind her softly.

The moon floods the room with cold, brilliant light, casting long shadows as she moves swiftly through the space, first running her hand over the top shelf of the armoire, then pulling open the wide drawer at the bottom. She even feels inside the pockets of the two winter coats hanging there. Then she checks each drawer of my bureau, which holds neatly folded blouses and skirts, un-touched since my death. She lifts and replaces the items care-fully. Next she lifts the lid of my storage trunk, releasing the scent of mothballs, rummaging all the way to the bottom, beneath the piles of winter clothing and blankets.

Finally she shuts the bedroom door and steals down the path to the outhouse. She disappears behind the screen of oleander shrubs. But instead of entering the outhouse, she slips to the other side and in a few seconds is at the orchard gate.

Inside the orchard, the silkies cluck softly in their coop, then fall silent again. Nanmei pushes open the cottage door. Moonlight shines through the small windows, casting a leafy pattern of shad-ows which wavers with the breeze. She pulls a candle from her pocket and lights it. Looking around, she dribbles some wax on a broken tile and presses the candle onto its cracked surface. With her makeshift lamp in hand, she searches the cottage, reaching under the old bed, groping in drawers, even lifting up the dirty mattress. She sets the candle down to search the wardrobe, and unrolls the musty sheets and quilts I had stowed there for my trysts with Hanchin. Finally, with a sigh, she blows out the candle.

Outside, she leans against the trunk of a peach tree, ex-hausted. She's shaking, and I know it has nothing to do with the evening chill. Nanmei returns to her room, silent and un-observed. She curls up in bed and sobs quietly, the quilt pulled over her head. She doesn't sleep, just dozes fitfully as usual. This tormented young woman who holds her secrets so close bears no resemblance to the lively, spirited girl who was my best friend.

Not every night, but a few times each week now, Nanmei searches the unoccupied rooms of the house. Each of her forays is brief, a few minutes at most is all that she dares. When Baizhen takes Meichiu and Weilan to the movie theater one afternoon, Nanmei takes her time, searching their rooms while Little Ming gossips in the kitchen with Old Kwan.

I know why she is searching. If only she would dream.

∽∾∽

In the new year, an event of supreme importance brings Gong Gong back from his self-imposed exile. The moment Meichiu goes into labor, Jia Po sends Little Ming running for the midwife while Baizhen sends a donkey cart to Infant Mountain to bring his father home. The cart driver, pleased to be part of a joyous event that will bring him a good fee, slaps his animal's flanks with a willow stick and sets it trotting. The cart makes the trip at top speed and within a few hours Gong Gong is at the front gate, bellowing at Old Ming to open the door.

Meichiu has done her duty, and very quickly too. Jia Po is so happy she leaves off scolding her husband.

"A healthy, big boy!" she cries, as soon as Gong Gong steps over the threshold. "Husband, we have a grandson!"

ᘓᗡᘉᗢ

When I married Baizhen, Gong Gong and Jia Po became my parents. Their wishes superseded those of my own father. Yet as a daughter-in-law, I had been less than a true daughter of the house, no matter how much my in-laws approved of me, no matter how much Baizhen loved me. Only bringing a grandson would have elevated my status, and in this I had failed.

Meichiu is now securely positioned in the family. For the moment, she is completely absorbed with motherhood, all of her waking hours spent in bed cuddling her son, or in the nursery watching him suckle at Little Ming's round breasts. Jia Po practically lives in the nursery, fussing over Meichiu and the baby, who has yet to be named. In fact, everyone seems to spend all their spare time in the nursery. Baizhen is as proud as a rooster when he holds the infant. Mrs. Kwan and Dali always find reasons to peek in. Weilan rushes in between lessons to admire the baby.

Only Gong Gong, temporarily absorbed in the important task of selecting a name for his grandson, doesn't join the crowd around the baby. He spends hours in his study consulting family genealogies; he visits his grandson only on occasion, as if for inspiration.

"Look at how his mouth pulls at her teat," Jia Po declares. "He won't be a fussy eater."

"How strong he is, see how his little legs kick," says Baizhen, smoothing down the soft black hair on the baby's round skull.

Sitting beside Little Ming, Meichiu says nothing, but smiles contentedly. Weilan leans over Little Ming's shoulder, a rapt, adoring look on her face.

"Isn't he a handsome little brother?" Baizhen asks, noticing her expression. She nods and carefully strokes the dark, downy hair with one finger.

Little Ming looks up at Baizhen reproachfully and whispers, "Young Master, you're tempting the evil spirits." Then, louder, she says, "This child is cross-eyed and will grow up to be bad-tempered. I can tell by the way he sucks."

From the other side of the room, Ah Jiao is crying, hungry for his lunch and for his mother's attention. Little Ming looks up, apologetic.

"There's some congee over there in a bowl," she says. "I'll feed him later."

"In the meantime, he's disturbing the baby," says Jia Po crossly.

Nanmei picks up Ah Jiao, puts him over her shoulder smoothly, and picks up the bowl and spoon.

"It's all right. I'll take him next door into Weilan's room and give him his meal in there."

Gong Gong finally names his grandson Lee Weihong. Then he composes a birth announcement and sends it out to be printed on sheets of red paper flecked with gold. When the order arrives my in-laws work in tandem, Gong Gong addressing envelopes while Jia Po stuffs them. As the envelopes pile up, their conversation grows more animated. There's no longer any hint of animosity between them.

❦

Enchanted by his son these days, Baizhen spends less time with Weilan. Who can blame him? What could be more joyful than the birth of a son? As for Meichiu, my worst fear had been that she would grow cold to Weilan, perhaps even turn cruel once her position in the family was secure. But so far nothing of the sort has transpired. Now that she's mother to the heir of the family, Meichiu concentrates on running the household. She asserts herself with a confidence that testifies to a lifetime of lessons passed down from a practical mother.

She begins with the housekeeping budget.

"You've spent enough years poring over the accounts," she says to Jia Po. "Please let me look after the expenses so that you can spend more time with your new grandson."

Jia Po gives in with barely a murmur of protest.

I used to do the accounts but only to record what we'd already spent, or to try to estimate just how poor we would be in a few years' time. Meichiu is from a newly prosperous merchant family and better understands how to rein in costs.

She takes an inventory of food supplies in the kitchen. She plans meals a week in advance, sitting with Old Kwan at the kitchen table with the cupboards open to see what the cook might need for the days ahead. Her menus are full of tofu and eggs, vegetables and fish. Pork is on the menu only once a week, chicken and beef very rarely.

She investigates closets and drawers, pulling out fabric stored for decades and shaking out packets of mothballs so old the naphthalene has evaporated down to tiny white granules like seed pearls.

"We don't need to buy any cloth this year," she says, holding up a length of silk brocade. "This material has been hidden away for such a long time, it should all be used."

"But, Daughter," protests Jia Po, looking at the pile of cloth. "This silk velvet is too good to use for ordinary clothing, and so is this fine embroidered cotton."

"How old is the cotton?" Meichiu holds up the fabric to display a number of moth holes.

"My own mother gave it to me the year I was married. It's European."

"Mother, if we don't use these fabrics, they will just go to waste. It costs less to sew what we have than to buy more cloth."

Soon Gong Gong receives a new jacket of silk velvet finer than any he has ever worn, and a small round cap to match. Meichiu sews blouses for Jia Po from the embroidered cotton, the pieces carefully cut to hide or trim moth holes. The blue silk brocade turns into a padded jacket for Baizhen. The leftovers are enough to make Weilan tunics and trousers.

Meichiu is good for the family, I have to admit this.

❦

No one dreams about me anymore. I've been dead just over a year. Meichiu's baby, Gong Gong's return. They have other things to think about.

Perhaps they do dream about you, my *yin* soul says. *You just don't happen to be in their dreams at the right time.* She wafts the fragrance of osmanthus blossom in my direction, but it fails to soothe me.

The family is completely besotted with the baby. I'm the last thing on their minds. Do you see how comfortable Baizhen looks with his new wife?

Are you jealous? my *hun* soul asks. *You were never in love with him.*

Well, of course I'm glad that he has a wife who's so good to him. And that he has a son. I just thought it would take him longer to forget me.

He remembers you. He loves you still. But he always was in awe of you, says my *hun* soul. *He just finds Meichiu simpler to understand.*

Perhaps he'll dream of you again, says my *yin* soul, *when the baby is older and the household has settled into a routine again.*

We all know this needs to happen soon.

How are you feeling? my *yang* soul asks. He's anxious. There is an iron tang in my mouth.

I'm all nerves, I admit. *Even when I'm watching Weilan sleep I feel restless and unsettled. It's driving me insane.*

There's a silence and I realize what I've said. *That's just a figure of speech,* I say quickly. *I'm nowhere near turning into an insane hungry ghost. Don't you think you'd be the first to know?*

∽∼∾

"Your brother-in-law is coming to visit," Gong Gong says, and hands the letter to Baizhen.

Baizhen hastens to explain to Meichiu. "It's from my first wife's brother, Weilan's Second Uncle. He introduced Teacher Wang to us."

Congratulations on the birth of your son. Although he isn't of my blood, it cheers me to know that you have an heir, and my niece a brother. I wish to convey our family's congratulations in person. I would also like to see for myself whether Miss Wang has proven a good tutor. I'll be in Shanghai on business on the fifteenth of this month. I'll take the train to Pinghu from there. I will stay only for one or two days.

How I wish the stories about ghostly powers were true. Then I could appear at will anywhere, in Changchow or Shanghai, even Hong Kong, to learn what my sisters are doing, to spy on Tongyin, to uncover what Nanmei is up to.

When she learns about Tongyin's visit, Nanmei sleeps even less. She's up every night searching the estate. She even looks in the chicken coop one afternoon when Weilan is out with Jia Po. If Nanmei can't tell me anything through her dreams, I'll have to wait for my brother. In a few days I can spy on his conversations with Nanmei, even try to enter his dreams.

Gong Gong decides that all three generations of the family must pay a visit to the Temple of Soul's Enlightenment to make offerings of thanks for the birth of little Weihong.

"But what will you do while I'm gone?" Weilan asks Nanmei, confident in the way children are that others can't function without them.

"I'll write letters. You've kept me so busy, I haven't written to my friends. They'll think I've vanished."

"Will you tell them about me?"

"Of course. I'll tell them you're short and bad at arithmetic."

An indignant shriek of protest and giggles, but before Weilan can answer, Little Ming calls up from the courtyard.

"Little Mistress, the rickshaws are here. We must hurry!"

"I'm coming, I'm coming!"

The rickshaws depart and the servants withdraw to the kitchen to enjoy a precious hour of leisure. They huddle around the kitchen stove, sharing gossip and a bowl of salted peanuts. Ah Jiao sleeps in Mrs. Kwan's arms, accustomed now to being passed around among the servants.

In the library, Nanmei sets out some writing materials. But she doesn't do any writing. Instead she steals again into my bedroom, opens all the drawers she's opened before. She even removes them to look beneath each one. She lifts pictures from the wall and pries open their frames, one by one.

When she first began these secret explorations I had suspected her of looking for money or jewelery. Now I'm certain she's looking for Hanchin's manifesto.

Could she be the courier assigned to collect the manifesto? But it was Tongyin who arranged for her tutoring job. Is she on the Nationalist side then, working for Tongyin?

Nanmei replaces my photograph in its frame and adjusts its cardboard mat, then hangs it back on the wall. She touches the glass over my face and sighs.

Next she opens the storage trunk containing my winter clothes and lifts them out, even though she's done this before. The plum-colored jacket, my blue student blazer, which I couldn't bear to give away, in the hope that someday Weilan would wear it to my old school. Nanmei takes out dark-hued winter vests padded with silk batting, a green velvet tunic and skirt embroidered with butterflies. She runs her hands over them all, searches in the pockets, and refolds them. At the very bottom of the trunk, beneath a stack of pillowcases, she finds something she hasn't seen in her previous, candlelit searches. A man's handkerchief, a much-washed green-and-gray plaid. She tucks the handkerchief into her vest pocket and with carefully controlled motions returns my clothes to the trunk.

Back in her room, she falls on the bed and sobs without restraint. She unfolds the square of faded cotton and holds it to her face, breathing in deeply. Tears run down her cheeks and she rocks back and forth in anguish, her face buried in Hanchin's handkerchief.

"Oh, my husband, my life's companion. Come back, come back to me!"

⌒⌒⌒

So that's who she really is. My souls and I stare at Nanmei as she muffles her sobs in her pillow.

After I realized how Hanchin had used me, I'd done my best to push him out of my mind. But jealous and angry thoughts, unpredictable as wreckage carried over rapids, would sometimes catch me by surprise. I had never stopped wondering what sort of woman he had married.

I wonder what Nanmei gave up for Hanchin's sake. My *yin* soul voices my thoughts. Her brow furrows in sympathy for Nanmei and she approaches the bed as if to comfort the weeping woman.

There was a time when you would have been jealous of her for marrying the man you loved but couldn't have, my yang soul says. He watches me carefully.

Now I'm dead. And when I see her cry, I grieve for her.

Ah, because she is a widow? my *hun* soul asks.

I shake my head. *No, because she loved a man who was unworthy of her.*

24

*N*anmei opens the top drawer of the old bureau in her bed-room and pulls out a diary with a detachable cloth cover. When she removes the cover, I see a pocket sewn to its inside, a pocket containing two small photographs.

The first is a wedding photograph, hand-tinted. The couple wears traditional high-necked tunics of simple design; Nanmei's bridal status is made obvious only by the artificial flowers she holds to her chest. She is joyous, her plump face beams out at the camera. Hanchin's familiar smile is a little ironic, patient. Nanmei sets this photo down gently on the bureau top. The second photograph is one I recognize. I have a copy myself. It's in an album I'd left behind in Changchow, along with just about everything else from my school years. In it, Nanmei and I are side by side at a podium. Behind us is a banner for the debate club. This image had been published in our school yearbook with the caption *Most likely to marry politicians*.

Nanmei studies our faces, our pert, confident smiles. Then

she takes from the drawer a sheet of flimsy blue paper and a pencil, and begins to write:

My dearest Husband,

I guessed you were here, that you came to Leiyin for help. Now I know you found her. I knew that even if you told her about us, she would still have helped you. She was a good friend and a good person. I regret nothing, Hanchin. I don't care that my family disowned me. I don't care about all those years in poor farming villages, living in mud-brick shacks. Even being apart so often, you in the city, me teaching in rural schools, I was happy. We were building a new China together.

But of course Hanchin never told me he was married, let alone to my best friend. He knew the depths of my infatuation, knew I would be jealous and angry, and manipulated me in his own way. Nanmei has a better opinion of me than I deserve. And now I know that she was teaching school in the country while Hanchin returned to soft beds and city life in Changchow and Shanghai, to run his spy network. But why is she writing a letter to a dead man?

She pulls out another sheet and begins writing again:

Dear Leiyin,

As soon as I met Hanchin, I understood why you loved him. You never knew I delivered all your letters to his office personally instead of putting them in the post. He was so kind, so attentive, so willing to take the time to chat with me. I told him I would be attending university in Soochow, a less prestigious school than yours. I envied you so much, your university, your romance, your future.

After I arrived at my aunt's home in Soochow, my sister let me know in a letter that your marriage, so sudden, was the talk of the town. Then Hanchin came to see me. He had taken a teaching job in Soochow and decided to look me up. I was so flattered.

Do you remember when we promised to write to each other every week? But we didn't, and now you're gone. I am so sorry. But I'm writing to you now.

She crumples up both letters and drops them in her waste-basket, an old tin bucket that's missing its handle. She lights a match and kneels down to watch the pages burn.

Outside, a babble of voices announces the family's return from the temple. Nanmei hides her photographs and slips the cloth cover over the diary. She pushes the book to the rear of the drawer and shuts it, and by the time Weilan bounds upstairs Nanmei is in the library, quietly writing letters.

∽∽∽

I ride in the rickshaw facing Baizhen and Tongyin. My brother descended from the train with two suitcases; he and my husband are sitting with their feet propped up on the luggage.

"My mother looks forward to seeing you again," says Baizhen. "Your last visit was the liveliest evening we'd had in years."

I remembered that visit. The *mah-jong*, the drinking. Tongyin telling me about Hanchin's wife.

"With your new son, the house must be quite lively every day."

"Yes, it is. But it's different. The whole household revolves around the baby."

"I hope your wife doesn't mind. After all, I'm a reminder of your first wife."

"Nonsense! You're my brother-in-law and Weilan's uncle. Death does not cut the ties of family. Why, do you remember the Wu and Kang families my mother mentioned on your last visit? They continue to call each other kin, even though the Kang boy died a few months after the betrothal."

"So the Wu girl is now considered a widow?"

"Almost, almost. Her parents are finding another husband for her, but the Kang family gets a say in the decision. A mere courtesy of course."

❦

When Tongyin appears for dinner, his arms are loaded with packages that he puts down on a side table before bowing deeply to Gong Gong and Jia Po.

"Please accept some gifts from our family, with congratulations on the birth of an heir."

Gong Gong is visibly moved. "Not a day goes by that we don't cherish the memory of your sister. Tomorrow, we'll show you her ancestral tablet in the family temple. Weilan can offer incense along with you."

"Exactly. Those were my intentions. To offer incense to my sister. Perhaps I could see the schoolroom tomorrow. I'd like to report back to my eldest brother that all is well with our little niece's education."

It's a sham on Tongyin's part, I'm sure of it. A letter of congratulations for the birth of little Weihong would have been enough. Perhaps a red envelope with some token amount of cash, or a gift of tea and ginseng—all this could have been arranged easily by Changyin's secretary. There was no need for Tongyin to come in person.

Old Kwan had been ordered to splurge on this meal. Fish soup thick with strands of beaten egg appeared on the table, a jellied pork terrine, fragrant tea-smoked duck, and river crabs steamed with ginger and wine. The liquor, once again, is fine cognac, a gift from Tongyin.

Weilan isn't present. She and Nanmei are eating in the nursery with Little Ming and the baby. After supper Jia Po sends for them. Weihong, in Little Ming's arms, receives most of his grandparents' attention and words of praise from Tongyin.

"Such healthy color in his cheeks. What a solid little arm."

That's the extent of what my brother can say about babies. He turns his attention to Nanmei.

"Teacher Wang, I hear your work is excellent. Yes, excellent," he says. "I look forward to talking with you tomorrow, perhaps when Weilan is taking a nap."

She bows her head. "Any time you wish tomorrow, Mr. Song."

Then she gives Weilan a tap on the shoulder, a small push forward.

"Good night, Second Uncle," my daughter says, her voice confident. "I'd like to recite some poetry for you tomorrow if you have time."

"I would be delighted, Little One."

I feel proud of Weilan's poise, and know that Baizhen feels the same because he pats Weilan's head approvingly when she passes his chair on her way out. Tongyin's eyes follow her.

"How is your stepmother?" Jia Po asks. "We used to enjoy her letters to Leiyin. So much useful advice."

"Ah, you mean my father's concubine. She is well, very well. As competent as ever, yes, still running the house like a general."

I have to smile. Even though Geeling is the clan matriarch now, she is no match for Stepmother and Head Servant Lu.

"Weilan is a lovely little girl," Tongyin says, clearing his throat. "Very lovely. Very bright. Have you thought about her marriage?"

I don't know why, but my heart lurches in fear at his words.

"I must confess," says Baizhen, "I haven't thought about it much; she's not yet seven years old. But one reason we wanted a tutor for her is that with an education, her prospects might be better."

Jia Po sighs. I know she's thinking about the dowry.

"So you're thinking of a local family?" Tongyin continues.

"Her mother" — and here Baizhen falters a little — "your sister hoped Weilan could marry a young man of good family from Changchow, or one of the cities. Someone with a university degree. That's only natural, coming from a family as sophisticated as yours."

"Since we're all family here," Jia Po interrupts, "let's be frank. All we can give Weilan is a small dowry and our family's good name. Only another Pinghu family would put any value on our name, so when the time comes, we'll probably arrange for Weilan to marry a local boy."

The air around her crackles with recriminations. With a grandson in the nursery, Jia Po is much happier, but there are still times when her bitterness toward Gong Gong wells up. Gong Gong stares into the deep amber liquid in his cup.

Tongyin smiles and leans across the table.

"I feel some obligation to help my dear sister's child. May I offer a suggestion?"

"We welcome your advice!" Baizhen cries. "We're just small-town folk."

"It's true that dowries still matter, alas. However, in some of the more progressive families, if there are strong personal ties between the families and good accounts of the girl's qualities, dowries are but a small part of the overall criteria."

He has their full attention and mine as well.

"You see, Mother," exclaims Baizhen. "Times are changing!"

"Take, for example, the Cha clan in Shanghai," continues Tongyin. "They're very progressive. General Cha was educated at West Point, a military school in America. He has four sons. His eldest is married. Two others are betrothed. I know for a fact that dowries were only a small part of the decisions. The youngest boy is not yet matched."

My spine is an icicle. If I had a voice I would be screaming by now. If ghostly hands had strength, I would be wringing Tongyin's neck.

"General Cha!" Gong Gong exclaims. "You know his family?"

"Yes, I do." Tongyin nods modestly. "Absolutely. Yes, I went to university with his son. We're also in business together." He helps himself to more duck.

"But what about the dowries?" Jia Po prompts impatiently.

"The Cha family doesn't need the money, you understand. Their first consideration is intelligence and discretion. Think of the social position the wives must uphold. They must know how to cultivate connections that help the Cha family."

Baizhen looks doubtful. "It sounds as though the girls must be exceptional."

Tongyin nods. "The girls are not only intelligent but also beautiful. You can count on a time when the young Cha wives will rule the elite of Chinese society."

"But Weilan is just a small-town girl," Gong Gong says, a note of dejection in his voice. "She won't be sophisticated enough."

"No, not true. Not at all. She's completely unspoiled, a clean slate." Tongyin laughs and slaps his knee. There's an oily quality to his voice. "After the betrothal, she would spend a few months of each year at the Cha estate, being trained in all the social graces. It's part of the marriage contract. She'll be groomed to be the perfect wife, whether the boy grows up to be a diplomat or a general."

The dining room is silent. My in-laws are beaming and hopeful, and even Meichiu nods.

I want to pound my fists on the table.

"This sounds too good to be true," Gong Gong says, finally finding words.

I want to scream at him. *That's because it is!*

"I believe Weilan has the right qualities. Yes, I truly believe this. If you're willing, I'll speak to my friend Cha Zhiming."

There's a hubbub of excitement at the dinner table. Gong Gong's eyes glisten at the thought of becoming allied to one of the most important men in China. He pours more cognac all around.

Only Baizhen seems hesitant. "I promised my . . . your sister that Weilan would go to high school. And she wanted our daughter to go to university as well."

"Surely there's a better future for her in the Cha family than as a schoolteacher," Gong Gong says with a trace of annoyance.

"Think of how much better our son's prospects would be with a sister married into such a prominent family," Meichiu adds.

I can see Baizhen wavering.

"Now, now," says Tongyin. "Nothing's settled. Nothing yet. All I can do is make the suggestion. But perhaps you could take Weilan to the photographer's tomorrow. I'd like to have some pictures to show Cha Zhiming when I speak to him."

"Nothing is settled," Gong Gong agrees, "but your kindness is already more than we ever expected. The least we can do is to arrange for some photographs of Weilan."

If I could shatter plates and bring down the roof beams, this entire house would be in ruins.

❧

He's selling my daughter! Tongyin must know what Cha Zhiming is like. How can he care so little about her fate? And the family's going along with it, even Baizhen is swayed.

They don't know what you know about the Cha family, my yang soul says. *Perhaps Tongyin doesn't really know either. Or he believes Cha Zhiming wouldn't touch his younger brother's fiancée.*

All Tongyin knows is that the Cha family once made an offer for Fei-Fei, my yin soul says, *and that gave him the idea.*

What Tongyin knows, suspects, or is ignorant about doesn't matter, says my *hun* soul. *Weilan mustn't end up with that family.*

I don't know how, but I must stop him, I agree. *At any cost.*

✶✶✶

Tongyin sits on his bed in the guest room and lifts up the quilt. Dali has placed two hot bricks wrapped in flannel at the foot of the bed. He sighs and undresses, throwing his clothes over a chair. He puts on silk pajamas and a robe of the same garnet red in a heavier silk. From his suitcase he pulls out a bottle of cognac and pours himself a drink.

He tosses and turns for nearly an hour before the hazy dream shadow forms over his head. Lifting its thin veil I step inside, wondering whether doing harm in a dream has any effect in real life, because all evening I've wanted to murder my brother.

In his dream, Tongyin pushes open the door to a long, brightly lit corridor. His footsteps echo on bare concrete and un-painted walls. There are no windows, only doors spaced far apart. Bare lightbulbs hanging from the ceiling swing back and forth in the draft that blows in from the open door. He's still wearing his garnet silk pajamas and he shivers in his bare feet. A sliver of light widens to a triangle as a door opens farther along the corridor. My brother hesitantly enters a dingy office where a Nationalist police captain is seated behind a desk. Other men are sitting in the dim shadows at the corners of the room, their faces indistinct, their figures dark and threatening.

"I don't have it. I don't have it." Tongyin looks frightened. "I'm sorry, I didn't know the document existed until after he was executed."

"It's the only thing that will save you." The police captain's face blurs and now I'm looking at Cha Zhiming.

"My sister would have known where to look," says Tongyin, "but now she's dead. I'm trying my best. I've sent Hanchin's wife to look. I didn't tell you about her, but that's what I've done."

Rising to their feet, the shadowy figures in the corners reach for their guns.

"Wait, wait. Cha, tell them." He looks at Cha Zhiming, pleading. "We're related, we're family. My niece is married to your little brother."

Cha Zhiming shakes his head. "Not yet." A gun appears in his hand.

Tongyin turns and runs into the corridor, which stretches out in an endless tunnel to nowhere. His movements are agonizingly slow, as though he is pushing through river mud, his pursuers always just a few steps behind. Then he wakes up, shuddering.

I've learned nothing except what I already know: Tongyin's frightened of Cha Zhiming and the Nationalist police. And Tongyin somehow knows about the manifesto. I can't be sure of anything else. Does Cha Zhiming also know about the manifesto? Does he know that Tongyin thinks it's hidden here?

Then I realize that my hand is still holding on to the edge of his dream shape.

Tongyin reaches for the packet of cigarettes on his bedside table. The table blurs, its color changes from a lacquered black to rich mahogany. Through the window, a noonday sun blazes down on a rose garden in full bloom. He's still dreaming. To escape his fear, he dreamed of waking up. Now he's started a new dream and he's in his bedroom in my family's Changchow villa.

Nanmei enters the room, a Nanmei dressed in drab peasant clothing, thin and dirty.

"Miss Wang, what progress have you made?" he asks, with no sign of the terror of his previous dream. A faint wisp of tobacco smoke curls upward with his words.

I will my dream-image to appear. I need to speak with him directly.

"You should ask Leiyin," says Nanmei's dream-image.

"I know she saw your husband while he was in Pinghu." He laughs, and it's not a pleasant laugh. "Yes, I would say she helped him quite a lot, my little sister."

Nanmei's features swim and now it's my dream-image that paces through the room, dressed in a school uniform, hair in two pigtails. I look about fifteen years old. So that's how my brother remembers me. The image begins to waver, but before it can shift back to Nanmei's figure, I step in. My body prickles all over, not quite a sting, not quite an itch. Then the sensation dwindles, my dream-image grows solid, and I face my brother to say what I've wanted to shout all evening.

"Don't you dare offer my daughter to the Cha family!"

Tongyin looks startled, then he smiles. "But I'm doing it to keep our family safe, Little Sister. If we're related to them, they can't arrest me."

"Arrest you for what?"

He doesn't answer my question. "Little Sister, where's Hanchin's manifesto?"

"Why? How does that document have anything to do with my child?"

He doesn't reply, just buries his face in his hands. I try again.

"If I tell you where to find the document, will that be enough to keep you safe? Will you forget about a marriage between Weilan and the Cha boy?"

"I need both, the document and a family connection to the Cha clan. Then I'll be safe."

"Tongyin, listen to me. The Cha men like little girls. If you send your niece to that family, she'll be abused and molested. Please don't mention my innocent child to those men."

He doesn't listen; he's weeping.

"Did you hear what I said about Weilan?" I shake him and he looks up.

"Yes, yes, I heard. She'll be fine, don't worry."

I slap him and he recoils, a look of astonishment on his face.

"Don't you dare marry off my daughter to Cha's little brother," I hiss. "I may be dead, Second Brother, but I will curse you from beyond the grave if you buy your safety with my daughter. I'll tell you where I hid the document, but only if you promise to leave her alone."

"It's not enough," he whimpers. "It's never enough."

He wakes up, this time for real. I'm standing over him, but am helpless now to make myself heard. He struggles to his feet and reaches for his cigarettes. I can't tell if he remembers anything about the dream—my pleading and then angry words. If only he weren't leaving Pinghu tomorrow. I'd haunt his dreams every night until he was more afraid of my ghost than of Cha Zhiming.

The servants at the far end of the estate are stirring. Dali is lighting the stove with coals kept hot from the night before, Old Kwan is throwing cold water over his face while his wife combs her hair into a tight bun. In the nursery, Little Ming is still asleep, Ah Jiao tucked against her side. Weilan is dozing, nearly awake, arms and legs sprawled beneath her quilts. A few rooms away, Baizhen has joined Meichiu and they talk softly, looking down at the baby between them, just as Baizhen and I used to do when Weilan was tiny.

Tongyin's presence menaces this little world, like a hostile wave that could carry away my daughter to dangerous shores. How can I stop him?

☙❧

I have to warn Baizhen. I have to warn Jia Po. I'll even try Gong Gong and Nanmei.

But what can Nanmei do? my *yin* soul replies, puzzled. She stands balanced on a newel post at the end of the stone balusters that surround the terrace, her pleated skirt fluttering in a cold wind.

I don't know, I don't know! I pace from the edge of the terrace to the door of the family shrine and back again, my mind confused. I've never felt so helpless. But I must do what I can, influence whoever I can find dreaming of me. I don't care if the family gets frightened by my ghost haunting their dreams.

Perhaps the Cha family will reject Tongyin's offer, my *yin* soul says. *Perhaps we have nothing to worry about.*

I can't take that risk. Once Tongyin has photographs of Weilan to show Cha Zhiming, the situation will be out of my control. Everything will happen away from Pinghu.

You don't have any control anyway, my *yin* soul points out.

We have another day, my *yang* soul says. The old gentleman looks tired again as he says, *When Tongyin and Nanmei are alone, perhaps we'll learn the true story.*

25

She doesn't have leather shoes to go with the dress," says Jia Po. "Only cloth."

She slips a pair of embroidered shoes over Weilan's feet, which are already encased in her best white ankle socks. Dancing around in the little plaid dress Jia Po made for her from the skirt of my school uniform, Weilan is pink with excitement at the thought of getting her picture taken and she twirls to make her skirt rise in the air.

"It's not a problem, no problem at all," says Tongyin. "Just tell the photographer to keep the camera above her knees or pose her behind something." Then, like a casual afterthought, he adds, "Have you had a family photo taken since Weihong was born?"

An hour later, the entire family has set out for Pinghu's one and only photography studio, Little Ming carrying baby Weihong. I have no interest in following the rickshaws. Tongyin has the house—and Nanmei—to himself and I am desperate to learn the truth about what is between them.

In the library, Nanmei looks tired. Tongyin slouches into a chair with practiced nonchalance and looks at her questioningly.

"I even searched the chicken coop," she says, not waiting for him to speak. "I was sure it would be in this house or the cottage in the orchard, somewhere close by. If it's here, it would be hidden indoors, protected from the weather."

"Is there someone else in Pinghu who might've been a contact? Hanchin still thought of Leiyin as a schoolgirl. I wonder if he would really trust her with something so important."

Nanmei considers this and shakes her head. "Perhaps it doesn't exist. He was captured just a few days after leaving Pinghu and never had the chance to send anyone a message. Perhaps he destroyed it when he knew he was going to be captured."

"That would be a pity. His manifesto would have given us all so much inspiration, especially now that he's a martyr to the Communist cause." Tongyin runs a finger over the books arranged on my bookcases. I can't believe Nanmei doesn't see through him, but then she's not familiar with that oily tone of voice. "Have you looked inside the books?"

"Yes, every one of them, and also inside the old exercise notebooks."

"I keep wondering about some other contact in Pinghu," he persists.

"Hanchin never told me anything about his contacts. He said it was safer that way." She sounds guarded.

"If the document had surfaced somewhere else I'm sure we would've seen copies distributed all over the country. You may be right. He probably destroyed it before he was captured." He twirls a pencil between his fingers.

"I had to try every avenue. I'm grateful you could get me here."

"I admired your husband very much. Very much." He actually sounds earnest.

"The one time he mentioned you in his letters, he said you'd given him a key to your apartment in Shanghai. You were a good friend."

Tongyin waves his hand. "Not at all, not at all. It was only a few rented rooms, not even in a very good part of town. Did he say anything else about our friendship?" His tone is casual, but I know there is emotion behind it.

"He didn't tend to reveal much in writing, as you know. I thought you were just an old friend until you told me you were one of his agents." Nanmei stands up and goes to the window. "I'll be leaving soon. I doubt the manifesto's here. There's no reason to stay. I must join my comrades behind the lines in Jiangxi."

With her back turned, she doesn't see the worried expression on Tongyin's face.

"Let me make arrangements to smuggle you to Jiangxi. Wait to hear from me. In the meantime, keep trying to find the manifesto. If you do, send a telegram to me in Shanghai. I'll come immediately and make sure it gets to the right people."

Everything I know about Tongyin is telling me that this is not the truth. All my instincts scream a warning. If Yen Hanchin's wife is a card he can play to regain Cha Zhiming's favor, he won't hesitate.

Nanmei's been duped, first by Hanchin and now by my brother.

My souls and I have congregated in Nanmei's small room, watching her sleep, waiting for a dream to materialize.

Perhaps Hanchin did love her, my *yin* soul suggests. *Surely he didn't marry her solely for some nefarious secret purpose.* She sits at the foot of the bed, cross-legged.

Do you think Nanmei suspects Hanchin had an affair with me? What would she think?

You're a ghost now, my *hun* soul reminds me. As if I needed reminding. *What does it matter what she thinks of you? But no, I don't think so. She believes in Hanchin absolutely. As much as you did.*

He did have that persuasive quality, didn't he? Of making people believe in him. My *yang* soul speaks like he's thinking out loud.

My *yin* soul speaks up suddenly. *Maybe Nanmei will dream of Hanchin! What if you meet him in one of her dreams?*

Let's worry about that when it happens. Right now, I just wish she would dream at all.

✦

After Tongyin's visit, Nanmei seems to relax a little. She no longer searches the house furiously at night. I don't know if Nanmei really trusts my brother, but if Hanchin ever told her about Young Wang the bookseller, she hasn't revealed this to Tongyin, so perhaps she knows enough about him to be cautious. There's so much I want to tell her. I want to warn her, to tell her to get away from Pinghu before Tongyin turns her in. But how can I talk to her when she never dreams? And how can I persuade her to help prevent Tongyin from offering my daughter to Cha Zhiming?

Over the next few nights I go to everyone's bedroom in turn: Baizhen, Jia Po, Gong Gong, Nanmei. Everyone dreams except Nanmei, but they never dream about me, or at least I never manage to enter their dreams at the right time. If only my souls could also walk into dreams. Then we could share the task of circling through the sleeping household, waiting for my image to appear.

No matter how often I enter his sleep-world, Baizhen doesn't dream about me anymore. All his dreams are of Meichiu, his son, and Weilan. I enter pleasant, uncomplicated scenes of picnics and birthday celebrations, of playing in the gardens, strolling beneath the trees that line Big Canal. I'm fading from his life as reality replaces memories, as contentment with his new family diminishes his sadness about my death. How can I even begin to warn him about Tongyin and the Cha household?

The horrible anxious sensation presses on me, growing stronger each day. Sometimes I can't tell whether this is the relentless pull of the afterlife or my own fear for Weilan's safety. Soon the photographs will arrive and Baizhen will mail them to Tongyin.

∽∾∾

Finally Nanmei's sleep becomes restful, and one night I detect at last a cold light gleaming around the outlines of her dream. It wavers at first, but slowly becomes substantial enough for my fingers to touch. I pull back and the shape balloons out, but the portal is dark. I can't see any shapes moving on the other side. I step through anyway, and find nothing but blackness, the dreamless sleep of utter exhaustion.

Why should I be surprised? She's been carrying a great burden of grief for her husband, and then she took on a nerve-racking mission to find the document that would be his legacy. Who knows what she endured getting to Changchow just to pick up Hanchin's trail. I step back out of her dream. Her face has softened and I can see again the sweetness of her features.

The next night, when there is movement behind the gauzy boundaries of the entryway to her dream, I prepare to step inside, then pause.

Does she dream of Hanchin?

My souls circle behind me, anxious, anticipating. I don't feel ready to see the two of them together. I don't know how I'll feel seeing Hanchin as remembered by his wife, to see them together and intimate, perhaps making love.

But for Weilan's sake, I must enter her dream.

Nanmei is in a dim, shacklike schoolroom. Its windows are no more than square holes cut from walls made of mud and straw. Twenty students—men, women, and adolescents in the tattered clothing of peasants—sit on the floor as she writes on the chalkboard the words for *China* and *revolution*. Hanchin stands by the door of the shack. Although I had prepared myself, his presence still jolts me. He holds a box of pencils and scraps of paper. I'm ready to face my fears, so I walk up to the dream-image of Hanchin and touch his shoulder, but he doesn't respond. He's only there in Nanmei's imagination.

Now Nanmei stands in a barn ripe with the odor of pigs and chickens. She holds up cards inscribed with large characters. The peasants sitting on dirty piles of straw repeat after her as she flashes the cards: *Field. Rice. Oil.* Hanchin stands by the door, again holding pencils and paper.

Nanmei is in our little library. Weilan is writing in a notebook. Three other children I don't recognize share the table, doing the same. Weilan wears the plaid dress and her hair is in pigtails. Hanchin stands by the door, holding a box of pencils and sheets of paper.

"How are your little students?" he asks.

"They're working on your manifesto," she replies. "I can't find it, so we must write another one."

"Ask Leiyin," says the dream-Hanchin, indicating the wall where my photograph hangs.

I will her to think of me. I beg her, silently.

Her hand on Weilan's shoulder, Nanmei pauses to look up at the wall. A woman appears at the door of the library, her face indistinct but wearing the dress and jacket from the photograph. Her face is blurry but surely the apparition is meant to be me. Before it can grow hazy or vanish, I hurry over, rush into the figure. There's a prickling sensation, the now-familiar all-over tingling, and as it recedes, I can tell from the changed appearance of my clothing, now clear and visible, that I fully inhabit my dream-image.

Hanchin's image merely continues to lean against the door frame.

I don't want to frighten Nanmei into waking up. This could very well be my only chance to speak to her. I smile as reassuringly as I can and approach the table very slowly. I stroke Weilan's hair. Nanmei smiles back at me and she is seventeen again, her face plump and pretty, her smile as wide as the horizon.

"I'm so happy to see you, Leiyin. I have so much to tell you."

I want to pour my heart out and talk for hours. But we're not teenagers anymore and we don't have hours.

"Oh, Nanmei, me too. But what I have to say is so, so important. Please try to remember this dream when you wake up. Promise that when you wake up, you'll write down everything I say in this dream right away, before it fades."

She cocks her head. "So we're dreaming?"

"Yes. Please remember just three things. First, don't trust Tongyin. He's the one who betrayed Hanchin. It was my fault too. I'm so sorry. I told Tongyin the route Hanchin was taking to Jiangxi."

"You? And Tongyin? You betrayed my husband?"

"If I had known what would happen, I never would have told Tongyin." She must believe me and I want her to forgive me. I'm dead but it still matters to me.

"Tongyin." She frowns, puzzled. I press on.

"Second, you must find a way to stop Tongyin from arranging Weilan's betrothal to General Cha's son. And third, the manifesto."

"The manifesto." Her face grows alert. "You're the only one who knows where it is. Please, tell me."

"Promise me, promise me first, that you'll prevent Tongyin from matching my daughter to the Cha boy. Nanmei, the Cha men like little girls. Weilan would have a terrible life."

"I promise. Tell me!" She stands up and takes my hand, gives it a squeeze.

"Look inside the trunk in my bedroom. The lid is lined with hard cardboard. Lift that out. Hanchin's document is underneath, in an envelope."

She claps her hands. "I should have just asked you in the first place."

"Please, Nanmei, repeat back to me what you must write down as soon as you're awake."

"Don't trust Tongyin, he betrayed my husband. Stop him from arranging a marriage for Weilan. Look in the clothing trunk, inside the lid." She recites the words with a big smile, not taking it seriously.

I want to tell her again, emphasize the importance of remembering, but the edges of the dream are softening. The walls of the room are blurring, running like watercolors in the rain.

"Nanmei," I say, reaching out to her, "please, remember this dream when you wake up."

But Nanmei is falling out of her dream and into a fitful doze, and I'm left standing in the middle of her room, my hand still outstretched. How much will she remember? I can only wait to see what happens when she wakes up.

Finally, the black rooster in the orchard greets the dawn with his call and Nanmei turns over, shivering a little. Her eyes open and she reaches for the coat she has spread over her blankets for added warmth. Her movements seem agonizingly slow as she settles it over her shoulders, then draws thick woolen socks onto her feet. She shuffles over to the chest of drawers and pulls out her diary and a pencil, then scribbles briefly. She sits on the cot again, staring at the page. *Leiyin. Tongyin. Trunk lid.* Nothing about Weilan.

In the schoolroom, Nanmei opens the shutters to let in the first pale rays of morning light. They fall on the framed photograph on the wall. She stands in silence for a moment to look at it, lost in thought.

Please, please, I beg. *Remember. Believe what I told you.*

But she writes nothing further.

As the morning progresses, my despair grows. Nanmei appears to have forgotten her dream. She takes Weilan into the orchard to let the chickens out of their coop before joining the rest of the family for breakfast.

Weilan finishes a page of math problems and Nanmei follows with a history lesson, stories about the lives of ancient emperors and heroes. They unroll a length of rice paper on the schoolroom table and draw a timeline of all the Chinese dynasties, from Xia to Qing, then the Republic of China.

Lunchtime, followed by nap time. Nanmei mends her clothes and sews a button back onto one of Weilan's pairs of trousers. More lessons, and then an afternoon excursion with Weilan to buy thread at the dry-goods store. Nanmei shows no sign of remembering what I've told her.

My chest is tight, my skin crawls as though I'm covered with invisible insects. The afterlife pulls at me. I'm a boat caught in a strong tide, my anchor line straining. I could snap and break at any moment.

The photographs arrive later that day, delivered to the house by the photographer's assistant. There are multiple copies of a family portrait, Jia Po and Gong Gong seated solemnly at the center, Weilan standing beside Jia Po. Baizhen and Meichiu stand behind them, Meichiu holding little Weihong in her arms so that he faces the camera. The photos are hand colored, Meichiu's cheeks a little too pink, a bit of shading added along her jawline to slim her face.

There's a portrait of baby Weihong propped up on cushions, looking up at just the right moment.

There are two portraits of Weilan. In one she poses beside a large vase filled with artificial plum blossoms. She's almost as tall as the vase. In the other, she looks out from a window frame decorated with elaborate latticework, the sort of prop every studio owns. Weilan looks exquisitely pretty, her smile happy and genuine. But she has been posed like a young woman instead of a little girl. Her body is angled and she looks over her shoulder at the camera. I hate the pictures.

But Weilan is delighted and asks for copies of her photographs to be framed and hung on the wall. Baizhen digs through drawers and trunks, turning up items that have been put away and forgotten over the decades. He finds a frame large enough to hold two pictures side by side. A middle-aged couple looks out from the wooden frame, their sepia-toned features solemn and joyless, as stiff and formal as their heavy brocade gowns.

"I don't even know who these people are," he says. He removes the photograph and gives the frame to Nanmei. "Maybe a distant great-aunt and great-uncle, or some twelve-times-removed cousins."

Nanmei helps Weilan mount the photographs, measuring and cutting out a cardboard mat. Then comes the important decision of where to hang the pictures.

"In your bedroom," suggests Nanmei.

"No," Weilan says. "I want to be beside my mother. Here on the library wall."

Baizhen returns to find Weilan's likeness hanging on the wall beside mine.

"Look, Papa. Look where we put my photographs."

"Yes, they look very nice, just the right place."

"Will Second Uncle like them?"

"I'm sure he will. I'll mail him a set tomorrow."

Weilan skips out, pleased with her efforts. Nanmei clears away the strips of leftover cardboard.

"Her uncle must be very fond of her. How nice of you to send him these."

"He's trying to arrange a marriage for Weilan, so he needs her photographs."

"Really? She's still very young." Nanmei's voice is matter-of-fact.

"Yes, she is. But the Cha family arranges their sons' marriages early. Perhaps you've heard of them? General Cha's family."

At this, Nanmei sinks into a chair, suddenly trembling. Baizhen, still studying the photographs on the wall, doesn't notice her distress.

"Did you say the family of General Cha?"

"Yes, do you know of them? Of course, it's too much to hope that Weilan could marry into such a family, but my brother-in-law promises to try."

He leaves the room and Nanmei stares up at my picture on the wall, her hands clutching the seat of the schoolroom chair. My face gazes down at her.

⁓⌣⁓

That night, Nanmei dreams again.

She is a little girl, visiting her grandparents in Soochow. I follow her out of a narrow house that backs onto a canal. Ancient willow trees grow along the banks, sweeping the water with the tips of their branches. She holds her grandfather's hand and follows him down broad stone steps to the water's edge. A waiting boatman lifts her into a long barge and her grandfather pats down the cushions before they sit. The boatman leans his weight against the massive oar at the stern and the boat glides through the water. The old gentleman hums to himself, a comforting familiar tune. The dream is so vivid and Nanmei so happy to be a child again.

"Grandfather," asks the child Nanmei. "Do you believe in ghosts?"

"Yes, of course. There are many kinds of ghosts. Most are just harmless spirits trying to make their way to the next life."

"Have you ever seen one?"

Her grandfather turns into Hanchin, who lifts up her small chin.

"You shouldn't be afraid if you do see one, Nanmei. They're just trying to talk to you."

With a heartrending cry, Nanmei throws her arms around him.

"Oh, Hanchin, I knew you'd come back to me!"

The edges of her dream crack and Nanmei wakes up, tears

soaking her pillow. I curse out loud. I didn't even have a chance to speak to her. It's just past two in the morning, so perhaps she will fall asleep again.

She whispers out loud in the still night air, "Come back to me, my life's companion. Oh, come back!"

Words without hope, only longing. *Nanmei, go back to sleep and dream again*, I implore.

But she lies awake, eyes open in the dark. Then she sits up and pulls on her coat and heavy socks. She takes out a stub of candle and some matches from the chest of drawers and drops them in her pocket.

With growing excitement I follow her downstairs to my bedroom. She lights the candle and kneels beside the trunk. Lifting the wooden lid, she rests it against the wall. Holding the candle closer, she inspects the inside of the lid, then runs her fingers across the leaf-patterned paper that lines the interior. The paper is glued to cardboard, just as I told her. Putting the candle on the floor, she gently pries one corner away from the inside of the wooden lid. It curls up slightly. Amber-yellow flakes of dried glue fall away as she runs her finger along the edges of the cardboard and then gently pulls it away.

She sits back on her heels and shakes her head with a rueful look. There's nothing on the underside of the wooden lid.

Keep trying, I urge. *Please, please, keep trying.*

With a sigh, she picks up the sheet of cardboard and fits it back into the lid of the trunk.

Please, please, Nanmei.

Then she pauses, pulls the hard sheet away again, and turns it over. A page torn from an exercise book is glued to the center of the board, like a pocket. There is a slight bulge in the paper. Nanmei tears it off and an envelope falls out. An envelope I never opened, because of my promise to Hanchin.

I expect her to weep or hold it to her chest.

But Nanmei does none of this. She tucks the envelope up her sleeve, pulls off the rest of the paper, and crumples the sheet into her pocket. Then she presses the cardboard liner back into the lid. She closes the trunk and blows out the candle. Silent as smoke, she makes her way upstairs to her room.

Only then does she collapse on the cot, shaking. She draws the envelope out of her sleeve and presses it to her cold lips. She holds it there for a long time, as though reluctant to face its contents.

Finally, she lights a candle and slides down to the floor to read. There's nothing written on the envelope, but there is sealing wax dribbled along the edges of its flap. Nanmei rummages in the chest of drawers. She fishes out a slim, bone-handled knife and slits open the short end of the envelope. She extracts three thin sheets of carefully folded paper.

The pages are covered in tiny, neat handwriting, miniature words of enormous import. She blinks away tears as she reads. I lean over her shoulder, casting no shadow, displacing no air with my ghost-breath. I read along with her.

She reaches the third and final onionskin sheet. This page isn't part of the manifesto. It lists names and details for contacts in Hanchin's network. Hanchin has set down on paper what his successor in the movement would need to know. The only name I recognize is that of Young Wang the bookseller. Nanmei turns over the paper and on the back is another list, the names of trai-

tors and spies known to Hanchin, enemies of the Communist
movement. I scan the list and near the bottom is Tongyin's name.
Nanmei reads slowly now, running her fingers down the paper,
muttering to herself. When she reaches Tongyin's name I hear a
sharp intake of breath.

She collapses to the floor.

"Are you here, Leiyin?" she whispers into the darkness. "Are
you here?"

I can't even make the candle flame waver in reply, but that
doesn't matter. Nanmei reaches into her dresser drawer and takes
out a sheet of paper:

Dear Leiyin,

*When Hanchin and I were married, my parents weren't
pleased, as you can imagine, so they gave me a dowry but
not a wedding. Then they disowned me. The only evidence
of my wedding was a studio photograph but I didn't care.
We left Soochow, and with my dowry we were able to carry
out our dream. We set up schools in Jiangxi, schools for
peasants.*

She is writing to me, telling me her story.

She was far more than a schoolteacher. She gave herself heart
and soul to the Communist Party and became a trained agent.
The schools were a cover for recruiting. These were the happiest
years of her life, even though she and Hanchin were apart a good
deal of the time.

*They trained us both to run a spy network. Can you im-
agine me a spy? But I did whatever was needed for the Party.
Then came the Encirclement Campaigns and our armies
began losing badly. Hanchin was ordered to Changchow
to organize better intelligence gathering while I continued
to work in the villages. It was dangerous to communicate
in writing, so I had to be content with the clues he put into
the poems and articles he wrote.*

Then *China Millennium* shut down and Hanchin vanished.
Everything happened so quickly. She went to Shanghai and
Changchow to find him. Then she read about his capture and
execution. All she had to track down his last hiding place, to find
the manifesto if she could, were a few clues from the head of their
network. She tried to find more clues in Hanchin's published
articles. Then she read the last poem he had written for the journal, its final two lines:

*Childhood friends and our love, years pass and they
        change not,
Like a cherished secret, when released, they return us to joy.*

She guessed he might have tried to find me. I was unknown
to the movement, with no connection to his circle of contacts. I
had also been her friend.

*I was grasping at straws when I suspected he was hiding
here, but I didn't have anything else to go on. Then I*

*learned about your death and I was in despair. But my
last duty as his comrade and his wife was to recover the
manifesto he'd been writing. So I went to find your brother,
whom Hanchin mentioned once in a letter.*

Arriving at my family's villa thin and poorly dressed,
Nanmei looked nothing like the schoolgirl who used to visit
me there. When she introduced herself as Yen Hanchin's wife,
Tongyin claimed that he himself had been not only Hanchin's
friend but a fellow agent. She had to risk telling him about
the manifesto but divulged only enough information to win his
help. She needed to get to Pinghu and into our home without
attracting attention. Baizhen's letter, asking for help finding a
tutor for Weilan, had arrived only the day before. Tongyin was
quick to make a plan.

*I feel like a superstitious peasant, Leiyin, writing a letter
to a dead person. Perhaps I'm only dreaming all this. But
you helped me find the manifesto. I'll find a way to stop
Tongyin. I won't let him put Weilan in danger. She's all I
have of you now.*

She puts down her pencil and reads over what she's written.
Then she touches the candle's flame to the paper and watches the
pages burn to ashes in the old bucket. She hasn't written down
everything I want to know but it's enough.

∽∽∽

Had I been in Nanmei's place, I would have run out the door as soon as morning dawned and the streets outside were busy with peasants on their way to market. Instead, she follows the usual routine, helping Weilan feed the chickens and overseeing my daughter's lessons for the day. But when Weilan settles down for a nap, Nanmei shuts herself in her room and makes a copy of Hanchin's document. She writes a short note to go along with it and folds it all into an envelope that she tucks inside the lining of her winter vest.

Then she puts on her coat and outdoor shoes.

"Going for a walk, Teacher Wang?" Old Ming asks as she enters the forecourt.

"Just a quick errand."

"That wind is bitter today."

"Don't worry." She smiles. "This scarf is very warm."

I follow her along Minor Street and across Three Lanterns Bridge. She stops once to ask the way, and then I know where she is going. At 24 Southern Harmony Road she steps across the threshold of the Thousand Wisdoms Bookstore and closes the door to a jangle of bells.

The interior of the shop is only slightly warmer than the street outside. The shelves are only half filled with books, as though the store hasn't been restocked in some time. There are no customers. Young Wang emerges from the storeroom as soon as the bells announce Nanmei's presence.

"You're the owner?" she inquires.

"Yes, Madame. I'm Wang Duchen. How may I assist you?"

"*The hermit in his solitary dwelling clears his mind of worldly cares.*"

He stares at her in astonishment, and then blurts out, "'*A solitary swan wings its way from the sea.*'"

They look at each other again, almost shyly. Wang is the first to speak.

"How may I assist you, Comrade?"

She reaches inside her coat and pulls out the envelope. "Can you get this safely to your contacts in Shanghai?"

He turns it over. "Yes. You can expect this to reach Shanghai within two days. Do you need to know when it reaches its destination?"

She shakes her head. "No, but I do need your help with something else."

Afterward, she goes to the post office to send a telegram.

⌒⌒⌒

Did you know? Did you guess what she would do? My *yang* soul waves his cane as he circles the pavilion. A searing peppery taste flares in my throat. *You should have waited. Cha Zhiming might have rejected a match between his youngest brother and Weilan.*

My *yin* soul perches in silent dejection on the pavilion bench. In summer this gazebo is wreathed in pink wisteria, but now, with its frame devoid of blooms and foliage, it's clear that the heavy vines twisting around the pillars are all that is holding up the roof. Half heartedly she conjures a weak wisteria scent.

I knew there'd be a risk. But I'm willing to take that risk for my daughter. Once Tongyin shows Weilan's photographs to Cha Zhiming, the situation will be out of my hands. I had to take whatever opportunity came my way and Nanmei was it. How Nanmei chooses to stop Tongyin is up to her. I will accept the consequences.

Don't you understand what could happen? My *yin* soul whimpers, a child in distress. This time, the odor of urine.

Hush now, says my *hun* soul. *Leiyin understands very well. Weilan's life is at stake. Her daughter. Our daughter.*

They fall silent. My *yin* soul rests her head against my *yang* soul's shoulder. He pats her hand and clears his throat. *Will you enter Nanmei's dreams again?*

No. *I can't change anything now. She's set things in motion. There's no turning back.*

26

*T*hings are different when you're a ghost. Alive, I might have hated Nanmei, considered her a rival. I might have told her about Hanchin's infidelities. But now my pride and hurt feelings pale next to my yearning to escape this twilight existence. It's stronger than any desire I felt while alive, more potent than my longing to escape to college, more frantic than my feverish agitation during the early months of my marriage, when I felt trapped in this house, this small town. It's stronger even than my infatuation with Hanchin. I have only the faintest notion of what might be in the afterlife, beyond the portal. I know I cherish hopes of seeing my father one more time. And I know I must transcend this existence before I become an insane and hungry ghost, tormented and senseless. Without my souls.

There's only one thing that matters more than rising to the afterlife: Weilan.

Whatever the cost to me and to my souls.

∽∾∾∾

The day after her visit to the Thousand Wisdoms Bookstore, before the morning light colors the sky, before the black rooster even stirs in its coop, Nanmei slips out the side door of the orchard. The wind blows colder than usual today and carries a promise of rain. She takes with her only a few clothes and her diary, all stuffed into a cloth satchel. A covered donkey cart waits at the top of the lane, silhouetted against the gray light. A hand flicks open its canvas flap and Nanmei climbs in. The driver's bamboo stick whistles in the air and the donkey sets off at a trot. Nanmei exchanges greetings with the two men inside.

"This is Comrade Ho," says Young Wang the bookseller.

"Comrade, all is ready." The other man twists a piece of rope in his hands. He is huge, with stubbled cheeks and big hands. He wears the clothing of a laborer, rough trousers and a worn, padded coat, his bare feet strapped into straw sandals. His accent, however, is that of an educated man.

"What's the spot you've chosen?" Nanmei hugs the satchel to her chest, looking more like a schoolgirl than a spy.

"There's an old warehouse not far from town," says Ho. "The owner went bankrupt years ago. The loading dock is on the Shanghai Pond River."

"Neighbors?"

"None. Just some fields gone to seed."

"And afterward?"

"A barge loaded with coal. Shanghai Pond River runs into

the Huangpu, near Damao Port, thirty, maybe thirty-five miles upriver from Shanghai."

"What's in the sacks?" Nanmei points at the rough jute cloth they are sitting on, mounds stuffed with something scratchy.

"Just straw."

"Thank you, Comrades, for organizing this on such short notice."

The cart stops. There's an exchange of voices outside. Nanmei's hands tighten almost imperceptibly around the satchel. Then the cart's flap opens and the driver's face appears, grinning.

"No need to go hungry while we wait. Best steamed buns in town. Two each."

He passes them a bamboo basket. Nanmei's hands relax. Outside, an icy rain begins a light, relentless thrumming on the canvas cover.

~~~

When my brother gets off the morning train from Shanghai, he resembles any other traveler, bundled up to face the cold day. For once, he is wearing nondescript clothing, an ordinary-looking padded jacket and long gown. The brim of his felt hat is pulled down over his forehead, and his scarf is wound up to his chin, hiding half his face. When he sees Nanmei pushing her way toward him he waves and points at the station exit. They wade through the crowd separately and meet out on the street, where rickshaw drivers shiver in their vehicles, sheltered under half-shells of oilcloth.

"I'm glad you could get on the overnight train like I suggested in my telegram." Nanmei opens an umbrella and they become just another pair of travelers, huddled close for shelter from the rain.

"Do you have the manifesto? That's the reason you wanted me to come, isn't it?" Tongyin is eager, animated.

"Yes, but let's go somewhere less crowded. And let's get out of the rain."

She leads him farther down the street, toward where the donkey cart waits.

"Ah, but this one already has passengers," says Tongyin, looking inside.

"No, no, we're just getting out," says the rough-featured man in laborer's clothes, cheerfully. "Let me help you in, sir."

He holds out a big hand to Tongyin, who pulls himself up through the open flap. Nanmei positions herself so that the umbrella obscures the opening and in that moment Comrade Ho throttles Tongyin from behind. He shoves my brother down to the floor of the cart. Tongyin cries out, but his face is pushed into a sack of straw and no one on the street appears to have noticed anything. Nanmei closes her umbrella and climbs in. Only the slightest shaking of her hands betrays any anxiety as she closes the canvas flap.

The cart driver flicks his switch and the donkey trots off. In such foul weather, the streets leading away from the train station are nearly empty. A few passersby hurry along, eyes cast down, watching for puddles, arms struggling to keep the wind from inverting their umbrellas. Tongyin protests, but his words are muffled. Young Wang sits with one hand firmly pressed down on Tongyin's head while Ho ties my brother's hands behind his back.

Then he turns Tongyin over and clouts him across the face with a giant fist.

"Now quit trying to talk or I'll hit you again. You'll have plenty of time to talk soon."

The large man stuffs a rag in Tongyin's mouth, gagging him. Tears stream down my brother's face and he stifles a cry. He stares at Nanmei, who is now slumped against a pile of straw-filled sacks, her face pinched and pale.

She closes her eyes and refuses to look at him. "Let me know when we're outside town."

The sound of cartwheels rolling over stone-paved streets gives way to a gritty grinding noise. The passengers lurch as the cart splashes through potholes filled with water, now bumping down a muddy country road. The large man nods to Nanmei.

Nanmei reaches into her satchel and holds up an envelope to show Tongyin.

"Here is what we've been searching for. This is Yen Hanchin's most precious work." Her voice is as even as her gaze, which is fixed on Tongyin.

Tongyin stares at the envelope, then back at my friend.

"But do you know what else was in this envelope, Mr. Song?" A threatening tone now. "The names of the spies in his network, information he had kept in his head and never written down until he was ready to return to the front lines."

She gestures to Ho, and Tongyin flinches as the large man reaches toward his face again.

"Stop cringing, you idiot," Ho says. "I'm just taking off your gag so you can answer our comrade's questions." He pulls Tongyin up to a sitting position and yanks out the gag.

Tongyin splutters, his breathing ragged. "I'm on your side! My name should be on the list of spies who worked *for* your husband!"

"Actually, Mr. Song, your name is on a list of double agents and traitors."

He gapes. "I swear to you, I was his friend. I rented an apartment for him in Shanghai, I subsidized the magazine. I took care of him! I kept him safe from the Nationalist Police!" Tongyin begins crying again, long choking sobs that shake his body.

My poor brother. I'm so sorry I set these wheels in motion, but the situation is out of my hands now.

Nanmei's face is hard, unrelenting. "You were the one who tracked him to the jail in Ningbo and revealed his true identity to the Nationalists."

Carefully she puts the envelope back in the satchel. She leans in to his face. "And what did you have in mind for me, dear Comrade? Were you going to add to your feats by turning in the wife of Yen Hanchin? Who else knows you're here?"

"No one knows about you, Comrade! I wasn't going to tell anyone about you, not until I was sure you'd found the manifesto!"

Ho hits him across the face. Tongyin cries out, blood gushes from his nose and mouth.

"I know, Song Tongyin. You were going to use the manifesto to get back in the good graces of your friend Cha Zhiming, the Nationalist Police captain."

He moans, spitting blood. "No, I swear. I'm only friends with Cha because Hanchin told me to watch him."

She nods to Ho and he smashes his fist into Tongyin's stomach. My brother gasps, winded and unable to scream. Young Wang flinches, but just presses his lips tight.

"You can tell me everything now," says Nanmei, "or you can wait until we get to our destination, where no one can hear you. Once we get there, my comrade won't feel the need for restraint. For the last time, who else knows you're here?"

They wait while Tongyin regains his breath, face contorted.

"No one, no one else knows! Why would I tell anyone? I'd just get in more trouble for not turning you in the day you showed up at our gates. Please, let me go, I won't say anything."

"Does anyone else know about the manifesto?"

"No, no. There were rumors, only rumors. I only knew for sure once you told me."

"Does anyone know about me? Does Cha Zhiming know you're using me to find the document?"

"No, no. I'm being more careful now. What if the manifesto wasn't here? It would have been bad to make promises I couldn't keep."

"Why did Hanchin leave Changchow so suddenly?"

"He gave me false information that I passed to Cha Zhiming. Cha lost face terribly. He was fed up with Hanchin, had had enough of my promises, so he raided the offices of *China Millennium* and arrested everyone. He may still arrest me, he says he can't trust me anymore."

"He's just playing with you," Nanmei says in disgust. "If Cha really believed you were a Communist sympathizer, he would've thrown you in jail already. Why are you so sure he isn't having you followed?"

"He thinks I'm a fool, not worth his men's time." His voice is

bitter. My brother wants so much to be part of something important, but no one takes him seriously.

"That, I'm willing to believe," Comrade Ho rumbles from the
corner of the cart.

"Please. Let me go. I'm just a small fish. I'm nobody. Please,
I have money."

"I don't want money." Nanmei's voice is cold. She leans forward and spits in his face. "I want revenge. You betrayed my husband and because of you, he's dead."

"No, no, your information's wrong! I didn't want him dead!
I didn't think they'd execute him! I never betrayed him. He's the
one who betrayed me. I loved Hanchin, I loved him!"

Stop, I say to my brother. *Don't say any more about you and
Hanchin. It won't help you.*

Nanmei waves her hand again.

Comrade Ho has a brick in his hand. He strikes my brother
on the back of the head and Tongyin falls unconscious, knees
drawn up to his chest, curled like a mouse in his nest of straw-
filled sacks. Outside, the rain keeps up its steady beat on the taut
canvas, filling the silence. For the next twenty minutes, Nanmei
and the two men say little to each other, but what they say is
enough.

The cart driver gives a shout and Ho leaps out. They have
stopped in front of a warehouse. He runs ahead to open the door.
The donkey clops inside, shaking its ears when the driver calls a
halt. Gusts of rain blow in through gaps at the far end of the roof
and lightning flashes as the men drag my brother off the cart and
toward the loading dock.

I remain behind in the cart. I have no wish to see any more.

I don't want to watch Nanmei and Ho climb into the covered barge that will take them to Shanghai's riverside slums. I don't want to see them hide Tongyin's inert body inside a coal sack, to be heaved into the Huangpu River as they approach the city's shoreline.

The driver and Young Wang return, soaked and shivering.

I return to town with them.

But I know exactly when my brother dies.

Because suddenly I'm lighter. I float closer to the glowing edges of the portal. My souls bob up like corks. They circle me in excitement, bright red sparks of anticipation and hope.

In the next moment, my mind's eye sees Weilan's future as it would have been if I hadn't done what I did. She's in an opulent house, looking through a long window at the parklike garden below, forbidden to go outside. She's miserable and lonely, the adults around her indifferent to her despair.

I see her pressed against a wide sofa, Cha Zhiming leaning over her, pulling up her plaid skirt, and whispering, "Tell Uncle Cha how much you love him."

I see Weilan as a teenager now, running terrified through the streets of a city in chaos. I see Shanghai neighborhoods surging with panicked crowds, Japanese airplanes overhead. I hear the din of machine-gun fire.

Then in the next moment, a jarring lurch, a sinking feeling.

I grow heavy, heavier than I've ever been. The glowing portal recedes until it's just an indistinct shadow. My souls scatter like startled birds, worry and fear dimming their brightness.

I witness the other consequences of my actions. I see the

future as it would have been for my brother if I hadn't helped Nanmei.

I see Tongyin strolling down a bustling Shanghai street, clad in a stylish wool suit. I see him enter a nightclub with Cha Zhiming, who claps him on the shoulder with a friendly smile. I see Tongyin while away the hours at an elegant café, taking his time over the newspaper, chatting with other customers. I see a life of leisure.

I see him boarding a steamship with Changyin and his wife, Geeling, Gaoyin and Shen ahead of them on the gangplank, herding children and nannies in a hasty exodus. I see the vessel pitching and rolling, making its way across the water to Taiwan, taking them all to a new home as the Nationalists retreat from China.

I see Tongyin older, much older, a handsome white-haired man promenading in downtown Taipei, dawdling in restaurants and shops, chatting with friends. I see a life of comfort. This is the future I have taken away from him.

✁⁓

A feeling of lightness, rising higher toward the shining portal. And then a long plummet into darkness, and now we are heavy, sucked down into the mud of my sins.

What crime could be worse than causing the death of a member of your own family? My *yang* soul is a dull speck of light in the dim family shrine. *How many more lives must you save now, to atone for your brother's murder?*

*But she didn't know for sure how Nanmei would stop Tongyin.
She only wanted to save her daughter.* My *yin* soul balances on the
tip of my name tablet. It's as though my souls are too tired now
to manifest as anything more than weak sparks. *Her motives were
good.*

There's no reckoning of motives good or bad, says my *hun* soul.
*There's only a life, a death, what was averted, what was caused. You
know that.* It's no brighter than the ashen tip of an incense stick,
on the verge of burning out.

*I knew the risks and I accept the consequences. Can you put a
price on Weilan's safety?*

◦⌒◦⌒◦

At home, Jia Po's indignation over Nanmei's sudden disappear-
ance has not been mitigated by the note she left behind.

"A sick mother, indeed," says Jia Po with a snort. "I thought
she was an orphan."

"Well, nothing's been stolen," says Meichiu, "so she wasn't a
thief. A thief wouldn't have left a farewell note."

"This is most distressing," says Gong Gong. "Our kinsman
will lose face if we tell him the tutor he sent us left under such
odd circumstances."

Weilan still goes to the orchard each morning and lets the
silkies out of the coop, scatters grain for them. Sometimes she
picks up the docile birds one by one to stroke their soft black
plumage. She spends the rest of the morning in the library, leaf-
ing through books and copying out words over and over. I hear
her speak of her missing teacher only once. When Meichiu looks

in on her one day, Weilan is gazing up at the photographs on the wall. Without turning to Meichiu, she says, "I wish I had a photograph of Teacher Wang."

"Come with me, Stepdaughter. It's nearly dark. Let's put the silkies back in their coop." I hadn't expected this gentleness from Meichiu.

∽∾∾∾

Nanmei's abrupt departure is a source of speculation in our home for only a few weeks. When a letter arrives from Changyin, addressed to Baizhen, the mysterious teacher is pushed out of everyone's thoughts by far more dramatic news. The envelope contains a card bordered in black, announcing Tongyin's death. Changyin's precise handwriting tells the story as he knows it:

> *My brother obviously cherished his friendship with your family, for he visited your home twice after the death of Third Sister, and in his rooms we found photographs of little Weilan. You should know that my brother was missing for weeks before his body was discovered. He didn't die of natural causes. Shanghai is a violent and dangerous city, so we doubt his murder will ever be solved. If only he had spent more time in Changchow, or in your peaceful little town.*

Baizhen weeps, for he had considered Tongyin a friend as well as his brother-in-law.

My in-laws decide it would be poor manners to ask Changyin

to speak to the Cha family about Weilan. The fact that her photographs were still in Tongyin's room was clear evidence that Tongyin had not yet approached the Cha family.

⌒⌒⌒

A feeling of lightness and then a plummeting drop.

There's no reckoning of motives good or bad. There's only a life, a death, what was averted, what was caused. This is what my *hun* soul said.

And yet. And yet.

When I was shown Tongyin's life as it should have been, an existence of idleness and comfort, I had felt a pause, a delay, as if a deliberation was in progress, a weighing. On every other occasion when I was shown the future, it was in quick splashes, each scene instantly washing out the previous one. This time, there was one scene from my brother's future. Ladled out slowly, it had remained before me for so long, like spilled water pooled on a table, that I was able to eavesdrop on Tongyin and his friends as they gossiped in a café. I had inhaled the fragrance of his coffee, breathed in the sweet stink of their cigarettes, hovered over his shoulder to read the headlines of the newspaper spread across his lap.

That's how I know there's more to do.

Cha Zhiming is no longer a threat but Weilan's life is still in danger.

EPILOGUE

Pinghu, 1936

*J*urry, hurry," says Little Ming. She lifts Ah Jiao into the donkey cart and he toddles over to Weilan, who is already inside. Little Ming climbs in to join them and Dali shifts to make room. The rest of the cart is filled with food and small items of furniture. Weilan is sitting beside a cloth-covered cage. Beneath the cloth, the silkies cluck hesitantly and she croons back at them, reassuring noises. The coolness of early morning has burned off and the sycamores overhead struggle to block the glare of the sun, which falls hard and bright on my family.

In front of them is another cart. Meichiu sits under its canvas cover, Weihong on her lap. Baizhen climbs up beside the driver, who snaps his switch at the donkey's rump. From the gate, Old Ming waves farewell.

"Why aren't Old Kwan and Mrs. Kwan coming with us?" asks Weilan.

"They're going back to their own village, it's not far away,"

Dali replies. "At the end of this week, we'll all come back to Pinghu."

"What about Old Ming?"

The old servant can't remember a time when he wasn't in service to the Lee family. He refuses to leave and has insisted to my husband that someone must stay behind to guard the property and look after the Master and Mistress. Jia Po and Gong Gong are also refusing to depart the estate.

"To go all that way, for just a few days," Gong Gong said. "All on a whim. The Japanese won't come here. We're an insignificant town."

"Not a whim, Father," Baizhen pleaded with him. "I've had the same dream about Leiyin so many times over the past few months and so has Ma. Leiyin warned us to get away from Pinghu before tomorrow."

"But your mother isn't leaving."

Jia Po snapped her fan shut.

"I'm not leaving because you're not leaving. You're my husband. What would people say? So we'll both die in this house because you won't leave your books and porcelain."

Baizhen squeezes Meichiu's hand.

"You'll see," he promises. "I'm not going mad. We'll be safe in the cottage at Infant Mountain."

"It's wise to listen to the spirits of the dead when they make an effort to help us," she says. "I lit some incense in front of First Wife's name tablet this morning."

The two carts clop along until the paved streets of Pinghu give way to a wide dirt road, baked hard as clay in the summer heat. I remember the first time I traveled this road, my feet dan-

gling over the back of the cart, Weilan in front with her father
and Little Ming beside me. I remember singing and playing word
games all the way to Infant Mountain. I think back to our climb
up the winding path to its summit, where I looked down on the
serene beauty of Pinghu and its lake, the graceful pagoda of the
Temple of Soul's Enlightenment on its shores.

Tomorrow morning, I will stand at the summit of Infant
Mountain once more and look down on Pinghu. And tomorrow,
my souls and I will know.

I believe I will see Japanese bombers fly in formation over the
town, on a practice run toward an inland target. One will struggle
and fall behind, its engines spewing black smoke, and the pilot
will drop his load of bombs in an effort to gain some control over
his aircraft. The town will light up in a series of explosions, each
one brighter than the last, seconds apart. Entire streets of houses
will burn. The young pilot will try for a water landing, but the
plane will fall from the air, spinning out of control until it crashes
into the lake and sinks in an eruption of oil and water.

☙❧

Until tomorrow, we won't know if a bomb will destroy our home.
But I believe that's what will happen.

My souls are dim sparks balanced on top of the cart. I feel
thin, translucent, like watered-down rice soup, my body stretched
out, in pain. It takes all my will to think clearly. It gets harder
every day.

Why else would the gods have allowed you that chance to read
Tongyin's newspaper? my *yang* soul says in agreement. *You saw the*

name of the town and the date. You saw the news about a damaged Japanese aircraft, bombs, fire, and fatalities.

We must believe you were being given a chance to save many lives, my *yin* soul says. *Enough lives to atone for the death of a brother, and the death of a lover. Oh, why wouldn't Jia Po and Gong Gong come with us?*

We can't control their fate, says my *hun* soul, *we can barely manage our own. But we can hope for tomorrow.*

Tomorrow, I say, *tomorrow we can hope for rebirth.*

And swaying with the motion of the cart, my souls and I look ahead, toward Infant Mountain.

ACKNOWLEDGMENTS

*T*he family stories and anecdotes my parents shared with me during my childhood have been the primary sources for *Three Souls*. Leiyin's character was inspired by my grandmother, whose ambitions might have been fulfilled had she been born just a decade later. Baizhen is a more sympathetic version of my grandfather, and Hanchin is loosely based on my grandmother's first cousin Qu Quibai. At one time Qu was de facto leader of the Chinese Communist Party; he met with the same fate as Hanchin.

Pinghu, my parents' hometown, is real. To the best of my knowledge, there was no Hangchow Women's University during the Chinese civil-war era. There were, however, at least two highly regarded women's universities during that time, one in Beijing, the other in Shanghai.

My thanks to the Authors of Asian Novels group for the lively online debate that convinced me to use Pinyin for the characters' names and Chinese Postal Map Romanization for the names of major cities. The Qing Dynasty officially adopted the latter for place names in 1906 and its use continued until 1949; it is the system that made "Peking" more familiar to the world than the Wade-Giles translation "Pei-ching."

China has been host to numerous belief systems. Many of its folk religions stem from ancestor worship, in which the notion of multiple souls is common, with varied interpretations of the souls' qualities. Daoism asserts that a person possesses three *hun* souls and seven *po* souls, but I felt three was quite enough.

To my mentor and classmates at the Writer's Studio, Simon Fraser University. I will always treasure Shaena Lambert's empathetic and thoughtful advice. My gratitude goes to David Blinkhorn, Claire DeBoer, Lara Janze, Lorraine Kiidumae, Toni Levi, Kacey-Neille Riviere, Anthony Patten, and Patricia Webb for workshopping the same damn story all year. Special thanks to Elizabeth Morwick, who handed me the winning ticket.

Robert McCammon and Nancy Richler had no reason to champion my book but they did, and I am forever humbled by their kindness. Many thanks also to Jennifer Pooley, whose talented guidance elevated *Three Souls* above the slush pile. Beverly Martin, thank you for the encouraging shove that put me on this path.

I am fortunate beyond words to have Jill Marr at the Dijkstra Agency representing me. Many, many thanks to Iris Tupholme and Jennifer Brehl for believing in *Three Souls*; also to Lorissa Sengara for her amazing and instructive editing. So many others have made my entry into the world of publishing an absolute dream of an experience—thank you Maylene Loveland, Shannon

Parsons, Noelle Zitzer, Allegra Robinson, Doug Richmond, Cory Beatty, Rebecca Lucash, Ben Bruton, and Molly Birckhead. To my husband, who took over the cooking and housekeeping so that I could write every night and all day on weekends: Geoffrey, thank you so much for the gift of time.

Insights,
Interviews
& More ...

Meet Janie Chang

JANIE CHANG is a Canadian novelist who draws upon family history for her writing. She grew up listening to stories about ancestors who encountered dragons, ghosts, and immortals and about family life in a small Chinese town in the years before the Second World War. She is a graduate of the Writer's Studio at Simon Fraser University. *Three Souls* is her first novel.

Born in Taiwan, Janie has lived in the Philippines, Iran, Thailand, and New Zealand. She now lives in beautiful Vancouver, Canada, with her husband and Mischa, a rescue cat who thinks the staff could be doing a better job. ∿

The Story Behind
Three Souls
An Interview
with the Author

You've said there's a lot of family history behind the story of Three Souls. *Can you talk a bit about your grandmother, who is part of that inspiration?*

Absolutely. I never knew her, but my paternal grandmother really is the story behind the story. And yes, she was one of three beautiful sisters. Her name was Qu Maozuo, and like Leiyin, she was from a wealthy, well-educated family. Also like Leiyin, she was trapped at the confluence of change. She knew there was more to life than arranged marriages and the closed-in world of courtyards. Young women of her generation were training to be teachers and nurses, and the Shanghai Women's Savings Bank had been set up by women for women, with a female president. But these were just pockets of freedom. Chinese society did not progress all at the same pace. It really depended on the family, and older, wealthy families could be very conservative. ▸

Are any of the other main characters based on real people?

It was hard keeping real people *out* of the novel! My great-grandmother really was the wealthy bride who came to the Chang family with a magnificent dowry. And her husband, my great-grandfather, really did squander it all, in just the way Old Kwan described to Leiyin. Fortunately, in real life, my great-grandmother inherited some money when her father died, or else the family could never have managed to send my father and his siblings to boarding school.

My grandfather was the model for Baizhen, but only in appearance and lack of education. Beneath his unremarkable façade Baizhen is a man of fine qualities. My grandfather, alas, was spoiled rotten and lazy— another reason to pity my grandmother.

And then there's Hanchin. He's based very loosely on my grandmother's first cousin, Qu Qiubai, one of the intellectuals of the early Communist movement. My father told me that my grandmother and her cousin were considered the two most intelligent children of the Qu family. Qu Qiubai had quite the career during his short life. He

> **❝** It was hard keeping real people *out* of the novel! **❞**

was the Moscow correspondent for a Chinese newspaper; he translated Russian works into Chinese (but not *Anna Karenina*!), wrote books about politics and social change, and developed a system for romanizing Chinese as an alternative to the Wade-Giles system. He is best known for being Mao Zedong's mentor, and for a time, chairman of the Chinese Communist Party.

Have you ever visited the small town of Pinghu?

Yes, and it's not a small town anymore! It's quite the modern city now. I've been to China twice, once with my father and once with my mother. Both times we visited Pinghu. The main canal still runs through the middle of the town, and there's a temple with a pagoda beside the lake, now beautifully restored. We weren't able to find my mother's home, but my father's ancestral home was still there. The houses and courtyards had been divided up with makeshift brick walls, and about two dozen families were living there. I've since heard that it's been torn down to make way for modern apartments. Unfortunately we didn't have time to try and find Infant Mountain, which my six-times- ▶

66 [My grandmother's first cousin] is best known for being Mao Zedong's mentor, and for a time, chairman of the Chinese Communist Party. 99

great-grandfather built somewhere in the countryside.

Speaking of your ancestors, your father's family has a recorded genealogy going back hundreds of years. How common was that?

More common than you'd think, because honoring ancestors was a big part of Chinese tradition and documenting genealogy was part of that. If a family was literate and could afford it, they would update the *jia pu*, the printed genealogy, every few generations. It was expensive because they'd have to hire artisans to carve new printing blocks, and then print and bind new editions to distribute to all branches of the clan.

At the same time, *jia pu* are not as easy to find as you'd expect because many did not survive war and migration. During the Cultural Revolution, many families destroyed their *jia pu*, out of fear they'd be accused of bourgeois proclivities. My uncle safeguarded ours, and when my father went back to China for the first time in forty years, my uncle gave him a copy to bring back to Canada. My father had always told me about this *jia pu*, but until then, he thought it had been destroyed, and with it all records of our

66 During the Cultural Revolution, many families destroyed their *jia pu*, out of fear they'd be accused of bourgeois proclivities. **99**

ancestors going back to the Song Dynasty, 900 years ago.

Your main character is a ghost. What made you decide to tell the story that way?

My grandmother's story has haunted me all my life. I suppose it was only natural that she would enter the novel as a ghost. The second reason is that women of that era were unable to affect outcomes in a direct manner: they had to work behind the scenes to influence their destinies and the lives of those they loved. Leiyin's ghostly existence parallels that helplessness. Finally, quite a few of my family's stories feature encounters with the supernatural: ghosts, immortals, and dragons—it just felt right!

What about those souls? How did you come up with three?

I didn't invent that notion! China is an ancient civilization: over thousands of years different religions have sprung up or found their way there. I've read about belief systems that say people have three souls, others say five souls, or seven. I think eleven was the highest count. So the notion of multiple souls was already there, and I borrowed the idea to ▶

> 66 Women of that era were unable to affect outcomes in a direct manner: they had to work behind the scenes to influence their destinies and the lives of those they loved. 99

The Story Behind *Three Souls* (*continued*)

create a fictional afterlife where souls could interact with their dead person. Besides, who would Leiyin's ghost talk to if she didn't have her souls?

You've published your family stories on your website. If readers want to learn more about the real people who found their way into the novel, which of the family stories should they read?

At www.janiechang.com there is a Stories section. I would recommend the following:

- "The Difficult Daughter": about my grandmother (Leiyin)
- "The Idle Son": about my grandfather (Baizhen)
- "The Wealthy Bride": about my great-grandmother (Jia Po)
- "The Spendthrift Husband": about my great-grandfather (Gong Gong)
- "The Artificial Mountain": about Infant Mountain and the ancestor who built it ∾

Questions for Reading Groups

1. Leiyin's three souls manifest three very distinct and different personalities. What do you think the souls represent, individually and collectively? What do you think their role is in the story?

2. Pre–World War II China was a time of great turmoil. What details and descriptions of ordinary life does the author use to evoke the social and political transitions taking place?

3. Think about the conflicts that women of Leiyin's generation experienced during this time of transition. How are they similar to the experiences of immigrant women today? How are they different?

4. *Three Souls* makes a strong statement about how women were treated in Chinese society. Of all the examples showing how women were oppressed, which affected you the most, and why?

5. What new information did you learn about Chinese history, society, or family dynamics? Were there any passages or scenes in the novel that you felt gave you fresh insights into that time and place? ▶

6. In Leiyin's memories of her times with Hanchin, what tips us off that he is just toying with her? Discuss what Leiyin doesn't see or won't acknowledge that she sees.

7. Throughout Part One, Leiyin is warned repeatedly to obey her father. What do we know about her father that might cause her to believe he will eventually give in to her or at least forgive her?

8. Many readers consider Stepmother the most interesting secondary character of the novel. Do you agree? What makes her so memorable and admirable— especially given the constraints of the era and her status in the family?

9. The female characters are not the only ones whose lives are constrained. Discuss how some of the male characters are also trapped by tradition.

10. In many ways this is a coming- of-age story—in which the final coming of age happens after the protagonist dies. In each of the three parts of the novel, how does Leiyin grow and mature? What does she learn about herself or the way the world works?

11. At the end of the novel, do you think Leiyin will succeed in ascending to the afterlife? Why or why not? Do you find the outcome satisfying?

12. Consider the structure of the novel. The author changes between past tense and present tense. Do you feel this is confusing or effective? ᴖ

Books and Movies about China during the Same Time Period as *Three Souls*

Nonfiction

Bound Feet and Western Dress
Pang-Mei Natasha Chang
The author tells the story of her quiet, reserved great-aunt, who married an iconic poet and defied tradition to run the Shanghai Women's Savings Bank.

Wild Swans
Jung Chang
A chronicle of three generations of women that spans the Chinese warlord era at the turn of the century to the 1970s, when the author leaves China.

Ancestors: 900 Years in the Life of a Chinese Family
Frank Ching
Ching traces his origins, and in doing so learns about how his ancestors were a part of Chinese history and, ultimately, the influences that shaped his father's life.

Shanghai: The Rise and Fall of a Decadent City
Stella Dong
The biography of a city whose name still conjures an era of glamour,

excess, corruption, and incredible wealth during a time when cultures were thrown together in China.

Fiction

Family
Ba Jin

Exactly what the title says: a portrait of an old family where four generations live under one roof, but with increasing conflict as China struggles to modernize.

Peony
and
Pavilion of Women
Pearl S. Buck

Any title by Buck is good. These two novels are about women who choose to live outside the norm.

Film

Raise the Red Lantern
Directed by Zhang Yimou (1991)

In 1920s China, a young woman is married to a wealthy older man as his fourth wife. This film is an unflinching portrayal of family politics and despair. ∽

Don't miss the next book by your favorite author. Sign up now for AuthorTracker by visiting www.AuthorTracker.com.